Adverse Events

Galveston Crime Scene Book Two

Leigh Jones

Galveston Crime Scene Press

Adverse Events by Leigh Jones

Published by Galveston Crime Scene Press

www.galvestoncrimescene.com

Copyright © 2022 by Leigh Jones

All rights reserved.

No portion of this book may be reproduced in any form without written permission from the publisher or author, except as permitted by U.S. copyright law.

This is a work of fiction. Names, characters, places, and incidents either are the product of the author's imagination or are used fictitiously. Any resemblance to actual persons, living or dead, events, or locales is entirely coincidental.

Cover by Elizabeth Mackey.

ISBN:

978-1-7334900-7-8 (paperback)

978-1-7334900-8-5 (hardback)

978-1-7334900-6-1 (ebook)

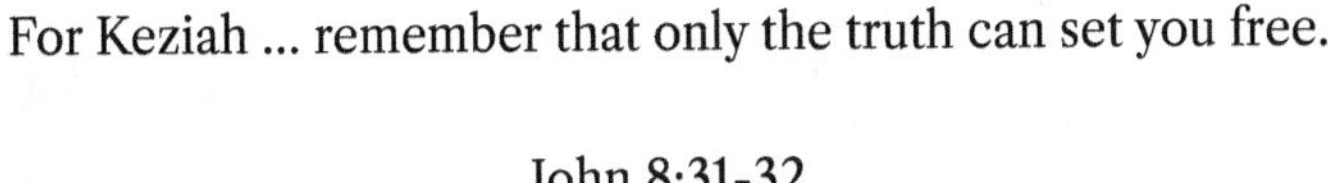

For Keziah ... remember that only the truth can set you free.

John 8:31-32

Chapter 1

Muddy brown waves rushed the beach, leaving a trail of foam as they danced back to the Gulf of Mexico. A full moon lit the wide strip of sand, infusing everything with a soft silver glow. It was a perfect night for a swim.

Detective Peter Johnson scanned the beach. A handful of Galveston police officers dotted the dunes, peering into the weeds. Several others stood near the waterline, gazing out into the sea as if it might suddenly spit the missing woman back on shore.

No matter what her friends said, she could not have just vanished.

"We were only five minutes behind her," the man standing next to him moaned. "Five minutes! There's no way she went out in the water and got in trouble in that amount of time. No way. I'm telling you, something's happened to her."

Johnson clapped his hand on the man's shoulder. "Take a deep breath, David. We'll find her."

The man nodded miserably and raked his hand through his hair. "I can't believe this is happening."

Johnson turned around and surveyed the row of houses behind them. Yellow light blazed from the windows of four properties. Curious residents stood on their decks to watch the search.

"Let's start from the beginning," Johnson said, more to give the distraught man something to do than because he needed to hear the details again. "Tell me what happened from the moment you guys finished dinner."

"We went out on the deck. Emily was wired—laughing, joking, pacing around. I guess she was just wound up about tomorrow's announcement." He stopped and looked at his watch. "Today's announcement. Oh, god. I can't believe this is happening."

"Were you drinking?"

"We had some wine, but I'm telling you, it was not enough to impair her. There was no way she was getting drunk the night before the biggest day of her life."

Johnson nodded. He believed David Knowles was telling the truth. But even a little wine on a heavy stomach could make swimming difficult. If his girlfriend had waded out into the water, underestimating the current and overestimating her own strength, she could easily have gone under and been dragged into deep water before she knew what had happened. Even in five minutes.

"What happened next?"

"We talked for a little while, and then Emily said she wanted to go for a swim. It was such a beautiful night. We all thought it sounded like a good idea. She ran back to our room to get changed. She was back in the living room with a towel before the rest of us even had a chance to get our bathing suits."

The young man shook his head, tears filling his eyes.

"She kissed me on the cheek and said she would see me down on the beach. I didn't even think to tell her to wait. It didn't seem like a big deal."

"Whatever happened here is not your fault," Johnson said. "No one can predict the future."

"How does someone just disappear?" David wailed. "We were only five minutes behind her."

Johnson looked out at the water, a seed of sorrow lodging in his gut. Most people had no idea how quickly those benign-looking waves could turn into killers. It probably would take a few hours, but he expected Emily Gibson's body to wash ashore before sunrise.

"At first, we thought she was punking us. Her towel was there, just a few feet from the water. We expected her to jump out from behind a dune or something. That's the kind of mood she was in. When she didn't appear after about five minutes, we started getting worried. We called her name and then walked up and down the beach. By that time, we were really worried. We started knocking on doors. But no one had seen her. That's when we called 9-1-1."

Two hours had passed since then. Officers had combed the beach, talked to neighbors, and interviewed the missing woman's friends. Beach patrol said there was no point putting a search team into the water after so long. If the waves had swallowed Emily Gibson, there was nothing anyone could do.

"I know you think she drowned," David said. "You're wrong. She's a strong swimmer."

Johnson nodded sympathetically. "I believe you. And I know this is not what you want to hear. But the most likely explanation is that she went into the water and got into trouble. Those currents can pull someone under faster than you realize. I'm really sorry."

The man put both hands over his face and bent over, uttering a gut-wrenching moan. "This can't be happening."

Johnson gently patted the man's back. Fed by his despair, Johnson's own sorrow had distilled into pity, searing his heart like alcohol poured over an open wound. The best he could hope for at this point was for the woman's body to wash ashore quickly and free her family and friends from the uncertainty of wondering what had happened to her.

"Listen, David, there's not much more we can do here until daylight. I'm going to leave a few officers with you, but I've got to put the rest of my guys back on patrol. At dawn, we'll get more people out here to go over the beach again."

"What about the news conference? They'll wonder where she is."

"If I were you, I would call her boss and let him know what's going on."

David pressed his lips together. His jaw ticked. "I have no interest in talking to him. Could you do it?"

Johnson frowned. "Was there a problem between them?"

"No, not a problem, exactly..."

Johnson raised an eyebrow. David swallowed and pursed his lips before continuing.

"Newhouse is a jerk. I've never liked him. Never liked the way he looked at Emily, or the late nights he had her working in the lab. She revered him. Never said no to even the most unreasonable request. He took advantage of her."

Johnson's frown deepened. That was a very different picture of the pair than the one painted in all the media reports. Dr. Aaron Newhouse was hailed as a brilliant epidemiologist whose Ebola vaccine held hope for millions of people facing a painful and almost certain death as the virus continued to ravage West Africa. Newhouse had introduced Emily Gibson as a talented researcher instrumental to the vaccine's development. Thanks to her boss, she was famous before she'd even earned her MD/PhD. She was supposed to be at his side later today when he announced the start of FDA trials for the vaccine, the last step before mass production.

"Let's wait until morning and see if we have any more information," Johnson finally said. "I'll give him a call then."

David nodded miserably, his gaze fixed on the waves.

"I just can't believe this is happening."

Reporter Kate Bennett yawned and stretched, quickly pulling her toes back from a pocket of cold air trapped under her comforter. She rolled over and pressed her face into her pillow, pulling the covers up over her ears. Crawling out of bed had gotten harder in the last few months. Every time she drifted back to consciousness, thoughts of the two men who so flagrantly flouted justice just a few months earlier assaulted her mind.

Her raging anger had burned down, but it flared again every time she thought about the sex trafficking ring. Thankfully, Eduardo

Reyes had kept a low profile since December, staying out of the media for what might have been the longest stretch since he graduated from college. But Kate couldn't so easily avoid Mayor Matthew Hanes. City council meetings had become biweekly torture sessions. Her soul smoldered as though she'd swallowed his burning embers of guilt while he acted like nothing had happened. She'd thought about asking her editor to take her off the city beat, but in the end she didn't want to give Hanes the satisfaction of another victory. She could only hope every time he saw her, his conscience twisted with the reminder that someone knew what he'd done.

Kate stretched again, threw back the covers, and swung her legs over the edge of the bed. The police scanner on her bedside table hummed. She pulled it into her lap and turned up the volume. The chatter suggested officers were conducting a search for a drowning victim on the West End. She glanced at her alarm clock. She didn't have time to make it out there before this morning's press conference at the University of Texas Medical Branch. And she had no intention of being late. Every media outlet in the country had converged on Galveston for the big Ebola vaccine announcement. She couldn't let a drowning victim distract her from what was likely to be the biggest story of the year.

"Dr. Newhouse? This is Detective Peter Johnson, with the Galveston police department."

"Yes? What is this about? I'm sure you understand I'm very busy this morning. In fact, how did you get this number?"

"From Emily Gibson's cell phone," Johnson said, swallowing his irritation at the doctor's arrogance. "I'm calling to let you know Ms. Gibson's missing. We think she might have drowned after taking a late night swim off one of the West End beaches."

"What? This must be a joke. Emily should be at my office any minute to get ready for the news conference."

"I wish it were a joke, sir. We've been looking for her all morning. Her friends called us shortly before midnight to say she was missing."

"My God! How did this happen?"

"She and her friends were spending the weekend at a house on the West End. They decided to go for a swim after dinner. Ms. Gibson left the house first, and when the others went out to the beach, she was gone."

"Gone? What do you mean, gone?"

"They couldn't find her, and we've been unable to find any sign of her since then. We presume she went into the water by herself and got pulled under by the current. I'm sorry to say it, but we're just waiting for her body to wash ashore."

"Good God. This is terrible. Terrible! I... I don't know what to say."

"Well, I'm very sorry to tell you over the phone like this, but I wanted to make sure you knew before the news conference. I figured you'd be wondering where she was."

"Yes. Yes, I would. The news conference! This is terrible timing, with the vaccine trial just about to start. What a shame."

Johnson, standing on the beach watching officers walk methodically down the sandy expanse for the second time, shifted uncomfortably from one foot to the other. "It is. A real shame. Look, I should let you get back to your preparations."

"Yes. Thank you, detective. Will you let me know when you find her?"

Johnson hesitated. Normally, he would only provide that kind of information to the family.

"I'm about to notify her family. It probably would be best to let them communicate with you from now on."

"I see." Irritation gave the doctor's voice a razor edge. "I'll let you get back to doing your job, then."

Johnson was about to respond when he realized Newhouse had already hung up. He huffed out an indignant sigh. David Knowles' dislike for the man wasn't so hard to understand after all.

Johnson trudged back up the beach-house steps as the sun started squinting over the water. Across the waves, a deep red glow seeped from the horizon to the shore. Knowles' bloodshot, red-ringed eyes told the detective he'd spent the pre-dawn hours mourning, rather than sleeping. His friends hovered, exchanging worried, helpless glances and tidying up around him. Drowning or not, they still had to be out of the house by 10 a.m. Although the other two couples were Emily's friends as well, none of them seemed particularly close to her. The girls sniffed occasionally and dabbed their eyes with tissue, but they weren't shedding tears drawn from a well of true loss.

Johnson offered to call Emily's mother, but Knowles said he should do it. He took a while to work up the courage, but finally, with the detective standing by his side, he punched her number into his cellphone. In a shaky voice, he delivered the news no parent is ever prepared to hear. The woman's sobs poured from the other end of the line. While Knowles told her the bare minimum of what they knew, Johnson stepped over to the window. The officers had gone about six houses down the beach and were coming back now. No sense of urgency indicated they'd found anything.

On the other side of the room, Knowles was telling Emily's mother he'd see her soon. As he hung up, he walked over to where Johnson stood.

"I'm going to meet her at Emily's apartment, since she knows where that is. But then I'll bring her out here."

"Okay. How long do you think it will take her to get here?"

"Maybe two hours. She lives in the Woodlands."

Johnson nodded. "I'll meet you here then. Listen, I know this is tough, but if my officers don't find anything, I'm going to have to call off the search. All we can do at this point is wait. Why don't you head over to Emily's apartment. Take a shower. Get a cup of coffee and something to eat. I promise it will make you feel better."

Knowles glanced back at his friends, who nodded their encouragement. Johnson hoped Knowles couldn't tell how relieved they looked at the prospect of having him gone.

"Okay," he finally said, his lower lip trembling. "I still can't believe this is happening. This is the kind of thing that happens to other people, you know?"

Johnson sighed. No police officer ever said that. This kind of thing, and worse, could happen to anyone.

Thirty minutes later, Johnson was back down on the beach, a semi-circle of officers in front of him. He had his notebook in one hand and a pen in the other, but none of them had anything to report worth writing down. They'd found nothing out of the ordinary. And no sign that Emily Gibson hadn't walked into the waves and to her death.

He was just wrapping up the meeting when his phone rang.

"Detective! Someone broke in to Emily's apartment."

"What? David, is that you?"

"Yes! The door was ajar when I got here, and the place is totally trashed. All the drawers are open. There's stuff everywhere. What the hell's going on?"

A tingle of shock charged up Johnson's neck, making every hair stand on end and temporarily shorting out his voice.

"Detective? Can you hear me?"

"I'm here. Have you already gone into the apartment?"

"I'm standing just inside the door."

"Okay. Don't touch anything. Go back outside and wait for me. I'll be there as fast as I can."

Barking out orders for several of the other officers to follow him, Johnson ran back to his car and yanked open the door. Possibilities wrestled with probabilities, churning a whirlwind of confusion in his mind.

Six hours ago, he felt sure Emily Gibson had drowned. Was the break-in at her apartment just a coincidence? Johnson shook his head as he mashed the gas pedal and sped down the street, spraying an arc of sand in his wake. A coincidence like that was possible. Possible, but not probable. And if the two incidents were connected, how likely was it the promising young researcher's disappearance really was a tragic accident?

Chapter 2

THE GLASS DOORS AT the hospital entrance slid open and the chatter of reporters tumbled out, blowing past Kate in a noisy gust. Women in tight pencil skirts clutched microphones as they preened in front of television cameras. Photographers focused long lenses on the empty podium, while radio reporters squabbled over the sound system's audio output jacks. The newspaper journalists clustered based on circulation, the industry's currency of importance. Kate recognized reporters from *The New York Times*, *The Washington Post*, and the journal *Science*. Writers from the smaller papers and magazines gazed longingly at their colleagues at the top of the food chain. But they didn't dare join their self-important conversations.

Kate rolled her eyes and picked her way across the room. She ignored dirty looks from reporters who'd established their territory before she got there and staked her claim to a gap in the crowd near the front of the room. The man standing next to her huffed out a drawn-out sigh every thirty seconds, crossing and uncrossing his arms and checking his watch. Kate leaned over to ask him how long he'd been there when the University of Texas Medical Branch press representative strode to the podium and gave a five-minute warning.

Flipping open her notebook, Kate scanned the questions she'd scribbled in advance. She'd tried to get an interview before the press conference with Dr. Aaron Newhouse, or even his ever-present sidekick, Emily Gibson, but the hospital kept a tight rein on its two stars. The vaccine development was the biggest thing to happen to UTMB in decades. As long as the trial succeeded, and based on the early reports there was no reason to think it wouldn't, Texas' oldest medical school soon would be a household name.

Newhouse and Gibson had already made the rounds of major television networks, giving interviews to all the nightly news programs. Kate's male colleagues made crude jokes about the relationship between the doctor and his researcher. They couldn't see past her shimmering red hair and bright green eyes. But the woman's intelligence and passion for her work crackled through every interview. She gave direct answers to the interviewers' questions and appeared totally focused on her work, not the attention it brought her. When she frankly, but kindly, told one television anchor she wanted to stop talking about the vaccine and get back to the lab to start testing it, Kate's heart swelled with every ounce of feminist pride she possessed. Despite her coworkers' jokes, she doubted Emily Gibson would be stupid enough to get involved with her boss. She cared too much about her work.

The chatter filling the room hushed abruptly when men in white coats filed out of a side door and made their way toward the podium. The press representative did a quick sound check and made sure the cameras were rolling before introducing the medical school president, Stephen Phillips.

"Thank you all for coming today. This is an important day not only for UTMB or this country but for the whole world. I knew when we recruited Dr. Aaron Newhouse from Johns Hopkins University he would be an immensely valuable asset to our staff. Little did I know the role he would play in saving so many lives from this terrible disease. We are honored to have him, and I am proud to pass the microphone to him now."

The much-vaunted doctor flashed a Cheshire-Cat grin as he shook hands with Phillips and took his place behind the microphone. He had good reason to look like he'd swallowed a canary. The Ebola vaccine had cemented his place in medical, if not world, history. He had the admiration of his colleagues and the satisfaction of being a future savior to millions of people.

Tall and trim, with wire-rimmed reading glasses hanging from a gold chain around his neck, Newhouse exuded quiet confidence. In the interviews Kate had watched, he appeared just slightly condescending, as though only willing to answer questions about his work for the greater good. With black hair swept high across his forehead and dark brown eyes, Newhouse was academically attractive. But Kate found nothing about his manner appealing.

"I have dreamed of this day for many years," Newhouse began. "When I started researching hemorrhagic diseases, they were a relatively rare scourge affecting only Africa. Today, the specter of Ebola overshadows the entire globe. No one is safe from its deadly threat. But our vaccine has the possibility to protect millions from an almost certain, excruciating death."

Behind Newhouse stood a group of his colleagues, hospital administrators, and local officials. Kate frowned as she scanned the crowd. Emily Gibson was not among them.

"After years of research, the vaccine is ready for human trials. I am grateful to FDA officials, who fast-tracked our request and approved this vital next step. As quickly as possible, I plan to be back here before you, announcing the vaccine's mass production."

As Newhouse finished his prepared remarks, the press representative returned to the microphone.

"Dr. Newhouse has agreed to take a few questions now. I'm sure he won't have time to get to all of you, but we'll try to take as many as possible."

Two dozen hands shot into the air, fingers wiggling in eager supplication. Kate did her best to catch the doctor's eye, but she didn't really expect him to pick her first. He knew his audience. Beaming, Newhouse acknowledged the reporter from *The New York Times*.

"How long do you expect human trials to take, and what are the risks to participants?"

The questions went on and on. Kate crossed them off in her notebook as the other reporters made all the queries she had thought up in advance. Newhouse answered each one carefully, giving away little new information. By the time she finally caught his eye, Kate couldn't think of anything about the vaccine trial left unasked.

"Yes, the representative from our local paper," Newhouse said, pointing at Kate.

She paused for a moment in panic. The only question that came to mind was the one she'd been wondering through the entire press conference.

"Where's Emily Gibson?"

"Ah." Newhouse cleared his throat. "Ms. Gibson was ... not feeling well this morning and couldn't join us. She has been a very important part of this team, and I'm sorry she couldn't be here to share this moment with us. Next question."

Kate frowned. She doubted Emily Gibson would miss this press conference unless she had some kind of debilitating illness. And even then, she had shown the force of will to overcome anything that might keep her from such an important event.

Newhouse took several more questions, all about the vaccine's development. No one else seemed interested in his researcher's absence. When the press representative returned to the microphone to thank everyone for coming, Kate headed for the door.

She had a busy day ahead. The story about today's press conference would anchor tomorrow's front page, and she had to write a separate version for the website. Ben Denison, the paper's main cops reporter, had a trial to cover, so Kate was stuck checking the daily police reports. Thankfully, they hadn't included any major crimes in the last few days, just the regular spate of arrests for drugs, disorderly conduct, and domestic violence. As she drove back to the newspaper office, she punched Detective Peter Johnson's number into her cellphone.

"Hey." The tension in his voice snapped through the speaker like a rubber band pulled too tight.

"Everything okay? You sound a little stressed."

"Well..." Johnson paused, and Kate's pulse ticked up with every second that went by.

"Are you still there?"

"Yeah. Look, I can't talk right now, but I may have something for you later. Give me a few hours."

"Okay. That will give me time to get my press conference story written. Is your thing a page three story, or is it going to bump my Ebola vaccine story off the front page?"

"I would tell your editor to save a spot next to it."

Excitement crackled across Kate's body. Every nerve ending tingled. But she tried to feign only mild interest.

"Oh yeah? I bet it's not that interesting. You guys always think even minor drug busts are worth a front-page story."

Johnson's wry chuckle tickled her ear, spreading warmth across her face.

"Suit yourself. If you guys want to rearrange the whole paper right before deadline, it's no big deal to me. How was the news conference?"

Kate laughed at his attempt to change the subject. "Boring. Totally scripted. No new information. I could have written the story last night. The only interesting thing was that Newhouse's researcher, Emily Gibson, wasn't there."

"Yeah..."

"Wait, what do you mean, 'yeah?'"

"Did anyone ask about her?"

"I did. Newhouse said she was sick and couldn't make it. Seemed more than a little strange."

"Hmmm..."

Kate's pulse pounded in her ears. "That's all you've got? What's going on? Did you know she wasn't going to be at the news conference? That can't be good."

"Call me in a few hours. I've got to go."

"Wait!" Dead air swallowed Kate's appeal. Johnson had already hung up. She tossed the phone into the passenger seat and gripped the steering wheel with both hands. Apprehension burrowed its way into her chest, a greedy prospector tapping a reservoir of dread.

Johnson knew Emily Gibson would not be at the press conference. If the police were involved, the researcher obviously wasn't sick. What had happened to her?

Johnson tucked his phone back in his pocket and looked at the mess around him. Overturned books and loose papers covered the floor of Emily Gibson's apartment. All her dresser drawers were open, as though they had voluntarily vomited the lacy underwear, T-shirts, and scrubs piled in front of them. Her mattress teetered half off its box springs. Long gashes tore across two pillows, their fluffy white stuffing covering the bed in a snowy blanket.

Someone had tossed the place good. What were they looking for?

"Detective, have you found anything?"

Johnson sighed and looked over his shoulder through the open front door into the hall, where David Knowles had been pacing for the last half hour. The poor guy had gone from the agony of thinking his girlfriend had drowned to the fear something even worse had happened to her. Sympathy pricked Johnson's heart. Still, he wished Knowles wasn't so underfoot.

"Nothing yet," he said, stepping carefully over Emily Gibson's possessions and out of the apartment. "My guys are taking pictures and lifting fingerprints. Hopefully, we'll get something to go on."

"I don't understand what's going on here. Why would someone do this?"

"That's what we're trying to figure out. Had Emily acted nervous in the last few weeks? Did she seem worried about anything?"

Knowles raked his fingers through his hair. "Maybe. I don't know. She seemed preoccupied. I chalked it up to all the hype leading up to the vaccine trials. She was doing a lot of interviews on top of her work. There was just a lot going on."

"But you weren't worried about her?"

"Worried? No. Not exactly."

Johnson raised an eyebrow. Knowles fidgeted.

"I mean, we'd been arguing a lot recently. She spent a lot of time with Newhouse. I couldn't shake the suspicion that something was going on between them. She always denied it, but recently the denials had been a lot less emphatic. She seemed evasive whenever I asked her about work. It's like she didn't even want to talk about it. Overall, I just felt her pulling away from me."

"Okay." Johnson looked back into the apartment, more to hide his face from Knowles than to survey the mess again. This morning, he thought of Emily Gibson's boyfriend as a bystander to be pitied. Now, he had to be considered a suspect, along with everyone else in the woman's life. But what motive would he have for trashing her apartment?

"Do you think she's still alive?" Knowles asked quietly, hope thinning his voice into a whine.

"I don't know, David. Right now, anything is possible. Whatever happened here might have nothing to do with her disappearance last night. It's still possible she went for a swim and didn't make it back to shore."

"But why would someone do this to her apartment?"

Johnson shook his head and shrugged. "Was there anything in her life, other than her work, that might have been a source of trouble? Family? Old boyfriends? Shady acquaintances?"

"No. Not that I know of."

Over Knowles' shoulder, Johnson watched an older woman with shiny copper hair, clutching a big purse in one hand and a wad of tissues in the other, walk toward them. When she got closer, he could make out her red-rimmed eyes and hear her sorrowful sniffing.

"David?" she warbled, her voice thick with tears.

"Mrs. Gibson!" The younger man opened his arms, and she collapsed into them. A stab of compassion knifed Johnson in the gut and he looked away. Constant proximity to other people's pain made it impossible to avoid some of the emotional shrapnel.

When Mrs. Gibson finally pulled away, mopping tears from her cheeks, she looked through her daughter's open door and gasped.

"What happened?"

Johnson took a step toward her and extended his hand. "Mrs. Gibson, I'm Detective Peter Johnson, with the Galveston Police Department. We're trying to figure that out."

"But David said Emily disappeared last night after saying she was going for a swim!"

"She did. But when David came back to her apartment this morning to meet you, he found this."

"Oh!" She hiccuped out a half sob and clutched her tissues to her face. "But I don't understand. Where's my daughter?"

"We don't know, Mrs. Gibson, I'm sorry to say. But we're trying to figure that out. As I've already told David, it's possible whatever happened last night had nothing to do with this. The timing could be coincidental."

The bewildered woman peered at him beseechingly. Johnson's heart sank. He had no idea what had happened to Emily Gibson, but he doubted she would suddenly waltz back into her life as though her absence was all a big joke.

"Right now, we consider your daughter a missing person. There's no sign anything bad has happened to her, but I don't think she would have missed this day voluntarily."

Mrs. Gibson shook her head vigorously and sniffed noisily. "Oh, no! She worked so hard for this, and she was so excited to start the vaccine trials. Please find her, detective. Please!"

Johnson groaned inwardly. The hardest part of his job was the inability to undo whatever horror had beset the victims of the crimes he investigated.

"We're doing everything we can," he said quietly. "I know this is difficult, but I'll need both of you to go to the police station so we can get your fingerprints to exclude them from whatever we find in the apartment. I'll also need to talk to you, Mrs. Gibson, about the last time you talked to Emily. As soon as my men are done, you'll be free to go in."

Mrs. Gibson nodded. "I'll start cleaning up. I don't want Emily to come home to such a mess."

"I'll help." Knowles said, squeezing the older woman protectively around the shoulders.

Johnson stifled a sigh. He understood why people tried to keep acceptance at arm's length, but it never made reality any easier to deal with when it finally evaded all avoidance tactics and came crashing in.

☣ ☣ ☣

Kate stared at the clock on her phone, waiting for the minute to roll over. Her fingers twitched with anticipation. She'd written her stories on autopilot, handing them over to editor Hunter Lewis in near record time. For the last thirty minutes, she hadn't done anything but wonder about Emily Gibson. She selected Johnson's number from her favorites list.

"Okay. I've given you two hours and four minutes. Spill."

Johnson's exasperated sigh didn't bother her a bit.

"Sometimes I wonder why I even answer the phone when I know it's you."

"Quit avoiding the question."

"You're like a little bulldog. A mean one."

"I take that as a compliment."

"Ha! Well, you can quit chewing on my ankle. I'm prepared to make a statement."

"A statement?! Whatever happened to our nice, comfortable chats? Do you plan to share this statement with others?"

"I'm sure as soon as you post your story, I'll get inundated with calls. So, yes. But I'm giving you the exclusive. Like usual."

"You know I appreciate it."

Johnson snorted. "You have a funny way of showing it."

"Okay, okay. I need to work on my source management skills. What have you got for me?"

Twenty minutes later, Kate hung up the phone, surprise, excitement, and dismay still swirling in her head. Four hours ago, she had chafed at being upstaged by the reporters from the big national papers, who got the interviews with Newhouse and Gibson that she couldn't get. Now they'd be following her on an explosive update to a story they thought they owned. Anticipation galloped up her spine and raced down her arms, leaving a trail of goose bumps. It had been months since she'd had a really good story to dig into. But underneath the exhilaration, a twinge of sadness perched like a hungry seagull that refused to take its beady eyes off a kid with a cracker.

She had rooted for Emily Gibson to succeed, to make her mark as a strong woman in a man's world. Now she probably wouldn't ever get that chance. She was a missing person for now, but not likely for long. Her body would turn up eventually. Johnson said it remained possible she drowned, but Kate would bet her next paycheck the woman's disappearance was no accident. She gritted her teeth as the familiar burning desire for justice caught fire in her gut. Last time she had a hunch about a story, she'd had to let it go. This time, she would not stop digging until she figured out what happened to Emily Gibson.

Ebola researcher missing

Police look for clues in disappearance of UTMB vaccine team's lead member | By Kate Bennett

EMILY GIBSON, THE LEAD researcher working on the Ebola vaccine with Dr. Aaron Newhouse, disappeared last night, hours before the serum was set to start human trials.

Gibson, 25, was staying for the weekend at a West End beach house with friends. When they decided to go for a swim after dinner, she left the house ahead of everyone else. By the time they walked down to the water, she was gone.

Police at first thought she waded into the water alone and drowned. But several hours later, Gibson's boyfriend discovered someone had ransacked her apartment.

"At the moment, we're treating this as a missing persons case," Det. Peter Johnson said. "We have no evidence of foul play. But we're asking anyone who might have seen Ms. Gibson or anything suspicious to come forward."

Gibson left her purse, wallet, and cellphone behind when she went down to the beach. Her friends and family don't know where she might have gone, if she went somewhere voluntarily, Johnson said.

Although investigators aren't ruling anything out, it's too early to say whether Gibson's work at the University of Texas Medical Branch might be related to her disappearance, Johnson said.

UTMB officials also expressed shock at the news.

"We're devastated to hear that Emily is missing," UTMB spokeswoman Claire Dupont said. "She is a valuable member of our community, and we're doing everything we can to assist the police in their search. Our thoughts and prayers go out to her family and friends in this difficult time."

Through Dupont, Newhouse declined to comment on the situation, except to say he hoped Gibson would return soon.

"As you can imagine, this has been a severe blow to our Ebola team at a very crucial time," Dupont said.

Gibson, who is working toward an MD/PhD, has spent the last year in Newhouse's lab, helping to develop his Ebola vaccine. He has credited her with overcoming some of the last hurdles to make the serum stable and get it ready for human trials. Gibson, who grew up in the Woodlands, graduated top of her class from the University of Texas at Austin.

During a recent interview with CNN, she said she knew early in her studies she wanted to work with infectious diseases. Galveston's National Biocontainment Laboratory, one of only two in the country, made UTMB her top choice for medical schools.

"There are so many things we know how to cure," she said. "I wanted to work toward finding a cure for diseases that have no cure and can wipe out entire communities. I wanted to spend my life doing something that would make a lasting difference for people who don't have the advantages of clean water, working sewer systems, and universally available health care."

Chapter 3

Johnson shifted on the white leather sofa outside Dr. Aaron New-house's office and laid his hand flat on his knee to keep from drumming his fingers. He'd waited ten minutes, with no sign of Newhouse. The doctor claimed he wanted to do everything he could to help find his missing researcher, but he had so far put more effort into postponing a meeting with police. At first, he said his work needed his full attention. Then he said he really had no information that could help the investigation. Johnson finally warned him any further attempts to delay an interview could be considered obstruction of justice.

After five more minutes ticked by, Johnson sprang up and strode toward the secretary on the other side of the room, ready to announce he would be back with a warrant. But before he could cover half the distance, Newhouse stepped through the door leading in from the hallway.

"Detective, my apologies," he said. "I had to deal with an issue in the lab that could not wait. I did not expect it to take this long."

Johnson nodded curtly, clenching his teeth against the cutting reply stampeding over his tongue. Newhouse led the way to his office and waved a hand toward the sleek red chairs in front of his desk.

"Please, make yourself comfortable," he said, walking around the wide glass tabletop and perching on the edge of an overstuffed, throne-like seat. Newhouse crossed his arms and leaned over them on the desk, narrowing his eyes as he looked at Johnson.

"Tell me truthfully, detective. Do you really think Emily is alive?"

Surprise widened Johnson's eyes and left him momentarily speechless.

"Why are you so sure she's not?"

"Detective, please." Newhouse waved his hand as though swatting away an incomprehensible insult to his intelligence. "When you called yesterday morning to tell me Emily was missing, you thought she had drowned. That seems the most plausible explanation, as terrible as it is. But the story in the newspaper this morning made her disappearance sound like a big mystery."

The suspicion itching at the edge of Johnson's mind began a full-scale scrabble for attention.

"We still consider drowning a possibility," he said carefully. "But someone ransacked her apartment. Until I can explain that, I can't rule out a connection to Ms. Gibson's disappearance."

"You don't think it was a robbery? Break-ins are not unheard of here, after all."

"Nothing of value was missing, that we can tell. It looked as though someone was looking for something specific. Did Emily ever take home anything related to the vaccine research?"

"Not that I know of. It would be highly irregular. We follow very strict security measures with the serum, and of course with the virus samples. Nothing like that could ever make it out of the lab."

"What about the data and any other written material? Test results, that kind of thing?"

"We maintain everything on computers in the lab. No one can copy the data to a computer outside the network without my permission. And only Emily and I have access to the most sensitive data. The lab technicians can only input data."

"Could someone print it?"

"Well, yes. But, detective, I don't see what any of this has to do with Emily's disappearance."

"Is it possible Emily took something from the lab that someone might have wanted?"

"You mean another researcher?"

"Perhaps a competitor?"

Newhouse sat back in his chair and gripped the arms, flexing and relaxing his fingers as he squinted across the desk. Johnson watched his face darken. The thought of his data being stolen seemed to catch him by surprise.

"Of course scientific espionage is not unheard of," Newhouse said slowly, as though still considering the possibilities. "But I cannot think of anyone who is close enough to us in vaccine development to benefit from our data. I suppose perhaps a drug company could be doing research that I'm not aware of."

Johnson nodded and looked down at the notepad in his lap. He wanted to let Newhouse chew on the implications and see where it led him.

"But, detective!" Newhouse rocked forward, his balled hands hitting the desktop with enough force to make the few items sitting on it jump. "You don't think Emily was working with someone trying to steal my research?"

"Do you?"

"I didn't until you suggested it."

"I didn't suggest it. You did."

Newhouse opened his mouth but snapped it shut without saying anything. He sat back in his chair. Johnson waited. He'd rattled the doctor. Good. Without his mask of composure, maybe Newhouse would actually share something useful.

"Until Emily disappeared and you came here asking all these questions, I never doubted her dedication to this effort," he finally said. "I haven't seen anything to make me suspicious in the least. But perhaps I'm too trusting. As you said, it's possible Emily could have been working with someone trying to gain access to our research. It wouldn't have been easy for her to take that material from the lab, but where there's a will, there's a way, as they say. That still doesn't explain her apartment."

Johnson nodded but didn't reply.

"Unless, of course, you think she had a falling out with whomever she was working with and they came looking for whatever she'd promised them." Newhouse's eyebrows arched in surprise. "That's quite a theory, detective."

Johnson smiled. "Tell me about the nature of your relationship with Ms. Gibson."

"I'm not sure what you mean. She was my researcher. That was the nature of our relationship."

"And that's it?"

"Of course."

Johnson locked his eyes on the doctor's face, tracing the lines across his forehead and the soft fall of his jaw. Newhouse fidgeted.

"Emily is a beautiful woman, and one of the most intelligent students I've worked with in a long time. Possibly the most intelligent. Definitely the most driven. That's what makes her disappearance so disappointing, detective. She would have been a leader in this field in a very few years, I have no doubt."

"It sounds like you admire her quite a bit."

"I suppose I do. Yes, of course I do. But that does not mean there was anything going on between us. It would have been highly inappropriate. Haven't you ever worked with a woman you admired but could not, or would not, pursue?"

Johnson pretended he couldn't feel the warmth spreading across his chest. He refused to admit he knew exactly what Newhouse was talking about.

Newhouse dismissed the unanswered question with another wave of his hand.

"Besides, Emily has a boyfriend. Have you talked to him? From what I could tell, he seemed like a fairly possessive fellow."

"He's the first person I talked to."

"Good. Frankly, detective, it would not surprise me to learn he had something to do with Emily's disappearance. I always thought he was not quite in her league. Maybe she finally figured that out, and he didn't want to let her go."

"I'll keep that in mind. Is there anything else you can tell me about Ms. Gibson that you think might be useful?"

Newhouse sat back again in his chair and sighed. "Not that I can think of. This is all a most unwelcome distraction from the very important work we're doing here. Emily will be missed. Deeply missed. But we will soldier on, as they say."

Newhouse stood abruptly and tucked his hands into the wide front pockets of his white lab coat.

"I wish you the best of luck in your investigation, detective. I really hope you find her."

Johnson stood slowly and fixed the doctor with another hard look.

"Thank you for your time, Dr. Newhouse. I'll be in touch if I have any follow-up questions. I don't suppose you plan on leaving the area in the next few weeks?"

Newhouse shook his head and smiled as though talking with a child.

"No, detective. I have too much work to do here, especially now that Emily is gone."

Johnson nodded and walked toward the door. He expected Newhouse to ask him for updates on the case. He never did. As Johnson closed the office door behind him, he took a deep breath. For all his claims of admiration and professions of disappointment, Aaron Newhouse didn't appear devastated by his researcher's disappearance. And while he latched on to the idea Emily might have been working with someone trying to steal the vaccine, he seemed more interested in having Johnson believe it than in believing it himself. He didn't act like a man who sensed a threat to his life's work.

As Johnson left the building, suspicion slithered after him. Nothing about the doctor's reaction struck him as appropriate. But he was sure of only one thing: Aaron Newhouse did not expect his valued researcher to return. What made him so sure she was gone for good?

Kate took a sip of her lukewarm coffee to hide a satisfied smirk as Kenton Mattingly, managing editor of the *Galveston Gazette*, paced back and forth behind his desk. His tie hung loose around his unbuttoned collar, and his shaggy hair stuck out at odd angles from his melon-shaped head. But Kate hadn't seen him take a swig from the Maalox bottle on his desk all day.

"Great job with this, Bennett. Great job. You stuck it to those snobs from New York. They don't own the news in this town, we do!" Mattingly stopped to slap the top of his desk for emphasis.

Kate snuck a sideways glance at Hunter Lewis, the paper's assistant editor and her immediate boss. From the chair next to her, he flashed a grin. The *Gazette* staff had finally recovered from last year's layoffs and the disappointment of the sex trafficking case conclusion. Watching the mayor and Eduardo Reyes, Galveston's favorite son, evade justice had devastated Kate. But she took a small measure of comfort from watching it cast a pall over the rest of the reporting staff as well. Journalists all cared deeply about justice. Her colleagues lamented the failure in their collective mission to proclaim the truth almost as much as she did.

After losing his battle with the publisher to avoid newsroom layoffs, Mattingly had chugged two bottles of Maalox a day for a week before his wife ordered him to take some time off to recover. Since then, he'd been grouchy and glum, keeping his office door closed for long stretches throughout the day. But eventually, his righteous journalistic fire burst into flame again. About a month ago, Kate and her colleagues sat transfixed as they listened to him wage a screaming match over the phone with a county official he'd skewered that morning with an especially vicious editorial. When he finally slammed the phone down, the newsroom erupted in applause.

"So what's your follow-up going to be?" Mattingly asked, swiping a bottle of spring water off his desk and taking a noisy gulp.

"A profile of Emily Gibson. I have an interview with her mom and boyfriend in a few hours. I've talked to some of her friends already, but they weren't that helpful. None of them seemed to have known her very well. Sounds like her work was her life."

Mattingly grunted as he sat down hard in his overstuffed leather chair.

"What about Newhouse?" Lewis asked.

"I've left several messages for him, starting yesterday and then again this morning. He hasn't called me back. Surprise, surprise." Kate rolled her eyes.

"Well, don't let him put you off like that, dammit!" Mattingly roared.

Kate cringed. "What do you want me to do, ambush him in his office?"

"Yes! That's exactly what I want you to do. Wait by his car in the parking lot if you have to. His top researcher is missing under suspicious circumstances. He can't just refuse to talk about it."

"Have you tried to reach out to UTMB's press person?" Lewis asked. "Maybe they can encourage Newhouse to talk. It's terrible PR if he doesn't."

"It's also suspicious as hell," Mattingly interjected. "Call UTMB, fine. But don't wait on their help. Put the screws to this guy. If he continues to put you off, we'll make that our headline: 'Missing researcher's boss silent on disappearance.' Let him chew on that for a few days."

Kate took a deep breath and nodded. Mattingly's fury lit a fire in her gut, conviction burning away the natural human impulse to avoid confrontation. Newhouse didn't have to talk to the newspaper, but it would be uncomfortable for him if he didn't. She'd be happy to deliver that message.

"I'd better go look over my notes one more time before I head out to my interview," Kate said, standing. "After I talk to Mrs. Gibson and Emily's boyfriend, I'll swing by UTMB."

"Good. Just remember, you own this story right now. Don't give these guys from New York and Washington any room to steal it from you."

Kate grinned, a bolt of competitiveness crackling across her mind like sheet lightning, illuminating her purpose.

"I won't," she said over her shoulder as she walked back to her desk.

Chapter 4

From her seat on Emily Gibson's couch, Kate couldn't detect any sign of the mess the unknown intruder had left the day before. The small space looked ready for a photo shoot in a decorating magazine. A short stack of medical journals fanned out on the coffee table. Vacuum cleaner tracks lined the carpet. And a slight floral scent permeated the air.

As Kate looked around, Pamela Gibson emerged from the kitchen with two mugs of tea.

"It took me all day to tidy up," she said, following Kate's gaze. "Whoever came through here left quite a mess."

Kate smiled as she took the cup Mrs. Gibson offered. She was glad to have something else to do with her hands while the sorrowing mother talked. Constantly scribbling in a notebook would only remind the woman this was an interview and Kate was an outsider looking in on her grief. She wanted Mrs. Gibson to feel as though she were talking to a friend. She was much more likely to open up if she could forget, even for a few moments, that Kate was a reporter.

Across the room from his perch on a wrought iron bar stool, David Knowles exhaled a heavy sigh. Mrs. Gibson cast a sympathetic, motherly look his way.

"David, are you sure you don't want some tea? It's Emily's favorite."

"I know," he smiled weakly. "I'll save it for her when she gets back."

Mrs. Gibson nodded. "We refuse to believe Emily's not coming back," she said to Kate, her voice catching over the words. "That's what's getting us through this. I wanted to clean up right away so she wouldn't have to see the mess when she comes home."

Kate winced. Denial was a cruel coping mechanism. It took every ounce of effort to play along.

"I'm sure she'll appreciate it. Everything looks great. Could you tell whether anything was missing?"

"Nothing seemed to be. And nothing was broken either. Emily will be glad about that."

"Is Emily a really tidy person?"

"Oh, yes! Always, from the time she was a child. She used to group her stuffed animals by type and color after she was done playing with them. Of course, she didn't play with them for too long. Once she discovered books, she was done with toys."

"She sounds like an early achiever."

"She definitely was. All of her teachers commented on how smart she was, early on. But her curiosity really set her apart. There wasn't anything she didn't want to know about. She read everything she could get her hands on. We had a hard time keeping her in books."

"Did she decide she wanted to be a doctor when she was little?"

"It was after her dad died, when she was ten. He had ALS. We spent so much time in the hospital it became like our second home. Everything the doctors and nurses did fascinated her. She constantly peppered them with questions. I think it was partly her curiosity and partly her way of dealing with a very difficult situation."

Kate swallowed down the lump in her throat. After losing her husband, this woman would probably have to mourn her only daughter as well.

"That must have been a terrible time."

Pamela sniffed. "At least we had time to prepare. It wasn't sudden or anything. And in a strange way, I think losing her dad gave Emily a perspective on life and a determination she wouldn't have had otherwise. I've never met anyone more determined. She just refused to quit at anything."

Knowles slid off the bar stool and came to sit next to Mrs. Gibson on the couch, putting his arm around her shoulders.

"That's right. She never quit," he said. "And she won't quit on us either. She'll come back. I know she will."

Mrs. Gibson nodded and patted his knee, sniffing back the grief that threatened to overwhelm her.

"I'm so glad Emily had David to love her and help look after her when I couldn't be here," she said, giving him a watery smile.

"Have you guys been dating for long?" Kate asked, turning to David.

"About 18 months. We met during a surgery rotation. We basically just stood around and watched what was going on. She was totally focused on the operating table. I couldn't take my eyes off her. It took me two weeks to convince her to have a cup of coffee with me."

Mrs. Gibson laughed. "I was pleasantly surprised when she told me she'd gone on a date. I thought she spent too much time focused on her studies. I wanted her to study. But I wanted her to have some fun too."

"I tried to drag her away from the lab whenever I could." Knowles smiled, but it looked like the effort threatened to shatter his composure.

"Was she already working with Dr. Newhouse when you met?"

Knowles snorted with disgust. Mrs. Gibson shot him a disapproving look. Surprise shredded Kate's carefully prepared interview script. She wasn't expecting Emily's boyfriend to show any hostility toward her boss.

Mrs. Gibson quickly picked up the narrative before Knowles had a chance to answer.

"Emily started working with Dr. Newhouse as soon as she got to medical school, which was a little unusual. She developed a fascination with these rare diseases when she was in college. She heard Dr. Newhouse speak at a conference and started following his work then. That was when he was still at Johns Hopkins. She was so excited when she found out he was coming to UTMB. After that, this is the only medical school she wanted to attend, even though she could have gone to a more prestigious place. She wrote to Dr. Newhouse after she applied and told him she wanted to work on his team."

"Wow, that's really bold."

"I thought so too. But I'm not sure that's the way Emily looked at it. She wanted to work with him, and contacting him was the most logical way to achieve that. She's very direct."

"It worked, so I guess she was right."

Mrs. Gibson laughed. "That's true. She's been so thrilled to be a part of this. And she couldn't wait to start the vaccine trials."

Next to her, Knowles grimaced.

"It seems like you were less than enthusiastic about her work," Kate said, turning to David.

"Not at all!" His eyes flashed with anger. "I just didn't like Newhouse, that's all."

"Oh, David, let's not get into that again."

"Why didn't you like him?" Kate pressed, her conscience giving only a little twinge of protest at pursuing a topic Emily's mother obviously didn't want to discuss.

Knowles looked at his girlfriend's mom and pressed his lips together. "I just thought he took advantage of Emily, that's all. She did a ton of work for him, basically carried the whole vaccine project. All for nothing."

"He gave her a lot of credit in the interviews they did together, though. Right?" Kate asked.

"Yes, he did," Mrs. Gibson interjected. "And Emily was more than happy with that. She's still in training, after all."

Knowles tapped his clenched fist on his knee. "I know. But what about after she graduates? And what will she get if Newhouse sells this vaccine?"

"Is that the plan?" Kate asked, puzzled. "I thought he wanted to turn the vaccine over to a nonprofit to make it available as cheaply as possible."

"That's what he's said publicly. But Emily told me a few weeks ago she'd discovered he was talking to a drug company."

"A company contacted him, but she didn't know whether he was seriously considering an offer," Mrs. Gibson said. "David, I really think you're making more of this than you should."

"But what if it has something to do with her disappearance? I don't want anyone to rule that out."

Excitement bubbled under Kate's veneer of mild interest. Money always made a good motive for murder.

"Do you think Dr. Newhouse did something to Emily?"

Mrs. Gibson shook her head at Kate and frowned at her daughter's boyfriend. "No! Of course not. That's silly."

"I don't know," Knowles said. "I wouldn't put it past him. Maybe that doesn't make much sense. But none of this is logical."

Kate looked at Mrs. Gibson, who had her eyes fixed on her mug. She hesitated over her next question. She hated asking it.

"Mrs. Gibson, what do you think happened to your daughter?"

Tears filled the woman's eyes. Guilt latched onto Kate's conscience like an angry dog and shook it until she had a hard time taking her next breath. For a fleeting moment, she hated her job with its callous disregard for other people's suffering.

"I don't know. I've been asking myself that for the last twenty-four hours." She put her hand over her mouth to stifle a sob. "I'm sorry," she whispered.

Knowles tightened his arm around the woman's shoulders and kissed the top of her head. Shame flushed Kate's cheeks. She'd made a grieving mother cry. She should be the one apologizing.

"I keep hoping she'll walk through the door any minute," Mrs. Gibson said. "I'm sure you think that's crazy. I may be the only one who thinks she's still alive. But I just can't believe she's gone."

Mrs. Gibson covered her face with her hands as tremors of agony shook her body. Kate stood and stepped hesitantly around the coffee table, lowering herself slowly onto the couch on the other side of the sobbing woman. She reached out and put a hand on her arm, hoping that minimal comfort would stem the emotional tide she had unleashed.

"I'm so sorry … so sorry I had to ask you that," she finally choked out. "I didn't mean to make you cry."

Mrs. Gibson hiccuped twice and gulped down a few ragged breaths. She tore some tissue from a box next to her and mopped the flood from her face.

"Oh, honey. It's not your fault. You're just doing your job. I didn't mean to lose my composure like that."

They sat for a moment in silence. Kate finally pulled her hand back and picked at the edge of the notebook in her lap while Mrs. Gibson blew her nose and dried the last of her tears. When she was done, she looked up at Kate with aqua, bloodshot eyes.

"You know, Dr. Newhouse hasn't called me. I'm sure he's very busy with everything. I just would have thought, after working with Emily for almost three years…"

Knowles snorted again. "That's what I'm saying. None of this, including his reaction, makes any sense. I told that detective he needs to take a really good look at Newhouse. Maybe they'll find something on Emily's laptop."

"The police have her computer?" Kate's voice shot up an octave, making it impossible to conceal her shock.

Knowles nodded. "They found it shoved under her bed, like she was trying to hide it. Weird, right? She always kept it on her desk."

Kate's pulse pounded in her ears. She wanted to jump off the couch and run out to the car to call Johnson. That computer could be the key to the whole case.

"Hopefully they'll have some leads to go on soon," she said, regretting the hollow platitude as soon as it left her lips.

Next to her, Mrs. Gibson let out a sigh that sounded like it came from the depths of her soul.

"I don't care what anyone says. Until I have definite proof otherwise, I'm going to believe Emily's still alive, out there somewhere."

"That makes two of us," Knowles said, smiling encouragingly and squeezing her shoulders.

Kate looked down at her notebook to hide her doubt.

"I hope you're right," she said. "I really hope you're right."

About fifteen minutes later, Kate pulled into the parking lot closest to Newhouse's office. She found an empty spot, killed the engine, and sat gripping the steering wheel. David Knowles thought Newhouse had something to do with Emily's disappearance. If he was right, she was about to confront a possible murderer. Kate took several deep breaths to steady her nerves.

She planned to start with the doctor's secretary and then stake out the entrance to the lab, if necessary. But as she stepped out of the car into the cool spring late afternoon, she spotted Newhouse striding out the door. He had his head down and gave no sign he saw her until she was right in front of him, blocking his path.

"Dr. Newhouse? Hi, I'm Kate Bennett, from the *Galveston Gazette*." Kate held out her hand. Newhouse ignored it and made a move to go around her.

Kate sidestepped in front of him again, forcing him to stop.

"I just have a few questions for you about Emily Gibson."

"I have nothing to say to you, Miss Bennett, which is why I didn't return any of your half dozen phone calls. Now, if you'll excuse me..."

"The researcher you've worked with for almost three years, who's been at your side for major media interviews about the vaccine trials, is missing under suspicious circumstances and you have nothing to say? Do you realize how strange that looks?"

Newhouse brushed past her and headed for the parking lot. Kate hurried to keep pace with him.

"The headline in tomorrow's newspaper—in big, bold type—is going to say, 'Newhouse refuses to talk about missing researcher.'

How do you think that's going to make you look? Emily's mother told me you haven't even called her."

Newhouse's face darkened. His forehead creased over a ferocious scowl. But he kept walking.

"Those drug company execs you're talking to might not be so eager to do business with you if they think you had something to do with Emily's disappearance."

Newhouse stopped suddenly and raised his hands as though he intended to grab her. Kate took a few steps back, her heart thundering in her chest. The doctor's face had turned a deep purple. The veins in his neck bulged.

"How dare you suggest I did anything to Emily!" His angry snarl revealed two perfect rows of pearly white teeth.

"If you had nothing to do with her disappearance, why won't you talk about it?"

"I don't have to explain myself to you."

"No. But if you don't, it looks like you have something to hide."

Newhouse's chest heaved as though the effort to wrestle his anger under control took all his energy and concentration.

"I have no idea what happened to Emily. I'm as shocked and disappointed as everyone else by her disappearance."

Suspicion clanged louder in the back of Kate's mind. It almost sounded like Newhouse blamed Emily for her own disappearance.

"Disappointed? I doubt she vanished to inconvenience you."

"Stop trying to twist my words. Emily's disappearance is a shame for many reasons. My inconvenience is only part of it."

Kate's next question caught in her throat, trapped momentarily by surprise. Either Newhouse had no clue how callous he sounded or he just didn't care. Either way, she had no trouble imagining he might have had something to do with Emily's disappearance.

"Why haven't you called her mother?"

"I've been busy," he hissed through clenched teeth.

"That's a really lame excuse."

"I have nothing else to say to you, Miss Bennett."

Newhouse stepped forward again, but Kate made no move to get out of his way.

"What about those drug companies?

"If you continue to harass me like this, I will call the police."

Kate snorted. "If that's how you want to play this, it's fine with me. I got what I needed. But if you really know nothing about what happened to Emily Gibson, you're not doing yourself any favors."

Newhouse glared but didn't say another word. Kate took a small step to the side, and he shouldered past, coming so close he almost bumped into her. With shaking hands and a pounding heart, she watched him slide into a sleek silver Audi, its engine barely roaring to life before it flew out of the parking lot. Kate took a deep breath to steady her nerves. She had just enough for a story and more than enough to steel her conviction Newhouse had something to hide.

She pulled her cellphone from her back pocket.

Johnson was so absorbed in the words and images on the screen in front of him that he didn't notice his cellphone ringing until the officer sitting at the keyboard asked if he was going to answer it. He took one glance at the phone and almost put it back down. But if he didn't take her call now, she would just call back, or worse, show up at the station.

"Hey. I don't have anything for you at the moment."

"Is that because you're too busy going through the files on Emily Gibson's laptop?"

Johnson put his free hand behind his head and closed his eyes. This was a headache he didn't need. "How did you find out about that?"

"I'm a reporter. It's my job to know what you're doing before you're willing to tell me."

"Ha!" Johnson shook his head but couldn't help smiling. "So since you know I don't have anything to share, why did you call?"

"I figured I'd give you a chance to unburden yourself. I would bet my next paycheck you found something good."

Johnson let several seconds of dead air hang between them before sighing. He stepped into the hall so the other detectives wouldn't hear him.

"All right. Look, Kate, I can't give you any specifics right now. But when I can, you'll be the first reporter I call."

Kate groaned. "Come on! Mattingly is going to chew my butt if I don't come back with something good."

"You've got something good. You know we're looking over her laptop. No one else knows about it."

"Yeah, but as soon as our story comes out, all the other piranhas will smell blood in the water. If one of them gets the details before I do, Mattingly will fire me on the spot."

"That won't happen. I promise. Trust me?"

He tried to take comfort from her silence. At least she had to think about it. But the longer she waited to respond, the more he realized he hadn't made as much progress with her as he'd thought.

"You're killing me, but fine. If you get a call from Ben in the morning, you'll know I'm out looking for a new job."

"If Ben calls, I'll tell him to let Mattingly know I'm only talking to you."

"Ohhhh-kay. But if someone else beats me on this, I'll never trust you again."

"Detective kills reporter's mustard-seed faith in something other than herself? I can't have that on my conscience."

Her dry laugh brushed away the disappointment that had blown in on the heavy wind of her earlier silence.

"Well, I have a lame story to write, so I'd better let you get back to whatever juicy discovery I interrupted."

"I'll call you in the morning."

"It better be worth the wait."

"It is. Trust me."

Newhouse mum on researcher's disappearance

Police search Emily Gibson's laptop for clues | By Kate Bennett

DR. AARON NEWHOUSE HAS so far refused to talk about his missing researcher, Emily Gibson, as the investigation into her disappearance enters its third day.

Although police aren't any closer to figuring out what happened, they have a new source of potential clues—Gibson's laptop. Det. Peter Johnson declined to provide any details about what investigators have found so far but confirmed the Galveston Police Department's IT team is looking through Gibson's files for indications about what might have happened to her.

Newhouse issued a statement Monday through the University of Texas Medical Branch (UTMB) press office but has ignored all requests for more personal reflections about Gibson, whom he previously described as an integral part of his vaccine research team.

Gibson disappeared late Sunday while staying with friends at a beach house on the West End. Police initially thought she drowned accidentally, but after finding her apartment ransacked early Monday, they began looking at other possibilities.

When confronted in the parking lot of his office Tuesday afternoon, Newhouse said he didn't know what happened to Gibson.

"I'm as shocked and disappointed as everyone else by her disappearance," he said.

The *Gazette* is not the only one Newhouse isn't talking to. Gibson's mother, Pamela Gibson, said her daughter's boss and mentor had yet to contact her to offer any condolences. Newhouse told the *Gazette* he'd been too busy to make the call.

UTMB spokeswoman Claire Dupont insisted Newhouse was just as devastated as everyone else by Gibson's disappearance.

"Any suggestion to the contrary is just ridiculous and, frankly, insulting," she said. "Dr. Newhouse is very busy launching this important vaccine trial that meant as much to Emily Gibson as it does to him and the rest of our team. I'm sure she would not want anything to interfere with the work into which she put so much effort."

Gibson, who had a special interest in rare diseases throughout college, began working with Newhouse as soon as she arrived at UTMB for medical school. Her mother said she wanted to come to the medical branch because of Newhouse and his work with the Ebola vaccine, which began FDA trials just hours after she vanished.

Once testing is complete, Newhouse has said he hopes to give the serum to a nonprofit or humanitarian organization that will make it available in Africa as cheaply as possible.

Chapter 5

THE NEXT MORNING, KATE perched on the edge of her chair, glaring at the silent phone on her desk. Johnson rarely ignored her calls. But twice her attempts to reach him had rolled to voicemail. The first time she hung up. The second time, she left a terse message, stopping just short of demanding he call her back. Ten minutes later, she fought the urge to dial his number again. It was like an itch in the middle of her back—impossible to ignore or satisfy.

She glanced up and caught Mattingly scowling at her from across the newsroom. Any pats on the back she'd earned for confronting Newhouse the day before got lost in the thrashing she'd endured for "letting" Johnson get away with keeping the contents of Emily Gibson's laptop secret. If a source refused to give up information, Mattingly always blamed the reporter. The resulting harangue usually began with, "When I was out pounding the pavement..." Back then, sources apparently tripped over themselves to spill their guts to reporters. Once Mattingly started down that road, it was all downhill.

Kate reached down and pulled out one of her file drawers, rifling through the documents to look busy. She was still bent over when the newsroom door scraped open. The insistent *tap-tap-tap* of ridiculously high heels headed straight for her desk made her grimace.

"Guess who's not the only reporter to get a scoop on the Emily Gibson story?" Business reporter Jessica Linton's soprano whine always hit Kate like a butter knife scraped across a dinner plate.

"What are you talking about?"

"I've got inside intel on the Gibson story. I'm about to tell Mattingly, if you want to join us."

Jessica swiveled on her red patent heels and tip-tapped toward the managing editor's office. Kate ground her teeth. She did not have the patience this morning for Jessica's pathetic attempt to be competitive. There was no way she had dug up anything Kate didn't already know. But watching Mattingly humiliate someone else might soothe her wounded pride, and take her mind off her still silent phone.

"What?" Mattingly snarled as Jessica marched into his office without knocking and set her designer handbag down on his desk. A few steps behind her, Kate smirked.

"I talked to one of my sources at UTMB this morning, and he gave me a scoop on the Emily Gibson case," Jessica said, shooting Kate a triumphant smile.

Kate rolled her eyes.

"So, let's have it," Mattingly barked. "What's this big scoop?"

"Dr. Aaron Newhouse has been talking to pharmaceutical companies about selling the vaccine he said he wanted to give away."

Kate snorted. "We knew that yesterday."

"But did you know..." Jessica looked from Kate to Mattingly and back again. "...that he's reached a deal with Phenalta Corp. to hand over the serum for $24 million?"

Kate's eyes popped open as a chill raced up her back and down her arms. Mattingly let out a low whistle and leaned back in his chair.

"That's news to me. Bennett?"

Kate reluctantly nodded. "Me too. Are you sure? How much do you trust this source?"

"Impeccably. As much as you trust your precious detective."

Anger flared in Kate's chest, burning away any trace of grudging admiration for Jessica in getting a good scoop. Her colleagues never seemed to tire of teasing her about her relationship with Johnson.

"How does this source know about the deal?" Mattingly asked.

"He's part of the team advising UTMB. Of course, they're going to get a cut as well. Not a huge cut, but it's something. There was evidently some resentment among administrators that Newhouse wasn't willing to give up more of his share."

"What about Emily?" Kate asked. "What was she going to get?"

"I don't know. They were still negotiating that. Evidently, it was tricky because she's essentially just a research assistant. She doesn't even have her PhD yet. But now that she's disappeared..." Jessica lifted her hands and shoulders in a dramatic shrug. "Problem solved."

Kate sucked in a slow breath as her heart started to pound. "That's motive."

"Believe it or not, that's exactly what I was going to say," Jessica said, brushing her long, blonde hair over her shoulder and putting one hand on her hip.

Mattingly jumped to his feet and paced back and forth behind his desk. Kate's mind lapped him, even as the implications of Jessica's revelation weighted her to the floor. If Newhouse fought to keep UTMB's share of the sale as small as possible, he probably didn't want to give Emily anything close to what she deserved. But was that really worth killing over? Kate thought about the doctor's impressive display of temper the day before. Maybe he got angry and killed her accidentally. But that still didn't explain how she vanished without a trace from the beach, or how her apartment got trashed.

Kate started when Mattingly stopped pacing and smacked the top of his desk. He fixed Jessica with a long, hard glare.

"We have to play this carefully. If we're wrong, Newhouse could sue the hell out of us. Are you sure we can trust this source?"

"Yes. Absolutely sure. I'm not interested in getting burned on something like this." Jessica looked more sincere than Kate had ever seen her.

"What motive does he have for telling you?"

"He thinks there's something suspicious about Emily Gibson disappearing right before news of this deal breaks. Evidently several of the bigwigs at UTMB are terrified Newhouse did something to her. He's put them in a really bad position. But without more evidence, no one would dare suggest anything."

Mattingly nodded and started pacing again.

"Call Phenalta and see if you can get them to confirm it. After that, we'll need to talk to UTMB, but I want to plan out our strategy first. Get back to me when you have something."

Jessica nodded, picked up her purse, and brushed past Kate on her way to the door.

"Good work, Linton," Mattingly called to her retreating back. She shot him an exultant grin over her shoulder.

Kate sighed. Jessica deserved her moment, but did she have to be so petty about it?

"What are you doing still standing here?" Mattingly snapped. "Go call your detective again and find out what was on that laptop."

Kate's cheeks flushed. Without saying a word, she spun on her heel and stomped back to her desk.

Johnson tossed a stack of photos and email printouts onto the gleaming desk in front of Aaron Newhouse. The papers slid across the glassy surface and fanned out in a damning black-and-white indictment. From an 8x10 photo in the middle of the desk, Emily Gibson smiled seductively, her finger hooked around her bra strap, frozen in time as she prepared to slide it off her shoulder. In another photo, Newhouse stood in front of a mirror, clad only in what looked like silk boxers. His awkward smile suggested he hadn't mastered the art of electronic flirtation.

The doctor cast a wary eye over the spread but made no move to pick up any of the photos. If he felt the impact of the discovery, he didn't show it. Johnson planted his fists on the desktop and leaned toward Newhouse.

"Strictly professional, huh? Coulda fooled me."

Newhouse slowly took off his glasses and leaned back in his chair.

"This is not what you think, detective."

"Maybe not, but I know what it looks like. And that's bad enough."

Johnson pulled one of the desk chairs close and sat. Newhouse leaned forward and tentatively slid the smiling photo of Emily toward him. The hint of a smile flickered across his face. Disgust rolled Johnson's stomach.

"Have you ever been thoroughly admired by someone who truly sees your worth? Not fawning adoration, but true esteem?" Newhouse looked up from the photo with gleaming eyes. He sucked in a slow breath. "It's intoxicating, detective."

Newhouse exhaled a wistful sigh, as though reliving a treasured memory.

"Sounds to me like you took advantage of someone who worked for you. Legally speaking, that's sexual harassment."

Newhouse snorted. "It wasn't like that at all. Emily was not the kind of person who could be harassed, much less taken advantage of. Believe me."

"So what happened? She seduced you?"

"Not exactly. Emily was beautiful, as you can see, and amazingly intelligent. She was genuinely fascinated by my work. I've had assistants who tried to impress me by reading up on my research in an attempt to appear smarter than they were. Emily's interest was unaffected. I was flattered, of course. But over time I came to realize just how meaningful her admiration was."

Newhouse leaned back in his chair, apparently lost in another memory.

"I've read the emails, so I know all about her meaningful admiration. How did that turn into this?" Johnson waved his hands over the photos.

"We spent many hours together in the lab. The more she worked with me, the more I...appreciated her."

"The more you wanted her, you mean."

Newhouse's thin lips curled into a serpentine smile. "Call it what you want, detective. One night in the lab, I kissed her. After that, it was like water over a dam. For both of us."

Johnson grimaced.

"I knew on some level it was a bad idea, but as I said, it was intoxicating. I couldn't help myself."

"How long did this go on?"

"About six months. We were getting closer to the final stages of the research then. I think we both realized it would be best to avoid any distractions. She actually broached the subject one night, after... Well, let's just say it had been a long night in the lab. She seemed a little apprehensive at first. I'm sure she was worried about how I would take it. But I was a little relieved, to be honest. As much as I enjoyed Emily, I did not want to get into anything serious. It was much easier to have her suggest we return to a more professional relationship."

"You're quite the gentleman."

"Please, detective. What does that even mean these days? Emily and I both got what we wanted. That's all that matters."

Johnson shook his head. He knew a lot of people felt that way, even if few had the nerve to say it with so much brutal honesty. But his moral compass pointed in the opposite direction. Even if it didn't, he'd too often seen the consequences of unrestrained lust to know it rarely ended with everyone walking away unharmed. Playing with fire almost always left someone blistered and bleeding.

"So, what happened after that? Things just went back to the way they were before? No ripple effect?"

"I wouldn't say things went exactly back to the way they were. No. But it was not awkward or difficult between us, if that's what you mean. If anything, I think we worked even better together after that. We understood each other better, if you know what I mean."

"If that's true, why lie about it?"

"Because I knew how it looked, what people would think. And I didn't think it was the kind of thing Emily would want people to know about after she was gone."

"So now you're protecting her honor?"

Newhouse rolled his eyes. "It's not the kind of thing I want people talking about either, detective. I trust, since this has no bearing on your case, you won't be making this information public."

Irritation exploded in Johnson's gut, propelling him to his feet. "I'm not convinced this doesn't have any bearing on the case. And I'll release whatever information I think is necessary to help figure out what happened to Emily Gibson. What you want is irrelevant."

Newhouse sprang from his chair and rounded the end of the desk, stopping barely two feet from Johnson. A red sheen of anger spread from his neck to his face. His eyes narrowed into vicious slits. Johnson took a step back in surprise and quickly regretted it.

"Emily Gibson drowned, detective. Case closed. You must be desperate for a promotion the way you keep trying to come up with some nefarious reason for her disappearance. If you weren't so blinded by your own ignorance, you'd see there's no mystery here."

Johnson stepped toward Newhouse and locked his eyes on the doctor's face. He clenched his fists to check his own rising anger.

"I'm beginning to think you're hiding more than your relationship with Emily. Everyone else who cared about her wants us to keep digging until we figure out what happened. You're the only one who wants us to stop."

Newhouse's chest heaved, but he said nothing. Johnson leaned over the desk and scooped up the papers and photos. He tapped them twice on the desktop to straighten the stack before striding out the door.

Kate shook her head in disbelief. Disappointment knocked her breathless. How could Emily Gibson be so stupid?

"Kate? Are you there?"

"Yeah. Yeah, I'm here. I just... I can't believe this. For months I've had to listen to people make crude jokes about Emily Gibson and Aaron Newhouse. I defended her! Said she was too smart for that. I called them all misogynist pigs. I can't believe she proved them right!"

Johnson sighed. "She was human, Kate. That doesn't make her accomplishments any less valuable. Nobody's perfect."

"You're sure he didn't force her into it?"

"Judging from the emails, no. I would describe her as more than a willing participant."

Kate groaned. "Newhouse is a total egomaniac. That doesn't say much for her taste."

"No argument there. But maybe it was easier for her to overlook his flaws since she was able to relate to him on an intellectual level."

"So, where does that leave the case?"

Johnson paused. "I'll give you the on-the-record answer first. We are continuing to investigate all aspects of Emily Gibson's life, including her personal and professional relationships. At this point, we have no definite suspects. But every detail we learn about Ms. Gibson's life will hopefully get us closer to the truth about what happened to her."

"So, Newhouse is not a suspect? On the record..."

"We have no specific reason to believe Dr. Newhouse did anything to harm Ms. Gibson."

"And off the record?"

"It's suspicious as hell. But there's nothing in those emails that suggests animosity between them after their affair ended. It's hard to believe no one had any hard feelings, at least a twinge of disappointment. But I don't have any evidence of that."

"I just find it impossible to believe Newhouse's ego could survive the blow of having Emily no longer fawning over him."

"Well, just because we didn't find anything in her emails, that doesn't mean there's nothing there."

A question about the drug company contract caught in Kate's throat. Johnson hadn't mentioned it, which probably meant he hadn't heard about it. She knew better than to pre-empt Jessica's story by talking about it before it appeared in print. Johnson could be trusted not to tell another reporter, but Kate couldn't be sure he wouldn't tell the chief, or start asking questions at UTMB. Once that bombshell escaped the newspaper office, it was impossible to guarantee they wouldn't be scooped on it. As much as Kate disliked Jessica, she would never sabotage a good story.

"You have mastered the art of the long pause," Johnson said. "Are you trying to fake me out? I don't have anything else to tell you."

Kate huffed out a short laugh. "No, I was just thinking about all the possibilities. Oh! What about David? This is going to crush him."

"Yeah..."

"Are you going to call him?"

Johnson sighed. "It's tricky. I think I'll be communicating primarily with Emily's mother from this point forward."

His words, heavy with unspoken suspicion, rolled across the phone line and landed with a thud on her notebook.

"Wait. Is David a suspect now?"

"On the record, we have no suspects at this point. Off the record, this development gives him a motive to harm Emily. Think about it."

"But he had an alibi!"

"That doesn't mean he didn't have help."

Kate opened her mouth to defend the grieving boyfriend, but her own suddenly awakened skepticism cut off her protest. She exhaled slowly.

"He seemed genuinely devastated by her disappearance. I'm sure he loved her."

"Sometimes selfishness breaches the line between love and hate until it's impossible to tell the difference anymore."

Kate snorted. "So it does. Well, I've got a story to write. I'm counting on this to get me out of the doghouse with Mattingly. You're giving me an exclusive, right?"

"Only because you're my favorite reporter."

"Ha. Thanks." Kate filled the word with as much detachment as she could muster. But she smiled as she hung up the phone.

Johnson sprang to his feet as the crack of splitting drywall echoed through the small apartment. David Knowles, trembling and red-faced with rage, pulled his hand from a hole in the wall. A shower of plaster floated to the floor.

"Take it easy, man!" Johnson stretched his left hand out in a soothing motion while his right hovered near his holstered gun. He had expected David to be upset. He did not anticipate an emotional explosion.

"I knew it. I knew it!" David seethed through clenched teeth. "Emily swore there was nothing between them. It was all a lie."

He launched himself toward the door, and Johnson thought he was about to run out of the apartment, until he spun around and strode back toward the kitchen. He made that circuit three more times before Johnson attempted to break through his vortex of anger.

"Look, I know you're upset. You have every right to be. But I need to ask you a few questions."

David stopped pacing, but as evidence his boiling anger still needed an outlet, he rhythmically pounded his balled right fist into his left hand. Johnson slowly lowered himself to perch on the edge of the couch, hoping David would follow suit as his fury burned itself out.

"You said before you wanted us to look at Newhouse. Do you have any specific reason he might have wanted to hurt her, or get her out of the way?"

"You said she broke it off with him, right? I'm sure he didn't like that very much."

"Right. That's possible. But you were suspicious of him before we found out about this. Was there a specific reason?"

"I just knew it wasn't right between them. I knew there was something there! She denied it. But I still had this uneasiness in the back of my mind, you know?"

Johnson nodded in sympathy as he thought about how to ask his next question.

"Did you ever consider breaking up with her? I mean, it sounds like your suspicions were a big issue. If you thought she was lying, why didn't you just walk away?"

David stopped pounding his fist and stared at the photo of him and Emily hung prominently above the couch. They were on the beach, sun-tinged cheeks pressed together as they grinned at the camera while the waves lapped the sand behind them. His face softened as he stared at the image. His shoulders began to sag.

"I believed her because I wanted to," he finally said. Bitterness saturated every word. "I kept thinking as long as she stayed with me, I hadn't lost her completely. For a while, things got better. I guess that's when she broke things off with Newhouse. Then she started to pull away again. I told myself she was just distracted by the pending vaccine trial and all the attention. Do you think they started...whatever...again?"

"I don't see any evidence of that in her emails."

Johnson watched as anger, sadness, and disbelief battled for supremacy, the emotions rolling across his face like dark clouds over a flat sea. He finally collapsed onto the couch next to Johnson with an agonized moan.

"She humiliated me! Why couldn't she just break up with me and be done with it? How am I going to face people once this comes out? They're all going to be laughing about how she played me."

Johnson cleared his throat to hide his surprise at the turn in the conversation. It hadn't taken David long to go from worrying about

Emily's fate to fretting over his own reputation. No matter what she'd done to him, she was still missing—presumed dead. Did he no longer care about that, or had his sorrow been an act all along?

Newhouse admits intimate contact with missing researcher

Photos, emails appear to show the relationship was consensual | By Kate Bennett

DR. AARON NEWHOUSE HAS admitted to having an intimate relationship with his lead researcher, Emily Gibson, who went missing Sunday.

Newhouse had maintained his contact with Gibson was strictly professional. But investigators discovered photos on Gibson's computer that suggested otherwise.

"The photographs are of a private, intimate nature," said Det. Peter Johnson, who declined to describe them in detail or make them public.

Investigators also discovered emails between Newhouse and Gibson that confirmed the relationship went on for months. Johnson said all the evidence indicated the relationship was consensual.

But Gibson worked for Newhouse, and he had significant influence over her academic career. Such relationships violate the University of Texas Medical Branch's faculty code of conduct.

"This is a serious breach of policy, and we will launch an internal investigation," UTMB President Stephen Phillips said in a statement. "Faculty members should never compromise their position of authority over students by engaging in personal relationships, even if they're consensual."

Newhouse and Gibson were working on the development of the Ebola vaccine. It is set to begin FDA trials next week. On Wednesday, Phenalta Corp. confirmed it had reached a deal to buy the vaccine for $24 million. UTMB will get a portion of the money, but the bulk of it goes to Newhouse. It's not clear what amount Gibson would have earned.

The researcher has been missing for four days, and investigators still don't know what happened to her. Even with the latest revelation about her relationship with Newhouse, Johnson said he had no specific reason to believe the doctor did anything to harm her.

"We are continuing to investigate all aspects of Emily Gibson's life, including her personal and professional relationships," Johnson said. "At this point, we have no definite suspects. But every detail we learn about Ms. Gibson's life will hopefully get us closer to the truth about what happened to her."

UTMB Spokeswoman Claire Dupont described the entire situation as troubling, especially in light of the personal relationship between Newhouse and Gibson. She said the university was cooperating fully with the investigation.

"We are as anxious as Emily Gibson's family and friends to find out the truth," Dupont said. "This whole situation has been devastating to our entire community."

Chapter 6

K ATE AWOKE THE NEXT morning with a dull ache just getting comfortable across the top of her head. It felt like it was settling in for a day of misery. She had stayed up too late the night before. And had too many glasses of cheap red wine. She had brooded over what she considered Emily's betrayal of the code that bound all strong women. Work hard. Succeed. Don't let anybody say you can't. And don't let any man take advantage of you.

She knew her disappointment was irrational. She hadn't even known Emily, had only met her once at a press event. But she'd admired her from afar. Cheered her on as a champion of the ideals she felt sure they both believed in. So much for that.

She rolled gingerly out of bed, her pulse pounding the back of her forehead with each step. Clear, bright sunlight streamed through the nearly floor-to-ceiling windows of her loft efficiency. She groaned and shaded her eyes as she fumbled with the coffeepot. As the fog-clearing brew slowly dripped into the carafe, she walked to the front door and swung it open. Today's paper sat on her mat, the headline of Jessica's story shouting in 48 point type: *Newhouse cashes in on vaccine success.*

Kate unfurled the tightly rolled pages and spread them out on her kitchen table. She smiled slowly at the thought of Newhouse choking on his fancy espresso when he saw it. She didn't even begrudge Jessica her prominent position on the front page. Her own story about the photos discovered on Emily's computer sat in a smaller column next to Jessica's bombshell. All in all, it was shaping up to be a terrible day for Newhouse.

The oppressive thudding at the top of Kate's head became a little more bearable.

By the time she sauntered into the newspaper office, her headache was gone and she was ready to browbeat Johnson into giving her new information that would bump Jessica out of the prime real estate she'd claimed on today's front page. Before heading to her desk, she stopped by the panel of old metal mailboxes where the receptionist deposited anything that came in for the reporters. She cringed as her stubborn drawer let out a squeal of protest when she tugged it open. Jammed into a space too small to hold it was a large manilla envelope. The sender had printed her name and the newspaper's address across the front in neat block letters. But it had no return address.

Frowning, Kate walked to her desk and slung her messenger bag across the back of her chair. Tape sealed the envelope shut, as though whoever sent it feared its contents might escape before reaching their destination. Kate worked the tip of a pen into the corner of the flap and tugged at the seam until it gave way and she could slide her finger along its length.

She reached in and pulled out a stack of papers. The top page contained a spreadsheet filled with numbers. But it was the soft yellow sticky note attached to the middle of the page that caught her attention. In the same careful block lettering, someone had written: *It's all lies. Look at the data.*

Kate quickly thumbed through the pages. Every one contained columns of numbers.

"What the hell?" she muttered as she stared at the pages.

She was so focused on trying to make sense of what she was looking at that she jumped when Hunter Lewis knocked on her desk to get her attention.

"You look like you've just been handed a pop quiz over material you've never seen before," the editor said with a smile, sipping coffee from a cup emblazoned with the slogan "World's best dad."

"Ha! It kind of feels like that. What do you make of this?"

She held up the stack so he could read the note. His eyebrows shot up then scrunched into a perplexed line over the bridge of his nose. She set her elbows on her desk and rested her chin on her clasped hands while he flipped through the pages. A suspicion had lodged itself in the back of her mind. It elbowed through her doubts and objections until she could no longer refuse to look it square in the face. Goosebumps swept across her arms.

"Do you have any idea what this is?" Lewis finally asked, handing the sheets back to her.

"It looks like data from a vaccine trial to me." She tried to hide her growing excitement, but she couldn't stop the grin from tugging at the corners of her mouth.

Lewis nodded. "That's what I thought, too. But where did it come from?"

Kated picked up the envelope and carefully looked it over, front and back. The only thing besides her name and the newspaper's address was the postmark. She was about to set it down again when the number in the circular stamp caught her eye.

March 11.

Kate shot out of her chair, gripping the envelope in both hands as she held it up.

"This is postmarked the day Emily Gibson disappeared."

Lewis examined it himself and a slow whistle escaped his lips. Then he frowned, squinting at the envelope as he lay it back down on her desk.

"That may be a coincidence. We don't know who sent it, or why."

"True..." Kate said, drawing out the word in exasperation. "But it's a possibility."

Lewis tapped the stack of spreadsheets. "Focus on the why and that will go a long way to telling you who."

He glanced over his shoulder into Kenton Mattingly's office. The managing editor had his door shut, phone pressed to his ear.

"Let's let the boss finish up his morning calls and then see what he thinks. In the meantime, see if you can figure out what all these numbers mean."

Kate nodded and managed to suppress a groan until her boss made it back to his own office. This was sure to resurrect her headache. She always joked with her dad that her stunningly poor performance in high school algebra had sealed her career fate. She had no chance of succeeding in anything technical or numerical. But English was another matter. Diving into literature, deconstructing meanings, and swimming back to shore with a perfectly organized and punctuated essay produced an unbroken string of straight As. She concluded early on that she was destined to make a living with words. The lure of journalism came naturally after that.

After poring over the spreadsheets for forty-five minutes, she'd concluded that the rows were test subjects, and the columns were readings of various biological markers. Each page held readings from a different day. The numbers rose over time but then leveled off and eventually plummeted close to their original values. The most recent sheet was dated from about a month ago.

Kate looked up when she heard Mattingly's door open. The managing editor stood in the doorway with his hands on his hips.

"What are you looking at, Bennett?" he barked. "Shouldn't you be on the phone trying to get more information about this missing researcher? Or do you just plan to give Linton your spot on the front page permanently?"

Kate's cheeks burned. Kenton Mattingly could be a first-class jerk. But he was also a first-class news man, and that covered over a multitude of sins.

Hunter Lewis strode through his own office door as Mattingly stalked back to his desk. Lewis motioned for Kate to follow him into the lion's den.

"Kate got an interesting package in the mail this morning," he said, settling into one of the two chairs facing the managing editor. Kate perched on the edge of the other one, clutching the envelope and stack of papers tightly in both hands. Her heart picked up speed as her excitement grew. Mattingly cocked one bushy eyebrow at her.

"Well?"

"Twenty pages of what looks like data from the vaccine trial. The envelope has no return address. But it's postmarked the day Emily Gibson went missing, which probably means someone dropped it in a mailbox the day before. And stuck to the top page was this note."

She held it up for him to read.

"Well, I'll be—"

"We don't know who sent it," Lewis cut in before Mattingly could finish. "So let's not jump to conclusions. And we don't even know what these numbers mean. They could even be fake."

"Why would someone send us fake data?" Kate asked. "Would anyone think we would print something without verifying it?"

Lewis shrugged. "Why would someone send it to us in the first place?"

Kate opened her mouth to reply but couldn't think of a good response. After a few moments, Mattingly's gruff voice broke the silence.

"Because they wanted us to keep digging."

Kate grinned at him triumphantly. That's why she'd wanted to work for Mattingly, despite his tendency to shred his reporters' dignity.

"I don't really understand what these numbers mean. But I can see that the levels of whatever they were monitoring went up and then went back down again. Seems like that could be a bad sign?"

"Mmmmmm..." Mattingly grunted, leaning forward and tapping his pen against the calendar that covered half his desktop.

"The note says it's all lies," she continued. "What if that's a reference to the trial results? What if the vaccine doesn't really work?"

Kate glanced between the two editors. A pause stretched between them so long she wondered if she'd speculated a step too far. Mattingly tapped his pen a few more times before throwing it down and looking directly at her.

"That would be one hell of a story," he finally said. "One hell of a story."

A dizzying surge of adrenaline pumped through Kate's heart. Mattingly couldn't have made her happier if he'd offered her a raise and a promotion.

"It's also a solid motive for murder," Lewis muttered.

Kate scooted back in her chair and took a few deep breaths to slow her skipping pulse. Mattingly nodded at Lewis.

"Whoever sent this, assuming the data is real, has the ability to blow up this whole project," Mattingly said. "I can't imagine Aaron Newhouse would sit by and let it go public."

"But surely he knows someone will figure it out eventually, especially now that he's supposed to hand everything over to Phenalta," Kate said, trying to make sense of the possibilities swirling around her mind.

"I don't suppose it's possible he doesn't know?" Lewis asked, the doubt threading through his question, effectively answering it.

Kate snorted. "Not likely. But I could easily imagine him doing whatever it took to keep it quiet as long as he could."

"So where does the missing researcher fit into all this?" Mattingly asked, bringing the speculation back to the place it started.

"Well... if Emily Gibson knew about this and threatened to expose him, I bet Newhouse would find a way to shut her up."

Kate shuddered at the thought of what might have happened to a woman she'd written off as a traitor to the sisterhood just hours before. The thought of the researcher defending the truth and possibly even dying for it certainly redeemed her.

"So you think Emily Gibson sent this to you, knowing she was in danger?" Lewis asked, lines of worry creasing his forehead.

"Maybe it was her insurance policy."

"Humph," Mattingly said, but it sounded to Kate more speculative than dismissive. "Don't get ahead of yourself. The first thing we need to do is figure out if these numbers say what you think they say. After we know that, we can figure out what to do with them."

Kate pressed her lips together as she thought about how to verify the data. Sharing it with anyone opened the possibility that word would get out. She refused to get scooped on a story like this.

"So, do you know anyone you could trust to review it and keep quiet?" Mattingly prompted, as though he'd read her mind.

Kate shook her head and tried to ignore the tickle at the back of mind that reminded her that wasn't true. She cursed her luck and sighed.

"Well, actually, I might. I dated a doctor last year who might be willing to help. He's not a researcher, but he's probably looked at enough things like this to at least let us know whether we're on the right track. And I know I could trust him."

I'm just not sure I want to make that call, she added silently.

"Good!" Mattingly barked. "Let's start there. Then we'll figure out what to do next. In the meantime, don't either of you say a word about this. I don't want even a whisper to get out. This will be the story of the year if we get it right."

Flutters of excitement swirled in Kate's stomach as she walked back to her desk. She'd be content to expose Newhouse for a fraud, but writing the story of the year would be a pretty nice bonus.

Two hours later, Kate pulled into an empty parking spot outside the UTMB Emergency Room. It had taken her about 20 minutes after leaving Mattingly's office to finish composing a text message to Brian Dougherty. She hadn't seen him for months. The last time they'd talked, she'd told him she wasn't ready to take their relationship any further. She didn't know whether he'd moved on, or found another companion for his regular dinners at Frank's. The thought of him sharing his seared scallops and expensive white wine with someone else conjured a pang of regret. She missed him.

Anyone else probably would have ignored her text. But she counted on Brian's uncommon decency, and he didn't disappoint. He texted back about ten minutes later to say that he was in the middle of a shift but could meet her for a coffee in the hospital cafeteria during his break. Now she sat in the parking lot taking deep, even breaths to calm her nerves.

She didn't immediately see him when she walked into the cafeteria, so she methodically scanned the room. She hadn't expected to beat him here.

"Kate! Sorry I'm a few minutes late."

The voice behind her sounded warm, confident, and not the least bit perturbed. Kate cursed her pounding heart. She tried to fix a casual smile on her face and turned around.

"Brian, hey. Thanks for agreeing to meet me." Her smile faltered at the happiness that danced in his eyes. She held out her hand awkwardly, but he stepped forward and wrapped his arms around her. His short, tight hug suggested he wasn't taking anyone else to Frank's.

"It's good to see you," he said. "Here, grab a table while I get us some coffee."

Kate scanned the room for the most secluded spot and chose the table farthest from the door. She sat where she could see who came in, just in case. She felt a little silly to even think about taking such a precaution. But if whatever she had in her bag prompted Emily Gibson's disappearance, maybe it wasn't that silly.

Brian set two paper coffee cups on the table and sat down in the chair across from her. He just looked at her for a few moments, smiling.

"Great story this morning. That's all anyone around here's talking about. It doesn't look very good for Newhouse. I really hope he didn't do anything to Emily Gibson."

He frowned and shook his head.

"Did you know her?"

"Emily? No. I've never met her. But it seems like she was a brilliant researcher. If she's dead, it's definitely a loss for the medical community."

Kate nodded. How much worse would it be if Newhouse had killed her?

"So, you said you needed help. What can I do?"

Kate pulled the envelope containing the spreadsheets out of her bag and laid it on the table in front of her. She took a deep breath.

"You have to promise me you won't say anything about this. To anyone."

He raised a quizzical eyebrow. Then he smiled and raised his right hand, holding up three fingers. "Scout's honor."

Kate rolled her eyes and laughed.

"Okay, okay. But I'm serious. If this is what I think it is, it's a huge story. I don't want to get scooped."

She slid the pages out of the envelope and briefly explained how she'd gotten them. His eyes widened with surprise when she showed him the note.

"So, I think these spreadsheets are evidence that the vaccine doesn't really work. I know this isn't your specialty, but do you think you'd be able to tell if I'm on the right track?"

"I don't know. Let's take a look."

She pushed the papers across the table and wrapped her hands around her coffee cup while he inspected sheet after sheet. When he got to the end, he flipped back through them, comparing different columns of numbers as he went. His eyes narrowed in concentration.

With growing impatience, Kate glanced away. It took all her self-control not to interrupt him. When she glanced back, he was looking at her, a worried frown creasing his forehead.

"I can't say with 100 percent certainty," he paused and took a deep breath. "But I think you're right. If these numbers are correct, it shows an immediate immune response to the vaccine, like you would expect. But then all the markers return to normal within a few days. That means the immunity didn't last."

His words set off an explosion of excitement she had a hard time suppressing. It rumbled through her chest like an earthquake and almost lifted her out of her seat.

"So the whole thing's a sham?" she asked, lowering her voice even though they were alone. "How is that possible?"

"I don't know. But this definitely isn't the data they provided to the FDA. There's no way they could get human trials started based on this."

"So that means they must have submitted fake data."

"Assuming this data is correct, yes. But that's impossible to know. I mean, it's easy to fake a spreadsheet."

Kate pursed her lips in frustration.

"Well, at least I know what these numbers show. Now I just have to figure out if they're real."

Brian sighed. "I can't help you with that."

Kate gave him a rueful smile. "You've helped a lot. I really appreciate it. I didn't have anyone else I could trust to keep it a secret."

For a few seconds, she looked into the familiar questioning eyes. He had been patient to a fault the whole time they'd dated. He hadn't pushed, hadn't tried to force his way into her inner fortress. Just held his ground and waited. But she could feel her defenses wearing down. That's when she'd turned tail and run.

He reached across the table and took both her hands in his.

"I've missed you," he said.

She felt her face get hot and looked away. He let her hands go and sat back in his chair.

"Sorry," he said. "When I got your text, I just hoped..."

She looked back and smiled. "It's okay. I... I miss you, too."

The words both surprised and relieved her. Maybe it was time to stop running.

He leaned toward her with bright eyes and a wide smile.

"What are you doing Saturday? Want to go to Frank's?"

Chapter 7

Kate sat in her car in stunned silence. She'd walked out of the hospital with a date and a stack of spreadsheets that suddenly felt like they were burning a hole in her messenger bag. Both were equally exciting... and terrifying. She allowed herself a moment to recall Brian's exultant smile when she'd said yes, the way his eyes crinkled at the corners as he squeezed both her hands. Then she forced herself to set it aside and focus on the more pressing problem. How was she going to figure out whether the data was real or a very detailed hoax?

She stared up at the building across the street where she knew Newhouse had his offices. She should go back to the newspaper and confer with Mattingly and Lewis. This was not the time to get distracted. But she couldn't help entertaining a little mental fantasy of confronting him, just to see his reaction. If he casually dismissed her, he probably had nothing to worry about. But if his guilty conscience flared up with righteous indignation, she'd know she had something. She longed for a bombshell that would blow that arrogant smile right off his face.

The longer she sat in her car, the easier it was to believe dropping by his office was a good idea. He probably wasn't even there. But maybe she could wheedle some information out of his secretary. Kate opened her car door and got out. She thought about locking the envelope in her trunk but decided she couldn't let it out of her sight. She slung the messenger bag over her head and shoulder and trotted across the street.

Her footsteps echoed off the walls of the building's empty lobby when she stepped inside. The directory listed Newhouse's office on the fifth floor. As the elevator doors closed, the tiniest kernel of unease took root. If Newhouse really had done something to Emily Gibson, she needed to be very, very careful.

When the elevator doors slid open, she tip-toed across the hallway to what looked like an elegant office suite. She paused outside the glass-paneled door and took a deep breath. Then she twisted the handle and swung it open.

Soft light permeated the reception area, but the chair behind the front desk sat empty. Kate looked around, held her breath, and listened. She thought she could hear the faint murmur of a voice toward the back of the suite.

"Hello?" she called out tentatively. When no one came, she said it a little louder.

Still nothing.

Kate crossed her arms and counted to one hundred. Still standing alone on the fluffy area rug in front of the receptionist's desk, she debated her options. She should probably leave. What if the receptionist was just down the hall in the bathroom and came back to find a reporter poking around in Dr. Newhouse's inner sanctum? Not good. But she thought she'd heard a voice in the back. Shouldn't she at least check? After all, it wasn't her fault someone had left the office door open for anyone to walk in.

She peeked around the corner and down the hallway. She slowly put one foot in front of the other until she was standing in the middle of the corridor, closed doors on her right. No light emanated from the spaces at the bottom. But around a slight bend in the hallway, she found another door. This one had a yellow glow beneath it.

Kate's heart pounded as she lifted a lightly clenched fist and placed her knuckles softly against the smooth wood. She held her breath and knocked twice.

"Yes? Who is it?" Kate instantly recognized the thin, whiny voice of Aaron Newhouse.

She squared her shoulders, swung the door open, and stepped inside.

Newhouse leaned back in a big leather chair. A pair of reading glasses dangled from his fingers as though he'd just taken them off to look up at the intruder. For an instant, he just looked surprised. Then an angry scowl contorted his face.

"Hi Dr. Newhouse. Kate Bennett, from the *Galveston Gazette.*" Kate boldly crossed the space between the door and the desk until she was standing about 10 feet in front of him.

Newhouse sat up and glared at her.

"I know who you are. How did you get in here?"

"The front door was open. I waited for someone to come. I even called out, but no one answered."

Newhouse looked like he'd bitten into a rotten lemon.

"Well, you can turn around and walk right back out. I have nothing to say to you."

Indignation burned Kate's face. She refused to be dismissed so easily.

"Would it help if I took my shirt off and sent you trashy photos?"

Newhouse jumped up and marched around the desk. Fear jolted through Kate's body, but she didn't step back. She crossed her arms to keep herself from trembling. Newhouse had turned the color of beets.

"How dare you say that to me! Get out."

"What did you do to Emily Gibson, Dr. Newhouse? You know it's only a matter of time before the police figure it out."

He seized her forearm and spun her around toward the door. Kate yelped and stumbled, wrenching her arm free as she regained her footing. Her breath came in short, shallow gasps. Fury and disbelief made her voice warble.

"Touch me again, and I'm calling the police. That's assault."

"Get out!" Newhouse screeched.

Kate's fear ebbed just enough that she could take an even breath. He hadn't tried to grab her again. She had an advantage.

"Fine, I'll leave happily. You may not have anything to say to me now, but you'll have plenty to say after the newspaper publishes my next story. Of course, by then you'll probably be in police custody."

She gave him a smirk and walked back down the hall. She had almost made it to the foyer when she heard his footsteps behind her. She spun around.

"What are you talking about? What story?"

"Wouldn't you like to know?"

"I'll sue you for libel if you print anything that gets in the way of this trial."

The adrenaline surging through her body made Kate feel light-headed. She knew she should walk away. But she just couldn't resist getting in one more dig.

"Gets in the way of it? It's going to blow it out of the water."

Newhouse stepped around her, blocking her exit. Kate's triumph melted. He'd turned the tables.

"What do you think you have?" he hissed.

Kate crossed her arms over her chest. Newhouse no longer looked apoplectic. But his now restrained fury felt much more threatening. Her mind raced. She had to get by him and out that door.

"Oh, nothing much. Just proof that your miracle drug is nothing more than snake oil."

Newhouse crossed the space between them in an instant and seized both of Kate's arms above her elbows. He gave her a slight shake.

"That's rubbish. You're bluffing."

Terror squeezed Kate's throat as she tried to twist free.

"My editors know I'm here, and if I don't make it back to the newspaper, the police will know exactly where to start looking. I doubt you can make two women disappear and get away with it."

Newhouse pulled her to him until their noses were just inches apart.

"You're pathetic. You have nothing. You're just fishing for your next front-page headline to give your sad little existence some meaning."

"Pathetic, huh? Just wait until we publish this data showing you're a fraud."

Kate didn't realize she'd moved her hand over the front of her messenger bag until Newhouse's eyes darted down. Suddenly, he let go of her arms and grabbed the strap across her chest.

"Data? Is it in here?" An evil snarl split his face as he tried to pull the strap over her head.

"Hey! Let go!" Kate yanked backward and stumbled, her heel catching on something. She put one hand behind her as she tumbled backward, her other hand stretched out to ward off Newhouse. His snarling face was the last thing she saw before a blinding pain exploded in the back of her head and everything went black.

Kate groaned as a wave of nausea washed over her. She lay absolutely still until the heaving in her stomach subsided. She tried to open her eyes, but the light stabbed into her brain like ice picks. She put her hands over her face and took deep breaths. Where was she?

Slowly, the afternoon's events came back to her, replaying through her mind almost like a slide projector. The envelope. The meeting with Brian. Walking into Newhouse's office. *The envelope.* Still not daring to open her eyes, Kate felt around her with growing dismay. She had to get up and find her bag.

She took a few deep breaths before rolling onto her side. Her throbbing head screamed in protest. Her stomach heaved again and she stifled a sob. When the pain and nausea ebbed, Kate slowly inched herself into a sitting position. Shading her face against the glare, she slowly opened her eyes. She was sitting on the fluffy rug in front of the receptionist's desk. One corner was flipped over. That must have been what tripped her.

In the middle of the room, she spotted her messenger bag. She sobbed with relief. But as she sat there steeling herself to crawl over to it, a growing sense of dread snuffed out any comfort the sight of the bag brought her. What was the chance Newhouse had just dropped it and run, without looking inside?

Tears flooded her eyes. How could she have been so stupid?

She inched toward the bag, tears now flowing freely down her cheeks. How was she going to explain this to Mattingly and Lewis? She could kiss her story of the year goodbye. When she got close enough to the bag to reach inside, she felt nothing but air.

The folder was gone.

She fumbled with the zipper on the front pocket and slid out her cellphone. She pulled up her favorite contacts list and tapped the name at the top.

The phone rang twice before he picked up.

"How's my favorite reporter? You must be busy since you haven't called once today to harass me for information."

The deep, warm voice soared through the phone's speaker like a lifeline.

"Peter," she said, her voice cracking. She couldn't remember ever calling him by his first name before. "I need your help."

"What?!" Johnson yelled, jumping up from his chair. "You've got to be joking."

"Please don't yell. My head..." Kate's tear-filled, muffled voice only supercharged his suddenly pounding heart.

"I'm on my way," he said, already jogging down the hallway toward the station's back door. "But Kate, don't hang up. Just set your phone down on the floor. I want to make sure I can hear what's going on, in case he comes back."

Just thinking about Newhouse slinking back into his office, with Kate lying defenseless on the floor, made him shudder. He flipped on his lights and siren as he rocketed out of the parking lot. The afternoon exodus of UTMB employees heading home to the mainland made for a steady stream of traffic going the other way. But his route was mercifully obstacle free.

"You still with me?" he asked as he neared the hospital campus.

"Barely," she croaked. "Those sirens are ripping my head apart."

Johnson smiled at the flicker of her normal sass and flipped off the siren.

"Almost there," he said as he screeched to a stop outside the office building. He took the stairs two at a time and drew his gun as he got to the fifth floor. Newhouse had likely fled a while ago, but he wasn't taking any chances.

He slowly opened the door and peered down the hall. It was empty. He stood still and listened for a few seconds before striding over to Newhouse's office door and swinging it open.

Kate sat against the opposite wall, her phone clutched to her chest.

"It's the cavalry," she rasped. Her flippant tone suggested she was trying to be brave, but her trembling lip and tear-filled eyes gave her away.

Johnson holstered his gun and knelt down beside her.

"How's the head?"

"It hurts like hell, but I don't think it's broken."

He chuckled and shook his head. "Your sense of humor is intact, so that's probably a good sign."

She rewarded him with a wan smile. "Thanks for coming."

He pressed his lips together at the memory of her frantic call and resisted the urge to take her hand. Instead, he pulled out his notebook.

"What happened?"

The anger quenched briefly by worry boiled over again as Kate told her story. He almost snapped his pen in fury when she recounted Newhouse grabbing her. But he also shook his head more than once in exasperation at her own part in the confrontation.

"I know it was stupid!" Kate said. "Okay, I know! I was just hoping to tell by his reaction whether he thought he had anything to worry about."

"Well, I guess he did."

"Fat lot of good that does me now. The data's gone."

"Maybe so, but that doesn't mean you don't have a story."

She started to laugh and then groaned as she raised a hand to her forehead.

"Very funny," she whispered.

He sighed. He could lecture her for 10 minutes about her carelessness and stupidity. But maybe this time experience could be the bad guy.

"We really need to get you downstairs and have someone look at your head."

Kate frowned. "Why, so they can tell me I have a concussion? I know the drill. Ice and ibuprofen. I'll be good as new in a few days."

"The fact that you can even say that about a head injury is disturbing. You know that, right?"

She flashed him a grin that was almost as bright as normal.

"Help me up?"

He stood and reached down, grasping both her hands in his. Then he lifted her gently to her feet. She scowled and screwed her eyes shut, gripping his hands tightly.

"Kate..." he started, gritting his teeth against the impulse to scoop her up and carry her down to the emergency room.

"No, no. I'm fine." She took a deep breath and opened her eyes. She glanced at their hands and a smile tugged at the corner of her mouth. "Sorry. I just needed to get steady."

She let go of his hands and took a step to the side. He frowned.

"I'm fine. Really. Let's get out of here."

He picked up her bag and carefully draped it over her head and shoulder.

"You're sure it's not bleeding?"

"It's not bleeding. I checked before you got here."

"Fine," he huffed. "If you can make it out of the building, I'll let you go. But only to your apartment. I'm not letting you get in your car. I'll drop you off."

"But I need my computer!"

"Someone can bring it to you. You're in no shape to drive."

Kate glared at him, but she didn't protest as they walked down the hallway.

An hour later, Johnson pulled up to the edge of Aaron Newhouse's immaculate emerald lawn. Two cruisers pulled up behind him. The officers followed him to the front door, standing about five paces behind. He didn't know what to expect. He had a hard time imagining the doctor trying to resist arrest, despite his attack on Kate. Newhouse viewed her as someone he could push around. Johnson doubted he'd try that with three armed police officers.

He curled his fingers into a fist and pounded on the door. He tried not to think about how satisfying it would be to do that to Aaron Newhouse's face.

The door swung open, but the doctor was not on the other side. The man on the threshold wore a soft grey suit, shiny oxfords, and a light blue tie. A matching handkerchief peeked out of his jacket's front pocket.

"Detective Peter Johnson?" The man smiled politely. "My name is Bruce Castleman. I'm Dr. Newhouse's attorney. Please come in. We've been expecting you."

Johnson frowned as the lawyer walked calmly down the hall toward what appeared to be an open living room. Had Newhouse called his lawyer as soon as he fled his office, leaving Kate lying motionless on the floor? Had he known she was just knocked out, or did he think she was dead? Johnson tamped down the seething anger that threatened to boil over. He turned to the officers behind him and motioned them to follow him inside.

The living room looked out over the backyard. Immaculate landscaping surrounded a glistening pool. Next to a wall of windows overlooking his personal paradise, Newhouse sat in a sleek black leather chair, his feet propped on a matching ottoman. Half an inch of dark amber liquid swirled in the bottom of the crystal tumbler he held in his hand. He slowly lifted it to his lips and finished off the drink, pressing his lips together in appreciation. Johnson watched him through narrowed eyes. Newhouse smirked.

Johnson's face flushed hot and his heart pulsed. He took a deep breath and counted backward from ten. He refused to let Newhouse provoke him into doing anything that might compromise the case. But he allowed himself one small smirk of his own as he unclipped a plastic tie from his belt and stepped forward.

"Aaron Newhouse, you are under arrest for assault, failure to render aid, and theft."

Johnson continued to recite the Miranda rights as Newhouse stared up at him. He wasn't smiling anymore. When he was done, Johnson waited expectantly, but Newhouse made no move to stand.

"Get up," Johnson said through clenched teeth. "Unless you want my officers to assist you."

Castleman, who had been standing a few feet away, hastily stepped over and put a hand on his client's shoulder.

"That won't be necessary," he said. "Aaron, I'll be right behind you. Don't say a word. I'll have you out as soon as possible."

Not if I can help it, Johnson thought.

Newhouse put his tumbler on the coffee table and stood. He pressed his lips into a thin line, as though it took every ounce of self-control to keep his mouth shut.

"Turn around and put your hands behind your back," Johnson said.

"Detective, surely that's not necessary." Castleman said. He sounded like he was used to turning questions into statements that people readily agreed with.

Johnson looked at him for a few moments, as though considering. Then he looked back at Newhouse and smiled.

"It's necessary."

Newhouse arrested, charged with assault

Scuffle with reporter sparked by dispute over vaccine claims | By Ben Denison

GALVESTON POLICE ARRESTED DR. Aaron Newhouse on Thursday night. He's charged with assault, failure to render aid, and theft after attacking *Galveston Gazette* reporter Kate Bennett.

Bennett went to Newhouse's office at the University of Texas Medical Branch to ask him about an anonymous tip sent to the newspaper. Spreadsheets of data mailed to Bennett seemed to show the Ebola vaccine is not as effective as Newhouse claims.

Bennett said when she told Newhouse about the data he demanded to see it. When she refused, he grabbed her messenger bag and tried to pull it over her head. In the ensuing scuffle, Bennett tripped over a rug and fell backward into a desk. She hit her head and blacked out.

When she woke up, Newhouse was gone and so were the spreadsheets.

Well-known island defense attorney Bruce Castleman represents Newhouse.

"My client is a respected member of the local community, not to mention the global medical community," he said. "We are confident that when the whole story is told, Dr. Aaron Newhouse will be exonerated."

UTMB spokeswoman Claire Dupont said administrators were shocked to learn of Newhouse's arrest.

"Obviously, this is an extremely unusual and unfortunate situation," she said. "Dr. Newhouse is presumed innocent until proven guilty. But clearly this is not a circumstance we would want any of our faculty members to be in."

Newhouse's arrest comes just a day after university officials announced they were launching an internal investigation into his relationship with missing researcher, Emily Gibson. Photos and emails on Gibson's computer show the two carried on an affair for months, in violation of university policy.

On the same day, pharmaceutical company Phenalta Corp. confirmed it had reached a deal to buy the vaccine for $24 million.

A company spokesman declined to comment for this story.

Dupont said she had no information about claims the vaccine's efficacy might have been exaggerated.

"This is news to us, but if true, it would be devastating to everyone, not to mention the communities in Africa hoping for protection from this devastating disease," she said.

Castleman declined to answer any questions about the missing spreadsheets or the vaccine.

Gazette Managing Editor Kenton Mattingly called the attack on Bennett an assault on the free press.

"For a member of the media, simply doing her job, to be attacked over information, it's unbelievable," he said. "We have no way to investigate the tip sent to us, since the spreadsheets are gone. But if they're right, Dr. Aaron Newhouse has plenty to answer for. And we will make sure he does."

Galveston police are continuing to investigate Gibson's disappearance.

Chapter 8

JOHNSON WOKE BEFORE SUNRISE the next morning. Without switching on the light, he pulled on sweatpants and a T-shirt and slipped on his running shoes. His two dogs hopped and spun circles with excitement as he took their leashes from their hooks by the front door. A hazy pre-dawn sheen covered the cars and gave the buildings a ghostly aura as they trotted up 12th Street toward the seawall. After they descended the steps onto the sand, Johnson unclipped the dogs and let them burn through their first shot of energy by tearing off toward a flock of seagulls. The birds rose with a thrum of alarm that made Johnson chuckle. They were in no danger of being caught. But the dogs never seemed to tire of the game, despite their continual lack of success.

After they'd made sure no stray bird had dared to return, the dogs loped back to their master, dripping tongues hanging out of their mouths. He re-clipped their leashes and began his own run down the beach, the dogs trotting obediently at his side. His shallow breaths deepened and fell into rhythm with his pounding feet. They ran toward the east, where a sliver of orange peeked above the horizon.

Johnson wondered how Kate had fared overnight. He'd texted her after booking Newhouse into the Galveston County Jail. Her response still made him laugh: *Put him in a cell with someone big and mean.* As much as he would have liked to, Johnson had Newhouse put in a single cell for the night. Ben Denison had called about 30 minutes later to get a quote for his story. He said Mattingly had given Kate the night off. Although breathing heavily from his run, Johnson couldn't help but smile at the thought of how Kate must have responded to that.

Now he had to figure out his next move. He knew Bruce Castleman would clamor for a bail hearing first thing this morning. But he hoped he could get a warrant for Newhouse's computers first. If the data Kate described was real, the doctor would do everything he could to erase all traces of it. Assuming he hadn't done that already. They needed to get a look at his computers before he could access them again.

Police Chief Sam Lugar was already in his office when Johnson arrived at the station about an hour later. He had a copy of the *Galveston Gazette* spread out on his desk. Johnson could just make out the headline of Ben's story from across the room. He tapped lightly on the doorframe. Lugar waved him in.

"Helluva story," he said, picking up the paper and opening it to read the final few paragraphs on page four. When he was done, he folded it up again and laid it aside. "Bennett has an uncanny knack for finding trouble."

Johnson laughed. "She does, occasionally, let her enthusiasm co-opt her better judgement."

"Humph," Lugar grunted. "That's just a long-winded way of saying she's a trouble-maker. What's your gut on Newhouse?"

"I think he's hiding something. Maybe it's just about the vaccine. If it's a dud, he certainly wouldn't want that coming out. Although he can't hide it forever. Once the FDA trials start, someone's going to figure it out."

"If that's his biggest problem, that's not our concern. Peddling a fraudulent vaccine isn't a criminal offense."

"Right. But killing your lead researcher to hide evidence of your fraud is."

"I'm listening."

"Kate Bennett thinks Emily Gibson might have mailed that data to the newspaper before she disappeared. If Gibson knew that the vaccine was a hoax, Newhouse had every reason to want her gone."

"Twenty-four million reasons."

"Exactly. Right now, we have no evidence that he did anything to her. But we haven't looked either. This gives us a possible motive, and I think that's enough to persuade a judge to let us at least take a look at his computers."

Lugar leaned back in his chair and pursed his lips as he thought it over.

"It's a fishing expedition. And you don't have a direct tie to Emily Gibson's disappearance. No reason to think anything on those computers pertains to her."

"That's true. But if there's a problem with the vaccine, what are the chances she didn't know about it? That means she was an accomplice or a whistleblower. Either way, she was a liability."

"That gives you a motive and a theory, but it's not evidence. It's not even circumstantial evidence."

Johnson sighed in exasperation. "I know. But it's a piece of the puzzle."

They sat in silence for a few moments while Lugar thought it over.

"I don't object to you giving it a try, if you can convince the judge," he finally said. "I don't think UTMB will put up much of a fuss, but you never know. If they're willing to cooperate, it will help. Once you get your warrant signed—if you get your warrant signed—see if they'll send over someone who can interpret this stuff."

"On it. Thanks, chief."

"Just remember, we don't know for sure that we're dealing with a murder here. There's still a possibility that Emily Gibson drowned accidentally."

Johnson nodded and stood to go. He knew it was possible. But the more he learned about Newhouse, the less probable it seemed.

It took some convincing, but Johnson finally persuaded the judge to sign his warrant. Bruce Castleman met him at Newhouse's home, where officers found one laptop and one iPad. The officers dispatched to UTMB brought back two desktop computers from Newhouse's office and four from the lab.

Although UTMB's in-house counsel had protested over the computer seizure, he hadn't protested much. Johnson got the feeling university administrators wanted to get to the bottom of this almost as much as the police did. If the vaccine was a fake, they were as much a victim of Newhouse's deception as anyone. They had readily agreed to send over a statistician to assist with the investigation.

Dr. Gwen Zhou arrived about 30 minutes after the police department's IT team had finished setting up the computers in the conference room. Johnson met her in the foyer. Her sharp black eyes swept over him as he walked up to her.

"Thanks for coming," he said, shaking the small hand she held out to him. "We've only just started to look at the files. But all these medical readings don't mean much to us."

"Don't worry, detective. I should be able to tell pretty quickly if anything looks amiss. I've followed Dr. Newhouse's work, so I know what the data should say."

She pressed her already thin lips together disapprovingly. Johnson thought she wanted to say something else, but she just shook her head as if she still found the whole thing hard to believe.

"Okay," he said, gesturing toward the door behind him. "Follow me and I'll get you set up."

Johnson introduced Dr. Zhou to the technicians and then stepped back to let them work. For the next two hours he hovered at the edges of the room, watching the digital investigators tap at keyboards and point at screens. Gwen Zhou sat shoulder to shoulder with one of the officers in front of a computer taken from Newhouse's lab. They hadn't found any evidence of problems with the data, as far as Johnson could tell by their reactions.

Niggling doubt about the success of his fishing expedition had started to tug on his mental line when Officer Dylan Conner waved his hand.

"Heeeeyyyyy, boss? You need to see this."

Johnson almost ran to the table where Conner sat hunched over Newhouse's laptop. He stared at the screen.

"I found nothing in his regular email, nothing unusual anyway," Conner said. "But I figured a guy like Newhouse's gotta have a private email address. Know what I mean?"

Conner raised his eyebrows and nodded knowingly. Johnson rolled his eyes.

"Come on, what did you find?"

"I'm getting there!" Conner looked slightly offended, but he was in his element. His impish grin gave that away. "So I did some digging and found references to a web-based email service. It wasn't in his history, mind you. He wiped that clean. But we have ways of un-wiping, right?"

Johnson took a deep breath as he pulled up a chair and sat down.

"What did you find?" He said each word slowly, hoping Conner would get the message.

The young officer's smile disappeared. He sat up straighter and cleared his throat.

"Right. Well, I found another email account and I've been sitting here trying to figure out the password. I finally got it."

His fingers swept across the laptop's track pad and a new browser window appeared on the screen.

"You probably better just read the messages for yourself, starting here."

Conner clicked on a message near the bottom of the inbox. It was about two months old.

A, There's something wrong with these readings. Can you take a look? E

Newhouse had responded a few hours later.

That can't be right. Run the tests again.

Over the next few days, the emails flew back and forth. Then they stopped for about a week. The next one made his breath catch.

A, I've run everything twice and the results are the same. Something is seriously wrong here. We can't keep pretending everything is fine. E

Emily had sent that message on a Friday afternoon. Newhouse didn't respond until Sunday evening.

Keep working on it. We're not going to lose everything we've worked for. Don't say anything to anyone unless you want to throw away your career before it even gets started.

Johnson tried to picture Emily Gibson's face as she read that message. Was it a threat or just a reflection of Newhouse's belief that if the vaccine failed, it would end both their careers? Her next message came through the following Friday.

A, I'm getting out of town for the weekend. I need a break from all this. I'm begging you to reconsider. I don't think the reaction will be as bad as you do. It's a setback, but we'll figure it out. If we don't say something now, they're going to figure it out eventually. What will we say then? E

The messages stopped for two weeks. Then Emily made one last appeal.

Aaron, we cannot go through with this. You have to tell the FDA that the trial failed. They need to know. It might delay the next step, but we'll figure it out and get back on track. If you won't tell them, I will.

Newhouse never responded.

Johnson sat staring at the screen. Emily Gibson had begged and pleaded for weeks to go public with the vaccine trial problems. What would Newhouse have been willing to do to keep her quiet?

"Get me printouts of those messages, and give Dr. Zhou a copy of that first data file Gibson sent," he told Conner, standing up. "Let's see if she can tell us what went wrong."

An hour later, Johnson sat across from Aaron Newhouse and Bruce Castleman in one of the police station's interrogation rooms. He slid the printouts across the table and watched as Newhouse scanned the pages. He took off his glasses and rubbed his hand over his face.

"So, did she?"

Newhouse looked tired. His defiance from the day before had melted into something closer to resignation.

"Did she what, detective?"

"Rat you out to the FDA."

Newhouse snorted. "No, obviously not."

"And why is that?"

Castleman held up his hand. "You don't have to answer that."

Johnson fixed his eyes on Newhouse's face. The doctor stared back through narrowed lids. It looked like he was trying to decide whether to take his lawyer's hint to keep his mouth shut.

"Because I persuaded her not to," he said, his voice flat, matter-of-fact.

The hair at the back of Johnson's neck stood on end. Was that a confession?

"Aaron, as your lawyer, I'm advising you not to say anything else," Castleman said. Clearly, he thought it sounded like a confession, too.

"I know what you're thinking, detective," Newhouse said with a scornful glance at his attorney. "But I didn't do anything to Emily. We talked. That's all. I persuaded her she had as much to lose as I did and that our best bet was to figure out what went wrong and fix it."

"Seems like you already tried that, and it didn't work."

"It will work!" Newhouse banged a clenched fist against the tabletop. "We just need more time. We will figure this out."

"We who?"

Newhouse glared at him. "I will figure it out."

"Not from in here, you won't," Johnson said, crossing his arms and leaning over his elbows on the table. "What happened to Emily Gibson?"

"I told you I didn't do anything to her." A hard edge of anger punctuated his words. "I have no idea what happened to her."

"But it sure was convenient for her to go missing, just before she could have done the most damage to your pet project."

Newhouse flushed crimson and jumped to his feet, chest heaving. Johnson eyed him warily and eased out of his chair, keeping his hand on its back as he rose to his feet. If Newhouse charged him, he would use it like a lion tamer. Castleman just gaped at his client, too surprised to intervene.

"This is not some pet project!" Newhouse screeched. "This is my life's work. And I will not let it fail!"

The air in the small room crackled with intensity. It reminded Johnson of being outside in a thunderstorm, just before lightning ripped open the sky. Castleman finally broke the silence.

"Aaron, please, sit down." He patted Newhouse's chair as if he were talking to a child. "This isn't helping."

Newhouse took several ragged breaths as he struggled to wrestle himself under control. He passed his hand over his face again. Johnson eyed him warily until he slowly lowered himself back into his chair.

"I didn't do anything to Emily Gibson, detective. Her absence hurts me more than anyone else."

Except maybe Emily, Johnson thought.

He spent the next hour in the chief's office.

"It's not enough to charge him with murder," Lugar said after they'd reviewed all the evidence. "If she'd gone missing from her apartment, maybe. But the DA will never be able to make a case for murder when there's still strong evidence that she drowned. I know the timing is suspicious as hell. But I've seen stranger coincidences."

Johnson sat back in his chair and laced his fingers together behind his head. He blew out a breath in frustration. He knew Lugar was right. But he wanted Newhouse to pay for what he'd done to Kate and what he'd mostly likely done to his researcher, even if they couldn't prove it.

"Are the techs done with the computers?" Lugar asked.

"They're still working on them. I'm going to have them review Emily Gibson's computer again, too, now that we know there may be another set of emails to look for."

Lugar nodded.

"What did the doc who reviewed the data say?"

"She confirmed the vaccine doesn't work like it's supposed to. I didn't ask her to explain the science behind what went wrong. Since Newhouse admitted there was a problem, I didn't think we needed the details."

"Humph. I probably wouldn't understand it even if you had. We'll let the folks at UTMB explain all that. No doubt they're conferring with their lawyers and their media consultants as we speak."

Johnson recalled the hard set of Dr. Zhou's mouth when he told her what they'd found. If all the hospital administrators were half as disgusted as she looked, Aaron Newhouse needn't expect any support from his former colleagues. He'd dragged the hospital's name through the mud, a stain that would dirty everyone associated with the institution. Newhouse's scandal was personal for all of them.

"Speaking of the media..." Johnson let his words trail off to give his boss a chance to follow his train of thought.

Lugar raised an eyebrow.

"Kate Bennett had this information until Newhouse attacked her and stole it. Seems only fair to give her an exclusive on the story."

"That seems like playing favorites to me."

"Come on! She got a concussion chasing down this information. I think she earned it."

Lugar shook his head. "I'm pretty sure she brought that whole thing on herself. But I'm happy to curry a little favor with the local press."

"Yes, sir. I'll start putting together a news conference for tomorrow morning."

He rose to go but only made it halfway to the door when Lugar called him back.

"Reporters can be allies, but they're not our friends. Don't lose sight of that."

"Yes, sir."

With the chief's caution still ringing in his ears, Johnson walked down the hall to his office. He waited until he'd shut the door behind him to pull his cellphone out of his pocket. He stared at Kate's name on his favorites list. Lugar would probably tell him to erase it. But that wouldn't do any good. He had the number memorized.

He touched her name lightly with his finger and lifted the phone to his ear.

"How's my favorite reporter?"

Vaccine hoax

Developer admits Ebola shot a failure after police find evidence of doctored data | By Kate Bennett

THE EBOLA VACCINE DEVELOPED by Dr. Aaron Newhouse is a fraud, police revealed Friday. Investigators looking for clues about Newhouse's missing researcher found evidence of the fraud on computers seized from his lab at the University of Texas Medical Branch.

Hospital administrators confirmed the discovery.

"We are profoundly shocked and disappointed," UTMB President Stephen Phillips told the *Gazette* late Friday. "We have no idea how this happened, but we are cooperating with the police in their investigation."

Researcher Emily Gibson disappeared late Sunday. Police initially thought she'd drowned during a late-night swim on the West End. But her boyfriend found her apartment ransacked on Monday, leading to suspicions of foul play.

Det. Peter Johnson is leading the investigation into Gibson's disappearance.

"We still don't have any evidence that points to what might have happened to Miss Gibson," Johnson said. "But we are exploring every possibility, including her connection to the vaccine."

Emails discovered on Newhouse's personal laptop showed Gibson discovered a problem with the vaccine and alerted her boss about six weeks ago, Johnson said. When they couldn't quickly figure out the problem, Gibson urged Newhouse to make the information public. Newhouse refused.

The doctor's attorney, Bruce Castleman, insisted his client is innocent of any involvement in Gibson's disappearance.

"He is as mystified as everyone else, and just as disappointed," Castleman said. "Dr. Newhouse believes the problem with the vaccine can be fixed. That would be much easier with Emily Gibson's help than without it."

Castleman declined to comment further on problems with the vaccine, although he said Newhouse sincerely believes the vaccine will eventually produce the long-term benefits he initially promised.

"It's absurd to think he would try to pull one over on the entire medical community," Castleman said. "As soon as the FDA began looking at the data, they would have discovered something was wrong. My client simply hoped he could fix the problem himself before anyone else found out. Obviously, in hindsight, that was a grave error of judgment. But that doesn't make him guilty of anything worse."

Officials with the FDA could not be reached for comment.

Newhouse remains jailed on assault charges stemming from an unrelated incident.

Chapter 9

AFTER HE'D TALKED TO Kate on Friday night, Johnson sent the tech team home for a good night's rest. Now that they had a thread to pull, he wanted them all at full strength the next morning. The adrenaline high he'd been riding since Kate called him from Newhouse's office had finally run out. He'd fallen into bed almost as soon as he got home and slept for a dreamless 10 hours.

Wispy clouds clung to the horizon as he drove up Seawall Boulevard the next morning. The damp, predawn chill rolled through his open window, making him shiver. He didn't normally take the long way to the station, but today he needed a little extra calm before walking into the media storm.

His phone started buzzing shortly before 6 a.m. with numbers from New York, Washington, Atlanta, and Houston. It seemed like every reporter in the country wanted to pump him for information on the Newhouse case. He'd texted them all the same reply: "News conference at 10 a.m."

He counted five satellite trucks in front of the station as he pulled into the back parking lot. Inside, the building was nearly deserted. But from the conference room where they'd set up the computers seized Thursday, Johnson could hear a faint humming. It took him a few moments, standing in the doorway, to locate the source. In the far corner of the room, Dylan Conner sat hunched over a laptop. He was humming along to whatever he was streaming through his earbuds. Johnson chuckled. As he watched, Conner broke into a rousing chorus, jumping up and clutching an invisible microphone to his lips and pointing at a crowd only he could see. He ended the song with a flourish, hands raised to accept the adoration of his imaginary fans.

Johnson clapped loud enough to break through the young officer's soundtrack. Conner's cheeks turned bright pink, but he grinned sheepishly.

"Sorry, boss," he said, pulling out one earbud. "I got a little carried away."

"Looked like a rousing performance," Johnson said with a laugh. "You'll have to invite me to your next show. What are you doing here so early?"

"Well, I couldn't stop thinking about that email account we found on Newhouse's computer. And that got me thinking about Emily Gibson. We didn't look for secret accounts when we went over her computer before. But if he had a private way to communicate, what are the odds she did, too? So I thought I'd get a jump on the search."

"Good man. Let me know if you find anything." Conner could be a little rough around the edges, but what he lacked in experience, he made up for with enthusiasm. Johnson smiled as he walked the rest of the way to his office, humming the chorus to Conner's song.

He spent the next hour going over his notes and typing up his statement. The chief wanted to review it before the news conference. He was almost done when his phone buzzed with a text message.

Can I bring you a coffee? You're probably going to need a little extra caffeine today!

He smiled, first at her unusual thoughtfulness and then at what Sam Lugar would say if he caught him accepting gifts from an "ally" he was supposed to keep at arm's length.

Thanks, but I'll be tied up in meetings until the presser. You'll be there?

Not even gonna dignify that ridiculous question with an answer. I'll be the one heckling from the front row.

Johnson laughed. He could picture her making faces at him, trying to break his concentration.

"Something funny, detective?"

Johnson jumped as Sam Lugar's stern bass boomed from the doorway.

"Nothing in particular, sir. I'm almost done with this statement. I'll bring it down to you in five minutes."

"I've already had half a dozen calls from UTMB this morning. President Phillips will be here, along with the head of the epidemiology department. I told them we'd let them have their say after you're done talking about the investigation."

"Are they taking questions?"

"I told them I thought they should, unless they want to spend the rest of the day taking follow-up calls."

Johnson nodded.

"Five minutes," Lugar said, holding out his hand with his fingers spread wide as he walked out the door.

Three minutes later, Johnson hit print and headed down the hall to pick up the copies on his way to Lugar's office. He was scanning the pages as he emerged from the workroom and almost collided with Dylan Conner. The pink that had tinged his cheeks when Johnson caught him singing had spread over his entire face. His wide bright eyes and parted lips made him look like a little boy who's just discovered a hidden stash of Christmas presents.

"What is it, Conner?"

"You won't believe it," he said, excitement making him a little breathless. "You just have to see it."

Johnson's heart jolted as though he'd taken Kate up on her coffee offer and downed three shots of espresso in one gulp. He followed Conner back to the conference room. The younger officer gestured for Johnson to take the chair in front of Emily Gibson's laptop. Conner rolled another one over from a neighboring table and perched on the edge.

"So, I was looking for a hidden email account, and I was digging through her cached files. Most people think you can erase them, but you have to try pretty hard to delete all traces."

"Conner!" Johnson barked, anticipation sparking an eruption of frustration. "I'm supposed to be in the chief's office right now. Give me the history later. What did you find?"

Conner pursed his lips in disappointment but reached around to tap on the laptop's track pad. A browser window swept into view.

"Chat messages between Newhouse and Gibson. He threatened her, boss. Said if she told anyone about what she'd discovered about the vaccine, he would kill her."

For a moment, the only thing Johnson could hear was the blood whooshing through his ears. He leaned over the keyboard and clicked on a thread that started about two weeks before Gibson disappeared.

EG: We can't keep this up. They're going to figure out something's wrong.

AN: We'll solve the problem before then.

EG: We won't. We need more time.

AN: We can stall.

EG: I won't keep lying for you. It's totally unnecessary. These kinds of setbacks happen all the time. Most people just admit it and go back to the drawing board.

AN: I'm not going to admit defeat.

EG: If you keep trying to hide this, it will blow up in your face.

AN: If you say anything, it will blow up more than your face.

The messages stopped for about a week and then picked back up just a few days before the announcement about the FDA trial approval.

AN: I've been watching you cozy up to the team from the FDA. If you know what's good for you, keep your mouth shut.

EG: What's that supposed to mean?

AN: I will not let you ruin everything I've worked so hard to build.

EG: I've worked hard on this, too. And I will not have my career ruined by your pride.

AN: You will regret it if you say anything. I'm not joking. If you value your life, you'll keep this to yourself.

EG: Is that a threat?

AN: I promise you I will not let you do this to me. Save your career. Save your life. Keep your mouth shut.

A few days after that, Emily Gibson disappeared.

All the pieces to the puzzle that had been milling around in Johnson's mind for days clicked into place. He looked up at Conner with a grim satisfaction.

"Good job with this. You may have just figured out what happened to Emily Gibson."

Kate frowned as she pulled her phone out of her back pocket for a third time to check the clock. The news conference should have started ten minutes ago. The annoyed buzzing of the other reporters filled the room. They assumed Johnson kept them waiting because he didn't respect their time. But punctuality was part of his law-loving nature. He wouldn't be late unless he had a reason.

She pulled her pen out of the spiral at the top of her notebook and began filling the top sheet with swirling doodles while her mind wandered through the possibilities. Maybe the UTMB administrators were still trying to perfect their statement. Or maybe the IT team had found new evidence. She hadn't expected to learn anything new today, since Johnson had given her the exclusive the night before. But maybe today was about to get a lot more interesting than she expected.

"Hey, Bennett!" one of the TV reporters called from across the room. "You seem to have a direct line to the detective working this case. Could you give him a call and tell him to hurry it up?"

He grinned as a snicker rippled over the crowd.

"Maybe he's giving you time to get your head out of your—" Kate cut her insult short when the door at the far end of the room swung open and the media liaison for the District Attorney's office strode to the microphone.

"Sorry to keep you waiting, folks," she said. "We've had an unexpected development in the case this morning. I can't tell you anything more than that at the moment. But I do apologize for the delay. And if you stick around, I think I can guarantee it will be worth your while."

The reporters' shouted questions bounced off the woman's retreating back. Kate was too breathless to bother. A hurricane of butterflies beat against her ribs. Then a wave of nausea washed over the excitement. What if they'd found Emily's body? She scooped up her bag and picked her way around television cameras and cables until she reached the front doors.

"Where's Bennett going?" she heard someone say as she pushed her way out into the bright sunshine. She walked far enough away from the door that no one could eavesdrop, but stayed close enough to see through the glass in case the conference suddenly started. She flipped through her notebook pages until she found the one she was looking for and pulled out her phone.

The butterflies felt like angry hornets swarming in her chest as she listened to it ring.

"Hello?"

"Hey, David. This is Kate Bennett with the *Gazette*. I'm sorry to bother you. Are you busy?"

Emily Gibson's boyfriend snorted into the phone, an angry sound that made Kate think of a bull about to charge.

"No. No, I'm not. It's a little hard to be busy when all I can think about is Emily and what Newhouse did to her. There's no way the police can still believe she drowned. Not with everything that's happened in the last few days."

Kate hesitated. She didn't think Johnson believed Emily drowned, but she didn't want to give false hope, either.

"I know," she finally said. "I'm sorry I wasn't able to give you a heads up on that story. It came in late and I was just scrambling to get it written up before deadline."

"It's fine. I know you've got your own stuff to deal with. How's your head, by the way?"

"Better, thanks." The truth was, she still felt a little off kilter, like she'd just spent a day at sea and hadn't gotten her balance back. "Listen, I'm down here at the police station. They were supposed to have a news conference 20 minutes ago. But they've delayed it and won't tell us what's going on. I thought you might have heard something."

On the other end of the line, David Knowles caught his breath. Kate winced. Guilt pinched her conscience. She was trying to get an angle on a story, but any definitive news about the missing researcher would probably bring nothing but grief to her family. It didn't matter whether Newhouse had killed her or she'd drowned. The end result was the same.

"Like what?" he asked, his voice thin. "Do you think they found her?"

Kate swallowed the lump forming in her throat. "I don't know. That's the first thing I thought of. But if you haven't heard anything, that's probably not it. They would definitely call Emily's mom before they made any public announcement. If she hasn't called you, then..."

Her voice trailed off. She wasn't exactly sure how to finish the sentence. Then there's still hope? But she doubted if David really believed Emily was still alive.

"I haven't heard from her," he murmured. "But I'll give her a call. I won't say anything about what you told me. I'll just see how she's doing. I was going to call her today anyway. I just hadn't worked my way up to it."

Kate tried to read between the lines. They had seemed pretty close when she'd interviewed them together after Emily disappeared. She settled on a vague question he could easily dismiss if he didn't want to be specific.

"Is something wrong?"

A heavy sigh blew over the phone's speaker. "No. I mean, not really. It's just been a bit awkward since.... well, you know, those photos. I was so mad. And I don't think she knew what to say."

"I'm sure she was shocked." Kate tried to imagine how her father would react if he'd learned in such a public was that she'd been sleeping with her boss.

"Yeah, and disappointed. And sorry for me, which didn't exactly make it easier, you know?"

"I can imagine," Kate murmured sympathetically.

"I loved her so much," David said, his voice breaking. "How could she do that to me?"

Suddenly, Kate wanted to get off the phone as fast as she could. She had no idea what to say to this man who'd had his heart and pride ripped to shreds while the whole world watched.

"I'm so sorry, David."

"Me, too," he said, bitterness making his sorrow razor sharp. "I would give anything to have one last conversation with her."

Kate frowned. It seemed like an odd thing to say, but he probably just meant that he had so many unanswered questions he wanted to ask.

"I think most people who've lost someone they love feel that way," she said, trying not to think of her teenage self filling page after page of her journal with questions she wished she could ask her mom.

"Yeah..."

"Listen, I should probably go. Hang in there."

"Will you let me know what they say?"

Kate hesitated. She didn't have time to give a personal report to everyone who wanted one. But she knew how desperately David and Emily's mom wanted answers.

"Sure, I'll text you. I won't have time for much detail because I have to write my story fast, but I'll let you know the basics."

"Okay. Thanks."

After she hung up, Kate continued staring at the phone, thinking about what David had said. *One last conversation.* What would he say? Emily had betrayed him and used him. Played him for a fool. And now he would spend the rest of his life wondering what would have happened if she hadn't disappeared. No wonder his emotions ping-ponged between sorrow and seething.

She sent a text to the copy desk editor, letting her know not to expect the story for a while but to hold a front-page spot. Next, she texted photographer Doug Cowel to let him know he might want to head her way. Then she went back inside to wait.

Another hour passed before the DA's press secretary walked back to the microphone. Reporters scrambled to their feet while cameramen frantically waved at her to wait until they could get their feeds hooked up.

"No rush, no rush," she said, holding up her hand as though to calm the suddenly roiling sea of journalists. "We'll be getting started in about five minutes. That should give you time to get all set up."

Excitement tingled up Kate's arms as she flipped her notebook open to a fresh page. She gripped it so tightly it bowed slightly.

Almost exactly five minutes later, the door at the back of the room swung open again and a long line of people filed in. Kate had expected Johnson to lead the pack, but District Attorney Nathan Mahoney made his way toward the podium first. Kate scanned the line of other officials until she found Johnson. His lips pressed together in a grim line, but something about his eyes suggested satisfaction. He held her gaze for a few moments and nodded just slightly. Not enough that anyone but her would notice.

Her heart beat faster with anticipation.

"Good morning," Mahoney said as he adjusted the microphone closer to his mouth. "I guess it's almost afternoon now. I'm sorry to keep you waiting. But as you know, there were some unexpected developments this morning, and they have substantially changed this case."

Camera shutters clicked as he paused for effect. Kate resisted the urge to roll her eyes. District attorneys were as much politicians as they were lawyers. They knew better than anyone how to play to an audience.

"Today, I am filing first-degree murder charges against Dr. Aaron Newhouse."

Kate's mouth dropped open as a murmur rolled through the crowd.

"We already knew that Emily Gibson tried to persuade Dr. Newhouse to come clean about the failure of his vaccine. He refused. But we now have evidence that he threatened to harm her if she tried to go public with what she knew."

Another pause. Kate scribbled frantically. The sudden surge in her pulse made her head throb.

"It is our belief that he did just that," the district attorney continued. "We still don't know what happened to Emily Gibson, but we believe Dr. Newhouse can shed some light on that, and we hope he will do so quickly."

Kate caught Johnson's eye and raised an eyebrow. He didn't so much as twitch a muscle. Kate tapped her pen on her notebook. What would they offer Newhouse to confess to Emily's murder? First degree murder would be hard to prove when the defense would likely argue she had drowned.

When Mahoney opened for questions, Kate shot her hand in the air and fixed him with her best I'll-remember-this-at-campaign-time stare.

"Ms. Bennett." he said, nodding her way.

"Is Dr. Newhouse cooperating with the investigation?"

"Cooperating?" Mahoney chuckled. "I can't say that he is cooperating at the moment. But I hope he will reconsider his position sooner rather than later."

The other reporters peppered him with questions related to the information she already had in this morning's story. She listened distractedly to make sure she didn't miss any fresh detail. How likely was Newhouse to give in? Based on his arrogance, she bet he'd fight tooth and nail to protect what remained of his reputation.

Forty-five minutes later, Kate turned onto Broadway and headed back to the newspaper office. She pulled out her phone and called Johnson. When he didn't answer, she counted to five and dialed again. Voicemail. Another five count, more ringing. He finally picked up on her fourth try.

"Kate, what gives? Are you trying to get me fired or something?" His exasperated sigh tickled her ear.

"There's no way he's going to confess."

Johnson paused so long she thought he'd hung up.

"Hello?"

"I'm here. I don't know if he'll confess. If he doesn't, he's looking at a very long court battle."

"Mahoney is up for re-election in two years. Is this his poster case? Even if he doesn't win, he can at least say he gave it everything he had."

Johnson laughed. "You're such a cynic. Don't you think the district attorney wants justice for a young woman who tried to do the right thing?"

Kate snorted. "Sure, especially if it sounds good in campaign ads. But seriously, murder one's going to be really hard to prove. Newhouse could end up walking away scot free."

She cursed the tremor in her voice and tightened her grip on the steering wheel.

"Kate, I promise you I will do everything I can to make sure Newhouse pays for what he's done. To Emily Gibson and to you."

She swallowed and blinked back tears.

"I just don't want to see one more murderer go unpunished," she said through gritted teeth.

"I know, Kate. I know."

Chapter 10

Kate spent the rest of Saturday and all Sunday holed up in her apartment. She'd postponed her date with Brian until Tuesday. Her head still ached, and she was nursing an even more debilitating case of anxiety over Newhouse. In her fitful dreams, he walked out of the Galveston County Courthouse a free man, fixing her with a smug smirk as he waltzed by the reporters gathered to witness his victory over justice. Once, the dream had morphed into a nightmare. She was locked in his office, frantically searching for a way out as he came toward her, a syringe in his hand.

By Monday morning, her head had stopped pounding, but her mood hadn't lifted.

"Good morning, sunshine," Hunter Lewis raised an eyebrow over his "World's Best Dad" coffee cup when she stalked into the newsroom. "Doesn't look like your weekend of rest did you any good at all."

She glared as she swiped a copy of the day's paper off a table and stomped to her desk. Lewis followed at a distance.

"Do you need another day off? Did you get in to see a doctor?"

Kate tried to smooth out her scowl to ease his own worried frown.

"I'm fine. Really. Just stressing about this case. I do not want Newhouse to get a pass."

Lewis nodded. "Mahoney is taking a gamble on the charges. But he's not interested in losing a big case right before his next election, so he must think it's a risk worth taking."

"He'll never get a conviction as long as Newhouse's lawyer can convince a jury Emily might have drowned. He won't even have to fight the murder charges. All he has to say is, 'prove there even was a murder!'"

Before Lewis could respond, the newsroom door scraped open and Delilah Peters swept in, followed closely by Ben Denison.

"Heads up, kiddo," Denison said. "Judge held a bail hearing for Newhouse on the sly first thing this morning. Looks like he's going to be bonding out in a few hours."

"What?!" Kate jumped out of her chair, nearly knocking it over. "How could he do that? The hearing wasn't scheduled until this afternoon!"

"Castleman called in a favor. I guess Newhouse didn't like his accommodations very much."

"So they're just going to let him go?"

"My source told me he's getting fitted with an ankle monitor. Home confinement. Mahoney got that concession, at least. He'd better hope the pressure of being locked up at home, as pleasant as I'm sure that is for a doctor, will encourage Newhouse to spill his guts."

"Unbelievable." Kate's anxiety boiled over into seething anger. The adrenaline coursing through her body made her tremble.

"You'd better double check that bit about the ankle monitor. I didn't get it official."

Kate spent the next 30 minutes trying to get Mahoney on the phone. When he finally answered, he sounded almost as aggravated as she felt. After stipulating they were off the record, he spewed a string of profanities about the judge and his lack of judiciousness.

"On the record?" Kate finally asked when the tirade slowed.

"On the record, while I'm certainly disappointed by this turn of events, I respect the judge's decision. My office is already hard at work on this case, and we will be ready for a trial as soon as the judge sets a date. But I am still hopeful Dr. Newhouse will do the right thing and tell us what happened to Emily Gibson. Her family deserves the answers that only he can provide."

Kate cringed as she thought of Emily's mother. The poor woman had to know by now her only child would not be coming back to her perfectly tidied apartment, no matter how long she waited. Her only hope now was to find out what had happened to her.

Kate thanked Mahoney and hung up. She needed to call Mrs. Gibson to get a comment, but she dreaded dialing in to the woman's anguish. Other people's sorrow always threatened to bore into the well of mourning she kept carefully buried year after year.

Reluctantly, she tapped the numbers on her phone.

"Hello?" The warbling, watery voice almost made Kate hang up.

"Mrs. Gibson? This is Kate Bennett, with the *Gazette*."

"Oh, I saw the area code and thought it might be someone from the police department calling with news."

"I'm so sorry. I don't have any news about Emily. But Aaron Newhouse is getting out of jail this morning. The judge set his bail at \$5 million, and of course he didn't have any trouble meeting that."

Mrs. Gibson sniffed. Kate groaned silently.

"I still can't believe he did something to Emily," the distraught mother whispered. "But I can't believe any of this. It's just like a nightmare that's happening to someone else."

"Emily never said anything about him making threats or about problems with the vaccine trial?"

"No. She'd seemed more stressed the last month or so. But I just chalked it up to her being focused on the project. She never seemed to have time to talk, until just a few days before she disappeared. She called me and apologized for being so distant. She told me she missed me and she'd see me soon. But she never hinted that she feared for her life."

Mrs. Gibson ended with a hiccup and a soft sob. Kate tried to swallow down the lump that sprang to life in her own throat.

"I'm so sorry," she murmured, pausing to weigh her next question. "If you could speak to Aaron Newhouse, what would you say?"

"Oh! I don't, I mean, I hadn't thought..." She sniffed a few more times before continuing. "I guess I would say, if you know anything about what happened to Emily, please, please tell us. I just want to know what happened to my baby!"

Kate wiped the corners of her eyes as Emily's mom sobbed on the other end of the line. The phone suddenly felt like it weighed 10 pounds. It took all her effort to keep it pressed to her ear.

"I'm sorry. I didn't mean to fall apart like that," Mrs. Gibson said after what felt to Kate like an eternity. "I know you have better things to do than sit here and listen to me cry."

"It's okay. I'm sorry I called to bother you."

"Oh, honey, I know you're just doing your job. I appreciate you caring so much about what happened to Emily. If you keep writing about it, maybe we'll get some answers in the end."

"I hope so. I really do." Kate cleared her throat. "I'd better let you go now. But if I hear anything, I'll let you know."

After she hung up, she laid her head down on her desk. She counted to twenty as she stuffed the agony of loss and helplessness back into the emotional lockbox where she kept them safely contained most of the time.

"Bennett!" She jumped as Kenton Mattingly barked her name from across the room. "That Gibson's mom you were talking to?"

She nodded.

"Good. I need a story to post within the hour. Get cracking!"

Kate nodded again and suppressed a sigh.

Forty-five minutes later, she turned in her story, scooped up her car keys, and headed for the door. The soft spring breeze lifted her hair off her neck and caressed some of the tension out of her shoulders. The grey skies that had added to the weekend's oppressiveness had lifted. Bright sunshine washed everything in a hopeful hue. Vibrant pink and white flowers covered the azalea bushes that lined the median on Broadway. In spite of herself, Kate smiled.

She headed downtown to her favorite coffee shop. Latte for lunch seemed like a great idea. Coffee in hand, she drove over to City Hall and picked up the packet of information for Thursday's council meeting. Then she made her way to the seawall and drove slowly back to the newspaper. The novelty of coastal living hadn't worn off after more than a year. She still marveled that she could spend her lunch hour watching the waves roll over the beach while pelicans made kamikaze plunges into the gulf.

When she got back to her desk, she settled in for the mind-numbing process of reading through the council agenda. Thirty minutes later, her lunchtime caffeine infusion was the only thing keeping her awake. The bleating of her desk phone roused her from a near stupor. She shook her head to clear it as she lifted the receiver to her ear.

"Thanks for calling the *Galveston Gazette*. Kate Bennett speaking."

"Miss Bennett, this is Bruce Castleman." Her eyes snapped open in surprise. "I'm representing Dr. Aaron Newhouse."

"I know who you are." Her pulse sounded like a jackhammer in her ears. "What can I do for you, Mr. Castleman?"

"Dr. Newhouse would like to meet with you."

Kate almost dropped the phone. She stood up to catch her breath. Suspicion pricked the back of her neck.

"Excuse me? Why would he want to do that?"

The lawyer paused, like he was trying to choose his words carefully.

"Dr. Newhouse would like to tell you his side of the story. He hopes he can convince you he's innocent."

Kate stood staring at nothing, her mouth hanging open. She knew she hadn't misheard him. But his words seemed completely nonsensical.

"I'm sorry, what did you say?" she finally asked.

Castleman sighed. It sounded like he had a hard time believing his words, too.

"Dr. Newhouse has a theory that he'd like to share with you, about what happened to Miss Gibson."

Kate's eyes narrowed.

"The DA's pretty sure he knows what happened to her. Given the evidence, and Dr. Newhouse's behavior, his case is pretty convincing."

"That will be for a jury to decide."

"You know, the last time I talked to Dr. Newhouse, it didn't go so well for me."

Castleman cleared his throat. "Yes, well, I'm sorry about what happened between you and Dr. Newhouse. But that doesn't make him a murderer. And, as you know, there are always two sides to every story."

The thought of being in the same room with Newhouse again made Kate's stomach twist. But curiosity won the brief tussle with her fear. How could she resist an exclusive interview with a murder suspect? Talk about click bait. The publisher would be in raptures. And she would get a chance to let Newhouse, in his own words, show the world what a conceited, self-centered pig he was. No one would believe his claims of innocence after she got done with her story.

"I'll have to clear it with my editor," she said. "But I'm interested."

"Good. Give me a call back once you've talked to him."

Kate dropped the handset back in its cradle and strode over to Hunter Lewis's office. By the time she knocked on his open door, she was grinning.

"You'll never guess who just called me."

Lewis raised an inquisitive eyebrow.

"Aaron Newhouse's attorney."

Lewis's second eyebrow shot up to match the first one. "What did he want?"

"He's offering me an exclusive, or rather, Newhouse is offering me an exclusive. He wants to tell his side of the story."

Lewis let out a low whistle.

"At first I thought there was no way I would put myself in the same room with him again. But think about the story! Everyone's going to want to read it. I'm sure the *New York Times* wouldn't say no."

Lewis laughed. "No, I don't suppose they would. What did you tell him?"

"That I had to talk to my editor."

He chuckled. "Well, let's go see what Mattingly thinks."

Kate recounted her conversation with Castleman for the managing editor. He leaned back in his chair as she talked, his bushy eyebrows kissing over the bridge of his nose.

"So I told him I had to clear it with you. What do you think?"

"It's a helluva plan. Wonder what game Castleman's trying to play."

"What do you mean?"

"He's trying his case in the press. Why? How does that benefit Newhouse?"

"Well, I got the impression he wasn't all that excited about it, to be honest. Seems like it's something Newhouse wanted."

"Castleman wouldn't allow it if he thought it would hurt his case."

Kate looked over at Lewis, seated in the chair next to her.

"You don't think we should do it?" he asked.

"I'm not saying that. But if we're going to get used, I wanna know why. I also don't want Bennett called in as a witness in a murder trial."

Kate frowned. She hadn't thought about that. But if the DA thought she had information that would help his case, he wouldn't hesitate to issue a subpoena.

"So, how do we avoid that?" she asked.

"Not sure we can. We might just have to risk it. Readers will eat this story up. And I don't want him taking it to someone else."

"So that's a yes?"

"With a few ground rules." Mattingly held up a finger. "First, Lewis, I want you to go with her. I don't want him trying anything funny. Second, you tell him anything he says is fair game. If he doesn't want to see it printed in black and white, he'd better not say it. We're not doing anything off the record. That's our best defense against a subpoena."

The excitement building behind the dam of Kate's doubt began to trickle over the spillway. A little shiver shot up her back. Knowing she wouldn't have to face Newhouse alone squashed any remaining hesitation.

Now all she could think about was what Newhouse would say. And how she could make him look like the lying murderer he was.

"Alright then. I'll call Castleman back and set it up."

She was halfway to the door when Mattingly called her back.

"Don't let your history with Newhouse get in the way here. Of course, you don't believe he's innocent. Neither do I. But you'll get a better story if you use that skepticism like a scalpel, not a sword. Cut through his crap, but don't lop off his head."

Kate laughed and gave her boss a thumbs up as she retreated to her desk.

On her way home, Kate debated calling Johnson. She wanted to know if he'd found any more evidence, but she wasn't sure she should tell him about the meeting with Newhouse scheduled for the next morning. She considered Johnson as a co-belligerent in the fight for justice. But that didn't mean their battle plans always aligned.

Eventually, the desire to hear a friendly voice won over her hesitation.

"I was wondering when you were going to call me," he said by way of greeting.

She wasn't sure when they'd dropped the need for formal hellos, but it made her smile every time.

"Oh, I thought you needed a break from being badgered," she said breezily.

"Right. You must have been busy today. I saw your story about the bail hearing. I hoped Mahoney would push harder to keep Newhouse locked up, but I guess that wasn't likely given his resources."

"At least he's not free to roam or skip town."

"That's true. But I'm sorry we couldn't make him a little more uncomfortable, to make up at least a little for what he did to you."

Kate smiled. "Thanks, but given what he probably did to Emily Gibson, I guess I shouldn't really complain."

"Ha! Well, still. I know how you feel about people not getting what they deserve."

"He's going to stand trial for murder. That's something."

"Let's just hope Mahoney can get a conviction. Or that Newhouse has an attack of conscience and confesses."

"I don't think that's going to happen."

"Why not?"

Kate hesitated. "He's doubling down on his claims of innocence."

"What does that mean?"

Kate took a deep breath. "I can't believe I'm actually saying this, but this is off the record."

"What?" Johnson burst out laughing. "That's my line."

"I know! But you have to promise you won't repeat this. It will all come out Wednesday morning anyway, so you don't have to wait long."

"Okay..." He drew out the word in an unspoken question.

"I got a call from Bruce Castleman today. Newhouse wants to tell me his side of the story. An exclusive interview. But it's definitely not a confession. Castleman said he has some theory about what might have happened to Emily."

Johnson groaned. "And I'm sure you're going to do the interview, right?"

"Yep."

"Kate, haven't you had enough of his lies and intimidation? You already know what he's going to say. He's just using you to taint the jury pool."

Anger bristled in her chest. "I'm not an idiot. I know he's playing a game. But I'm not about to let him give his exclusive to the *Times*."

"Even if it means you might help him get off? I thought you wanted him to pay for what he did to Emily Gibson."

"I do! But if he wants to tell his story, he'll do it somewhere. Why not let the *Gazette* get credit for it?"

"And is the *Gazette* going to take credit for helping him beat a murder charge? Seems like you're undermining your campaign for justice."

His accusation knifed through her self-assurance. Indignation flushed her cheeks.

"What happened to your insistence that things would work out in the end?"

"What happened to your belief that everyone has a duty to see justice served?"

Kate gritted her teeth. "That's what I'm doing. Believe me, no one who reads my story will vote to acquit if they get picked for a jury."

Silence. For a moment, Kate thought Johnson had hung up.

"So, you're planning to do a hatchet job on purpose to influence the trial?"

"It's not a hatchet job if it's true! We both know he killed Emily Gibson. I'm just doing my part to make sure everyone else knows it, too."

"Kate..." He trailed off.

"What?" The defensiveness in her voice grated on her ears. Why couldn't he see that she was trying to make the DA's job easier?

"I do think Newhouse did something to Emily. But I've been wrong before. It's not up to us to decide whether he's guilty. That's the jury's job."

"But they're only going to hear his lawyer's description of him as a fine, upstanding citizen. And obviously, he's biased!"

"But you're biased, too." He said it so quietly she almost didn't catch it all. "And you might not be any closer to the actual truth than Newhouse's lawyer. Look, do I want to see him convicted? Yes. But not at the expense of true justice. If we don't have the evidence, I'd rather him walk free."

Kate flinched. Watching another murderer go free would shred her last morsel of hope in humanity. Johnson sighed, almost as though he could read her thoughts.

"I don't think that's going to happen. And I'm going to do everything I can to make sure it doesn't. Believe me, I want to show you that sometimes justice does get served the way you think it should."

Tears pricked the back of Kate's eyes. He understood. Even though he didn't depend on immediate justice, he knew it was her gospel.

She cleared her throat.

"I promise I won't let him win," she said huskily. "I promise."

Chapter 11

WHEN KATE'S ALARM WENT off at 6 a.m. the next morning, she wasn't even tempted to hit snooze. She put the coffeepot to work before jumping in the shower. Considering how fitfully she'd slept, she felt surprisingly alert.

Most days, she considered her clothing selection inconsequential. Her wardrobe was functional and practical, nothing flashy. But today she debated for fifteen minutes over what to wear. She wanted to look as professional and competent as possible. Newhouse would have no reason to sneer at her today. After pulling on fitted black slacks and buttoning up a pale blue blouse, she twisted her hair into a knot at the nape of her neck.

For the next hour, she pored over her notes and reviewed the questions she'd written down the night before. Two cups of coffee later, she strode into the newsroom to meet Hunter Lewis.

"Well, it looks like you're ready," he said after taking in her outfit. "How do you feel?"

"Good. I'm ready. I'm going to nail him to the wall."

Lewis raised an eyebrow.

"What?" she demanded.

"That doesn't sound very objective."

"Do not tell me you think he's innocent."

Lewis pursed his lips and locked his hands behind his head as he leaned back in his chair.

"It doesn't matter what I think. I don't want him to use us to get off. But I'm also not interested in prematurely convicting him on the front page. That's not our job."

"Our job is to tell the truth!"

"The truth we know, not the truth we believe."

"Sometimes they're the same thing."

Lewis smiled and stood up. "And sometimes what we believe turns out not to be true. Only time will tell."

Newhouse lived in Cedar Lawn, a neighborhood that dated back to the 1920s. Like most of the island, it contained an eclectic mix of houses. And many of them had a history. Some, like the one designed for Sam Maceo, even had a place in history. The same architect had designed Frank Sinatra's home in Palm Springs. Newhouse lived in a Mid-Century Modern bungalow that perched on an immaculate expanse of emerald green grass. It didn't share the opulence that oozed from its Colonial Revival neighbors, but it had a snappy panache that suited its owner.

Kate took measured, deep breaths as she led Lewis up the sidewalk. They paused for a moment in the entryway before ringing the doorbell.

Seconds after the chimes died away, Bruce Castleman opened the door. A guarded smile stretched his lips but didn't touch his eyes.

"Come in, come in. Thank you for coming."

They stepped into a small foyer that managed not to feel cramped, thanks to white walls and light wood trim. An abstract oil painting in dark blues and yellows hung over an angular glass and iron side table.

"Can I get you some coffee? No? Alright, let's go into the living room. Aaron is waiting."

Castleman led them down a short hallway that opened into the home's main living area. Kate glimpsed glittering water and bright tropical flowers through the tall windows before a movement drew her attention to Newhouse. He stood as they approached but made no attempt to step forward and shake hands. She glanced at his ankle, where a thick black band sat conspicuously above his shiny wingtips.

He grimaced and his eyes narrowed just slightly.

"It's a small price to pay for getting out of that wretched hole," he said, gesturing at his foot. "But it's totally unnecessary. I have no intention of going anywhere until this is all cleared up."

As though the thought of the fight ahead exhausted him, Newhouse abruptly sat down again and closed his eyes.

Kate glanced questioningly at Lewis before Castleman jumped into the awkward silence.

"Please sit down. Make yourselves comfortable."

Kate perched on the edge of the leather sectional and dropped her purse at her feet. Newhouse watched her through narrowed lids as she opened her notebook to a clean page and balanced it on her knees. His steady, calculating gaze made the hair on the back of her neck stand on end.

"Mr. Castleman didn't think you would come after what happened the other day," he said. "I told him I didn't think you could resist. Figuring out what happened is like putting together a puzzle for you. Am I right? You just can't let it go until all the pieces fit into place."

Kate tried to ignore her thumping heart. A sudden surge of nervousness made her tremble. She laced her fingers together in her lap so he wouldn't see her hands shake and stared back at him until she was sure her voice wouldn't betray her rising unease.

"I do want to know what happened to Emily Gibson. It's only a puzzle because someone keeps trying to hide the pieces."

Newhouse snorted. "Well, I suppose that's true. The question is, who?"

"That's what I'm here to find out."

"Yes, but I'm afraid I don't have all the answers for you. Maybe after we're done today, you'll realize there are still other pieces left to find."

Kate was about to respond when Lewis interrupted. She was so absorbed in Newhouse's cryptic word game she'd almost forgotten he was there.

"Dr. Newhouse, I'm Hunter Lewis. I'm Kate's editor. Before we get started, I just want to remind you that we will consider everything you say here on the record. If there's anything you, or Mr. Castleman, don't want to see in print, please don't say it. We will not agree to leave anything out, under any circumstances."

"Thank you, Mr. Lewis," Castleman said. "As you can imagine, I have advised Dr. Newhouse that doing this interview might not be in his best interests. But he insisted. And we understand the terms."

"Poor Bruce!" Newhouse barked a humorless laugh. "I'm not exactly a model client. But since it's my neck on the line, I think I should be allowed to have my own way."

Castleman spread his hands in front of him as though surrendering the argument.

"Now, Ms. Bennett," Newhouse said, returning his narrowed gaze back to her face. "As you are here to ask questions, I suppose I should let you do it. But I just want to say one thing first."

Kate's nervous tremble had subsided into a hum of energy that ricocheted through her brain like a double shot of espresso. She focused all her attention on the man sitting across from her. Every gesture, every glance held a clue about how much of what he would say was truth and how much was a lie. She held her breath.

"I did not do anything to Emily Gibson. I didn't harm her in any way. Did we disagree about how to handle the vaccine trial setback? Yes. But I had absolutely nothing to do with her disappearance. And I have no idea where she is."

Kate kept her eyes glued to his face as he spoke, looking for any tell, any tick. His gaze never wavered.

"You say you disagreed over the vaccine trial. Why don't we start there. What happened?"

Newhouse sighed, his lips pursed.

"I still don't know what went wrong. All of the indicators looked promising. They were right where we expected them to be. But after we'd already sent the data to the FDA, Emily began running the experiments again. It's standard procedure. But the results were not the same. The levels all looked fine at first. Then they began to taper off, indicating that the immune response was not consistent or prolonged enough to offer any meaningful protection."

"In layman's terms, it didn't work."

Newhouse shot her a withering look and tapped the arm of his chair impatiently.

"It did work, Ms. Bennett. But for some reason, we couldn't duplicate the results. Something went wrong in the testing or the analysis, but it did work."

"So, what did you do when you discovered the problem?"

"Emily discovered it. She brought the numbers to me, and she was distraught. I'd never seen her so rattled. She wanted to contact the FDA right away and tell them there was a problem."

"But you didn't."

"No. I was sure we could figure it out and amend the data we'd sent them for review. This kind of thing is not uncommon."

"That seems a bit deceptive, if not dishonest."

Newhouse's lip curled in contempt. "That's what Emily said. But I didn't see it that way. Everything had been so perfect. I was not going to just give up. I was sure we could figure it out and get back on track."

"But you didn't."

"No, we didn't." Newhouse said it flatly, as though that settled the whole question.

"And how did Emily take it? She had as much to lose as you did."

"Not as much to lose, Ms. Bennett, but..." Newhouse waved his hand in the air dismissively. "But enough, I suppose. She thought this would be a brilliant beginning for her brilliant career. And so it should have been."

"Did she keep pushing to tell the FDA?"

"She pushed, yes. We argued. But," he held up a finger. "She would not cross me. She knew that this was my life's work. And she respected that. She kept quiet out of loyalty."

"You're saying she cared more about you than her own career?"

Newhouse frowned. "No. But she trusted me. She believed we could figure it out."

"What about the threats the district attorney says he's found? Did you threaten to harm her?"

Newhouse shook his head slowly.

"I don't know what the DA thinks he's found," derision dripped from every word. "We haven't seen the evidence yet. But I never threatened her. Never."

Kate scribbled a question in her notebook for Johnson. The DA would eventually have to show his hand. Hopefully, she could get Johnson to tell her first.

"So if you didn't do anything to Emily, what do you think happened to her?"

Newhouse glanced out of the windows to his left, where a breeze rustled the bright pink flowers on the other side of the glass.

"It is possible that she drowned, you know," he said after a long pause. "That's what the police initially thought. And there's been nothing to show that's not what happened."

"It's possible," Kate said, repeating his words slowly. "But it's a little too convenient, don't you think?"

Newhouse met her gaze again and held it. She sensed he was weighing his next words.

"I do, actually. But what if it wasn't an accident?"

Kate's eyebrows shot up. "You mean, like she drowned herself on purpose?"

"No," Newhouse scoffed dismissively. "I do not believe Emily would take her own life. What for? She had far too much to live for."

"Then what? Who besides you would want to hurt her?"

"I've told you already I had no interest in harming her," he snapped. His knuckles turned white as he gripped the arms of his chair. Warning bells jingled in the back of Kate's mind. She had no interest in watching Newhouse lose his temper again. She considered scooting closer to Lewis.

But Newhouse closed his eyes and took several deep breaths. His grip on the chair relaxed as he regained control of his emotional flare up.

"Emily was confident, driven. She knew what she wanted. You wrote about how she contacted me before applying to medical school because she wanted to be a part of my research team. She was incredibly focused. And she channeled all her energy and intelligence through the idealistic filter of youth. She wanted to change the world and had the audacity to believe she had the power to do it."

He paused, glancing out the window again.

"She reminded me of myself at that age."

Kate rolled her eyes. The man's narcissism knew no limits.

"But in one respect, we were very different." He paused again and fixed his eyes on Kate's face. "Emily had periods of doubt, Ms. Bennett."

Kate frowned. "Doesn't everyone?"

Newhouse smirked as though she'd asked him whether the earth was flat.

"No. They don't."

Irritation flared in her chest, but Kate snuffed it out. She refused to let him see she understood the insult.

"What did she have doubts about?"

"Whether the path she had chosen for herself was the one she wanted to walk down for the rest of her life."

"I think that's a question a lot of people struggle with, especially at Emily's age."

"Perhaps. But Emily was not like most people. Her doubts undermined the foundation of who she was. She had defined herself by what she planned to do. Doubting her purpose meant doubting herself."

"That's pretty philosophical."

Newhouse shrugged. "Call it what you like. Emily fascinated me, and I studied her. At first it was like looking in a mirror. I searched for signs of myself. I wanted to mold her into an even better version of me."

Kate wrinkled her nose at his unapologetic arrogance.

"So realizing she had these doubts must have been pretty disappointing."

"More like surprising. It was a completely foreign concept to me."

Newhouse paused, lost in thought. Kate studied him in the silence. The more he talked, the more he sounded like a crazed megalomaniac.

"What does any of this have to do with her disappearance?"

Newhouse hissed out an exasperated sigh, as though explaining all of this to someone who couldn't keep up had pushed him past his last reserve of patience.

"The problems with the vaccine trial brought all of Emily's doubts back with a vengeance. Success can stifle doubts. But Emily thought we had failed. And failure created a crisis of belief."

"And? I still don't see what this has to do with what happened to her."

"I believe Emily decided to walk away, Ms. Bennett."

"What do you mean, walk away?"

"I mean, leave everything behind and start over. Or at least take the time to figure out who she was and what she really wanted."

Kate shook her head, incredulous.

"You've got to be joking. You want me to believe that she just ran away? That's absurd."

"It's not, if you think about it from Emily's perspective. She believed she had failed at the one thing she'd set out to do. She saw nothing left for her here."

"What about her mother, her boyfriend?"

Newhouse snorted. "David Knowles is an idiot. Emily could never truly love him. As for her mother, I don't know. I don't suppose she's done anything to make you think she might really know what happened to her daughter?"

Kate thought about the woman who'd eagerly taken her phone call the day before, hoping it was the police with news, and then broken down in tears talking about her child.

"No," she said emphatically. "That's ridiculous. I've never thought her grief wasn't anything but 100 percent sincere. She's completely heartbroken."

"Well, as I said, I don't know what to tell you about that. I suppose it's possible Emily plans to contact her after the immediate furor dies down."

"You mean you think she would let her mother believe she was dead, for any length of time? Who would do something like that?"

"Perhaps someone who didn't fully think through the consequences of her actions."

"I thought Emily was smart. That seems like a pretty basic consequence to overlook."

"She is smart. But she's also having an existential crisis."

"According to you."

Newhouse sighed. "Yes, Ms. Bennett, according to me. You find it completely unbelievable because you're starting from the assumption that I killed Emily. But I know I didn't. So if she didn't drown and no one else harmed her, what is the other logical option?"

Kate just stared at him. The conversation had gone so off-script she didn't know how to get it back on track.

"What about your relationship with Emily?"

"What about it?"

"It was a little more involved than you suggested earlier."

Newhouse's mouth curled into a smirk that made Kate's skin crawl.

"We had a brief sexual relationship, yes. That's true. But it has nothing to do with any of this."

"You were her boss. It was highly unethical."

Newhouse rolled his eyes. "What are ethics, Ms. Bennett, except for the rules that a minority tries to impose on the majority? Only I can judge for myself what is right."

Kate raised her eyebrows.

"I don't expect you to understand," he continued, waving his hand dismissively. "Although you strike me as the kind of person who will do what you want no matter what anyone else thinks, as long as you think it's justified."

Kate thought about her conversation with Johnson the night before. Her cheeks burned. She mashed her lips together and tried to wipe every trace of emotion from her face.

Newhouse gave her a knowing smile before looking out the window again.

"I was drawn to Emily, as I've already said. And she was drawn to me. At first, it was strictly professional. But the more time we spent together, the more the barriers between us fell away."

Across the room, Castleman cleared his throat. Newhouse swiveled to face him.

"Alright, Bruce, alright. I'm not going to say anything you think is dishonorable."

For a moment, he seemed lost in his memories. A hint of what might have been wistfulness softened the corners of his eyes.

"I already told you, looking at Emily was like looking in a mirror. It was the same for her. She saw in me a reflection of her future. Eventually, looking wasn't enough. She wanted to come as close to experiencing it as possible."

Kate didn't even bother to hide the disgust that contorted her face.

"That is the most narcissistic thing I have ever heard."

Newhouse shook his head as though entertaining an annoying child.

"Call it what you like, Ms. Bennett. You asked me to describe my relationship with Emily. That's what it was like."

"So who got tired of whom?"

"It wasn't like that. It was just that we'd gotten what we wanted, and it no longer held the power that it did in the beginning. At that point, our work was all-consuming, and it required all our attention."

"Are you suggesting she used you?"

He snorted. "Hardly, no. I don't know that Emily herself even understood why she was drawn to me. I think it was partly to silence her doubts."

He paused thoughtfully.

"It might have worked if we hadn't run into problems with the trial."

Kate shook her head at the convoluted logic.

"And then you think she ran away. Because she couldn't handle the failure."

Newhouse narrowed his eyes as he looked at her.

"I think she decided she was on the wrong path. So she left in search of the right one."

Kate shook her head again.

"Of all the things that could explain Emily's disappearance, that is literally the most improbable."

Kate flipped her notebook shut and slid it back into her purse. She glanced at Lewis.

"I don't have any more questions. I think I have what I need."

She stood to go. Lewis and Castleman followed her lead. Newhouse did not. A ferocious scowl filled his face.

"Obviously, I haven't convinced you, Ms. Bennett. But if you want to solve this puzzle, you'll think about it. Just ask yourself, if you were Emily, what would you do?"

She hesitated only a moment before answering with as much conviction as she could force into the words. "I would stay and fight for what I thought was right."

"And what if you didn't know what was right?" Newhouse leaned forward and stared at her intently. "What then?"

She returned his gaze for a few moments before turning on her heel and heading for the door.

Chapter 12

Kate leaned back against the headrest and watched the Victorian-era mansions on Broadway zip by the passenger window of Hunter Lewis's car. She was glad she'd agreed to let him drive to the interview. Resisting Newhouse's vortex of self-absorption for nearly two hours had drained her energy. She closed her eyes and tried to conjure up a tranquil image of waves washing over latte-colored sand. She was more than halfway to a power nap when a chuckle from the driver's seat broke the spell.

She shot her boss an annoyed look. "What?"

"The whole thing is just so bizarre."

"You think? I knew he was an arrogant jerk. Now I realize he's crazy, too."

Lewis laughed again.

"Well, it's going to make quite a story. And I don't think you need to worry about it benefiting his defense."

"You don't think a jury will buy his story about Emily walking away?"

"Seems pretty far-fetched."

"For sure."

"I mean..." Lewis paused as he checked his rearview mirror and moved over onto the off-ramp for Teichman Road. "It's possible. But it doesn't seem very plausible. Personally, I would be more inclined to believe she was the victim of some random abduction totally unconnected to any of this."

"Oh, come on! What are the odds of something like that happening?"

Lewis shrugged as he pulled into the newspaper parking lot. "Random crime does happen. I'm not saying that's what I think happened. I'm just saying that might be more believable than the story Newhouse is peddling now."

"At least they're equally impossible to prove."

They trudged up the stairs to the front door, buffeted by the warm spring breeze.

"Well, if she really ran away, someone must have seen something. I mean, she couldn't just blink herself off the island. And eventually, she'd have to turn up somewhere."

"True," Kate said. "And if someone had seen her or knew something, you'd think they'd have come forward by now. Right?"

"You'd think."

Kate shook her head. "You're right. He's never going to sell that to a jury."

It took her four hours to finish her story. After Lewis did an initial edit, he passed it off to Mattingly for his approval. Kate sat in front of the managing editor's desk while he read. She squirmed every time he grunted or stabbed at his keyboard to slice off an offending word or phrase.

"That's quite a story," he said when he got to the bottom.

"Thank you?" She wasn't sure whether he was commenting on her work or Newhouse's claims. Mattingly rarely handed out compliments, so she decided she'd chalk it up as a one.

"Since Lewis has already read through it, I'm assuming you didn't make this guy seem any crazier than he really is."

Kate grinned. "Nope. He did that all by himself. It was really odd. For someone who's so smart, he sure seems disconnected from reality."

"Maybe he is. Or maybe this is one of those stories that's just so crazy it's true."

"That's one theory," Kate said lightly. Her story was about to get a green light for the front page, and she could feel the weight slipping from her shoulders. She stood to go.

"Wanna suggest a headline?"

Kate stood thinking for a moment, phrases forming and reforming in her mind as she tried out different options. "How about, 'Disappearing act? Accused murderer claims victim still alive.'"

Mattingly grunted his approval and typed it at the top of the document.

Two hours later, Kate sat on the wide windowsill of her loft apartment, watching the seagulls wheel above the port. The sharp tang of salty air wafted through the open window. A languid calm had replaced the intense focus that had driven the day. Exhaustion blocked out any anxiety about her date with Brian. Or so she thought. But his knock whipped up a swirl of butterflies in her stomach.

She took several deep breaths as she crossed the open space to the door. The butterflies ignored her efforts to banish them. She fixed what she hoped was a serene smile on her face and opened the door.

He said nothing for a few moments, just stood smiling at her. His eyes sparkled over the bouquet of spring flowers he held in his hand. He looked so much like a giddy little boy, she couldn't help but laugh.

"Come in," she said, standing aside. "Let me put those in water and then we can head out."

He paused as he walked past, bent down, and softly kissed her cheek. Warmth flooded her chest, leaving behind the tingle of longing. The crisp scent of his cologne filled the kitchen. She could feel his eyes on her as she pulled a vase down from a shelf, filled it with water, and crammed in the bouquet. She looked sideways at him, heat suddenly filling her cheeks.

"Let me just close the window and we can go."

When she turned to walk back toward the kitchen, she caught him rearranging the flowers. She laughed again.

"I'm terrible at that kind of thing, remember?"

"Oh, I remember." He flashed her a grin that made her heart skip. "Ready?"

"Yep, let's go. I'm starved."

They made the short drive to the seawall in a companionable silence. When they arrived at Frank's, she opened the door and hopped out at the same time he did. She stopped short when she saw him frowning playfully at her.

"You know, I would have gotten that for you."

"Sorry," she said, half sheepish, half defiant. "I'd forgotten about your archaic manners."

He shook his head. "Letting a man open your door doesn't actually diminish your independence, you know. I've read all the research. No scientific link at all."

She laughed. "I'm ill-prepared for this skirmish. Let me look into this supposed research and I'll get back to you."

He grinned and offered her his arm as they walked into the restaurant. The hostess greeted Brian by name and ushered them to a secluded table in the back of the dining room. Kate resisted the urge to ask him if he'd brought someone else in the five months they'd been apart. It was none of her business. And if he had, he obviously hadn't found someone permanent or he wouldn't have asked her out tonight.

"Shall I order us some wine?" He peeked at her mischievously over the top of the menu.

She rolled her eyes. "Of course. You don't want me ordering it."

"No, definitely not." He gave a mock shudder.

As if on queue, the waiter appeared at Brian's elbow. He took the order with a murmur of approval and padded deftly away. Kate watched his retreating tuxedo-clad back wistfully.

"It's just not the same without Slava."

"Ah, Slava. He definitely made each meal memorable. I do miss hearing him call you Louis Lane."

Kate laughed. "I know he had to go home, but I wish he could have stayed."

The Ukrainian waiter had shepherded their regular trips to Frank's for months. He had regaled them in clipped English with the trials of life in the international student worker program. And he'd been instrumental in helping Kate break up a major prostitution ring. But even those heroics couldn't delay the expiration of his temporary visa. He left Galveston in December and made it back to Kyiv just in time for Christmas.

Thinking about Slava reminded Kate of a few things she'd rather forget. Shaking away the memories, she smiled across the table. Brian was watching her carefully.

"So, tell me about you," she said. "How's work?"

Brian had an endless supply of entertaining stories from the emergency room. He kept her in stitches through the appetizer and main course. It wasn't until they'd ordered dessert that he turned the conversation to her.

"How are things at the paper? Better, I guess, since you have another big story to follow."

Kate snorted. "Yeah, the publisher is happy, I'm sure. He hasn't threatened to lay anyone else off, so that's a bonus."

"You've done a great job covering all the Newhouse drama. I don't see how he could complain."

"It's all about his bottom line," Kate said, trying not to sound as bitter as she still felt about the last round of layoffs and the publisher's spineless refusal to take on local powerbrokers caught in a scandal.

Brian cocked his head and looked at her through slightly narrowed lids.

"How are you doing?"

Kate waved her hand dismissively. "I'm fine."

He raised an eyebrow. "It's got to be hard to have to stare down the mayor every other week at council meetings."

Kate pressed her lips together. This was the last thing she wanted to talk about.

"It sucks. But there's nothing I can do about it."

The waiter saved her from having to say anything else by delivering two slices of key lime pie. But not before Kate caught a fleeting look of exasperation cross Brian's face.

They ate in silence for a few minutes before Brian tried again.

"How was your trip home? Your parents must have been happy to see you."

Kate's face flushed. In all the months they'd dated, she'd never told him about her mom. She'd always deflected questions about her family, her past. He hadn't pushed. It was one of the things she'd appreciated about him. And probably the only reason they'd lasted as long as they had.

She stared at him. How could she tell him the whole story now, even if she wanted to?

Brian frowned. "I guess you don't want to talk about that either."

"Can I get you anything else? Coffee?" The waiter had impeccable timing.

"No, thank you." Brian gave him a tight smile. "I think we're all done."

Kate's key lime pie felt like a lump of concrete in her stomach. She watched silently as Brian took two $100 bills out of his wallet and tossed them next to the empty wine bottle. He stood, walked around the table, and slid her chair back so she could stand. He offered her his arm again, but the gesture lacked the warmth of their walk into the restaurant.

The silence of the drive back to her apartment was much less companionable. When he pulled up outside her building, she took a deep breath and steeled herself.

"Brian, I'm—"

"Look Kate," he interrupted. "I can't force you to open up to me. I waited patiently last year. I thought I'd eventually earn your trust. But you shut me out every chance you got. I don't know what you're running from, but I won't keep chasing you."

"I'm not—"

"Yes, you are," he said firmly, opening his door. He walked around to her side of the car and opened her door.

She clenched her teeth and swallowed against the lump filling her throat. Before she could step up onto the curb, his hand gently circled her arm. Regret filled his eyes as he looked down at her.

"When you finally decide to stop running, let me know."

An hour later, Kate was still pacing her apartment. She kept replaying their last conversation. His conversation, really. Because she hadn't said anything in her own defense. Of course, she could think of half a dozen smart responses now that he was gone. But when he confronted her, she just froze.

Brian was wrong. Totally wrong. She wasn't running. She was just protecting herself from emotional entanglements that inevitably ended badly.

"Ugh!" Her exasperated cry echoed off the brick walls of her apartment. She felt like a tiger pacing a cramped zoo exhibit.

She stomped to the door, grabbed her car keys off the hook on the wall, and flung open the door. The warm night air caressed her cheek as she pulled out of the parking garage, windows down. She drove toward the seawall and parked in one of the empty slots parallel to the beach. A full moon cast a warm glow over the sand. The white light made the tops of the muddy waves sparkle.

She got out of the car and picked her way down the steep stairs that led to the beach. She slipped off her shoes on the bottom step and sank her bare feet into the sand. In 30 steps, she stood at the edge of the lapping tide. The cool water tickled her toes and sent a wave of goosebumps up her legs. She retreated to a safe distance and sat down.

The short drive had taken the edge off her anger. But it hadn't changed her conviction.

"You're wrong," she said, the sudden sound of her voice startling several seagulls into flight. "I'm not running."

The hypothetical Brian in her head didn't back down.

Oh yeah? Then why won't you talk about your family? Why don't any of your relationships last longer than six months?

"Because I'm not interested in anything serious." She said out loud, flipping her hair over her shoulder for emphasis.

Really? You seemed pretty interested four months ago.

A memory of tangled sheets and the scent of warm skin floated through her mind. She dug her fingers into the sand at her side and flung a clump at the water. Tears pricked the back of her eyes.

"I'm not running."

Then why are you sitting here alone?

She drew her legs up to her chest and wrapped her arms around them, resting her forehead on her knees. She'd barely been a teenager when her mom died. Back then, she was so fragile she felt like she would shatter at the slightest disturbance. So she'd built an imaginary glass box to keep herself safe. She could see out. Everyone on the outside could observe from a distance. But no one could touch her.

Still, that wasn't running. That was just self-preservation.

She picked up her head and watched the waves roll ashore. Who wouldn't do whatever it took to protect themselves? Hadn't she just witnessed a prime example of that today? Aaron Newhouse had killed Emily Gibson to protect his precious vaccine trial. And now he was spinning a crazy theory about her disappearance to save himself from a murder conviction.

She let her mind wander back over their conversation. He'd said the vaccine trial failure had demolished the foundation Emily had built her whole life on. That might have been the only thing he'd said that wasn't hard to believe. In fact, Kate had no trouble believing it at all. She knew exactly how that felt.

This morning, she'd listened to Newhouse's theory through the filter of logic. But she knew better than anyone that logic didn't apply to someone whose world had just shattered.

She closed her eyes and drifted back to her 13-year-old self. It was a week after her mother's funeral. She had just come home from her first day back at school. And she was determined never to go back. The familiar desperation swamped her as she relived the memory. Her dad wasn't home from work yet. She'd grabbed an old backpack from the bottom of her closet and stuffed it with clothes. She was headed out the front door when he came home. One look at his face and she knew she couldn't leave him all alone.

But if he hadn't come home right then, she would have been gone.

She would have just disappeared.

Kate's breath caught in her throat. Suddenly, Newhouse's theory didn't seem so far-fetched.

Of course, as Lewis had said after the interview, Emily Gibson didn't just blink herself off the island. She'd run out of that beach house in a bathing suit, carrying nothing more than a towel. If she really had planned an elaborate ruse to disappear, she had help.

And that meant someone had to know something.

It still wasn't the most likely explanation, but it wasn't as preposterous as she'd thought six hours ago. And if Emily wasn't dead, a jury might actually convict Aaron Newhouse of a murder that never happened.

Kate's stomach lurched like she had just crested the top of a rollercoaster. Justice misapplied was just as bad as justice denied.

She jumped to her feet, heart pounding, and pulled her phone out of her pocket. Was she letting her own bias talk her into something crazy? She could only think of one person she trusted to give her an honest answer.

Chapter 13

Johnson rubbed both hands over his face to wipe away the last traces of drowsiness. He'd been about to climb into bed when his phone rang. Kate was talking so fast he could barely understand her. But one thing came through clearly: she wanted to see him. Right then.

Alarm had snapped him awake, and he'd peppered her with questions until he was sure she wasn't in any danger. When she'd finally convinced him she was fine, his tide of exhaustion had rushed back in. He was sitting on his front step, elbows resting on his knees, when she pulled up in front of the house.

The wind whipped her hair in a swirl around her head as she trotted up the steps. Her eyes sparkled with a feverish intensity. If she noticed his lack of enthusiasm for still being awake at this hour, she didn't show it.

"You want to come inside?" he asked as she rubbed her hands up and down her bare arms. The spring night had turned cool and the damp wind made it feel about 10 degrees colder than it really was.

She nodded. "That would be great. Thanks."

An image of the police chief's disapproving frown flitted through his mind. No doubt this looked like a slightly less than professional visit. He glanced around as Kate stepped inside. None of his neighbors were out and about at this hour. He sighed and followed her inside.

"Can I get you something?" he asked.

"No, I'm good," she sounded distracted as she slowly looked around the room.

His mother's paintings hung on every wall. It was like having a window to home. But also a reflection of the past. Some days, he wished he could just take them down.

"These look just like the one in your office," she said. "Are they by the same artist?"

He nodded. "My mom."

She tilted her head to the side and looked at him for a few moments in silence. Afraid she would start asking questions he didn't want to answer, he motioned toward the couch.

"What's all the excitement about this time?" he asked.

She eyed his disgruntled tabby, who was curled up on the opposite end of the couch. He chuckled.

"She won't bite, probably. Just give her a wide berth. She doesn't like her routine being disrupted."

Kate arched an eyebrow at him and sat down on the opposite end of the couch. He perched on the ottoman in front of his favorite armchair. The one he'd almost been asleep in when she called.

"I met with Aaron Newhouse today."

"And? Did he convince you of his innocence?"

She laughed. "No, not exactly. In fact, he spun a story I found completely unbelievable."

She paused, clasping and unclasping her hands in her lap.

"And?"

"Well, now I'm not sure."

"About what?"

"About whether it's really that unbelievable."

"Okay. So what's the story?"

Kate took a deep breath and let it out slowly. "Newhouse insists he didn't do anything to Emily Gibson and that he has no idea what happened to her. So if she didn't drown, he claims that leaves only one option: She disappeared on purpose."

"What? That's ridiculous." He'd heard a lot of excuses from criminals trying to get out of a conviction. But they usually tried to pin the crime on someone else, not claim that a crime hadn't actually been committed.

"I know. That's what I thought, too."

"So why are you suddenly not sure?"

Kate looked down at her hands but glanced at him sideways, like she was trying to decide how much to tell him. He resisted the urge to push.

"I... I was thinking about some of my own experiences. It's just... " She jumped to her feet and started pacing. "Newhouse said Emily was plagued by doubts about whether she really wanted to be a researcher. He said when they ran into problems with the vaccine trial, it ripped the rug out from under her. It basically threw her whole world into chaos. She felt like there was nothing left for her here but misery and humiliation. So she decided to run."

She stopped pacing and looked at him, her grey eyes pleading.

"I know it sounds crazy. That's what I told him. But when I put myself in her shoes, suddenly it didn't seem so crazy."

Johnson frowned as he looked up at her. Eyebrows drawn together, she was gazing at the painting closest to where she stood. In it, a young boy led a big white cow down a red dirt road.

"Haven't you ever... just wanted to disappear?" she asked, her voice almost a whisper.

He shifted uncomfortably, suddenly self-conscious. Not only had he wanted to disappear, he actually had.

"Maybe," he hedged. "But I never would have left my family. I wouldn't have let the people who loved me think I was dead."

Kate looked down, but not before he caught the shimmer of tears in her grey eyes.

"What if you felt like that was your only option? Like you had no other choice?"

He looked across the room at a painting of a field, men and women stooped to gather in the crop. It looked so peaceful. But that was before the attacks. Before the retaliation. Before his late-night flight in the back of the plane that carried supplies to remote villages. He'd disappeared from the only home he'd ever known, but he hadn't left his parents behind.

"No," he said firmly. "I couldn't have done it."

Kate sighed in exasperation and sat back down on the couch.

"Besides, Kate, we have evidence that Newhouse threatened her. This is off the record, okay?"

She nodded, her eyes glued to his face.

"He threatened to kill her. He said he would never let her expose the vaccine trial as a failure. If we didn't have that, I might believe what you're saying. But it's hard to buy his claim that he did nothing when he warned her he would."

Kate chewed on her bottom lip.

"There's no way that could have been planted?"

"By who?"

"Emily! Look, I know it sounds like something out of a spy novel, but if she really planned her own disappearance, wouldn't she want it to look like something had happened to her? Wouldn't she want people to think she was dead so no one would come looking?"

He threw up his hands. "You're right. This does sound like a spy novel."

She huffed. "It's not like no one has ever faked their own death before."

"Faking her own death would have been making people think she drowned, which we did, at first. What you're talking about is making us think she was murdered."

"Maybe that was her way of getting back at Newhouse."

He shook his head. "I understand why this sounds possible. It is possible. But it's just not plausible. Not based on the evidence we have."

"And you're positive that evidence is real?"

"I never had any reason to doubt that it was."

"Until now."

He crossed his arms. Exhaustion made his brain sluggish. He was not going to spin around on an argument merry-go-round all night.

"I will find out tomorrow how sure the techs are that Newhouse really sent those threats. But Kate, most cases are built on circumstantial evidence. There's no way to know for sure whether someone is guilty. That's why it takes 12 people to get a conviction. It's actually not that easy."

She sighed, and suddenly she looked as tired as he felt.

"I know. I just want to make sure we're not missing something. I don't want Emily Gibson to get away with murdering herself any more than I want Newhouse to get away with murdering her."

He chuckled. "That's definitely something I've never had to worry about before."

She smiled, and they sat staring at each other in silence. Now that they'd stopped arguing, he didn't want her to leave. Which probably meant she needed to leave. Reluctantly, he stood up. So did she.

"Thanks for talking it through with me. I know it sounds crazy. I guess I just... for a minute, I thought maybe it wasn't so impossible."

"Talking it through, huh? I thought you were trying to twist my arm into investigating a disappearance."

She grinned. "I have no idea what you're talking about."

He stood at the top of the stairs and watched as she walked toward her car. He shivered, suddenly feeling exposed. The cool night air seeped through his T-shirt. Before she climbed into her car, she waved. That simple, familiar gesture wiped away the last traces of his detachment. And for a moment, he didn't care who saw her leaving his house close to midnight.

The next morning, Kate's cellphone rang before she'd finished her first cup of coffee. David Knowles's name flashed on the screen.

She stared at it vibrating on her kitchen table, trying to decide whether she really wanted to answer it. She finally picked it up before it could roll to voicemail.

"Hey, David."

"Kate! I just read your story. This guy is completely wacko. There's no way Emily just disappeared. No way."

"I get it," she said, holding the phone away from her ear to muffle the intensity of his voice. Ever since her run-in with Newhouse at his office, she started the day with a low-grade headache.

"Then why did you write it?" His belligerence caught her off guard.

"Because that's what he told me." She didn't bother hiding her irritation. "Just because he said it, that doesn't make it true. I think that's pretty obvious."

Knowles was silent for a moment.

"I just don't want him to get out of this."

Kate frowned. That seemed like an odd choice of words. The kernel of suspicion planted last night sprouted again. What if Emily hadn't disappeared without letting the people closest to her in on her plans?

"Hey, David, I tell you what. Why don't we meet and I'll interview you for a story in response to Newhouse's claims? I can call some of Emily's friends, too. But of course, you knew her best."

"Um... sure? I mean, of course. Yes, I would be happy to. Anything that helps everyone see how crazy this guy is. There's no way Emily would just walk away without telling me. Without telling her mom!"

Kate's throat started to thicken. She thought about her own father's face when he'd caught her trying to leave the house with her backpack slung over her shoulder.

"No, of course not."

"So, where do you want to meet?"

Kate considered the possibilities. "Would you be willing to meet me at Emily's apartment? Maybe we could look through some of her things so we could say conclusively that nothing showed any sign that she planned to go anywhere."

He hesitated. "I guess. I mean, the police have already gone through everything."

"I know. But they were looking for evidence that someone did something to her, not evidence that she ran away."

"She didn't run away!"

"I know, I know. I'm just saying, it would be great if I could say a search of her apartment showed no signs that she'd been planning to leave."

"Okay. Yeah, sure, that makes sense. Can you be there in an hour? I have to be at the hospital for a shift at noon."

"Yep, I'll see you then."

Kate set the phone down on the table and took a sip of her coffee. It was probably a wild goose chase. But at least she could say with certainty that she'd done everything she could to disprove Newhouse's claim.

Knowles was leaning against his car outside Emily's apartment when Kate drove up. She studied him as she climbed out of her own car. Dark half-moons mottled the skin under his eyes. His shoulders slumped, and a scowl of misery marred what otherwise would have been a handsome face. He looked like someone had repeatedly kicked him in the stomach.

If he did have any inkling Emily was still alive, he was a fantastic actor.

"Hey, David. Thanks again for meeting me."

"Yeah, sure. I called Emily's mom to let her know we were meeting here. Somehow, it didn't feel quite right to just barge in."

"Oh, good. Yes, that was a good idea. I'm glad you thought of it."

He pushed himself off his car and approached the door. The hand holding the key trembled just slightly. He sighed.

"You know, the last time I was in here, I thought she might actually come back."

Kate took a step closer and put her hand gently on his arm.

"I'm really sorry. We don't have to do this if you don't want to."

He shook his head. "No, it's fine. I just... some mornings I wake up and it takes me a minute to remember what's happened. It's like living it all over again."

Kate sighed. She knew how that felt.

David gripped the key tighter and thrust it into the lock. The door swung open and Kate followed him inside. He stood in the entryway for a moment, slowly looking around.

"It's like she never left," he whispered. He took several long strides across the room and threw himself on the sofa.

Kate continued to look around the room. She wanted to give him a moment to collect himself, but she didn't also want to waste any time she could use to search. For what, she had no idea. She wandered over to a bookcase in the corner and glanced along the neatly grouped volumes. Most appeared to be medical textbooks. Only one shelf contained novels. Spy novels, she noted with a smile. She would not forget to share that detail with Johnson.

She glanced back at David. He'd taken his hand off his face and was watching her.

"Did Emily do much reading for fun?" she asked.

"Not much. We have so much studying to do in med school. But every few months she would say her brain needed a break. She would start a new book on a Friday night and just lose herself in it until she'd read the whole thing. She called it her escape."

She smiled, and David snorted.

"Not like an actual escape. A mental escape."

"No, I understand," Kate said. "Sometimes I do that, too."

She wandered over to the desk in the opposite corner of the living room.

"Do you mind if I look through a few desk drawers?"

He eyed her with what looked like suspicion.

"What are you looking for?"

She shrugged. "Honestly, I have no idea. I just thought I should at least look in the most obvious places for anything that might disprove Newhouse's theory. We can do it together."

David pressed his lips together like he was considering saying no, then he heaved himself off the couch. He motioned for her to take the desk chair while he stood behind her. Kate slid open the middle drawer. Nothing but pens, pencils, paperclips and notepads of various sizes and colors. All were blank.

The second drawer contained a stack of cards that had obviously been sent to her. David sucked in a breath when he saw the one on the top of the stack. It contained a bouquet of flowers tied with a ribbon that formed the word "love." His hand shot out, and he scooped up the stack. Kate glanced over her shoulder at him. Tears filled his eyes.

"I gave her this last month for Valentine's Day," he mumbled.

Kate didn't know what to say, so she turned back to the drawer. She was half afraid he would tell her to stop at any moment. She spotted another stack of cards that appeared blank, probably for notes Emily needed to write to others. The next drawer contained files with labels like, "Student Loans" and "Bank Statements." A little tingle zipped up her neck at the thought of going through her financial documents. Would they show Emily was squirreling money away in preparation for leaving?

"I don't see anything there that looks interesting," David said decidedly, sliding the drawer shut before Kate could take one of the files out of its place.

She cursed silently and turned to the other bank of drawers. The top one contained a set of rechargeable batteries and a small camera in a bulky plastic case.

"That's the underwater camera we bought before we went to Cozumel for a long weekend."

"Did you dive?"

He shook his head. "Just snorkeling. It's really relaxing. Emily loved it. She'd never been before."

"Sounds like a great trip."

He just nodded. She had one more drawer to go through. It contained phone charging cords, an adapter, an empty cellphone box, and some documentation that looked like it might have come with a new laptop. It also contained a bright yellow CD-sized box emblazoned with the words "Rosetta Stone—Spanish."

"Oh, was Emily learning Spanish?"

David shook his head and frowned. "No. I mean, we all have to take some medical Spanish, but it's pretty basic. Emily knew enough to ask directions and order food when we were in Mexico."

"Looks like she was using Rosetta Stone to brush up. I've heard it's a really good program."

David shrugged. "I guess so. She never mentioned it."

Kate sighed and slid the drawer shut. She hadn't expected to find anything glaringly obvious, but she was still disappointed that her search had turned up absolutely nothing. She swiveled around in the chair and looked up at David. He was clutching the cards in one hand and frowning.

"I wonder why she never mentioned it," he said. Then he sneered. "Maybe because she was too busy lying to me about everything else in our relationship."

He tossed the cards onto the desk, where they fanned out in a colorful montage. Kate spotted birthday cards that looked like they'd come from Emily's mom, as well as a few others that looked romantic. She was sure all of those were from David. Newhouse definitely wasn't the type to send cards.

David turned around and walked back to the couch, blowing out a long breath as he went. He put his hands behind his head and laced his fingers together.

"Look, I know you have to get to the hospital soon," Kate said. "Why don't I just ask you a few questions and we can get out of here?"

He nodded, lowering himself to the edge of the couch. He leaned his elbows on his knees and stared at the coffee table.

"You told me on the phone that Newhouse was wacko. What makes you so sure Emily didn't just leave?"

His eyes flashed as he looked up at her. "She never would have done that to the people who cared about her. To make us all think she was dead? What kind of person would do that? No. Emily was not heartless."

Kate did not want to ask the next, obvious question. But she had to.

"I know this is hard, but it seems like Emily hid a lot of things from you. And from her mom. What makes you think she might not also have hidden this?"

He glared at her with an intensity that made her arms flush with goosebumps.

"I'm sorry to have to ask you that. Really. But it's something people will wonder when they read this story, so we might as well answer it for them."

David's jaw muscle flexed several times and the tendons in his neck stretched tight. Kate's heart thumped insistently. He looked like an angry snake startled out of the comfort of its den. Finally, he took a deep breath.

"Emily did hide things from me. But she wasn't cruel. She could have dumped me at any time, but she didn't. She loved me. I don't think she would have wanted to put any of us through this torture."

"So you think Newhouse made the whole thing up?"

"Yes, absolutely. He obviously did something to Emily. This is all part of some scheme to cast doubt about whether there's even anything to charge him with." His voice steadily rose until he was almost shouting. "But there is! I know there is. He killed her and he's going to pay for it!"

He jumped off the couch and towered over her, his chest heaving.

"David?" Kate tried not to sound as scared as she felt. Her heart pounded in her ears.

He shook his head and turned away abruptly. "Sorry," he mumbled. "I just can't stand the thought of him getting away with anything."

Kate took slow, steady breaths to calm her racing heart.

"I understand. Really, I do. Listen, I've taken enough of your time this morning. I should be going."

"Sure," he said, sheepishly. "I'm sorry I got so worked up. I didn't mean to scare you."

Kate felt the blood rush to her cheeks. So much for hiding her fear. She gave him a tight smile and hurried to the door.

"Thanks again for meeting me here. I hope the rest of your day gets better." It sounded so lame, but she couldn't think of anything else to say.

"Me, too," he said as she opened the door. "Me, too."

Chapter 14

KATE SAT AT HER desk, staring at a blank computer screen. She was supposed to be writing her follow-up story based on her conversation with David. But she kept replaying their odd encounter over and over again in her mind. He almost seemed unstable. Had he always been that volatile, or had all of this pushed him over the edge? Who wouldn't be a little unbalanced after everything he'd had to endure in the last week and a half?

"I don't think the *Gazette* is getting its money out of you this morning."

Kate jumped and then laughed. The paper's senior reporter, Delilah Peters, stood in front of her desk, looking critically at the empty screen.

"Do you think the publisher will demand my head on a silver platter?" Kate asked, giving her a sly smile.

"He might," the older woman chuckled. "And we no longer have a sacrificial lamb to offer him."

She snagged the back of the chair at the empty desk next to Kate's and plopped down in it with an "humph." Six months ago, the paper's education reporter sat there. But she'd been a victim of last year's layoffs—the sacrifice that ensured the rest of them could keep their jobs.

"I've watched you try to get a start on that story for the last 45 minutes. What's bothering you?"

Kate sighed. "Did you read today's story about Newhouse?"

"Of course I did. Great story. That doc is totally crazy. He's got 30 years to life written all over him."

Kate grimaced. The thought of Newhouse rotting in jail offered no comfort this morning.

"I know the whole idea makes no sense. I just can't get it out of my head. What if he's not crazy?"

Delilah arched a heavily penciled eyebrow. "Are you still suffering the after-effects of your concussion?"

Kate rolled her eyes. "Maybe. I don't know. Yesterday, when Mattingly read it, he said it just might be crazy enough to be true."

"Well, Galveston has spawned some crazy tales. Robert Durst is just the tip of the iceberg."

Kate grinned. Delilah had covered the Durst trial and written a true crime book about the case. Kate was pretty sure that's how she could afford her beach house on the West End. It wasn't a mansion by any means. But it wasn't affordable on a reporter's salary either.

"See? If I'd have told you a New York real estate heir was going to come down here in disguise, kill his neighbor, and cut up his body to hide the crime, you would have called that crazy."

Delilah sucked on her front teeth. "That's true. So, what's bothering you about this case?"

"I don't know. I can't put my finger on it. It's just a feeling."

"A gut feeling?"

Kate laughed. "Yeah, something like that."

"What did I tell you about that last year?"

"Trust my gut."

"And was I right?"

"Yeah, you were."

"I was. So if you have that same feeling about this case, and you haven't been getting breakfast burritos at that place I told you to avoid, then you owe it to yourself to do a little digging."

Kate laughed. "No more breakfast burritos, I promise."

"Okay then. So, what's tripping you up the most?"

"Just the idea that Emily Gibson might actually have run away. If she did, I don't think her boyfriend knew anything about it. He's so upset about this whole thing, he's almost unhinged."

Delilah shook her head. "Poor guy. She played him for a fool."

"So if he didn't help her, who did? Where did she go? And how did she get there?"

"You should ask your detective if they found any clues on her computer."

"Delilah, seriously. He's not my detective."

"I bet he would be if you asked him."

Kate's face flushed. "Come on, knock it off."

Delilah held up her hands. "Okay, okay. But just remember, you heard it here first."

"Anyway, I asked him what he thought about the possibility that Emily isn't dead. He's pretty convinced the evidence says otherwise."

"Well, the cops aren't always right."

"Yeah, I know. That's why I asked Knowles to meet me at her apartment this morning. I wanted to see if I could find anything that suggested she'd been planning to leave."

"He agreed to that? Does he think that's what happened?"

"No, not at all. I kind of persuaded him it would be good to say in the follow-up story that I looked through her apartment and found nothing unusual."

"And did you?"

"Did I what?"

"Find anything unusual."

"No. It was super awkward to have him there while I looked through her stuff. He teared up when we found a stack of cards he'd given her. Then he kind of lost it when I found some CDs for a foreign language software. He didn't know she was trying to learn Spanish. Then he said something about it being just one more thing she hadn't told him."

Delilah nodded thoughtfully.

"What?"

"Did he seem to think that was significant?"

"The software or her not telling him?"

"Both, I guess. But mainly I meant the software. I mean, why would she need to learn Spanish?"

"Doesn't everybody need to know Spanish? I sure wish I did."

"Yeah, but it's not like its something she would use in a research lab. She wasn't going to interact with patients, right? She was going to spend her career peering into a microscope."

Kate frowned. "Maybe it was just something to exercise the parts of her brain she didn't normally use. I also found a nice collection of spy novels that Knowles said she liked to use for a weekend escape when she'd had enough of studying."

"Maybe. Or maybe she needed it wherever she was headed."

A shot of adrenaline coursed through Kate's chest, like she was riding in a car that had just gone from zero to sixty in 5.3 seconds. Eyes wide, she stared at Delilah.

"Do you really think..." She suddenly felt too breathless to finish the sentence.

Delilah shrugged. "It's a thread. Maybe you should try tugging on it."

"Tugging on what?"

Kate's mind was spinning so fast with possibilities that she hadn't noticed Hunter Lewis amble over.

"Oh, Kate and I were just playing a little game of 'Where's Emily Gibson?'" Delilah winked at her.

"Yeah? You mean assuming she's not at the bottom of the ocean?" Lewis asked.

"Well, if she drowned, or if the not-so-good doctor killed her and dumped her body in the water, she'd wash up eventually. Kate's had plenty of experience covering those, huh?" Delila said.

Kate grimaced. "Right. And I can't see Newhouse trying to bury a body. How else could he have disposed of it?"

"I guess he could have pulled a Robert Durst and chopped her up," Delilah suggested.

"And done what with the pieces?" Lewis asked.

"Maybe he's hiding them in his refrigerator."

Kate groaned. "Gross."

Delilah laughed. "You haven't been doing this long enough if that makes you queasy."

"Whatever. Back to the question at hand: If she's not dead, where is she?"

"Kate found some Spanish learning software at Emily's apartment," Delilah told Lewis. "Her boyfriend didn't know anything about it, so we were just wondering if that could be..." Delilah tapped her fingers on the desk like drumsticks. "A clue."

Lewis arched an eyebrow. "You think she might have planned to go somewhere she would need to know Spanish?"

"Exactamente."

"Well, there are plenty of places just a short plane ride away."

"Yes, but she'd need to use her ID to get on a plane," Kate pointed out. "And that would show up as soon as the police started looking for her."

"Fake ID?" Lewis suggested.

"Maybe, but her photo's been all over local and national news," Kate said. "Unless she was wearing a disguise, don't you think someone would have recognized her?"

"Mmmmm," Lewis said, pursing his lips and scrunching his eyebrows together in concentration. "Could she have gotten on a private plane at the airport here?"

Delilah nodded. "That's possible. Especially if someone offered to sneak her on board. It shouldn't be hard to find out what planes took off the day after she disappeared, assuming she left right away."

"Wait," Kate blurted. "If she was willing to sneak on board something, isn't a ship the most obvious option?"

Delilah's eyebrows shot up, and she wagged her chin up and down. "A stowaway. Like the girls trafficked from Mexico."

The familiar tourniquet of anger and despair squeezed Kate's heart. She still agonized over the case that had exposed a human trafficking ring operating out of the Port of Galveston.

Lewis frowned. "I think the cruise ships have tightened their controls since last year. I doubt anyone could sneak on board one of them at this point."

"But what about all the other ships at the port?" Kate asked. "Ships sail to and from Central and South America all the time."

"That's true," Delilah said, sucking her teeth again. "And in that case, she probably wouldn't have been a stowaway."

"Why not?"

"Well, if she could pay for a cabin and give the captain a little extra, he might not have asked too many questions about official documentation."

"How hard would it be to find out what ships left port on the Monday after she disappeared?"

Delilah shoved herself up from the chair and marched back to her desk.

"I'll make a few calls."

"Let me know if you find anything interesting," Lewis said, wandering back to his desk with a wave.

For the next ten minutes, Kate listened to her colleague make an excruciating amount of small talk with her source at the port. She had to sit on her hands to keep from making impatient motions urging her to hurry along the conversation. But finally, Delilah let out a series of grunts, punctuated by the scratch of her pencil across her notepad. It took all Kate's self-control to keep from running over to see what she had written.

"Yeah, thanks. This is very helpful. You, too. Bye now."

Delilah hung up but continued making notes. Kate couldn't contain the nervous energy building like a nuclear reaction in her chest.

"Well?" she finally exploded. "What did you find?"

The senior reporter grinned, her mischievous eyes peering at Kate over the top of her reading glasses.

"Patience, my young Padawan."

Kate groaned. "Delilah, you're killing me."

"I think this is worth the wait." She stood and waved at Kate to follow her into the news editor's office. "Let's see what Lewis thinks."

"Got something?" he asked, when they sat down in the chairs in front of his desk.

"I think so," Delilah said, wiggling her eyebrows at Kate infuriatingly.

Kate just shook her head. But excitement bubbled in her gut. Delilah was enjoying this too much for it not to be really good information.

"Out with it!"

Delilah grinned. "Three ships left Monday, not counting the cruise lines. One cargo ship headed to Guatemala to get its regular load of bananas. One carrying wheat sailed for Mexico. And the last one…" She paused for effect. "Was headed to Cuba."

"Cuba?" Kate asked. "Is that legal?"

Lewis laughed. "Yes, it's legal. The embargo doesn't keep everything out of Cuba."

"So you have three possibilities," Delilah said. "And all to Spanish-speaking countries."

Lewis slapped the top of his desk. "My money's on Cuba."

"Why?" Kate asked, surprised to see him suddenly so interested in what he'd suggested was a wild goose chase not 30 minutes before.

"Med school."

"Ooooo, that's right," Delilah said. "I'd forgotten about that."

"What are you guys talking about?" Kate's head spun like she'd just stepped off a Tilt-a-Whirl.

"Cuba's got a pretty solid medical training program," Lewis said. "It's probably their biggest export, come to think of it. The Castro government started it not long after the revolution. They send doctors to developing countries in South America and Africa. And they bring students from those countries to train at their schools. Some Americans even go down there to study. That's why

I remember it. We did a story a few years ago about one guy who came back and managed to get a residency at UTMB."

The hazy possibilities in Kate's mind began to crystalize into a credible picture.

"So, what, she goes to Cuba and just picks up where she left off?" she asked.

Lewis shrugged. "Maybe, or something close to that. It's even possible she told them about her work on the vaccine and suggested she could continue her research there. I'm sure the Cubans would love to get their hands on that to shove up Uncle Sam's nose."

"And there would be an added bonus for her," Delilah said. "If she did end up getting charged with anything here, say fraud, for her role in the vaccine deception, she wouldn't have to worry about extradition."

"I guess that would make Cuba appealing even if she didn't want to continue her research," Kate said. "Remember, Newhouse claimed she was having doubts."

"True," Lewis mused. "But even if that was her eventual plan, her knowledge about the vaccine was still her biggest asset. What else did she have to trade to get her out of the country?"

Kate stared at Delilah, then at Lewis. She couldn't believe they had come up with a possible solution to the whole case. One nobody else had thought of. A slow grin spread across her face.

"I told you that thread was worth pulling," Delilah said, winking at her again.

"So what now? This all sounds great. How do I prove any of it?"

Lewis, who'd been leaning back in his chair, staring into space, sat forward and fixed his eyes on Kate's face. His normally easy-going expression was unusually earnest.

"The first thing you have to do is see if you can dig up any evidence that this actually happened. She would have had to make contact with the ship's captain somehow."

"The Broadside," Delilah said suddenly. "A lot of the crew members hang out there when they're in port."

Kate knew about the bar but had never been there. Every few months, it showed up on the police logs for a disturbance call. She could imagine Emily Gibson would have attracted quite a bit of attention if she'd gone in there alone.

"Alright," she said, drawing the word out as she thought about her options. "If I can connect her to a cargo ship, then what?"

"Then, you get to play 'Where's Emily Gibson?' for real," Delilah said.

Johnson had spent most of the day catching up on cases he'd neglected while dealing with the Gibson disappearance. But by midafternoon he could no longer ignore the question lurking at the back of his mind since the night before. He picked up his phone and dialed Officer Dylan Conner's number.

"Yeah, boss, what's up?" The young officer's normally eager voice sounded tired.

"Long shift?"

"Something like that. I'm about to head in."

"Stop by my office before you head home. I have a question for you about the Gibson case."

"Sure thing!"

Nearly an hour later, Connor tapped on his door. When Johnson waved him in, he all but collapsed in the chair. Johnson smiled sympathetically. Some days, when he was stuck behind his desk, he wished he could be back on patrol. But then he remembered beat cops had to deal with too many people who either forgot their own humanity or refused to recognize it in anyone else.

"I won't keep you long," he said. "I'm sure you've more than earned your night off."

Conner groaned in agreement.

"I just had a few questions about those chat messages you found on Emily Gibson's computer. Any chance someone could have planted or faked them?"

Conner sat up straighter, sharp-eyed interest wiping away the near stupor that had covered his face moments before.

"I mean, it's not impossible," Conner said. "We were basically looking at a saved chat thread, so I guess someone could have faked it."

"How would someone go about doing that, theoretically?"

Conner took a deep breath and laced his fingers behind his head. He studied the ceiling for a few moments while he thought.

"Well, I guess you could create two profiles and send messages back and forth between them until you had a thread saying what you wanted it to say. Then just save it."

Johnson frowned. That sounded way too easy.

"So how would we go about figuring out whether all the messages came from one person?"

Conner scrunched his eyebrows together in concentration. "You'd need to track down the originals on the chat platform and see if you could get the company to give you a log of IP addresses or the unique IDs of the devices used to send the messages. If they all came from the same device, you'd know for sure."

"But if someone knew what they were doing, they could use different devices to send the messages. Right?" Johnson didn't like where this was headed. "It would be virtually impossible to prove who sent—or didn't send—the messages."

Conner nodded. "Unless that person used the same account to send other messages that could be verified or tracked."

Johnson leaned back in his chair and closed his eyes. The air-tight proof he thought would disprove Kate's theory had sprung a leak.

"Sorry, boss. I guess the DA's gonna have a hard time proving Newhouse killed her, huh?"

"It's not Newhouse I'm worried about at the moment. But thanks, Conner. I appreciate the explanation."

"Sure thing. Let me know if you need anything else."

Johnson waved as the officer ambled out the door. His niggling question was gone, but the seeds of a headache had taken its place.

If it wasn't that hard to fake chat messages, he couldn't dismiss the possibility that Emily Gibson might have orchestrated an elaborate plan to disappear. But without evidence, it was still just a possibility. And it didn't seem any more plausible than it had last night, even after reading Kate's story this morning. Newhouse came across every bit as crazy as Kate initially claimed he was.

But if there was a chance he hadn't killed Emily Gibson? Johnson sighed heavily. He had no idea how to go about proving someone wasn't dead. But he had to try. He knew Kate would never forgive him if she thought he'd given up on justice again.

Chapter 15

KATE DABBED DARK PINK lipstick across her bottom lip. She stared at herself in the mirror. A tight black tank top hugged her curves and showed just a sliver of skin over the top of her jean skirt. Not the kind of outfit she would normally wear alone to a bar. But Delilah assured her she'd get better information if she looked like someone the men wanted to talk to.

After first giving her some pointers on where to go and how to broach what could be a tricky subject, the senior reporter had announced she was coming along.

"Not because you need a chaperone," she'd said. "I just can't stand to miss out on all the fun."

Kate put on a show of protest, but truthfully, she was glad to have Delilah with her. She'd never been comfortable sauntering into a bar on her own. She'd been to her share of nighttime hotspots with groups, or with dates. But never alone.

A long horn blast blared from somewhere below her window. She rolled her eyes. What was wrong with a text? She grabbed her phone, her purse, and her keys from the kitchen table and headed downstairs. Delilah's car was idling at the curb, windows down, Jimmy Buffett blaring from scratchy speakers.

"There you are," Delilah said when Kate opened the door. "I thought maybe you'd fallen asleep."

Kate laughed. "Are you kidding? Girls night out with you is the highlight of my week."

"Humph," Delilah grunted as she whipped the car into a tight U-turn in the empty intersection. She gave Kate a sideways glance. "At least you look better than my usual date."

"Speaking of, how did you convince Ben to stay home?"

Delilah snorted. "He's not home. He went to Millers. He'll probably behave himself. Mostly. I know the bartender. She'll keep an eye on him and let me know if he gets out of hand."

Kate shook her head. Ben Denison was the paper's longtime cops and courts reporter. He knew almost everyone on the island. And the people he didn't know, Delilah did. They made a formidable reporting team.

It took less than 15 minutes for Delilah to drive to the Broadside. The bar sat between a barber shop and a storefront with plywood covering the windows. It was just five blocks from the port, an easy walk for crewmen who didn't want to pay for a cab.

"Alright, remember we need to have at least one drink before we start asking questions," Delilah said as she put the car in park and rolled up the windows.

Kate nodded.

"And smile. You want to look approachable, friendly. It wouldn't hurt you to flirt a little either."

Kate rolled her eyes. "Seriously, Delilah. I have worked a source before."

"Yeah, but this is a bit different from managing local politicians."

"Ok, master dive bar hopper. Show me how it's done."

Delilah grinned. "Watch and learn."

Smoke billowed out the door when Delilah pushed it open. Kate tried not to cough. The owners clearly weren't concerned about the city's no smoking ordinance. Dim lights punctuated the bar's dingy interior with puddles of yellow. A short counter stretched to their left. Small tables filled the center of the room. Booths lined the back wall. And two pool tables sat at the far end of the room. Eighties hairband music screeched from speakers in the corner.

Kate plastered what she hoped was a friendly and flirty smile on her face and followed Delilah to the bar. The older woman squeezed between a bushy-haired man wearing tattered cargo shorts and a faded T-shirt and a clean cut man wearing the dark blue coveralls of a dockworker. The bartender nodded in her direction and leaned over to get her order. When he glanced in Kate's direction, she smiled and flipped her hair over her shoulder. He gave her what she took for an appreciative smile before turning his attention back to Delilah.

A few minutes later, he handed over two long-necked beer bottles. When Delilah turned away, he winked at Kate.

"Let me know when you're ready for another round," he said.

Delilah handed her one of the bottles and motioned toward the pool tables.

"Let's go watch the games, see what everyone's talking about. You can come back up here in a bit and see if the bartender's feeling chatty. I think you got his attention."

Kate grimaced. "Mission accomplished?"

"Not yet, but it's a start."

They weaved between the tables, smiling at the men as they went. Kate spotted a few other women, but not many. Now that she was here, she was even more grateful that Delilah had insisted on coming with her.

The men surrounding the first pool table made way for them to join the circle. Two men, both wearing coveralls, were about halfway through what looked like an evenly matched game. Her fake smile still plastered to her face, Kate glanced at the other spectators. They were a mix of nationalities. Some had the angular noses and chins of Eastern Europeans. Others looked to be from the Philippines.

Delilah was already chatting with the man to her left. Kate smiled at the man to her right. He grinned back, revealing two gold teeth. Before she could think of anything to say, he turned his attention back to the game. The other spectators seemed equally focused on the table. Delilah leaned over to whisper-shout in her ear.

"They've all got money on the outcome."

Kate nodded. That made sense. They watched the two players sink ball after ball. The onlookers kept up a running commentary with each shot. Kate couldn't understand any of it, but it seemed good-natured enough. Maybe no one was betting enough to get upset about losing it. When the winner sank the last shot, about half the crowd cheered while the others let out a chorus of groans. The losers tossed their money on the table's worn green felt. About half of them melted away, making trips back to the bar or returning to the smaller tables.

The winner of the game leered at Kate and Delilah.

"You like play?" he swept his hand over the table invitingly. Kate tried not to look as repulsed as she felt.

"Sure," Delilah smiled at him. "But not for money. We're just here to have a little fun."

The man grinned and wiped chalk-stained fingers across his chest. Then he gestured at Delilah.

"Just fun. We play."

Delilah handed Kate her empty beer bottle. "I'm out. Be a dear and get me another one. But don't rush back." She looked pointedly at the bartender.

Kate dropped Delilah's bottle in a trashcan on her way back to the bar. As if on cue, one of the men camped out on a bar stool slid down as she approached. He tossed a $20 bill on the bar, waved at the bartender, and shuffled toward the door. Kate hopped into the empty seat before anyone else could take it. She took a long swig from her bottle and set it down empty in front of her.

The bartender looked over and grinned. "Back so soon?"

"Evidently, my friend and I were more thirsty than we thought," she said with a sly smile.

The bartender sidled over to stand in front of her, folding his long arms on the top of the bar. He leaned toward her with a suggestive smile.

"I've never seen you in here before," he said. His eyes raked over her, making the hair on the back of her neck stand on end.

She forced herself to keep smiling. "It's my first time."

"That so? Well, I guess it's my lucky night."

Kate glanced back over her shoulder. Delilah was laughing with the man at the pool table, who was setting up his next shot. She couldn't tell who was winning.

"Doesn't seem like you get many women in here," she said, turning back to face him.

"Not usually," he drawled. "But the word must be getting out. You're the second sight for sore eyes we've had come in recently."

"Oh, yeah?" Kate tried to sound as casual as she could, but her heart had picked up speed.

"Yup. I thought the last girl to come in here was a professional, if you know what I mean," he said with a wink.

Kate cocked her head to the side and smiled hesitantly. She has no idea what he was talking about.

"A professional?"

"You know, a working girl?"

Kate felt her cheeks flush. She tried to laugh off his obvious suggestion. "Oh, that. And was she?"

"Nope. At least, I don't think so. The guys weren't sharing that info if she was."

Kate affected a giggle. "Too bad for you, I guess."

"That's right. Too bad for me." He grinned at her again and whipped the white towel off his shoulder to wipe at a spot on the bar. "So, what about you? What's your story? You're not here on... business... are you?" He arched an eyebrow suggestively.

Kate shook her head and tried her giggle again. "No, sorry. I'm not. Just here for a little change of scenery."

"Oh yeah? Well, I hope it's to your liking. It certainly is to mine."

Her smile felt brittle. She tapped her beer bottle lightly. "How about another round?"

"Sure thing. Coming right up."

She watched him carefully as he pulled the bottles out from under the bar and popped the tops. Both billowed condensation, reassuring her they hadn't been opened previously. In college, she'd written a series of stories about girls unknowingly taking date rape drugs while out at bars. She had no intention of becoming a victim.

He placed the bottles in front of her, a slow smile spreading across his face as she picked one up and took a swig.

A chorus of good-natured whooping and peals of laughter snapped her attention to the pool tables, where Delilah was doing a little victory dance.

"Looks like your friend beat Ivan," the bartender said, surprise rippling through his voice. "I hope she wasn't betting. He can get pretty mean when he loses."

Alarm prickled up Kate's back. She hoped Delilah knew what she was doing. She turned back with another forced smile.

"She told him no betting. But I'd better go make sure she's ok."

She snagged both beer bottles and hopped off the bar stool. Delilah spotted her coming and waved at her with a big smile.

"'Bout time! I was looking for that." She took the bottle and tipped it back.

Ivan waved his stick at them. It would have been menacing if he hadn't been grinning from ear to ear.

"Your friend is good," he said to Kate. "She no play for money. Too bad!"

Kate laughed. "But she beat you!"

"I let her win!" he said with a guffaw. "Next time, I win."

"Then I don't have much incentive to play again, do I?" Delilah said with a wink. "You'll have to find another victim."

"Okay, okay," he said, waving her off good-naturedly. He took his post by the table and looked around the room while grinding the square of blue chalk onto the tip of his cue. A skinny man with a shock of red curls and a mosaic of freckles across the middle of his face finally stood to meet the challenge.

Onlookers quickly gathered around, whispering wagers. Delilah scooted closer to Kate while the men were distracted.

"Did you get any info?" she asked in a low voice.

"Maybe. The bartender said I was the second girl to come in here worth looking at. Could be Emily. That's about all I got before I came over here to see what all the hollering was about."

Delilah rolled her eyes. "So, basically, you got nothing."

Kate huffed. "I was working on it."

"Well, if you want to get out of here with any solid info, you need to work a little harder."

Delilah nodded back toward the bar. Kate pursed her lips but swiveled on her heel and walked back the way she'd just come.

"Looks like your friend did just fine," the bartender said when she sat back down on the empty bar stool.

Kate laughed. "It was just a friendly game. She doesn't play for money. Ivan didn't seem to mind. He's found someone else to take on."

The bartender nodded knowingly. "That's a frequent match up. Reynaldo isn't bad. But he loses to Ivan pretty regularly."

"He loses, and he still wants to play?"

The bartender shrugged. "He's a glutton for punishment. But he takes his beatings like a man. Better than he takes his heartbreak."

Kate laughed. "What's that supposed to mean?"

"That girl I told you about? Reynaldo fell for her the minute she walked in the door."

"Oh, yeah?" Kate tried to look as nonchalant as possible.

"It was the hair."

"The hair?"

He leaned on the bar and raked his eyes over her again. "Redhead. Just like him. His buddies convinced him it was a match made in heaven."

Kate sucked in a breath. A redhead. What were the odds?

"So what happened? She wasn't interested?"

"Nah. She was friendly enough, but she was looking for something different, I guess. He keeps hoping to see her every time his ship comes into port, but she hasn't been in here in weeks."

"Poor guy," Kate said. Her mind raced with questions. "I wonder what happened to her."

The bartender shrugged. "No idea. She got all buddy-buddy with some of the crew from a boat that left out of here last week. I think they're due back before too long. Maybe she'll reappear then."

"You think she stopped coming in because her friends left?"

"Maybe. Who knows?" He said it like he really meant, who cares?

She was losing him. She leaned forward again and smiled admiringly.

"You must know these crews pretty well."

His face lit up and his chest puffed out. "Sure thing. Most of the men who come through the port end up here eventually," he said with a smirk.

"You have quite the international establishment." She batted her eyelashes at him.

"It has its perks."

"Oh yeah? Like what?"

He leaned in even closer and motioned for her to turn her ear toward him. She could feel his breath as he whispered, "Sometimes they bring me a little somethin' somethin'."

Kate arched her eyebrows and tried not to breathe through her nose. His breath reeked with the sharp tang of nicotine.

"Really?"

"Uh huh." He looked at her through half-lowered lids and traced a circle on the back of her hand. "That interest you?"

Kate laughed and leaned back, tucking a strand of hair behind her ear as an excuse for pulling her hand away.

"Maybe. Depends what you have to offer."

"What are you looking for?" he countered.

Kate smothered her frustration at the verbal game. She needed more information. He had to keep talking.

"I'm up for just about anything," she said with what she hoped was a sly smile.

"That so? Well..." He trailed off, licking his lips as he raked his eyes over her again. "I don't have anything special right now. But in a few weeks, it will be a whole other story."

"Oh, yeah?"

"Yeah. You like to smoke a little?"

Kate shrugged up one shoulder but smiled suggestively. He motioned her to lean toward him.

"You haven't smoked hash until you've smoked Cuban hash."

Kate's heart leapt. "Cuba? I didn't know ships came here from Cuba. Isn't that illegal or something?"

He laughed. "Naw. They come here regular. And it's a lot easier for them to smuggle in the good stuff. Fact, that's what I figured Reynaldo's girlfriend was after. That was the crew she attached herself to."

"Oh, yeah?" Kate gripped the barstool with both hands to keep from falling off. It took every bit of her self-control to contain the vortex of excitement spinning in her mind.

"She had to be gettin' something out of it, if you know what I mean," the bartender said with a wink.

Kate grimaced, and he laughed again.

"Don't worry, baby. Stick with me and you won't have to do any favors for these dock rats."

Kate forced herself to laugh and looked over her shoulder at the pool tables. Delilah was chatting away with several of the men. When she turned back around, her source was at the other end of the bar, dealing with another customer. She slid off her stool and hurried to the back of the smoke-filled room.

"Where's my beer?" Delilah demanded. "Here I am dying of thirst while you were over there flirting. Shameless hussy!"

Kate rolled her eyes. Several of the men around her laughed.

"I got ya, mami," one of them said. "Be right back."

When the others turned their attention back to the pool table, Delilah raised her eyebrows in inquiry. Kate nodded slightly, amazed her excitement wasn't written all over her face. The older woman grinned.

"Good work," she said in a low voice. "We'll stick around for a bit longer and then make ourselves scarce."

For the next forty-five minutes, Kate chased possibilities around in her mind. When Delilah finally said goodbye to her new friends, they made their way to the front of the room. Kate hoped they could make it out the door without the bartender noticing, but he waved them over before they could escape.

"Where ya going, baby? I thought you were going to come back to see me." He affected a pouty face that made him even more unappealing, something Kate didn't think possible.

"Oh, we'll be back," Delilah said, pulling some bills out of her back pocket and dropping them on the bar. "Don't you worry."

Kate smiled and gave him a flirty little wave as she followed Delilah out the door. She could hardly wait until they had climbed into the car to spill everything she'd learned. Delilah listened without interrupting. When Kate was done, she let out a low whistle.

"There it is. Cuba."

"It's got to be her, right?" Kate asked.

"If not, it's an incredible coincidence."

"But is that enough to convince Mattingly?"

Delilah sucked on her front teeth. "I guess we'll find out tomorrow."

Chapter 16

KATE TOSSED AND TURNED through the few hours she had to sleep before making her case to Mattingly. She had no doubt Emily Gibson had escaped to Cuba. But would her boss give her what she needed to prove it?

If she could resurrect the dead researcher, she'd have the story of the year.

Kate beat Delilah to the office. Both editors were on the phone. She got a cup of coffee and scrolled absently through emails for thirty minutes before the senior reporter finally walked through the door to the newsroom.

"About time!" Kate burst out before she could stop herself.

Delilah chuckled. "I figured you'd be here at the crack of dawn. Relax. Mattingly needs time to get through his voicemails before you hit him up, anyway."

Kate glanced through the window into the managing editor's office. He slammed the phone down in its cradle and leaned back in his chair.

"See there," Delilah said, dropping her computer bag in her chair. "My timing is perfect. Now he's ready for us."

Kate took a deep breath and forced herself to walk toward Mattingly's closed door. Butterflies swirled in her stomach. Two steps behind her, Delilah called into Hunter Lewis's office.

"We got the goods! We're about to tell Mattingly."

The news editor jumped up and followed them next door.

"What?" Mattingly growled as Kate and Delilah sat down in the chairs in front of his desk.

"Kate's been doing a little digging on the Emily Gibson story," Delilah said. "She's got a lead that will blow this whole case out of the water."

Mattingly's bush eyebrows scrunched together over his beaked nose. His temporary unibrow somehow conveyed interest and skepticism at the same time. Kate smiled despite the nervous energy coursing through her body.

"Let's hear it then," he said.

Kate started with her own doubts about Newhouse's claims and recounted her visit to Emily's apartment with David Knowles. She told him about her brainstorming session with Lewis and Delilah and ended with their trip to the bar. Mattingly listened without interrupting. She wasn't sure if that was a good sign or not. When she was done, he looked from her to Delilah to Lewis.

"Interesting," he said, leaning back in his chair and lacing his hands behind his head.

"The bartender did everything but give us her name and show us her photo," Delilah said.

Kate nodded. "Like Delilah said last night, if it's not her, it's an incredible coincidence."

Mattingly grunted. "Wouldn't be the first. Why didn't you show him a photo?"

"Didn't want to spook him," Delilah said. "If he knew this had anything to do with a police investigation, he'd probably deny ever seeing her, especially if he thought she was trying to make a connection for drugs."

Kate's heart thumped uncomfortably when Mattingly fixed his narrowed gaze on her.

"So, what's the ask? What do you think you should do now?"

She swallowed to keep her voice from shaking. "I want to go to Cuba to find her."

The managing editor barked out a laugh. "That's what I thought. No."

"What? Wait! You didn't even think about it."

He scowled. "I did think about it. There's no way I'm sending you to Cuba on a wild goose chase. I don't have a line item in the budget for that. And the publisher would never approve the expense."

Anger flushed Kate's cheeks. Budgets again. She glanced over Mattingly's head at the awards lining his wall.

"Then I'll pay for the trip myself," she said, balling her hands into fists in her lap. "If I'm right, this will be the story of the year. That kind of thing used to matter around here."

Mattingly glared at her in silence.

"She's right about this being a big story," Lewis said. "If she can find Emily Gibson, it will be a big scoop for us. Even bigger if she'll agree to an exclusive interview."

"That's too many ifs," Mattingly said. "And those are on top of the biggest if: If she really did run away to Cuba. It's a great story. But it's hardly the most plausible explanation."

Mattingly looked at her like he expected her to run down the list of other possibilities. Kate crossed her arms and mashed her lips together.

"What if she was looking for drugs in that bar? What if one of the crew members killed her? What if she got the drugs, took some the night she disappeared, and overdosed in the water? And let's not forget that this all started because the man charged with killing her claims she's not really dead. You're not dealing with any solid evidence here."

Kate's face burned. Her watertight theory was full of holes and sinking fast. Mattingly leaned forward on his elbows and sighed.

"Look, kiddo, I know how badly you want this story. And I haven't forgotten what that feels like, believe it or not. But I cannot afford to send you to Cuba. And even if I could, I wouldn't. It's not safe. In case you've forgotten, Americans aren't exactly welcome in Havana."

Tears of frustration pricked the back of Kate's eyes. She stood abruptly, heart pounding.

"So that's it? End of story?"

Mattingly glared up at her. "As far as I'm concerned, yes. End of story."

Without saying another word, Kate spun around and strode out of her boss's office.

Johnson drained the last of the coffee from his cup and set it down with a thump on his desk. He'd tossed and turned half the night thinking about Emily Gibson. If she was clever enough to attempt to frame Newhouse for murder, how likely was it that she had left any obvious clues about where she was headed? Financial records would be a good place to start. She would need money no matter where she planned to go. Assuming, of course, that she had gone somewhere and wasn't lying in a shallow grave on the West End.

Johnson sighed. It wasn't the first unlikely lead he'd ever chased down. But it was definitely the most unusual.

Before he started filling out the paperwork for a bank account subpoena, Johnson popped his cell phone out of the clip on his belt. He pulled up his favorites list and tapped the name at the top. The phone rang so long he was about to hang up when Kate finally picked up. He heard her take a deep breath as she raised the phone to her ear.

"Hey," she said on the exhale. He hadn't heard her sound that dejected in months.

"Hey back. What's up? You sound like you need more coffee."

Kate huffed. "I'm not sure that will help."

"Rough morning?"

"Yeah, you could say that."

"Not something a latte could fix?"

"Doubtful."

Johnson frowned. "Well, let's give it a try. My treat. Can you meet me on the seawall in 20 minutes?"

She hesitated so long he was sure she would say no.

"I guess," she finally said. "Make it a double."
"You got it. I'll meet you around 19th Street."

He spotted Kate's car as soon as he turned on Seawall Boulevard. The wide sidewalk atop the wall that ran for 17 miles along the island's gulf side was nearly empty. The early morning walkers had gone home. And the tourists hadn't flocked to the beach yet. Kate sat on one of the concrete benches facing the water, her face turned toward the sun as though trying to draw encouragement from its warmth.

He sat down and handed her a coffee cup without saying anything. For several minutes, he watched the waves roll in and listened to the seagulls wheeling overhead. A few times, he glanced at her out of the corner of his eye. The steady breeze blew her hair back from her face, adding to the wildness of the fierce scowl that left deep furrows across her forehead. Although she looked out over the water, all of her concentration focused inward.

"Is it helping?"

She looked sideways at him. A small smile tugged at the corners of her mouth as her frown relaxed just slightly.

"Is what helping?"

"The coffee. I ordered an extra shot of enthusiasm, just for you."

She smirked. "Is that an off-menu item?"

"Law enforcement special. You know, we need all the enthusiasm we can get."

That finally produced a laugh, and the last of her brooding mask crumbled. He smiled down at her as she pushed her sunglasses up on her head and looked at him with her clear grey eyes.

"Thanks." She sounded so sincere he had to squash the urge to put his arm around her and give her a comforting squeeze. He took a swig of his coffee instead.

"Aren't you even curious about why I called you?"

"Now that you mention it, I am. You never call me unless you need something."

"Hey! That's not the least bit true. I even bought you coffee!"

"Okay, okay. Now I'm dying to know. Why did you call?"

He grinned at her. If this didn't cheer her up, nothing would.

"I've been thinking a lot about what you said the other night about Emily Gibson. And you're right. I don't want her to get away with murder any more than I want Newhouse to."

Kate's eyes lit up, and she leaned toward him. "You think she's still alive?"

"Now that enthusiasm's kicking in," he said with a laugh. "I'm not sure I'd go that far. But if it's possible, it's worth investigating. Now I just have to figure out where to start."

A huge grin split her face from ear to ear. "Maybe I can help with that."

He raised an eyebrow in surprise.

"Have you ever been to the Broadside?"

He frowned. "Not voluntarily. Why?"

"Emily Gibson started hanging out there about six weeks before she disappeared. Coincidentally, most of the people who frequent the bar are cargo ship crew members."

His pulse started to skip. "And how do you know this?"

"I did a little reconnaissance last night," she said, shrugging. But her flushed cheeks and sparkling eyes ruined any attempt to feign nonchalance.

"What in the world made you go there?"

"Yesterday morning, I met David Knowles at Emily's apartment. I noticed a box of Spanish language learning software in one of her desk drawers. David said he had no idea she was trying to learn and couldn't think of any reason why she would need to. So that got me thinking maybe she knew she was going to need it wherever she was going. But if she was headed somewhere they speak Spanish, how would she get there?"

His mind raced with the possibilities. "You think she was trying to get a berth on a cargo ship?"

"Well, she couldn't fly without identification. And she'd be easy to track that way. But if she found a cargo ship captain willing to take her, no questions asked, she could probably skip town pretty easily."

"What made you think of the Broadside?"

She smiled a little sheepishly. "Delilah Peters. She checked with some of her sources at the port and confirmed three ships sailed out the morning Emily disappeared. All of them had Spanish-speaking destinations. Delilah said if she wanted to make discreet inquiries about getting an off-the-books cabin on one of those ships, she would start by cozying up to the crew members. And she said the Broadside was the best place to do that."

Johnson shook his head in amazement. In the time he'd spent debating what to do, Kate had found enough evidence to give her theory legs.

"So, what did you find?"

"The bartender said a woman who sounded a lot like Emily Gibson had started coming into the bar. She began hanging out with a crew from a ship going back and forth to Cuba."

"Cuba!"

"They're pretty proud of their medical training program, so I'm told." She took a swig of her coffee, her eyes locked on his over the top of her cup.

"So you think she went to Cuba to continue her training?"

Kate shrugged. "I don't really know. Maybe? It would also be a great place to continue her vaccine research, if she wanted to. Maybe she offered her knowledge and research to get her foot in the door. It would be a major coup for Cuba to get a working vaccine before the United States."

Johnson gave a low whistle. "Medical espionage?"

"It's the best bargaining chip she has. And Cuba is the perfect place to hide out. If U.S. officials ever decided to file charges over the vaccine fraud, she'd be totally safe from extradition."

For a moment, he couldn't think of anything to say. Kate was dragging him into the plot of an international spy thriller. He wanted to dismiss her theory like he had the other night. But he had that solid feeling in his chest he always got when he was on the right track.

"So, what's your next move?"

Storm clouds rolled over Kate's face again. Her eyes narrowed into determined slits.

"Mattingly refused to send me to Cuba. He said there were too many ifs, and he didn't have the budget for it. He also claims Cuba's dangerous, but I don't know how much he really believes that. He's probably just trying to scare me."

Johnson chuckled. "Clearly he doesn't know you that well."

Kate glanced sideways at him out of the corner of her eyes and flashed a grin.

"I've been trying to decide what to do. I just can't let this go. If I'm right, it's a huge story."

A tingle of apprehension pricked the back of Johnson's neck. "What are you thinking?"

"I told him I would pay for the trip myself, but that didn't make a difference. He won't give me his blessing. So I guess I'll have to go without it."

The tingle roared into a fire of fear in his belly. "Kate, Mattingly's not wrong about Cuba being dangerous. My parents have friends there. The government keeps a tight rein on everything. You wouldn't be able to go busting in and ask a bunch of questions."

She humphed indignantly. "I know that. I'll go as a tourist. That's possible, right? I'll have to fly to Mexico or something. Then I can just wander around Havana for a week and see what I can find out."

"But if they suspect you're up to something, they'd have no problem arresting you. Or just making you disappear. Kate, it happens. The Cuban government isn't accountable to anyone."

A savage frown creased her face. "Then that's all the more reason to go. I'll never find out what happened otherwise."

Johnson took a deep breath and tried to ignore the alarm bells blaring in his head. Kate was a grown woman and could make her own decisions. Before he could say anything else, her phone chimed. She pulled it out of her purse and cursed softly.

"I'm supposed to be at City Hall right now. I forgot all about this profile I'm supposed to be working on." She stood and pulled her sunglasses back over her eyes. "Thanks for the coffee. And for listening."

Reluctantly, he stood, too. "Keep me posted, ok? Maybe Mattingly will change his mind."

She snorted. "I doubt it. I think I'm on my own on this one."

"Kate," he called out as she turned to go. "Don't say that. You're never alone."

For the rest of the afternoon, he wrestled with what to do. After he left the station for the day, he took the dogs for a long run on the beach. The setting sun cast an amber glow across the waves and sand. His feet pounded rhythmically, beating down his anxiety, solidifying his resolve. He hadn't felt such a strong conviction about a case in years. He knew exactly what he had to do.

When he got home, he took a long, hot shower, and changed into jeans and a casual long-sleeved shirt. It was just long and baggy enough to cover the gun he clipped to his belt.

Stars dotted the night sky when he pulled up outside the Broadside. But it was still early for the regular crowd. The bar was mostly empty when he pushed open the door. The bartender nodded to him, a hint of suspicion tightening his shoulders. It was almost imperceptible, but Johnson knew he'd been made. No surprise there. He couldn't deny he looked every inch a cop.

The bartender ambled over. "What can I do for you?"

"I'll take a Corona," he said, perching on one of the well-worn stools.

The bartender disappeared through a side curtain and returned a moment later with the bottle. He popped it open and put it in front of Johnson.

"That all?" he asked as Johnson took a swig of the golden liquid.

Johnson smiled ruefully. Clearly, the guy wasn't a fan of cat and mouse.

"I'm looking for someone," Johnson said. He unclipped his cellphone and laid it face down on the bar.

"Not many people here right now," the bartender said evasively, casting a glance around the room as if to prove his point.

"Someone who might have been here recently."

"What makes you think that?"

"A friend of mine told me I should look here."

The bartender leaned back against the opposite counter and crossed his arms.

"I've got a photo on my phone," Johnson continued. "I just want to know if you recognize her."

He turned the phone over and swiped the screen open. Emily Gibson's smiling face glowed in the dimly lit room. The bartender glanced at it and narrowed his eyes. He didn't say anything, but the twitch at the corner of his mouth gave him away. A surge of excitement made Johnson catch his breath.

"You do recognize her," he said.

The bartender shrugged. "Pretty girl."

Johnson nodded. "Pretty hard to miss. When was the last time you saw her?"

Another shrug. Johnson waited. The bartender pursed his lips like he might not answer.

"Few weeks ago," he finally said. "What's she done?"

"Nothing, that I know of. She's missing."

The bartender's eyes widened, and he uncrossed his arms. "I don't know nothing about that."

Johnson raised his hands soothingly. "I'm not saying you do. I'm just trying to trace her last steps before she disappeared. How long has she been coming here?"

"I don't know. Maybe a month. She seemed to like hanging out with the crews from the port."

"Any one in particular?"

The man hesitated. "You think someone did something to her?"

"No, I don't," Johnson said. "I'm just looking for someone who might know where she went."

He seemed to relax just slightly. "She spent the most time with a crew from Cuba. They sailed out of here about two weeks ago. I don't think I saw her after that."

Johnson's heart pounded. Just like Kate had said.

"They haven't been back in port since then?"

He shook his head.

"She must have stood out in here. You never wondered who she was or what she was doing here?"

The bartender shrugged again. "I keep my thoughts to myself. Asking too many questions is bad for business. Know what I mean?"

Johnson chuckled and drained the last of his beer. He stood and pulled his wallet from his back pocket, tossing a $20 onto the counter.

"Thanks for your help."

"So, who is this girl, anyway?"

"She's a researcher working on the big vaccine project at UTMB."

The bartender's eyebrows shot up in surprise. Then his eyes narrowed." You know, this is the second day in a row she's come up in conversation. You said a friend told you to come in here?"

Johnson nodded, a smile tugging at the corner of his mouth.

"Is your friend a killer tease with a really sexy smile?"

Johnson laughed. "I've never thought of her quite that way, but yeah, that was probably her."

The bartender groaned his disappointment. "Guess that means she's not coming back to hang out."

"Sorry, man. I think that's highly unlikely," Johnson said over his shoulder as he pushed the door open and strode out into the night.

Chapter 17

Johnson headed for the chief's office as soon as he got to the station the next morning. Sam Lugar waved him in with a grunt.

"It's pretty early, even for you, detective," he said by way of greeting.

"I have some new information in the Emily Gibson case. I wanted to run it by you and hopefully get the green light to keep looking."

Lugar raised an eyebrow. "Why do I get the feeling you're about to ask for something that's going to give me a huge headache and create a PR nightmare?"

Johnson grinned and held up his hands in mock surrender. "Not me! I'm just trying to make the department look good and maybe save the DA some trouble."

The chief gave a skeptical huff and leaned back in his chair. "I'm not sure the DA wants you to save him any trouble. What's this new information?"

"About six weeks before she disappeared, Emily Gibson started making regular appearances at the Broadside."

"That dive on the East End?"

"That's the one. The bartender confirmed it when I showed him a photo of her. But he didn't know who she was or that she was missing."

"She clearly had bad taste in entertainment. But what does that have to do with her murder?"

"Most of the Broadside's patrons are dock workers and container ship crews. She evidently spent quite a bit of time with men from the ships sailing back and forth from Cuba."

The chief frowned and Johnson rushed on before he could interrupt again.

"Newhouse told the newspaper he thinks Emily ran away to avoid the potential uproar over the failed vaccine. I know that sounds crazy, especially coming from the man charged with killing her. But since we don't have solid evidence to show that a crime was even committed, I figured I should at least think about how she might disappear, if that was her plan."

This was probably the time to admit the idea first came from Kate, but he didn't want to give the chief any more reason to dismiss it.

"The biggest challenge would be getting off the island," he said. "How could she do it undetected, with no ID, leaving no trace? Getting a berth on a cargo ship seems like a good possibility."

Lugar shook his head. "This doesn't make any sense. You think she wanted off the island and decided getting on a cargo ship was the best option? How many people even know you can get a cabin on a cargo ship?"

"I don't think she started with the cargo ship. I think she started with the destination."

"And what would that be?"

"Cuba."

"Cuba! Why?"

"Medical training. Vaccines. And extradition. No matter what you think of the Cuban government, they have a pretty world-renowned medical training program. So, she could continue her research, and she could be sure they'd never send her back to the U.S. to face any charges related to the vaccine, if it came to that. It's actually a pretty good place to hide out."

Lugar leaned forward and crossed his arms on his desk. "Do you know how far-fetched this sounds, detective?"

Johnson smiled. "I do. I was tempted to dismiss it myself until I talked to the bartender at the Broadside."

Lugar's eyes narrowed. "What do you mean you were tempted to dismiss it? You didn't come up with this hair-brained idea yourself?"

Heat flushed his face. He couldn't hide Kate's involvement now.

"No, sir. Kate Bennett actually came up with the idea."

Lugar threw up his hands in exasperation. "You're taking leads from a reporter now?"

"That's not it at all. I didn't take her seriously at first. But I decided to go to the Broadside anyway. Once I talked to the bartender, it seemed a lot less far-fetched. At the very least, we need to check it out. The case against Newhouse is based on circumstantial evidence, and pretty flimsy circumstantial evidence at that. I know the DA hoped he'd confess, but it doesn't seem like that's going to happen. And if he really didn't kill her, we shouldn't be putting him on trial for murder."

"What about those threatening messages on Emily Gibson's computer?"

"Those could be faked. And you can bet that Newhouse's lawyer is going to get an IT forensics expert who says they are. Unless we can find some data on Newhouse's phone or computers showing he sent those messages, there's always the possibility that he didn't actually send them."

"You don't think the DA considered that?"

Johnson shrugged. "I don't know. I'm sure he knows it's a possibility. He's going to be trying to prosecute a case with no body and no solid evidence that a murder even happened. I assume he knows it's an uphill climb. But he may eventually decide to drop the charges."

"So, where are you going with all this? What do you want?"

"I want to go to Cuba." He let that hang in the air between them for a few heartbeats. "We could just wait until the cargo ship sails back into port and question the crew members to see if she really did sail with them. But they don't have to talk to us. It's not like they committed any crime. The only way to know for sure is to actually go to Cuba and see if I can find her."

Lugar put his head in his hands and rubbed them over his face. "I was right. This is going to be a huge headache. I cannot send you to Cuba to investigate anything. As you already pointed out, Havana is not exactly interested in furthering U.S. law enforcement interests."

"Yes, sir. I know. That's why I would go in an unofficial capacity. I have family friends there. It wouldn't be strange for me to make a trip down there. I can stay with them and do some poking around. I'm not exactly sure what that looks like. But Emily Gibson would be easy to spot. I might just need to stake out the medical school."

Lugar raised another skeptical eyebrow.

"Carefully, of course. Very carefully."

Lugar took a deep breath and blew it out slowly. "And what if you start making the officials there suspicious? You could end up in jail, or worse."

Johnson chuckled. He'd said almost the same thing to Kate. "Yes, sir. I know that. But it's not like I haven't had experience navigating through hostile territory."

Lugar didn't look convinced. "I'm not interested in being responsible for creating an international incident. If something happened to you, it wouldn't just be the mayor who'd be breathing down my neck. I'd be dealing with the feds, too."

He swore at the thought.

"Yes, sir. I understand," Johnson said, grasping for anything that would alleviate the chief's concerns. "Like I said, I have friends there. I won't be alone. They'll be a big help. I have no intention of making any headlines. I just want to know if she's still alive. If so, case closed."

Lugar shook his head. "If you were asking to go just about anywhere else, I could do it. But Cuba! I can't authorize that."

Johnson took a deep breath. "I understand. I'd like to take a week of vacation. It's been a while since I've had any time off. I could use a break."

Lugar shook his head. "Detective, why are you determined to be a pain in my backside today?"

Johnson grinned. "Not at all, sir! I'm trying to get out of your hair. For a week."

Lugar laced his hands behind his neck and leaned back in his chair. After a few moments of silence, he sighed.

"I can't tell you what to do on your own time, detective." He sat forward again and fixed Johnson with a look that would have made a less experienced officer tremble. "But if you were to head out of the country, say for a beach vacation, I'd recommend you keep it to yourself. Wouldn't want to make the other men jealous."

Johnson gripped his knees to keep from showing his rising excitement.

"Yes, sir. Understood. Thank you."

He stood up to leave before the chief changed his mind. But before he could escape through the door, Lugar called him back.

"I know you can navigate your way around a delicate situation overseas. But still. Be careful."

"Yes sir, I will. Believe me, I will."

Kate marched into the newsroom just after 9 a.m. She'd slept late after staying up to research travel plans. She knew Mattingly wasn't going to be happy about her sudden vacation request. But she'd crafted a story she hoped he wouldn't question too much. After dropping her bag at her desk, she walked straight to his office and rapped on the doorframe.

"Hey boss," she said when he scowled up at her from his laptop screen. "Do you have a minute?"

"Thirty seconds," he barked, tugging off his reading glasses and tossing them on the desk.

"I need to take some personal time. My dad called last night, and he's really sick. I need to head home tonight to check on him and make sure he gets to the doctor. I'm worried it could be something serious."

Mattingly stared at her with a blank expression. Then he turned back to his computer screen.

"No," he said.

"What do you mean, no?" she asked, her heart thumping uncomfortably hard. "He needs me."

"Bull," Mattingly said, not even bothering to look up. "You're just trying to get off so you can follow this crazy scheme you tried to sell me yesterday. The answer is no. Get back to work."

Anger roared to life in her chest like a baited bear. "You can't tell me no! It's personal time. No questions asked."

Mattingly barked out a laugh. "Nice try. But I know you're lying. And if you don't stop, I'll get your father on the phone to prove it."

For a moment, Kate couldn't speak. Her pulse pounded in her ears. In all her planning last night, she hadn't anticipated Mattingly refusing to let her go.

"This is ridiculous," she finally sputtered. "You cannot keep me from taking time off. And it's none of your business what I do on my time."

Mattingly jumped to his feet with a suddenness that made her take a step back in surprise.

"I will not say this again. Do you hear me?" His voice was barely below a shout. "You are not going to Cuba to chase down this crazy theory you've cooked up. It is too dangerous. I knew a reporter who disappeared in Havana in the early 80s. His family still has no idea what happened to him. And guess what? The government didn't lift a finger to figure it out. Know why? He wasn't worth an international incident. At least he was working on a story that was worth it. But this? This is a wild goose chase! I guarantee you, that girl is buried somewhere on this island. If you went to Cuba, you would be risking your life for nothing!"

Kate trembled with indignation. "You don't know whether that's true! Do you really want someone to go to prison for a murder that never happened?"

"That's the DA's problem," Mattingly growled, his face flushing nearly purple.

"If we have evidence that Emily Gibson is alive, it's our problem, too! I couldn't live with myself knowing I didn't do everything I could to figure out what really happened."

"You are not going to Cuba, do you hear me? If you don't drop this right now, I'll have no choice but to fire you."

Kate gasped. "What?"

"You heard me," Mattingly said, raising a finger in warning. "Think about it, Bennett. Real hard. Is this really worth losing your job?"

Mattingly's words hit her like physical blows. She grabbed the back of the chair in front of her to keep her suddenly wobbly knees from buckling. A voice somewhere in the back of her head screamed for her to turn around, go back to her desk, and get on with her day as though none of this had happened. But a much louder voice roared in rage at her boss's lack of faith in her. Tears stung her eyes, and she swallowed down the lump in her throat.

"Fine," she said through clenched teeth. "I quit."

Before she could change her mind, she spun around and marched determinedly back to her desk. She yanked open her drawer and pulled out her voice recorder and several mostly empty reporter's notebooks. Then she slid her laptop out of her messenger bag and set it on her desk.

"Kate?" Delilah's voice echoed across the newsroom, her question hanging unanswered in the air.

She waved dismissively at her surprised colleagues as she marched out the door. She made it halfway down the front steps before the tears cascaded down her cheeks.

Johnson spent the next hour clearing his vacation request through HR and briefing the lieutenant on cases that might need someone's attention while he was gone. By the time he was headed back home, it was nearly lunchtime. His whole body tingled with anticipation. He hadn't been out of the country in several years. Even if he came home empty-handed, the adventure would refresh his spirit.

As he cruised down Broadway, windows down, he pulled out his phone and hit Kate's number. Just like the day before, it rang so long he thought it would go to voicemail. He almost didn't recognize her voice when she answered.

"Kate? What's wrong?"

She sniffed before answering. "Well, it looks like you'll have to find a new favorite reporter. I quit this morning."

He was so surprised he fumbled his phone and almost dropped it. Her voice, thick with tears, squeezed his heart.

"What? Why?"

"Mattingly refused my request to take a week of personal time. He knew I was planning to go to Cuba. He told me if I didn't drop it, he'd fire me. So I quit."

By the time she reached the end of her explanation, some of her usual fire had burned through the weepiness that seemed to overwhelm her when she answered the phone. He smiled in spite of himself.

"Where are you now?"

"At home. Researching plane tickets."

"Be there in 10 minutes."

"What? What do you mean?"

"Sounds like we've got some travel planning to do."

Silence filled the line. For a minute, he thought he'd made a mistake saying something over the phone. Then he heard her take a quick breath.

"Pick up lunch, would you?" she said. "I'm starving."

Twenty minutes later, he knocked on her door, bag of burritos in hand. She grinned at him when she opened the door and ushered him in. But her red-rimmed eyes and puffy face told him just how much the morning had cost her. He set lunch down on the table and smiled. He wished he could wrap his arms around her and give her a hug.

"How you holding up?"

She shrugged dismissively. "I don't want to talk about it. I just want to focus on getting to Cuba and finding Emily Gibson. If Mattingly doesn't want the story, I'm sure *The New York Times* will be interested."

He nodded. He admired her resolve, and he wouldn't badger her with questions. At least not now. Maybe some day she'd open up to him, but he sensed today was not that day. He slid two burritos out of the bag and held one up to her.

"Lunch is served. How bad are the plane tickets on such short notice?"

She flashed him a grin, taking the greasy package and motioning for him to follow her into the living room.

"They're not cheap, but not as bad as I thought they'd be. I was just trying to decide whether to go to Mexico City first, or Cancún."

"Cancún. Smaller airport. Less hassle."

She arched an eyebrow at him as she unwrapped her burrito. "Alright, spill. How do you know that and how are you honing in on my trip?"

"Our trip," he grinned, warmth flooding his chest. He liked the sound of that. "I guess we had the same idea this morning. My boss was just a little more forgiving than yours. Or maybe less worried about my safety."

Kate snorted. "I thought you were in Mattingly's camp. What changed your mind?"

"I went to the Broadside last night. Talked to your friend the bartender. He's crushed that you were just pumping him for information, by the way. Poor guy really thought you were coming back to spend some quality time."

She rolled her eyes but flashed a wicked grin. "I'll bet. Did you show him Emily's photo?"

"I did. And he confirmed it was her. I didn't get anything new out of him, other than that confirmation. But I just decided you were right. If there's even a possibility that Emily Gibson went to Cuba, I have to see if I can find her. As much as I think Newhouse may deserve some time behind bars for general character improvement, I don't want to be part of sending an innocent man to prison."

Kate stared at him with shining eyes. For a moment, he had a hard time taking a deep breath.

"Thank you," she said. "For believing me. For taking a risk. I know this may not pan out. But I don't think we'll regret it."

"Me neither," he said, clearing his throat against a sudden tightening. "Hey, at the very least, we'll get a nice trip out of it."

Kate laughed. "True. I'll try not to think about having to come back and look for a new job."

"What are you talking about? When we find Emily Gibson, you'll be negotiating a big raise." He paused, another thought suddenly forming a knot in his stomach. "Or you'll be fielding offers from the New York Times and the Washington Post."

"Ha, let's not get ahead of ourselves. We have to find Emily Gibson first. And we haven't even booked our plane tickets."

"Let's get to it then," he said with a smile, trying not to think about the possibility that their trip would end with her moving to a bigger paper.

"Right. Which brings me back to Cancún. How do you know that's the best route?"

"I've done it before. My parents have friends in Cuba. They're going to be a huge help. Give us a place to stay, transportation. We'll be set."

Kate raised a doubtful eyebrow. "Who are they?"

"Cuban pastor and his wife. They live in Havana. And they'll be happy to put us up and give us a cover story. We're just two people visiting friends."

"A pastor, huh? You know, I don't know anything about your family. How do they happen to know a pastor from Cuba?"

"Denominational connections. My parents were missionaries. We lived in Africa, but we met people from all over. When we went on furlough—that is, vacation—we visited other churches all over the world. The Pérezes became good friends."

"Africa," Kate shook her head. "I should have known. All those paintings. How long did you live there?"

He shifted uncomfortably. The last thing he wanted to do was recount his own history.

"Most of my life. I grew up there. But that's another story for another day. Right now, we have plane tickets to buy."

Kate stared at him for a few moments. Just when he thought she was about to press for more details, she picked up her phone.

"Right. Let's get booking."

He suppressed a sigh of relief. He had so much he wanted to tell her. And so much he hoped she'd never find out. Taking her to meet old friends came with risks. She would no doubt learn more about him than he'd felt comfortable sharing with anyone since he'd returned to the States. But she'd also be exposed to a community of people willing to risk everything for what they believed in. If that opened her eyes to the truth, it would be worth it.

Chapter 18

KATE SAT ON HER windowsill the next morning, sipping her coffee as she looked out over the port. She'd slept long and hard, exhausted by the emotional whiplash of the previous day. She had walked out of the newspaper office in the depths of despair. By the time Peter left, long after the sun set, hope filled her heart. If she'd believed in a higher being who listened to prayers, she would have poured out her gratitude for a friend willing to take a risk with her, for her.

Peter. She smiled and shook her head. For the last year, she'd thought of him only as Johnson. Reporters almost always referred to police sources by their last names. That was how the officers referred to each other, and it hinted at both the precarious camaraderie and the professional distance journalists liked to have with their sometimes adversarial sources. But somewhere over the last few days, Kate had started to refer to him in her own mind by his first name.

She'd never taken comfort in companionship. But planning the trip with Peter cast a warm, welcome glow across her horizon. Doing life alone had left a void. And she was only just beginning to feel its depth.

Before Peter went home, they had plane tickets and a plan for their first few days of travel. He'd called his friends on Whatsapp and chatted for about 20 minutes while she heated tomato soup and made grilled cheese sandwiches for dinner. Listening to him talk in a mix of English and halting Spanish set her pulse skipping. She knew so little about him.

She shook her head and stood up, stretching. By this time tomorrow, they'd be on a plane to Cancún. But she had work to do today. As she and Peter had talked over the case, they kept coming back to Emily's mom. Was it possible that Emily could really let her mother think she was dead? What kind of person would inflict that kind of pain on someone who loved them?

Kate wanted to believe the best about Emily Gibson. She'd admired her from the day she'd learned about her involvement in the vaccine research. Emily's intimate relationship with Newhouse cast a shadow over Kate's admiration, but she wasn't convinced Emily wasn't a victim. Newhouse had clearly taken advantage of her. And Kate certainly identified with Emily's desire to flee. But she had a hard time reconciling her mental image of the strong, independent researcher with a hard-hearted narcissist.

Surely her mother knew something.

Before going to bed, Kate had texted Mrs. Gibson to ask if she could stop by today to ask her a few more questions. The grieving mother had agreed. She seemed eager to talk about her daughter. That was helpful, but Kate had to admit it didn't bode well for the possibility she was hiding something.

She took a long, hot shower and tried not to think about the text messages her colleagues had sent her the day before. Jessica Linton had been as fake as her hot-pink fingernails. "Kate! I can't believe it! I will miss you so, so much!! I'll let you know if I hear about any openings. I know the job market's pretty tight right now. Best of luck!! Keep in touch. xoxoxoxo" Delilah's had been much more honest and practical. "Take your break. Get your story. Then come back in triumph. Mattingly won't hesitate to give you your job back."

She still couldn't revisit the scene in her managing editor's office without feeling the sting of tears in her eyes. What had she been thinking? She scrubbed her hands over her face. She hadn't been thinking. Fury had driven her to take a stand she now regretted. She could only hope Delilah was right.

Thirty minutes later, she was driving over the causeway, headed for Houston. An hour later, she pulled into Mrs. Gibson's driveway. The unassuming, ranch-style home looked much as it probably had when it was built fifty years earlier. But flowers filled the front beds, creating a cheery welcome. Kate took a deep breath before knocking on the door.

Pamela Gibson opened the door with a wan smile.

"Kate! It's good to see you. Come in, come in. You must be tired after such a long drive. I'll put the kettle on and we can have some tea."

Kate wandered around the perimeter of the living room while Mrs. Gibson rummaged in the kitchen. Photos of Emily covered every wall. Kate took a steadying breath as her eyes swept over a panoply of the woman's life. Shots of her as a kid, her arms wrapped around the neck of a man with matching red hair. There he was teaching her to ride a bike. Presiding over an erupting volcano in the driveway. Then he disappeared, and Emily stood alone in the photos. In one prominent shot, she held a trophy at what looked like a science fair. In another, she posed in her cap and gown, diploma held high.

"Emily hated my little photo collection," her mother said, trembling lips pulled into the ghost of a smile. "She said it was embarrassing. But I was so proud of her."

A rush of sympathy bowled over Kate's doubts. If Mrs. Gibson knew her daughter was alive and well, she deserved an Oscar. She reached out and took the older woman's hand, squeezing it briefly.

"I'm so sorry," she said. That seemed appropriate, whether Emily was alive or dead.

Mrs. Gibson swallowed and blinked back tears.

"Thank you, dear," she said, giving Kate's hand a returning squeeze. "I know you are. And I appreciate it. Let me just get our tea and you can tell me what you need."

Kate sat down on the couch and watched as Mrs. Gibson carried in a tray covered with a teapot, cups, a sugar bowl, and a plate of cookies. She gave no sign of any self-consciousness or hesitancy about whatever this interview might bring. Kate chewed her lip while Mrs. Gibson filled two cups and offered her a cookie.

"Now," the older woman said as she settled back into the cushions, clutching a steaming cup to her chest. "You said you had some questions?"

The bite of cookie Kate had just swallowed seemed to stick in her throat for a moment and she had to take a sip of her scalding tea.

"Goodness! Be careful. That's hot," Mrs. Gibson said, peering at her with what seemed like genuine concern.

"Sorry," Kate sputtered. "That went down the wrong way."

She cleared her throat and took another, more careful sip of her tea, searching the older woman's face over the top of her cup. When she felt she couldn't delay it anymore, she plunged in.

"Did you know Emily was learning Spanish?"

Mrs. Gibson's eyebrows shot up. "No, I didn't. Who told you that?"

Kate briefly recounted her visit to Emily's apartment.

"Well, I didn't know. But I'm not surprised. Emily was always looking to learn something. No doubt she thought it would be useful. She took Spanish in high school. But like most people, I don't know that she learned much that she could actually use. She got a little practice when we went to Cancun the summer after her sophomore year. But she wasn't fluent or anything like that."

"Mrs. Gibson, I hate to even ask this, but do you think it's possible that Emily was preparing for a long stay in a Spanish-speaking country?"

The woman's face betrayed nothing but surprise. "Well, I don't know. She never said anything about that. And honestly, I don't know what country that would be. She sometimes mentioned China as a possibility for a future research trip. The Chinese are pretty advanced in their research, you know."

"Sure," Kate said, taking a sip of her tea while she thought of how to phrase her next question. "I just wondered whether Emily might have been considering leaving the country, anticipating fallout from the vaccine trial problems."

Mrs. Gibson's eyes widened. "You mean like Dr. Newhouse suggested? Running away?"

Her voice cracked on the last word, and Kate flinched.

"Well, not running away, exactly. But perhaps considering her options. I mean, if she couldn't convince Newhouse to admit to the vaccine trial's problems, maybe she thought she needed an escape plan, so she didn't get caught in the fallout of his conceit."

Mrs. Gibson stared at her blankly. Several uncomfortable heartbeats passed.

"What are you saying?" she finally asked. Her voice sounded pinched, like someone had clamped a clothespin over her vocal chords.

"I don't know, exactly," Kate said, squirming miserably under the older woman's mournful gaze. "I just wondered whether it was possible that Emily was planning to go somewhere."

"Without telling me?" Mrs. Gibson looked like she might cry. "And what about David? I can't imagine her leaving him. What did he say?"

Kate frowned. It was like Emily's mom had blocked out knowledge of her daughter's relationship with Aaron Newhouse. Didn't she realize Emily wasn't as devoted to David Knowles as he was to her?

"Well, he thinks it's nonsense, of course," Kate hedged. "But he also knows Emily wasn't 100 percent truthful with him."

Mrs. Gibson stared at her for a few moments before looking down into her cup.

"I see," she murmured. "I suppose that's true. Emily often kept her thoughts to herself. Whenever she was thinking about something important, she tended to withdraw. Where other people might seek advice or talk about their problems, Emily kept her own counsel. She rarely asked for advice. She just pulled into herself. I called it brooding. She called it analyzing. She would finally emerge when she'd made a decision, and she never seemed to question whatever path she'd chosen."

Kate set her cup down on the tray on the ottoman and leaned forward, her elbows on her knees. She searched the older woman's face intently.

"Mrs. Gibson, I have evidence that Emily made an effort to get to know crew members on a cargo ship making regular trips between Galveston and Cuba. Do you think it's possible that she might have been trying to find a way off the island without anyone knowing about it?"

"Oh!" the woman said, as her tea cup bounced off her knee and landed with a muffled thud on the carpet. Bronze liquid splashed over her pants and the couch.

"Let me get a towel," Kate said, jumping off the couch and heading into the kitchen. When she returned to the living room, Mrs. Gibson looked as though she hadn't moved. Her face was frozen in pinched shock, eyebrows drawn together, mouth slacked open. Kate quickly dabbed at the carpet and the couch cushions. When she had done all she could, she sat back and pondered what to say next.

"I'm sorry to ask you that. I realize it's a shock," she said. It sounded like a lame excuse, but she plowed ahead. "I just, I mean, I'm trying to put myself in Emily's shoes. What would I have done? And there was a time, when I was younger, when I thought it would just be easier to disappear. I know it doesn't make logical sense. But when you feel cornered, sometimes running just seems like the best option."

Pamela Gibson slowly looked up to meet Kate's eyes. She looked like a dog who'd been kicked one too many times.

"Emily never ran away from anything in her life," she said, her voice trembling. "She dug in. Always. She was incredibly stubborn. It was maddening. She never quit. Never."

Kate nodded. She understood that level of determination. But she also knew it was possible to dig in on the outside and give up on the inside.

"What if she didn't see it as quitting," she whispered. "What if she saw it as regrouping to continue the fight?"

Mrs. Gibson shook her head. "What does it matter, anyway? If she was planning to leave, Aaron Newhouse obviously made sure she didn't."

"What makes you say that?"

The older woman's mouth scrunched into an "o." Suddenly she understood what Kate was getting at.

"You think Emily did leave. You think Newhouse is telling the truth and that she's alive somewhere out there."

Two spots of bright pink flushed Mrs. Gibson's cheeks. Kate couldn't tell if she was about to start yelling or burst into tears. She raised a shaking hand to her mouth. Her eyes darted back and forth as her mind processed the possibilities. Kate willed herself to stay quiet. Mrs. Gibson had given no sign that she was hiding any secrets. But if she was, now would be the most likely time for a betraying word or motion. Tears welled in her eyes.

"If Emily is alive, then she's fooled all of us. She was willing to let everyone believe she was dead. Even me." Her voice caught on the last word and Kate's heart lurched.

"So you haven't heard from her?" Kate asked quietly.

Mrs. Gibson shook her head, tears spilling down her cheeks. "If I knew Emily was really alive, there's no way I could keep that a secret."

Kate believed her. "I'm guessing Emily would know that? I mean, if she was alive but wanted to keep it a secret, she probably knew she couldn't tell you."

Mrs. Gibson nodded, her lower lip trembling. Then she looked at Kate imploringly, through watery blue eyes.

"It's hard to believe," she faltered. "Hard to believe a child would do that, isn't it? But if she really believed she had to, I think she would."

Kate's throat tightened. If Emily's mother knew her daughter was alive, she would never admit to the possibility that she could be. Kate reached out and took her hand.

"I'm sorry. I hated to bring all of this to you. But I had to know if there was a possibility you knew anything."

Mrs. Gibson squeezed her hand tightly before leaning over to tug a tissue from a box on a nearby side table. After she blew her nose and wiped her eyes, she fixed Kate with another imploring look.

"Do you really think she's alive?"

Kate took a deep breath. "I do. So much so that I quit my job so that I could try to prove it."

"What? What do you mean?"

"I asked my boss to send me to Cuba to see if I could find Emily. He refused. I offered to pay for it myself, but he still refused. Said it was too dangerous. He told me if I didn't drop it, he'd fire me. So I quit."

Mrs. Gibson gasped. "So, what are you going to do now?"

"Go to Cuba. I leave tomorrow."

The older woman stared at her, as though of all the things Kate had told her, this is the one she just couldn't comprehend.

"You're going to Cuba to look for Emily?"

Kate nodded. "I don't want to give you false hope. But I do believe your daughter is alive. I don't have a lot of evidence to prove it. But my gut tells me she arranged for a cabin on that container ship and sailed off the island the day she disappeared."

"But why Cuba? And why not just fly there herself?"

"There's no way she could board a commercial airliner without being spotted. And she left everything behind. She couldn't be going anywhere she needed ID."

"But, Cuba?"

"It has a pretty world-renowned medical training program. She could continue her training, continue her research. Her knowledge about the vaccine would be a bartering chip for her to build a new life. It was just about all she had."

Mrs. Gibson shook her head in amazement. "Did you tell David any of this?"

The scene of his angry outburst flashed through Kate's mind.

"No," she said slowly. "I think this is all... a little more compli-cated for him."

"But if Emily's alive, he would want to know!"

Kate pursed her lips. How blunt should she be?

"I know David loves Emily, but he's also pretty angry about everything with Newhouse. If she is alive, it's hard to imagine them having a joyful reunion."

Mrs. Gibson frowned and looked down at her hands, now twist-ed into a knot in her lap.

"I suppose Emily has a lot to answer for," she said with a sigh. "I was shocked by what the police discovered. But I know David was devastated. I think he could forgive her, but maybe I'm wrong."

"Do you think Emily loved him?" Kate asked, unable to suppress her curiosity over what seemed like an obviously key piece of the equation.

Mrs. Gibson frowned. "I thought she did. But then I thought Dr. Newhouse was a nice man and Emily was dead!" She buried her face in her hands and let out a strangled cry.

Kate's chest tightened. She hoped with all her heart that she wasn't giving this poor, tormented woman false hope. She scooted closer to the hunched back and placed her hand on it gingerly.

"Mrs. Gibson, I hope I'm right about Emily. But you have to know, I could be wrong. I won't know until I get down there. And even then, if Emily's in hiding, I might never find her. Please, don't ... don't get your hopes up too much."

Mrs. Gibson heaved a shuddering sigh and pulled her hands away from her face. She looked at Kate as though she'd suggested they stop breathing.

"It's too late for that," she said. "Much too late for that."

Kate drove back to the island with a sense of dread hanging heavy on her heart. She'd convinced Mrs. Gibson that her daughter was alive. If she was wrong, the grieving mother would plunge into the pit of mourning all over again. Kate shuddered. She knew what kind of agony that meant. She would rather die herself than go through that again.

She stuffed the possibility into a corner of her mind she'd developed nearly complete control over in the last 15 years. She left things there she didn't want to think about. It was like a gun safe with a big silver wheel on the front. The kind her dad had in his closet at home. Nothing got out unless you had the combination.

Emily was alive. She would prove it.

Before driving back to her apartment, she swung by the grocery store and picked up some travel sized toiletries. Then she stopped at the ATM and made a withdrawal that left her feeling slightly nauseated. This trip would deplete all her reserves. If she came home with nothing, she would have nothing to fall back on.

She had just walked through her front door when her cellphone rang. One glance at the screen stilled her spiral of self-doubt.

"Hey," she said, pinching the phone between her shoulder and her ear. "Are you all packed?"

"I am! Are you?" His voice held a hint of mirth that told her he knew full well she wasn't.

"You bet," she said airily. "All packed."

Peter laughed. "You're a terrible liar. You haven't even started."

Kate smiled. "Believe what you want. I'm definitely not going to be up past midnight packing."

"I sure hope not! I'll be there to pick you up at 5:30."

She groaned. Why did the cheapest flights have to be first thing in the morning?

"I'll be ready, don't worry."

"I know you will be. I'll see you tomorrow."

Kate hung up and tossed the phone on her kitchen table. She opened her fridge and pulled out a long-necked bottle of beer. Walking to her window, she lifted the heavy sash. The warm evening breeze blew in, wrapping around her like a velvet robe. She perched on the wide windowsill and gazed out over the port.

The setting sun had painted the wispy tendrils of clouds a dusky rose against the pale blue sky. She took a long swig of the cool amber liquid and set the bottle down next to her.

Anticipation started to buzz deep in her soul. She had grasped the end of a very tangled thread. And she refused to let go until she worked out all the knots and pulled it through to the end. She'd risked everything to discover the truth. It had to be worth it.

Chapter 19

KATE'S EYES POPPED OPEN before her alarm went off. She showered quickly and threw a few final things in her duffel bag. They'd decided to travel light, only taking what they could carry. Even so, Kate had managed to squeeze in a week's worth of clothes. When Peter texted her at 5:25, she was ready.

He was leaning against his beat-up Jeep Cherokee when she pushed through her building's front door. She grinned at him, as the buzz building since the night before burst like a bubble in her chest. A tingle of electric excitement shot through her. They were actually going to do it. Even when she'd told Mattingly she would go, it seemed like a far-off dream. But now she was about to step into an adventure of her own making.

Peter grinned back and reached out to take her bag. Normally she would have rebuffed anything that hinted at chivalry, but his gestures never felt demeaning. She always had the sense that she gained something when he offered to help, never like she was giving up a part of herself. His hair was still damp. It made him look like a child whose mother had just smoothed down an unruly cowlick. Just the thought of him as a little boy sent a small thrill through her. She never would have wondered about his early life six months ago.

The comforting aroma of coffee billowed out of the SUV when she opened the door. Two paper cups from her favorite coffee shop sat in the console.

"You picked up coffee?" she asked incredulously when he climbed into the driver's seat.

"I figured you might be running a bit behind and probably didn't have time to make any," he said, glancing at her out of the corner of his eyes. A smile tugged at the corners of his mouth.

"I'll have you know I woke up before my alarm," she huffed.

"Is that a first?" he teased.

She punched him lightly in the arm. "Shut up. Most mornings are evil. But not this morning."

He laughed. "Excited?"

"Well, it feels like I've already had two cups of coffee, so I guess I am."

"Alright then! Here's to your third." He raised his cup and tapped it to hers before turning his attention to the road.

Kate watched as Broadway's jarring mixture of restored mansions, auto shops, and fast-food restaurants whizzed by her window. They drank their coffee in companionable silence as they sped over the causeway.

"From one island to another," Kate mused when they hit the flat stretch of freeway that would take them straight to one of Houston's two airports. "How long has it been since you last visited Cuba?"

He pursed his lips in thought. "Must be about 15 years. I was a teenager."

"And that's the last time you saw this family we're staying with?"

"Carida, yes. But Elian visited my dad when he was in the hospital here after we came home. Elian was on what they call a business trip. But his business was to connect with other pastors and get training. When he found out we were here, he came over from Miami before heading home."

Kate frowned. She knew nothing about Peter's parents.

"Is he," she faltered, trying to figure out what to say. "Is he ok? Your dad, I mean."

Peter tapped his fingers on the steering wheel. "He's recovered mostly. But he'll always have issues. Fortunately, my mom's a nurse, so he's in good hands."

Kate wanted to ask more, but his brief answer suggested he didn't want to talk about it.

"What about you?" he asked before she could change the subject. "When was the last time you left the country?"

"When I was in high school. Our senior class trip was to Cozumel. That's actually the only time I've ever been out of the country. We never really had the money to travel growing up. I've always wanted to, though."

"Why haven't you?"

She shrugged. "I guess I was just too focused on work. I figured I'd have time for things like that later."

"Well, maybe this will be the start of a whole new chapter," he said, draining the last of his coffee. "After this, there's probably no place you wouldn't go."

She laughed. "What's that supposed to mean?"

"Cuba is beautiful, and the people are amazing. But it's not Cozumel. Not even close."

They parked the car and made it through security with just enough time to grab a second cup of coffee before heading to their gate. Kate tried to look like she knew what she was doing. The people in the terminal around them chatted excitedly, no doubt anticipating a vacation in Mexico. Peter leaned against the wall, watching the crowd as he sipped his coffee. He looked completely relaxed, but she detected a watchful awareness in his eyes. His vigilance took the edge off her nerves. Whatever the next few days held, she would be with someone capable of dealing with just about anything.

As if he felt her looking at him, he glanced down at her. Cheeks burning, she looked away and slid her phone out of her back pocket. She knew she needed to text her dad, but she hadn't figured out what to say. They didn't talk often during the week.

But if he texted her and she didn't respond after a few days, she didn't want him to get worried and call the newspaper. She held the phone in front of her for a few minutes before finally deciding to call. He answered on the first ring.

"Katie!" he said. "It's a little early for you, isn't it? Everything ok?"

She cringed. She hadn't thought about how early it was. Good thing her dad had always been an early riser.

"Oh, yeah. Sorry. I'm at a thing for work and I'm just waiting for it to start. I've got a busy week ahead, and I thought I might as well call you now, since I probably won't have time later."

"Sounds like they're getting their money's worth out of you."

"Yeah, you know how it is. We've got a paper to fill every day."

"They still short staffed?"

"You mean after the layoffs? Yeah. We're still down a reporter. I don't see that changing any time soon."

Her father grunted. "Well, don't let them work you too hard. You tell your editor you need a vacation."

Kate tried not to laugh. "This from the man who never takes time off. I bet you're getting ready to go to the shop now."

"Just for a few hours. Then I'm going to take the boat out. I got a new jib I'm gonna try out."

"Yeah?" she smiled. Her father's sailboat was his happy place. "Did you get the tiller fixed?"

"Yup. It's as good as new. She turns like a dream now."

"Well, I hope you get some good wind."

"It's nothing like a sea coast breeze, but it'll do. Worked on any good stories this week? What about that missing researcher? They found her yet?"

"Not yet." Normally she would have filled him in on the latest details of the case. But she didn't want him asking too many questions.

"Huh. I thought that doctor would have confessed by now. He doesn't seem like the type to survive long in jail."

"Well, he says he's innocent. And I'm sure he knows without more evidence, the DA is going to have a hard time making a murder charge stick."

"Guess so. Should make an interesting trial to cover, anyway."

Kate laughed. "We'll see. Listen dad, my thing's about to start. I gotta go. I'll give you a call next weekend, ok?"

"Ok. Have a good day. Go do something fun tonight. Don't spend all your time working."

"I'll try not to. Love you."

"I love you, too, Katie pie."

She felt a twinge as she hung up. What would he say when he found out she'd been to Cuba and back without telling him? And what would he do if anything happened to her? She was all he had.

Shaking off a sudden feeling of foreboding, she turned back toward Peter, who stood holding both their bags. She mashed down the phone's power button until the screen went black.

"Time to board," he said, studying her face. "Everything ok?"

"Yeah, I just gave my dad a call. I told him I was going to be busy this week. I didn't want him texting me and getting worried when he didn't hear back quickly." She took her bag and slid the phone inside.

"We'll pick up some internet cards when we get there. We should be able to send messages if you want to let him know you're ok."

She nodded. "It's weird. I don't remember the last time I turned my phone off."

"Feeling disconnected? Just wait until we land."

Three hours later, they landed in Cancún. Kate slung her bag over her shoulder and stretched as they walked into the terminal. Peter had dozed the entire flight. She'd flipped through the in-flight magazine and watched the puffy white clouds slip past the window.

Peter looked at his watch. "We should have just enough time to get our visas and grab some lunch."

They threaded their way through the crowds filling the terminal and found the check-in desk for the small regional airline that would fly them to Havana. It took them only a few minutes to fill out the visa forms. Once they'd turned them in, they wandered back into the terminal.

"Take your pick," Peter said, waving his hand toward a bank of restaurants.

"It looks just like the airport in Houston!" Kate laughed.

"Gotta keep the American tourists happy," he said with a smile.

"And here I was, hoping for some authentic Mexican food."

"Don't worry. You'll get plenty of authentic food in the next week."

Kate surveyed the options. "Let's at least get some tacos. I can't begin this trip with a hamburger."

Once they'd ordered their food, they found a small table in the middle of the food court and sat down. Around them, sunburned tourists squabbled and jostled. Nobody looked thrilled to be going home. The sniping and noise cast a pall over their lunch.

"It's not the best ad for traveling," Peter said, snapping her attention away from a couple whose end-of-travel bickering had drawn her in.

She laughed uneasily. "I hope not! I was just wondering if they were on their honeymoon. How depressing!"

Peter glanced over at the couple. "It doesn't look that serious. They seem to be making up."

Kate turned her head in time to see the woman throw her arms around the man's neck and press her lips to his. Heat flushed her cheeks, and she took a bite of her taco to hide her embarrassment.

Peter chuckled. "I'm sure they're madly in love."

Kate rolled her eyes. "Charming."

"What? People fight. They make up. It's the circle of love."

"The circle of love?"

"Yeah, like the circle of life. The circle of love."

"How romantic!"

"Well, maybe not. But probably realistic."

Kate arched an eyebrow. "Are you speaking from experience?"

He groaned. "I guess I walked right into that, didn't I?"

Kate raised her other eyebrow. "That wasn't an answer."

Peter shook his head. "Not going to let it go, are you?"

"Not a chance," Kate said with a wicked grin.

He glanced at his watch. "I'm not sure we have time to detail all my epic romantic entanglements."

Kate's mouth dropped open in surprise. Was he kidding? She'd never pictured him with a long train of broken relationships.

Peter threw back his head and laughed. "I'm just kidding. You should have seen your face."

She threw a crumpled napkin at him and shook her head. But the sudden frown that creased his forehead stopped her from shooting the sarcastic barb forming on her tongue. He took a deep breath and fixed her with a much more serious expression than she'd expected.

"It's been a long time since I've been in love. I was just a kid, really. But we were…" His voice trailed off, and she had the feeling he no longer saw her, even though his eyes never left her face. "I think we would have gotten married if everything hadn't fallen apart."

He sighed, and his eyes refocused on hers. She managed a faltering smile. She'd never seen him look so exposed.

"I'm sorry," she breathed. It seemed hardly enough and yet the only thing she could say.

A wistful smile softened his face. "It was a long time ago. And I trust it was for the best."

Before she could say anything else, an announcement broke through the generic pop music playing in the background. Peter listened carefully.

"That's us," he said. "They're getting ready to board. We'd better head to the gate."

Kate stuffed the last bite of her taco in her mouth and balled up the wrapper. She studied his back as he carried their tray to the restaurant counter. She'd always thought of him as a hero, almost too perfect. Strong, dependable, generous, self-sacrificing. She'd never seen him vulnerable. But the softness in his eyes when he talked about his lost love reminded her he was completely human. What had she been like, the woman he'd once loved? And what had gone so terribly wrong?

They walked quickly to the gate, where other passengers were already lining up at the door to the gangway. Thirty minutes later, they had buckled their seatbelts and prepared for takeoff. Kate watched the ground crew scurry around on the tarmac.

"In a little over an hour, we'll be in Havana," Peter said. His voice sounded disconcertingly close in the tight space. She glanced over at him with a smile but quickly turned back to the window when she felt her face burning. She suddenly realized she'd never been this close to him. The fresh scent of his soap filled her nose. She laced her fingers together in her lap and closed her eyes.

She didn't open them again until they were in the air. She glanced over at Peter, half expecting him to be asleep again. But he was watching her.

"That was a fast nap," he said. "I figured your early morning wake-up call had finally caught up with you."

Kate shook her head. "Nah. Just thinking about everything that's ahead."

"And everything that's behind?"

"The newspaper, you mean? I'm trying not to think about that."

He nodded thoughtfully. "Don't worry. Once you're back safe, I'm sure Mattingly will relent."

She bit her bottom lip. "He'd better."

"You're going to nail this story, and then you'll probably have editors lining up with offers. This could be your big break."

How many times had she invested a story with that hope? She pursed her lips.

"I don't know. I'm not sure I want any other offers."

"Has Galveston grown on you that much? Or is there some other reason you don't want to leave?"

"What do you mean?" An uncomfortable flutter started to beat against her ribs.

"I just thought, I mean, Brian?"

"Oh, no," she turned to the window again to hide her discomfort.

After a few moments of awkward silence, he cleared his throat.

"Hey, I'm sorry. I shouldn't have asked."

She suppressed her knee-jerk reaction against talking about anything personal and turned back to him with a smile.

"No, it's fine. After I grilled you about your past, I had it coming."

He huffed a hesitant laugh. "It's none of my business. He just seemed completely infatuated with you. I know you were taking a break. But I didn't figure it would last long."

Kate sighed. How could she explain what happened with Brian?

"I hadn't seen him in months. But I called him when I got those spreadsheets with the vaccine data. He helped me look through them. And after that, we went to dinner. But..." she hesitated. "I don't know."

He looked at her but didn't interrupt.

"I broke it off last year because he wanted more than I could give him. Nothing's changed. He's a great guy. Amazing. I just..." she trailed off and shrugged.

He nodded but still said nothing. She bit the inside of her cheek and looked out the window. A sense of inadequacy burned in her chest. Never in a million years would she have had this conversation voluntarily. But she couldn't seem to stop talking.

"I know he loved me, or was close to it. But I couldn't love him back. It's not that I didn't want to." She broke off in frustration as she tried to put in words, for the first time, everything that had kept her from falling in love. "I just couldn't."

Peter never took his eyes off her face. He seemed to be looking right into her soul.

"There's a part of you that you don't want to share," he said after a few moments. "You keep it locked away and you don't let anyone get near it. Until you're ready to open up that room, you'll never be able to fall in love."

"How do you know?" She intended the question to sound forceful and demanding, but it came out in a strangled whisper.

He balled up his fist and put it over his heart. "I have one, too."

Kate stared at him in disbelief. She wanted to deny it. Tell him he was 100 percent wrong. But the words stuck in her throat. She swallowed and glanced out the window.

"I don't know how to open the door anymore," she said, her eyes fixed on the white clouds floating by underneath them.

"Yes, you do," he whispered. "You just haven't found anyone you want to let in."

Chapter 20

Peter studied Kate's profile as she continued to stare out the window. It took all his self-control not to reach out and take her hand, pull her back toward him. He felt every bit of her internal struggle as if she were actually writhing in the seat next to him. It had taken him a long time to diagnose his own relational struggles. But identifying the problem wasn't the same as embracing the solution.

The static-filled announcement asking the passengers to prepare for landing seemed to rouse Kate from her thoughts. She rubbed her arms and glanced over at him.

He smiled. "Won't be long now."

She nodded and seemed to be on the verge of saying something before changing her mind and looking out the window again. Her silence might have been unnerving. But her glance held no tension or animosity. Something had shifted though. He couldn't tell what, but it didn't seem to be for the worse.

Twenty minutes later, the plane glided onto the runway. Kate looked at him again, her eyes shining with excitement this time. He grinned back, the awkwardness of their conversation suddenly dissipating. As they waited for the flight attendant to open the cabin door, his own excitement started to build. He hadn't realized how cooped up he'd been, staying in one place for so long. He'd grown up traveling the world, and he missed it.

He followed Kate up the aisle and down the gangway into the terminal. Since they didn't have to wait for their bags, they were near the front of the line snaking through customs. While they waited, Kate set her bag down and pulled her hair into a ponytail.

"Feels just like home," she said, fanning herself with her passport.

He laughed. "I guess I should have warned you. But hey, we're used to it, right?"

"Yeah, just not usually inside," she said ruefully.

"Aw, it's not that bad. Think of it as part of the adventure."

"Speaking of adventure, I wish I could get my passport stamped," Kate said, flipping through the book's crisp, empty pages.

Peter glanced at his own, dog-eared version, its pages almost full. Every stamp told a story.

"Well, it won't exactly be a secret once you write your bombshell exposé," he said. "There's no reason not to get one."

Kate shot him a mischievous look. "True. I guess there's no going back now, come what may."

Once through customs they threaded their way past shops selling cigars and tall bottles of rum. When they reached the front of the terminal, Peter slowed, scanning the crowd milling around. He saw Elian just as the older man spotted them.

"Peter!" he cried in a deep, slightly raspy voice as he hurried over.

For a moment, Peter forgot Kate and the reason for their visit. He felt like the wide-eyed, tenderhearted teenager he'd been the last time he visited Cuba. Full of hope and dreams for what he could do as part of a community of difference-makers that spanned the globe. Everywhere he went felt like a small piece of home. He hadn't realized until now how much he missed that connection. He opened his arms wide and threw them around his old friend.

"Elian, it's so good to see you," he said, not even bothering to hide the emotion that choked his voice.

After a few long moments, he pulled out of the older man's embrace and smiled at him. Elian held his gaze for a few more moments, and Peter thought he saw a trace of sadness in his eyes.

"You are older, my son," he said. "It's about time you finally came to see us."

Peter chuckled ruefully. He felt older. Decades older.

"You must be Kate," Elian said, holding his hand out and shaking Kate's enthusiastically.

"I'm sorry," Peter said, suddenly feeling like an idiot for leaving her standing there so long.

"Kate this is Elian Pérez. Elian, my friend Kate. You have her to thank for this visit."

"And I won't forget it! You can believe," he said with the hearty laugh Peter remembered so well. "Welcome to Cuba, my dear. Welcome to Cuba."

"Thanks," Kate said. She seemed a little self-conscious. "I really appreciate you letting us stay. I mean, me stay. Because of course, Peter..."

She trailed off with a nervous laugh. Elian put his arm around her and ushered them toward the airport doors.

"Any friend of Peter's is a friend of mine. Come, come. Let's get home. Let me take your bag."

Kate hesitated only a little before handing it over with a gracious smile. Peter smirked to himself. He knew what an effort that took. Elian led them to an old Russian Lada. Although obviously decades old, the boxy car didn't have any dents or signs of rust. He directed Kate to the passenger seat and shooed Peter into the back with the two bags.

"You've had the tour before, Peter, and nothing's really changed since the last time you were here," he said. "We'll let Kate have the best view. It's all new to her."

Industrial sites near the airport gave way to open fields that eventually sprouted houses. The closer they got to central Havana, the more closely packed the houses got. Eventually, low-rise apartment buildings dotted the neighborhoods.

Elian chatted as they drove, pointing out landmarks and giving a synopsis of the island's history. Peter watched Kate's profile as she took it all in. A slight flush gave her cheeks a pink glow. He wondered if it was the heat or excitement. She listened attentively, inserting questions every so often. Ever the reporter, he thought with a smile. She couldn't help wringing the last detail out of everything. That might make for some painful conversations over the next few days. He felt sure Elian would bring up the past at some point. And Kate would no doubt expect him to fill in the gaps. Bringing her here had been a risk. He wasn't sure whether he'd suggested she join him in spite of that or because of it.

Forty-five minutes later, Elian pulled onto a side street, drove halfway down and pulled up outside a white stucco house with vines stretching up almost to the roof on one side.

Before they could climb out of the car, a short, round woman with sparkling brown eyes bustled out the heavy wood door.

"Oh, Peter!" she cried, throwing her hands up in the air as he climbed out of the car.

"Carida!" he said, laughing as she grabbed him by the shoulders and kissed him on both cheeks.

Not wanting to make the same mistake twice, he quickly turned to look for Kate and found her standing right behind him.

"Carida, this is Kate. Kate, this is Carida Pérez."

Kate held out her hand, but the older woman wrapped her arms around her enthusiastically. Kate's eyes widened in surprise, but she didn't protest.

"Come in, come in," Carida said, ushering them toward the door. "You must be tired and hot. Come in and have some nice, cold lemonade."

The warm smell of onions, peppers, and simmering beef wafted over them when their hostess opened the door.

"Ropa Vieja!" Peter said, his mouth watering as he sniffed the air appreciatively.

"Of course! I remember how much you love it," Carida said with a playful swat at his arm. "I think you ate your weight in it the last time you were here."

Peter laughed. She was probably right. He'd spent his days playing soccer with Elian and Carida's son, Macerio, and always worked up a ravenous appetite by dinnertime.

She showed them to their bedrooms, and they set their bags down before following her back into the main living area. She motioned for them to join Elian on the patio while she collected a tray of glasses and a pitcher full of lemonade.

The patio garden was exactly as Peter remembered it. An oasis of shade, with flowering vines clinging to the pergola and lush tropical plants nestled along the walls. In one corner, an ornate fountain gurgled. And at the other end, a dark blue hammock hung between two posts. You would never guess you were in the middle of the city.

Carida put the tray on a wrought-iron table and motioned for them to sit. But Kate stood staring at the lush greenery around her.

"This is amazing," she said, glancing from the fountain to the hammock.

"It's a great place to take a nap!" Elian said with a laugh. "We will make sure you have time to try it before you leave."

Kate took her seat as Carida handed her a tall glass of lemonade. She smiled gratefully and took a long drink. When Carida handed Peter his glass, she glanced between him and Kate, her eyes full of unspoken questions.

"I talked to your Papa after you called me," Elian said. "It was good to hear his voice. He seemed to be doing well."

Peter smiled. "He told me when he called right afterward to ask why I was coming to Cuba! I hadn't even had time to call him myself yet."

Elian bellowed out his bright laugh and made a disapproving clicking noise. "He said you don't call often enough. Now I believe it!"

Peter squirmed under Elian's gentle reproof.

"That's fair. I probably don't."

"And your mama?" Carida asked. "How is she holding up?"

"Good, I think. For the most part. I know it's not easy caring for dad. But I think the hardest thing is being back here, away from the people she spent so much of her life with."

"Hannah has a big heart," Carida said softly.

Images of his mom surrounded by women in colorful dresses, wide smiles across every face, danced through his memory. Serving the women of Africa had been her life. Tears suddenly filled his eyes, and he looked away, hoping Kate wouldn't notice.

"You miss it as much as she does," Elian said, compassion softening his voice.

Peter sighed. That one word seemed too small to describe how he felt when he thought of his old home. How could four letters convey all the longing, regret, and guilt he felt whenever he thought about it?

Across the table, Kate sat motionless, almost as if she wanted to disappear from what had turned into a deeply personal conversation. But her eyes never left his face. He felt them probing his every word and reaction for clues about what they were talking about. He cleared his throat and forced his lips into a smile.

"I do miss it," he said with false nonchalance. "But that's in the past. My life is in Galveston now."

"But your heart, eh? Where is that? Still in Africa, I think," Elian said.

Peter shook his head. "No. I can't. You know that."

Elian leaned forward, his compassion coalescing into something that was almost stern. Peter's heart beat faster. He had not expected to have this conversation so soon.

"What happened was not your fault," Elian said firmly. "That is not a burden you need to keep dragging behind you. Did you make mistakes? Perhaps. But you are forgiven."

"Forgiven is not the same as forgotten," Peter said quietly.

"No, but over time, it can be. And for you, who knows the truth of grace, it should be."

Peter drummed his fingers on the table. He lived in the tension between grace and guilt. He'd built safeguards so he wouldn't make the same mistake again. But living in a cage was a far cry from the freedom he'd once known. More than anything, that's what he longed for.

He felt Kate's eyes boring into him. She seemed on the verge of asking a question when Carida jumped in.

"Why don't you tell us what brought you here. Elian didn't say much, but what he told me sounds very interesting."

"That's Kate's story to tell," Peter said, smiling at her.

The slightest pink tint colored Kate's cheeks when their hosts looked at her expectantly.

"We're looking for someone," she said simply. "Someone we think faked her own murder and fled the country to start over."

For the next fifteen minutes, Kate recounted the details of Emily Gibson's rising star and sudden disappearance. Carida clucked her tongue and shook her head at some of the details, but neither of them interrupted her.

"So, we think she might have come here," Kate concluded. "And hopefully we can find her."

Elian and Carida exchanged glances. Peter took a sip of his lemonade and looked at Kate through the sheen of condensation on his glass. She'd seen their glance too and seemed to interpret it as doubt. She shifted uncomfortably in her chair.

"If she's here, and we believe she is, Kate thinks her most likely plan would be to go to one of the medical schools," he said. "So that's where we plan to start."

Elian sighed and shook his head. "She would probably stand out, but then so will you. You need to have a good reason for being there."

"I've thought about that," Kate said, straightening in her chair. Confidence washed away the drifts of doubt Elian's skepticism had blown over her. "I'm going to pose as a prospective student. We can tell anyone who asks that we're visitors and admirers of Cuban culture. We came to the island to see how we might like living here while I was in medical school."

Peter raised his eyebrows at her apparent intention to include him in her fictitious plans to settle in Cuba. Kate's face flushed.

"Since you're here, that just seemed to make the most sense," she said, an edge of defensiveness sharpening her voice.

Peter grinned. "No problem. I'm sure we can make it convincing."

Kate rolled her eyes. Elian chuckled but then grew serious.

"Convincing is very important," he said, looking back and forth between them. "If they think you're lying, they will bring you in for questioning. Or worse."

Worry creased Kate's forehead. But she swallowed and lifted her chin.

"We'll be fine," she said. "If it seems like they're suspicious, we'll leave right away and try to figure something else out."

"We will pray for your safety," Carida said soothingly as she reached over to pat Kate's hand.

Peter stifled a smile at Kate's mumbled thanks. Carida stood and gathered the pitcher and glasses onto the tray she'd used to bring them outside.

"Dinner won't be ready for a few more hours. Why don't you take Kate for a walk while it's still light? You should be able to make it down to the beach and back before dark."

Peter raised his eyebrows at Kate to gauge her interest, and she nodded. After getting a few directions from Elian, they headed out the gate. The sun-drenched street felt glaring and hot after the shady patio. But a sea breeze stirred around them, taking the sting out of the sun's rays. When they got to a main road, they took shelter in the dappled shade thrown by the trees that dotted the sidewalk.

They walked in silence for a while. Kate drank in everything they passed. The Vedado neighborhood was one of Havana's most eclectic. Stately old houses gave the neighborhood an air of faded glory. Their dull paint and pocked stucco suggested abandonment. Every so often, Peter spotted a boarded-up window.

"It looks a lot like Galveston," Kate mused. "That is, if the city fired all the code enforcement officers and everyone was broke."

Peter nodded thoughtfully. "I was thinking everything looked starved. Like it's slowly dying."

Kate grimaced. "That's bleak. But accurate, I guess."

"The people are such a contrast to their surroundings," Peter said, nodding toward the groups of chattering, laughing pedestrians on the other side of the street. "Joyful and resilient."

Twenty minutes later, they rounded the corner of an austere apartment tower and the sparkling blue Caribbean Sea stretched out in front of them. Kate took a deep breath of the salty breeze as she scanned the horizon. They waited for the traffic light to change and trotted across the Malecón to the seawall. They sat on the rough top and dangled their legs over the side.

"Just like home," Kate said with a laugh as the breeze lifted her ponytail off her neck.

"The water looks a little more inviting," Peter said, gesturing toward the azure waves.

"I'll give you that."

They sat in silence for a while. Peter scanned the horizon, looking for boats. When he glanced back at Kate, he caught her watching him. He looked away, hoping to avoid the interrogation she looked ready to spring on him. She didn't speak, but her curiosity filled the space between them like a lion coiled to pounce.

Peter sighed.

"I know you have questions. And I will answer them, eventually. But not right now."

He glanced at her again, and something in her eyes kept him from looking away. The guardedness that normally hung around her like a veil had vanished. Her face held an openness he'd never seen before. It was like she'd voluntarily pulled aside a curtain to see more clearly and be more clearly seen. Something stirred deep in his heart. He'd felt a twinge many times in the last year, but he'd squelched it unmercifully. Now it had come fully awake and there was no hope of beating it back.

They sat there, staring at each other, for longer than Peter would have thought possible. The weight of his unspoken story pulled harder than at any time in the last 10 years. He wanted to tell her what he'd witnessed, what he'd done. What he'd lost. Her wide, clear eyes spoke acceptance and understanding. Could he finally confess to someone who hadn't known him all those years ago what he'd been afraid to admit for so long?

A shout behind them made her jump and broke the spell. Peter looked over his shoulder. A group of teenage boys strode past them, laughing and joking with each other, unaware they'd interrupted anything.

Peter glanced back at Kate. She was looking over the water again, her usual guardedness back in place. His opportunity had rolled away like a wave retreating to the vast sea.

"We'd better start walking back," he said reluctantly. "Carida will have dinner ready soon, and I don't want to keep her waiting."

Kate nodded and smiled. "She seems pretty fond of you."

"I think Carida is fond of everyone," he said, standing and reaching down to help her up. She hesitated only slightly before placing her hand in his. It took just a moment for him to pull her to her feet. He let go immediately, but his fingers still tingled where they'd held hers. They walked back in silence. His missed opportunity trudged behind, pelting him with regret.

The mouth-watering tang of peppers and spices greeted them when they came through the gate.

"There you are! Just in time. It is ready," Carida said. "We eat on the patio."

They helped her carry bowls, cups, and spoons outside. When the table was set, they sat down and Elian stretched out his hands to his guests, palms up. Peter smiled and did the same, taking one of Elian's hands in his left and Carida's in his right. After a moment of hesitation, Kate did the same on the other side of the table.

"Let's pray," Elian said, bowing his head.

As his friend's words of thanksgiving poured over them, Peter wondered what Kate was thinking and feeling. He'd hoped being here would challenge her disbelief and open her eyes to a new way of looking at life. If it didn't? He'd have to root out that seedling of hope and yearning that had sprung to life. He knew it was foolish to feed something that could never bear fruit. But he also knew how painful it would be to walk away from something he suddenly wanted with all his heart.

Chapter 21

KATE SLEPT FITFULLY AND woke as the sun started to peek in at the window of her small room. She could hear voices in the kitchen and the warm slightly burnt smell of coffee beckoned. She dressed quickly and pulled her hair into a ponytail before opening her door. She nearly bumped into Peter in the narrow hallway.

"Good morning," he said, holding a steaming mug out to her.

She took it and smiled.

"I'm going to have a rude reality check when we get home and I have to get my own coffee again," she said.

He laughed, and the resonance of it strummed her still sleepy consciousness. She could listen to that sound all day. She followed him into the living area. Carida had set the table with bowls of fruit and thick slices of bread. Small glasses of juice sat at each place.

"Buenos dias!" the older woman said warmly as she ushered them to the table.

Kate took her seat, gripping her mug like an anchor. Peter looked completely at ease, while she was the outsider looking in. And yet at the same time, she felt like an actor on stage, every nerve awake with the sense that someone was watching her every move. She'd never had to depend on the hospitality of strangers.

She bowed her head when Elian said grace, but she peeked from under half-closed lids at the people seated around her. Carida and Elian radiated a quiet joy. Peter had propped his elbows on the table, resting his forehead on his clasped hands. Was this part of his routine, or was he flexing spiritual muscles he hadn't used in years?

While they ate, they discussed their plans for the day. Kate felt sure they would spot Emily on the medical school campus, or be able to get hints of a new American arrival if they played their parts right. She had rehearsed her story several times after she went to bed. It wouldn't be the first time she'd pretended to be someone she wasn't to get a story.

Elian had his doubts.

"You must be very careful, my friends," he said. "Very careful. If they think you're not sincere, they could decide you're a threat. If they think you might be CIA spies, they will have you arrested for sure."

"CIA spies?" Kate laughed, assuming he was joking. But the seriousness in Elian's face stopped her mid chuckle.

He sighed. "The CIA is the ever-present boogeyman. The Cuban government blames the CIA for everything that goes wrong, even droughts and crop failures. Cubans are taught from birth that our greatest enemy is the CIA. You are Americans. If they think you're lying about why you're here, they'll assume you are CIA spies."

Kate glanced at Peter, sobered by the thought of spending any amount of time in a Cuban jail. He gave her a small smile.

"We'll be fine," he said. "Worse comes to worst, we'll tell them the truth. It won't take them long to find Kate's stories about Emily Gibson online."

"And it won't take them long to figure out you're a detective, Peter," Elian said quietly. "You may convince them you're not with the CIA, but the truth might not be much better for you."

The thick slice of soft bread she'd just eaten suddenly sat like a rock in her stomach. She shifted uncomfortably in her chair, her eyes fixed on her plate. The last thing she wanted was to put Peter in danger just so she could get a great story. When she looked up, Peter's deep hazel eyes held her gaze. He stared steadily into her face.

"It's my job, too, you know," he said, as if he could read her mind. "I'm here to clear an innocent man's name."

Kate snorted at the irony.

Peter grinned. "Well, innocent of murder, at least. He's still guilty of being a class A jerk."

Kate laughed, and the tension that had settled over the table dissipated.

"Do you want to take the car, Peter? It's yours if you want it," Elian said.

"No. That would make it too easy for them to trace us. I thought we'd walk a ways and find a taxi. What better way to look like tourists than rolling up in one of Cuba's famous, classic cars?"

"Ah!" Elian said, jumping to his feet. "Let me call Marco. He has a beautiful 1957 Cadillac. He will take care of you. I won't tell him exactly why you're here, but I'll tell him you don't want anyone to know you're not just normal visitors. If anyone asks, he can say he picked you up and nothing seemed suspicious."

"Are you sure he won't mind getting involved?" Kate asked, unable to quell a ripple of worry over the possibility of putting someone else in danger.

"Marco has a servant's heart. He would do anything to help a brother, even an American." Elian clapped Peter on the shoulder and his rich laugh rolled over them.

Kate excused herself to finish gathering her things together in the small backpack she'd brought with her. Before leaving her room, she smeared a thin layer of sunscreen over her face and neck. She met Peter again in the small hallway. He'd put on a hat, and it gave him an air of boyishness she'd never seen before.

"Is that your tourist garb?" she asked, smirking up at him.

"No, it's my anti-sunburn garb."

She expected him to turn around and walk into the living area, but he just stood there, staring down at her. A flutter of nerves stirred in her chest.

"What?" she said. Her voice sounded slightly breathless, and she cursed the sudden lack of control she seemed to have over her reactions.

"Nothing," he said, the corners of his mouth curling up. "Are you ready?"

"Yep. Let's go find Emily Gibson."

As they walked through the patio on their way to the gate, they passed Carida sitting at the outdoor table. She had a large book open in front of her, a notebook sitting next to it. She reminded Kate of a college student sitting in a library. She wondered briefly if the older woman was taking classes somewhere. But then she realized the book was a Bible.

"I'll be praying all day for your safe return," she said with a gentle smile.

It seemed like an exaggeration, but as Kate looked into the woman's warm eyes, she sensed it wasn't. This woman she hadn't even known for 24 hours would spend the day praying for her. Kate didn't believe it would make any difference, but knowing she was willing made her feel like giving the woman a hug.

Peter gave Carida a quick kiss on the cheek and they stepped out into the bright morning sunshine. They walked more quickly than they had the night before. When they neared the Malecón, they slowed and commented on the things they passed. Peter stopped several times to take photos of the Hotel Nacional. They meandered through several shops before wandering over to the building where Marco had agreed to meet them. They spotted his bright red Cadillac right away. Marco was leaning against the door, reading a folded newspaper. Kate thought she saw recognition spark in his face when he looked up and saw them, but he continued to stare at the paper as though he wasn't expecting any particular customer.

"Hola," Peter said as they walked up. "Taxi?"

"Si, si!" Marco said, smiling widely. He wore a traditional guayabera Cuban shirt over faded khaki pants.

"My, uh," Peter paused, glancing back at her. "My girlfriend and I would like to visit the Escuela Latinoamericana de Medicina. Do you know it?"

"Si, I take you there," he said, opening the door and motioning for them to climb into the back seat.

"Un momento," Peter said, pulling out his phone. Before Kate realized what he was doing, he'd put his arm around her shoulders, spun her around so that the car was behind them, and snapped a selfie. Too surprised to protest, she scrambled into the back. Peter climbed in after her and flashed her a cheeky grin. As Marco started up the engine and pulled away from the curb, Peter draped his arm over the back of the seat behind her.

She tried not to think about his arm against her neck and his leg pressed against hers. Despite the constant teasing from her coworkers, and occasional snide remarks from other police officers, she'd never thought of Peter as anything more than a friend. But she'd never had a friend risk his life to help her chase down a story and save her job.

Once they were away, Peter leaned forward and chatted with Marco. His Spanish was halting, but Marco seemed to understand with no problem. After a few minutes, he sat back and shot Kate a confident smile.

"He's going to wait for us while we look around. We'll need to pay him a little more, but that's most likely what two visitors would do. He says there's a guard gate we have to pass through. We should probably just tell them you're a prospective student and want to look around."

Kate nodded. "Maybe they'll send someone who can give us a tour."

"That's what I'm hoping."

They drove for another 30 minutes along a highway that ran parallel to the coast. As they got farther from the city center, the space between the buildings widened and the trees grew closer together. By the time Marco slowed and turned on his blinker, Kate felt like they were in the country.

The school campus sat on a peninsula that jutted out from the coastline. Blue and white bunker-like buildings dotted a sparse landscape. But cheerful pink flowers dotted bushes packed with dense green leaves. It was the only nod to the school's tropical location.

The security guard who stepped out of the small gatehouse to meet them didn't look especially suspicious. He gazed at them through half-closed eyes, like he'd just woken up from a nap. Kate flashed him her brightest smile. Marco launched into an explanation in rapid-fire Spanish, gesturing at them and then at the buildings in front of them. The guard scratched his head. He seemed perplexed but eventually nodded and sauntered back into the tiny building.

"They must not get many requests for tours," Kate whispered.

"Un momento," Marco said, turning around to smile at them. He held his thumb and pinky finger up to his head, mimicking a telephone.

After a few moments, the guard came back out, said a few words to Marco and ambled over to the white crossing arm blocking the road. He leaned on the weighted end and it swung up into the air, clearing the way for them to drive through.

"Ha! We're in," Peter whispered triumphantly.

Kate's heart pounded as Marco put the car in gear and moved slowly ahead. But she smiled cheerily and waved at the guard as they rolled past, calling out, "Gracias!"

Marco said something to Peter, who nodded.

"Someone is coming to meet us. Sounds like they don't want us wandering around. That's good though. Maybe we can talk her into giving us a tour while we ask questions."

"Hopefully she speaks English," Kate said.

Peter just shrugged.

When Marco pulled up to the curb outside the main building, Peter climbed out of the backseat and held out his hand to help her. She expected him to let go after she stepped out of the car, but he didn't. Instead, he laced his fingers through hers.

"Gotta look the part," he said with an impish grin.

Kate fought the urge to pull away. The warmth from his hand crept up her arm like invisible molasses. Could he feel her pulse pounding in her palm? The surprise of their sudden, physical connection made her feel like she'd taken one too many shots of Cuban rum. But before she could succumb to her lightheadedness, the front door of the main building swung open. A woman in a billowy red top and black pencil skirt plodded down the steps toward them. Her shiny black hair was pulled back in a no-nonsense bun but big hoop earrings dangled on either side of her narrow face. She glanced between them, her sharp black eyes sliding over their clasped hands, and smiled tightly.

"Hola. How may I help you?"

She seemed to speak perfect English. Kate sighed with relief.

"Hi!" she gushed before Peter could say anything. If she was the one hoping to enroll, she'd better be the one to ask the questions. "Thank you so much for meeting us. I'm Kate, and this is Peter. I'm thinking about applying to med school here and we thought we would come check out the campus."

"You came all the way to Cuba to take a tour of the school?" The woman sounded dubious.

"Oh, no," Kate said quickly. "We wanted to come here just to see the island. We've been planning this trip for ages, haven't we, babe?"

She glanced at Peter, who nodded enthusiastically.

"It's only been in the last few months that I realized I didn't want to go to school in America. I'm not sure where I'll end up, but since we were here, I wanted to check it out."

The woman raised both her perfectly plucked eyebrows.

"We've enjoyed our stay here so much," Kate said, grasping at anything to thaw the woman's frosty reception. "It's so refreshing to be in a place where people come first. We could definitely see ourselves being here long term."

She squeezed Peter's hand in a silent plea for help.

"Cuba is an extraordinary place," he said, flashing the woman a lopsided smile. Kate always thought that made him look like he was 16. "It's nothing like we've always heard."

"We like it," the woman said.

"Well, we've told this to just about everyone we've met," Peter said. "But I would like to apologize for the American government's policies. It's not right that America has interfered with your way of life for so long."

The woman's face seemed to soften just slightly.

"If you ask me, I think American politicians are afraid if they end the embargo, Cuba will thrive and show everyone that this system is far superior to ours. They're just afraid."

"You don't love your country?" The woman's question was half challenge, half curious.

"We have so many problems!" Peter said. "And the politicians are just out for themselves. The rich keep getting richer, and the rest of us get left behind. I mean, just look at our healthcare system compared to yours."

Kate nodded. "Right! That's why I don't want to go to medical school in America. All doctors there care about is making lots of money and living an easy life. While the people who really need help can't pay for it. That's not how I want to live my life."

The woman smiled. "That's why a lot of Americans come here to study. Our system works for everybody. No one gets left behind."

Kate just smiled in response, willing the woman to drop the last of her reserve. After a few moments of silence, she extended her hand.

"My name is Nina. I work in the president's office. We don't normally give tours. But I can walk you around and answer a few questions."

"Oh, thank you so much!" Kate said. Every ounce of the relief that flooded her voice was genuine. She wrenched her hand out of Peter's grasp to shake the woman's hand. "I really appreciate it. I'm sorry if this isn't how you normally do things. I just got so excited after being here for a few days. We just fell in love with it."

"Come this way," Nina said, beckoning them to follow her. "I can show you one of our classroom buildings."

Kate scurried to keep pace with her, leaving Peter to trail them along the narrow walkway.

"It's a beautiful campus," Kate said, as they passed a bright pink bougainvillea in full bloom.

Nina nodded. "The most beautiful on the island. We have several other medical schools, you know."

"Yes, but this one is the best," Kate said confidently.

"I see you've done your research."

Kate beamed at her. "I love that you have so many students from all over the world who come here. It must be amazing to experience so many different cultures. Other people have so much to teach us."

Nina led them up an outdoor staircase and down a long hallway flanked with classrooms. It reminded Kate of the beach pavilions in Galveston. Open so the breeze could come through, but perpetually coated in the briny grime of the ocean air. It didn't look like a fit learning environment for grade school students, let alone medical students. She suppressed a smirk of satisfaction at the thought of Emily Gibson's reaction to her new circumstances. Of course, if she had planned her escape as thoroughly as they thought, she no doubt knew what awaited her.

As they walked, Kate peppered Nina with light questions about the school and life in Cuba. She peered into every room they passed and held her breath as they walked around every corner. She felt so sure they could spot Emily at any moment. She swallowed a sigh of frustration when they left the last building and began walking back toward the front entrance. It felt like two hours wasted.

"How many Americans do you have here at the moment?" Peter asked.

"I don't know," Nina said. "We always have some students from America. But we only take students who want to serve. Our students do not become doctors to get rich. Most of our international students come from Africa and Central or South America. Or other countries in the Caribbean."

"Given how things stand between our two governments, Americans must stand out," Peter said.

Nina gave him a tight smile. "We welcome all who want to learn in the spirit of the revolution."

"That sounds so perfect," Kate said. "That's just what I want. A purpose to live for and serve. Something bigger than myself."

"Then you would fit right in," Nina said.

"I'll start working on my application as soon as we get home," she said.

Nina smiled again, with a bit more warmth this time, as they stopped in front of Marco's candy apple red Cadillac.

"Would it be possible for me to talk to some of the American students? To get advice on my application and what I need to do to prepare?"

Nina frowned. "That's not the kind of thing we usually do. I'm sure you'll figure it out. Everyone does."

Kate smiled brightly to hide her disappointment.

"Oh, yes. Of course. Sorry. I'm just so excited and I want to make sure I do everything right, so I get accepted."

Nina held out her hand. Kate shook it firmly.

"Good luck," Nina said. "I hope to see you back here next year."

"Thank you so much," Kate said. "I really appreciate all your help."

She kept her smile plastered in place as Peter put an arm around her shoulders and guided her back to the car. As she climbed into the back seat, she glanced back and caught Nina watching them. Her narrowed eyes suggested suspicion. Kate waved cheerily as Marco fired up the Cadillac and backed out of the parking spot.

Kate waited until they were safely back on the highway before letting her mask of enthusiasm crumble. She closed her eyes and laid her head back on the seat. They'd just wasted an entire day with no sign of Emily Gibson. And without access to the campus, she had no idea what to do next.

Chapter 22

The next morning, Kate woke again with the sunrise. The sense of despair that had covered her like a wet blanket the night before had lifted. Hues of hope and possibility filtered in with the bright morning light. Determination drove her out of bed with a wakefulness that didn't even need a boost of caffeine.

She had come all this way to find Emily Gibson. And she would not give up after one day's setback. She was so absorbed in her silent pep-talk that the sound of a soft knock on her door made her jump.

"Is that my morning coffee delivery?" she quipped, as she swung open the door expectantly.

Carida's soft laugh and smiling eyes greeted her. Mortification flushed her cheeks.

"I'm so sorry!" she gasped. "I thought you were Peter."

Her host smiled. "He went for a run. I just wanted to see if you were ready for breakfast."

"Oh, yes. I'll be right there. I'm sorry if I kept you waiting."

She thought she'd gotten up early, but everyone else still had a head start! She raked her brush through her hair and pulled it back with a clip before following Carida. By the time she got to the table, the older woman had placed a steaming mug at her seat.

"Buenos dias!" Elian crowed as he came through the door to the patio.

"Good morning," she mumbled, suddenly self-conscious at finding herself alone with the couple.

"Peter will be back soon. He said he wanted to stretch his legs. Sit, sit," Elian said, waving at her chair.

She perched on the edge of her seat and wrapped her hands around her coffee cup. The warmth spread from her fingers to her chest. She took a sip and the creamy richness washed over her tongue.

"It's good?" Elian asked.

Kate nodded. "It's very good. I don't normally take my coffee with milk, but this is perfect."

"Cuban coffee is the best coffee in the world," he said proudly.

She smiled as Carida set a plate of sliced bread and fruit in the middle of the table. The couple bowed their heads in unison, and Elian said a simple prayer of thanks for the food. Kate bowed her head, too, but watched them through half-closed lids. She normally would have rolled her eyes in a moment like this. But something in their faces made derision impossible. They seemed so utterly content. She had never known peace like that.

"Peter doesn't say much about his work," Elian said after they started to eat. "But I would guess he's pretty good at what he does. What do you think?"

"He is," Kate said without hesitation. "He's one of the best detectives in the department, if not the best. And he's not like any police officer I've ever met. Detective, I mean. Sorry."

"Why is that?" Elian's warm eyes watched her intently.

"Well," she hedged. She suddenly didn't know how to put it in words. She tore off a piece of bread and dunked it in her coffee as she thought about how to explain it. "Most police officers have an edge. They're hard. They assume the worst about everyone. And they're full of their own authority. But Peter's not like that. Somehow he assumes the best and still has hope in ..."

She paused and glanced over at Elian. He was watching her expectantly. She pressed her lips together as she tried to pin down the elusive quality that made Peter so appealing.

"Something more, something greater?" Elian suggested.

Something more. Those words ricocheted around in her mind, ringing with the clarity of revelation. She felt like she'd just found one missing piece to the puzzle that was slowly taking shape in her mind.

"Yes, something more," she said. That was exactly what Peter had.

"I'm glad to see he hasn't lost it. He almost did, you know. Once."

Kate's pulse quickened. Peter had promised to tell her his story one day. She knew she shouldn't try to weasel it out of Elian. But she found the words tumbling out of her mouth before she could stop them.

"I don't, actually," she said. "He's never told me anything about his past."

Elian's eyebrows shot up. "Oh? Well, he will. In time. How long have you known each other?"

Kate considered. She'd interacted with him for more than a year. But she felt like she'd only just started to get to know him in the last few weeks.

"I guess not as long as I thought," she said.

Before Elian could say anything else, the back door swung open and Peter strode in. His sweat-soaked shirt clung to his chest, and a flush of heat and exertion covered his face and neck. But he beamed when he caught her eye.

"Good morning," he said between attempts to catch his breath. "I see you found your way to the coffee."

Kate laughed. "Yes. Carida took care of me."

"I knew she would. I'll just jump in the shower. Be right back."

Kate smiled at his retreating back. When she dragged her attention back to the table, she realized both Elian and Carida were watching her. She fumbled with her bread in embarrassment.

"Peter is a good boy," Carida said quietly. "I'm glad to see him so happy."

Kate's stomach twisted. Happy? Because of her? No. Carida had made a connection that wasn't there. Had Peter let his friends think they were dating? Her heart thudded uncomfortably. He wouldn't mislead them intentionally. If they'd gotten the wrong idea, it wasn't his fault.

But should she try to explain?

"So, yesterday you hit a dead end," Elian said, spearing two slices of mango from the fruit plate. "What will you do today?"

Kate gratefully stuffed her uncomfortable questions about Peter into the mental drawer where she consigned all untidy emotions and refocused on the reason for their trip.

"Nina, the woman we met yesterday, said the students often go to a nearby shopping area, especially the ones who are learning Spanish. They're encouraged to interact with people to practice their language skills. I thought if we hung around there for a little while, maybe we'd bump into some people we could talk to."

Elian nodded slowly. "What if that doesn't work? Have you thought about other schools? ELAM isn't the only medical school in Cuba."

"I know. But it's the best, right? I can't imagine Emily Gibson going anywhere but the best. She's truly brilliant. If she came here to finish her education, she wouldn't go to a second-rate school."

"This is an important case for you, no?"

Kate considered before answering. "It is," she finally said, taking another sip of her coffee.

"Peter said you can't stand to see an innocent man tried for a murder that never happened."

"That's true," Kate said, frowning as an image of Aaron Newhouse's condescending face floated through her mind. "But it's more than that. Emily Gibson has deceived everyone. I just want to know the truth."

"Ah, yes. The truth is all that matters."

Kate nodded emphatically.

"Is this a philosophical discussion or a practical one?" Peter asked as he slid into the chair opposite Kate. His wet, tousled hair softened his face. He looked more relaxed than Kate had ever seen him.

"Both!" Elian said with a laugh. "Kate was just telling us why she wants to find this Emily Gibson so much."

Peter flashed her a grin as he reached for a piece of bread. "Don't let her idealistic talk fool you. She's just chasing a headline. If she can prove this woman faked her own death to escape scrutiny over the vaccine trial and get back at her lying boss, Kate will have the story of the year."

She knew he was teasing, but his words still stung.

"You know it's not just that. Even if it's not the story of the year, I still want to know the truth."

"What are you going to do if you find her?" Carida asked quietly.

Kate glanced at Peter. He hadn't said whether Chief Lugar had given him any instructions about trying to talk her into coming back.

"I just want to talk to her," Kate said. "If we find her, we know she's not dead. But I want to know what happened and why she felt like she had to run."

"And what about the police?" Elian asked, turning to Peter with a smile.

He shrugged. "The only thing we really care about is whether she's dead. If the federal government wants to go after her for fraud related to the vaccine trial, that's up to them."

"So the CIA hasn't hired you for an elaborate kidnapping and extraction plan?"

Peter laughed. "Hardly."

Elian winked at Peter and drained the last of his coffee.

"Well, my friends, I have some church members to visit this morning. Good luck with your investigation."

"Thanks," Kate said, smiling up at him as he stood.

He hesitated, as though trying to decide whether to say what he was thinking. "Be careful. What you're doing is still risky."

"We will, don't worry," Peter said. "We can do some shopping for Carida if that would help. It would give us a good reason to be walking around stores."

Carida looked doubtful. "I don't know that you'll find much. But I can give you a list of a few things, just in case."

About an hour later, they climbed into the back seat of Marco's Cadillac. He drove them back down the same highway they'd traveled the day before. But before they got as far as the medical school campus, he turned into a neighborhood sandwiched between the highway and the glittering blue ocean. He pulled up and parked on a street dotted with stores. Kate could see what looked like a cafe in the distance and a small supermarket across the street.

"Looks like we can wander around here for a while without attracting too much attention," she whispered to Peter as he leaned forward to talk in low tones to Marco.

When he'd arranged for the driver to pick them up in about three hours, they climbed out of the car. As they ambled down the street, Peter caught her hand and laced his fingers through hers. She looked up in surprise. The warmth of his touch felt electric.

"I figure we need to keep up appearances," he said, flashing her a grin.

She raised an eyebrow but didn't pull away. She cringed to think what Delilah would say if she could see them. The teasing would never end.

They wandered in and out of stores for about an hour without spotting anyone who looked like a student, let alone an American student who might talk to them. At the end of the street, they stopped at a cafe and ordered two batidos de mamey. Kate wasn't a huge fan of milkshakes and had never heard of the pinkish colored fruit. Peter assured her she would love it. She expected something like mango, so the slightly caramel flavor that coated her mouth with the first sip came as a surprise. Peter laughed when she immediately took another long draw on her straw.

"I fell in love with these when I came here with my parents," he said. "I must have had one every other day."

They wandered back the way they'd come, on the other side of the street. Kate tried to focus on her drink and not their lack of success at finding anyone connected to ELAM.

"It's still early," Peter said, as though he could read her mind. "We still have plenty of time."

They were about halfway back to the grocery store when Kate heard the rumble of a bus. It pulled up in front of the market and emitted a hiss as the doors swung open. Kate caught her breath when a large group of young people swarmed out. They were laughing and talked as they filled the sidewalk. Several turned to wave at the driver as the bus doors swung shut and it pulled away from the curb.

Kate glanced at Peter. His hazel eyes focused on the group. It reminded her of a hunter sniffing out prey. As they drew closer, the murmur of their voices sharpened into distinguishable words. Kate's heart started to thud. Amid all the rapid-fire Spanish, she could clearly make out some English phrases.

"Bingo," Peter whispered, giving her hand a squeeze.

Excitement spread her answering smile as wide as she thought it could probably go. Peter tugged gently on her hand and they slowed to a saunter. By the time they got to the store, the group had disappeared inside.

Peter held the door open for her, and they stepped into the dim and slightly stuffy interior. Kate glanced around. The shelves that held the rum and cigars were full. The other shelves held noticeably fewer items. Peter pulled a folded piece of paper from his back pocket and glanced at the list Carida had given them.

"I'll see if I can find any of these things," he said. "You look for someone to talk to."

Kate walked in the direction of the laughing voices, trying to look like she was just perusing the shelves. When she got to the end of her aisle, she rounded the corner and almost ran right into two men looking mournfully at a limited supply of hair care products. One had close-cropped, sandy blond hair. The other had long ebony dreadlocks pulled back and secured with a band.

"Champu," the blond one said, reading the label of one of the bottles. "No translation needed. Why can't all Spanish words be so easy to understand?"

His companion chuckled and slapped him on the back good-naturedly. "You'll get it. Don't worry," he said in a lilting Jamaican accent.

"And if I don't, I can kiss my dreams of becoming a doctor goodbye," the blond man said with a sigh.

"Eh, you worry too much!" his friend said.

Kate plastered her brightest smile across her face and closed the gap between them in two strides.

"HI! Are you guys students at ELAM?"

The blond man eyed her suspiciously, but the easygoing Jamaican flashed her a saucy grin.

"That depends," he said. "Are you looking for medical advice or someone to show you the island's best nightlife?"

Kate laughed. "Neither. I'm planning to apply and I hope to get in by fall. My friend and I took a tour of the campus yesterday. It looks amazing!"

The blond man relaxed enough to smile.

"You're American, huh? Where are you from?"

"Texas. How 'bout you?"

"Northern California. What brings you to Cuba?"

"My friend and I are just taking a little break from school," Kate said with a giggle. "I've always wanted to see Cuba, so we thought, why not?"

"Well, if you don't know any Spanish, you'd better work on that," the blond man said. "ELAM gives you six months to pass their fluency test. If you don't, you'll be on the first plane home."

"Yikes! That sounds pretty intense."

"It's kicking my butt," he said with a groan. "I don't know if I'm going to make it."

"C'mon, man! You gotta stop worrying," his Jamaican friend said. "It's not that bad. If I can pass, you can pass."

"Sounds like you've been here for a while," Kate said with a smile.

"Just a year longer than this guy. It's not easy, that's true. But I know I didn't whine as much as him."

"Hey! Some friend you are."

"Who's helping you study then?"

"Yeah, yeah. Ok." He turned his attention back to Kate. "But seriously. Any prep work you can do will help."

"Good to know! Thanks for the tip."

"You bet. There's not many Americans here. It'd be nice to have a few more."

"I was wondering about that," Kate said. "I read that students come from all over the world. But I'm guessing they probably don't have a lot from the U.S."

"Seems like they might want more, but not a lot apply."

"Yeah, that makes sense. So do new classes all start at the same time? Or do people sometimes come in mid-semester?"

The men both shook their heads. "I never seen anybody new come except at the beginning of the school year," the Jamaican man said. "I don't know how you could come in the middle of classes. You'd be lost."

"Oh, for sure," Kate said. "I just wasn't sure if students transferred in from other places."

"I don't think so. I haven't been here that long, but I've never met anyone who's come from another school."

Kate nodded, trying to hide her disappointment. "I'm sure they would stand out, too. I bet you all know each other pretty well after a few months."

"Not all by name, but at least by sight."

"Well," the blond piped up. "I'm pretty sure you know all the pretty girls by name, at least."

His friend laughed and shrugged good-naturedly. "What can I say?"

"It must be so cool to be in a place where everyone knows everyone else. I go to the University of Texas. I almost never randomly run into anyone I know on campus."

"We're like one big family," the Jamaican man said.

As if on cue, another young man called to them from across the store. They waved and the Jamaican man called back something in Spanish that Kate couldn't understand.

"Looks like your friends are leaving," she said. "I should let you go. But thanks for the advice. Maybe I'll see you around next year."

"We'll look forward to it," the Jamaican man said, winking at her.

Kate forced herself to smile and wave as she wandered off, her eyes searching for Peter. A kernel of worry had just started to take root when he suddenly appeared next to her. He held a basket containing what looked like most of the things Carida had asked them to get.

"Let's pay for this stuff and then head outside," he said in a low voice. "Then you can tell me what you found out."

"Not much," Kate said, discouragement causing her voice to waver.

Peter slipped his hand over hers and gave it a squeeze. Despite her preoccupation with their so far fruitless search, Kate's breath still caught at his touch. She was having a hard time figuring out where their cover story ended and reality began. She trailed behind him as he walked to the cash register and pulled some bills out of his pocket.

A few minutes later, she was blinking in the bright afternoon sunshine. They walked back across the street and sat down on a bench in the shade. Peter pulled a water bottle out of his backpack, twisted off the lid and handed it to her. She smiled her thanks and took a swig.

"So, what did you learn?" he asked, after taking a long drink from his own bottle.

"They said they'd never seen anyone come in the middle of the semester. And it's a small enough place they'd definitely notice a newcomer. Especially a pretty, red-headed American. The one guy from Jamaica seemed like quite the ladies' man."

Peter laughed. "You didn't give him your phone number, did you?"

Kate rolled her eyes. "Seriously? He didn't ask."

"Sorry. I couldn't resist. Ok, so it sounds like ELAM is a dead end."

Kate groaned. "I was so sure we would find her here! Now I don't know what to do."

Peter leaned back and laced his hands together behind his head. "Well, this isn't the only medical school in Cuba."

"No, but it's the best."

He nodded. But before he could say anything else, Kate heard the rumble of Marco's Cadillac round the corner at the end of the street.

"Let's take this stuff back to Carida and talk things over with Elian. Maybe he'll have an idea."

Kate nodded miserably and stood up. Her dreams of a big scoop were melting faster than an ice cream cone in the blazing Caribbean sun.

She spent the rest of the afternoon swinging gently in the hammock in their hosts' patio garden. She pretended to read a book, but she mostly stewed on their failure. During dinner, she tried to focus on Elian's stories about his children, the church, and the challenges of living under the oppressive Cuban regime. But her mind kept replaying scenes from the last 18 months. She hadn't realized how much she loved living and working in Galveston. Had she really thrown all that away on what now seemed like hopeless grasping at straws?

When they were saying goodnight, Elian took both her hands in his and looked earnestly into her eyes.

"Do not despair, my young friend," he said. "I will pray that God will open a door. I do not think your search is over."

"Thanks," Kate said, offering an anemic smile. Under any other circumstances, she would have dismissed any offer of divine appeal. But at this point, she'd take all the help she could get.

Chapter 23

DAWN HAD JUST BEGUN to spread fingers of pale grey along the horizon when Peter woke up. He pulled on a T-shirt and padded quietly across the house to the patio door. The cool morning air contrasted so sharply with the warm afternoons that he would almost have called it chilly. He snagged a rough blanket off the living room couch and walked into the cool green garden. The hammock where Kate had spent most of the previous afternoon caught his eye and he walked over to it. He perched on the edge and rolled into its cocoon-like embrace. He thought he could smell lingering traces of Kate's shampoo where her head had been.

He closed his eyes and sighed. Their romantic cover story had stopped feeling like an act. It was getting harder to pretend he wanted to hold her hand and draw her close for purely tactical reasons. She never resisted, but he knew she wasn't completely comfortable either. Was it because of him? Or was she still battling feelings for Brian? Either way, did it really matter? They viewed the world so differently. He couldn't imagine a relationship working out. But that didn't stop his traitorous heart from surging every time he saw her.

A soft click drew his eyes to the back door. Elian emerged with a cup of coffee in one hand and a well-worn Bible and notebook in the other. He raised his eyebrows when he saw Peter in the hammock but didn't say anything. Instead, he waved a greeting and sat down at the table, facing the other direction. Peter watched as he opened the Bible and bowed his head over it. It had been a long time since he approached prayer with such abandon. But seeing his friend communing so effortlessly with God awakened a longing in his soul. He had felt empty for so long. Would it be possible to know assurance like that again?

His thoughts wandered back to his teen years, when everything seemed so much simpler. He traced the trajectory of his life, the joys, hopes, and dreams. He had almost gotten to the part where they all unraveled when Elian suddenly started and let out a little cry.

"Claro esta!" he said, standing up and turning toward Peter. "God has answered my prayer! Go wake up Kate. I have an idea."

Curiosity churned in his mind, but Peter swallowed his questions and swung his legs over the edge of the hammock. Kate was just coming out of her room when he walked inside. She had dark smudges under her eyes, as though she hadn't slept well. The half-hearted smile she flashed him seemed to take all her effort.

"Come outside," he said. "Elian has an idea he wants to share."

Carida poked her head around the wall separating the kitchen from the rest of the living space.

"I'll bring two coffees, uno momento," she said.

Peter squashed the urge to give Kate a hug as she approached. Instead, he turned and opened the back door for her. A warm, fresh scent tickled his nose and quickened his pulse as she walked by. Her hair hung loose, framing her face. It softened her features and made her look more approachable. That's probably why she rarely wore it down, he thought as he pulled the door closed behind them.

"Buenos dias!" Elian said with a hint of triumph as he stood and pulled out a chair for Kate.

Her answering smile wasn't wide, but it infused her eyes with warmth. Peter realized that despite her skepticism over Elian and Carida's faith, and her discomfort with strangers, she'd really come to like the couple.

"I have prayed that my God would come to your aid," Elian said when they were all seated. "And he has answered my prayer."

Kate raised a skeptical eyebrow.

"You doubt, but I am sure this is the clue you were looking for," he said.

"We're all ears," Peter said quickly, before Kate could say anything. "What is it?"

"BioCubaFarma." Elian said the word with finality and then sat back, clasping his hands in his lap with satisfaction.

"What's that?" Kate asked. A keen interest wiped out the skepticism that had filled her eyes moments before.

"Cuba's national pharmaceutical company," Elian said. "That is where all our medical research takes place. And it is where they make all our vaccines."

Kate's eyes widened. Peter could see the wheels turning as she thought through the possibilities.

"You thought this Emily Gibson would reach out to a school for help to defect. But if she really had something valuable to offer, I think she would go straight to the people who could use it immediately."

Kate leaned forward, eyes sparkling and lips slightly parted. "That makes sense! That could be it. I mean, of course! Why didn't I think of that?"

"Probably because we were looking for a situation here that mirrored what she had in Galveston," Peter said. "But I think you're right. This makes much more sense."

Carida emerged from the house carrying a tray filled with coffee cups and plates of bread and fruit. Peter jumped up to help her, putting a stop to their conversation while she laid everything out on the table. After Elian said a prayer and Carida passed plates around, Kate picked up the thread of hope Elian had offered them.

"So, where does that leave us? I'm sure we can't just walk up to a government company and ask for a tour."

Elian laughed. "No de hecho! That would be a bad idea."

"Well then, how will we have any way of knowing whether she's there?" Kate said, frustration sharpening her words.

"Could we try hanging around the building at the end of the day to see if she comes out?" Peter asked. He tried to sound optimistic, but it seemed like a long shot they didn't have time for.

"Ah!" Elian said, holding up his finger. "Again, God provides. Juan Carlos. He's the reason I thought of this in the first place."

"Oh, si!" Carida said, clasping her hands in delight.

"Who is Juan Carlos?" Kate asked. Peter cringed at the exasperation in her voice and hoped Elian wouldn't take offense.

"He is a member of our church," Elian said patiently. "His mother is sick, and I was praying for their family this morning. I was thinking about visiting her today, and then I thought I should wait until the evening, when Juan Carlos is home from work. That's what made me think about where he works."

"BioCubaFarma?" Peter asked, a bit bemused by his friend's circuitous explanation.

"Claro que si! The very one."

"What does he do there?" Kate asked, all traces of frustration gone.

"He's on the maintenance crew," Elian said. "So, he probably wouldn't have met this Emily Gibson, but he might know whether she was there."

"People who work in the background tend to know a lot more about what's going on in a place than the people running it realize," Peter said. "They make great informants."

"And sources," Kate whispered, excitement making her eyes shine.

"Exactamente!" Elian said. "See, I told you God would provide."

Kate opened her mouth to say something but then shut it again. Peter laughed.

"Well, I for one am grateful," he said. "How soon can we talk to Juan Carlos?"

"I will call him," Elian said, pulling his phone out of his pocket. "I should be able to catch him before he leaves for work. We will see what he can tell us."

Elian scrolled through his contacts until he found the name he was looking for. He stood up and strolled to the other side of the garden while the phone rang. Peter heard him say, "Juan Carlos!" but everything else got lost in a wave of rapid-fire Spanish. Peter looked across the table at Kate. She kept her eyes glued to Elian, a mix of hope and doubt playing across her face.

After what felt like half an hour, Elian hung up and walked back to the table. A pink flush of anticipation colored Kate's cheeks. Elian looked thoughtful, and Peter had a feeling he didn't have a definite answer.

"Juan Carlos has not been at work for the last week because of his mother's health. But he's going back today. He said he would ask around and see what he could find out."

Kate let out a sigh of disappointment. "So we'll have to wait until tonight to find out?"

"I'm afraid so," Elian said, sitting back down at the table.

Kate groaned and put her face in her hands. "Another day wasted!"

"It won't be wasted," Peter said. "We need to do some exploring while we're here, anyway. I want to take you to Old Havana, to see some sights. It will take our minds off the waiting."

Kate sat back and sighed. "I'm not sure it will take my mind off anything, but I do want to see the city."

"Muy bien!" Elian said. "Go, enjoy the city. By the time you get back, you will have your answer."

Marco picked them up and drove them into the city. They walked down narrow streets and admired the stately but crumbling buildings. They visited shops selling Cuban-made goods and picked up a few momentos to remember their trip. They listened to a group of men singing ballads in a square, their warbling voices echoing off the sun-baked walls around them. They visited the Museo de la Ciudad to learn about Havana's history and wandered the cavernous halls of the the mid-16th-century colonial fort, Castillo de la Real Fuerza.

Despite Kate's doubt about her capacity for distraction, she seemed completely engrossed by the history and beauty that surrounded them.

They ended their day at the Catedral de San Cristobal. The afternoon sun gave its stone walls an ethereal glow. Noisy crowds filled the square outside, but inside, the cool, quiet sanctuary beckoned them to stop and rest. As they sat in companionable silence, Peter marveled at the chain of events that had brought them to this point. He couldn't remember when he'd felt so much serenity. He'd spent the last 10 years trying to atone for a wrong he thought he could never make right. But being here with Elian and Carida, and Kate, had made him wonder whether his attempt at restitution had really been more about self-punishment. Maybe he could stop looking back and finally start living for the future.

He glanced out of the corner of his eye at Kate. Her head tilted back, her lips slightly parted as she gazed up at the vaulted ceiling soaring over their heads.

"It's beautiful," she whispered, turning toward him. "Thank you for today. I'm really glad we did this."

"Me, too. Were you sufficiently distracted?"

She smiled, and the warmth in her eyes sent a surge of longing through his chest. He wanted to put his arm around her and pull her close, just to feel her nearness. Instead, he unzipped his backpack and pulled out a bottle of water to give his hands something else to do.

"Part of me wishes we could stay here for hours," she said. "But the other part of me is starting to get anxious."

He flashed her a wry smile. "We should probably get going. Marco will be here to pick us up soon."

As they walked back down the aisle toward the cathedral's thick wooden door, Kate hesitated. She looked up at him with fear-filled eyes.

"What do we do if this is another dead end?"

Before he could stop himself, he put his hands on her shoulders. He wished he had an answer that would wipe away the worry and bring back the open-hearted enthusiasm that had filled her face all day.

"I don't know," he said reluctantly. "But I promise you I'll do everything I can to figure this out with you. We won't leave here until we've done everything we possibly can to find her."

Kate bit her bottom lip and nodded. As they began walking to the door again, she slipped her hand into his. He looked down at her in surprise, even as his fingers wrapped around hers.

"We've got to keep up our cover," she said with a sly smile.

When they walked back through the garden gate at Elian and Carida's house, they found their hosts sitting at the patio table talking with a young man who appeared to be in his late 20s. He wore dark blue overalls, and his wavy brown hair was slicked back away from his face. He grinned at them as they walked in, and Peter instantly recognized the look of a man who had something to tell. Elian also greeted them with a wide smile.

"Welcome back! How was your tour? Our beautiful city did not disappoint, I hope."

"It did not," Peter said, peeling off his backpack and setting it on the ground. "It's as beautiful as I remembered. We had a really good day."

Elian clapped him on the back. "Peter, Kate, this is Juan Carlos. He came here as soon as he got off work. He has something to tell you that I think will make your day perfecto."

Hope filled Peter's chest, and he glanced at Kate. Barely restrained excitement radiated from every part of her body. She looked like a kid who'd just discovered she was getting a puppy for Christmas. She practically dove into a chair and leaned toward Juan Carlos expectantly.

"I think I have seen the woman you are looking for," he said.

Kate clapped her hands in delight. "What does she look like?"

"Tall, red hair, and muy bonita," he said with a shy smile.

"That's her!" Kate exclaimed. "American, of course. Right?"

Juan Carlos nodded. "I don't normally go to the upstairs offices. That's probably why I haven't seen her before. But today, the entire maintenance crew was assigned to prepare for a big presentation. We moved furniture and helped set up chairs and tables."

"A big presentation?" Kate asked. "Do you know whether she is involved?"

He nodded again. "She's the one giving the presentation. They brought her in to show her the room and she pulled up some slides on the big screen at the front of the room."

"Sounds like she's going to explain the vaccine research," Peter said. "Did you hear what the presentation was about?"

The young man shook his head. "Only that everyone was very excited."

Kate sat back in her chair, grinning from ear to ear with satisfaction.

"So, we were right," she said, turning to Peter. "About everything."

He grinned. "Well, you were right about almost everything. She didn't go to ELAM, after all."

Kate waved her hand dismissively. "Minor details."

Peter threw back his head and laughed. "You've got your story now, that's for sure."

"Not exactly," she said, pursing her lips. "I've got to see her myself. Not that I doubt Juan Carlos. But I need to confirm it with my own eyes."

"Yeah, me too. I don't think the DA would be happy if I went back and said I talked to someone who said he saw her."

"What are our options?" Kate asked, worry lines once again creasing her forehead.

"They are having a big party tonight to celebrate," Juan Carlos said. "At La Guarida."

Elian let out a low whistle.

"What's that?" Kate asked.

"That is the best restaurant in Havana," Elian said. "A good place for celebration."

Peter looked at Kate, although he didn't need to ask what she thought. Her eyes shone with excitement.

"We'll go!" she said. "All we need to do is see her."

"It will be a big group," Juan Carlos said. "Not easy to miss."

"You'll need reservations," Elian said. "I will call."

"Do you know what time they plan to go?" Peter asked.

Juan Carlos shook his head.

"I will get you a table for 9 p.m. You can go earlier than that and have a drink at the rooftop bar. It is the best view in the city. Very romantic."

He winked at them and pulled out his cellphone.

Kate's cheeks flushed pink and Peter kicked himself for not being absolutely clear with his old friend that he and Kate were not dating. Elian had obviously drawn his own conclusions.

"Did you bring a dress?" Carida asked, turning to Kate.

She groaned. "I didn't! I don't have anything fancier than shorts and T-shirts."

"I brought a pair of pants," Peter said. "But I don't have any nice shirts."

"We can find something for you in some of Macerio's things," Carida said. "He always leaves clothes here for when he comes to visit."

"Do I have time to run to a store and buy something?" Kate asked. She had started to look a little frantic.

"No, but I have an idea," Carida said, pushing back from the table and standing up. "Let me call a few friends. You should go take a shower."

Peter shrugged when Kate looked at him questioningly. He didn't know what Carida was up to, but he trusted her.

"I have your reservation," Elian said triumphantly as he ended his call. "The woman I spoke to said they had a big party coming in to eat outside on the terrace. But they had a few tables left inside."

"Thank you for everything," Peter said, turning to both Elian and Juan Carlos. "Without you, we would have been out of luck."

"Ah, luck," Elian said, shaking his head with disapproval. "You know that has nothing to do with it."

Kate smiled, something she probably wouldn't have done at such a remark a week ago, Peter thought.

"Luck or not, we're grateful," she said.

Juan Carlos smiled, and Elian patted him on the back.

"I'd better go get in the shower," Kate said, standing up. "I can't believe we finally found her. I thought we were going to go home empty-handed."

Peter chuckled. "Me, too," he murmured as he watched her walk away.

"You have so little faith?" Elian said as Kate disappeared through the door. His eyes held a sadness Peter had never seen directed at him. He shifted uncomfortably.

"It's not that. It's just that I don't always see things as clearly as I used to."

Elian leaned forward and put his hand over Peter's. "That's because you have stopped looking. Open your eyes."

His friend's earnest gaze seemed to bore into his soul. He wanted to open his eyes. But what would he see when he did?

Thirty minutes later, Peter heard the bathroom door open and the door to Kate's room close. He'd found a guayabera in Macerio's closet that fit him perfectly. Just before he stepped into the shower, he heard a knock on the front door and Carida's exclamation of welcome.

The cold water sliced down his back and made him suck in a breath. He knew it was coming. Cubans considered hot water a luxury, but it still took his breath away, every time. The chill helped focus his thoughts on the evening ahead. Once he saw Emily Gibson with his own eyes, he had enough evidence to prove Aaron Newhouse wasn't a murderer. But how likely was that to be enough for Kate? She would have a long list of questions. He wanted her to get answers, but if Emily blew their cover, they could be in serious trouble. All she had to do was tell her new friends they were American spies, and they'd end up spending a very long time in a Cuban jail cell. Or worse.

He tried not to think about the possibilities as he dressed quickly and rejoined Elian on the back patio. The sun had set and a grey twilight gave the garden a dreamy aura. A few minutes later, he heard the door open again, and he turned around to see Kate step out. For a moment, all he could do was stare.

She wore a simple black dress that hung from her shoulders on thin straps. It accentuated every curve without being too tight or too revealing. A clip threaded with fresh flowers pulled her hair back from her face on one side. She looked stunning, but he couldn't figure out how to tell her that.

"Wow," he finally managed. "You look great. I mean, really great."

A tinge of pink crept up Kate's cheeks, and she smiled.

Elian laughed and held his arm out to his wife. "Well done, my dear. With Kate's help, I think Peter will just manage to get in."

Peter grinned. "I do feel a bit underdressed now. But I don't think anyone will notice me."

He walked to Kate's side and gazed into her face. Her smile faltered just slightly, and he wondered what she was thinking.

"We'd better get going," she said. "I don't want to miss her."

He nodded and held out his arm for her to take. Heat flushed his whole body as she threaded her arm through his. His mind reminded him that this was all part of their cover story. But his heart refused to believe it.

Chapter 24

Kate focused all her attention on keeping her ankles steady as she took Peter's hand and he pulled her gently out of the back of Marco's Cadillac. She rarely wore heels, and when she did, they usually weren't this high. As if sensing her unsteadiness, Peter put his arm around her waist before leaning down to say a few words to Marco. The warmth of his embrace held the hint of a growing intimacy. He let his arm drop when they turned away from the car to face the restaurant. But as he had for most of their public excursions in Havana, he laced his fingers through hers. It still made her heart flutter. How would they ever backtrack to their professional friendship when they got home?

She looked up at him. The traditional, white Cuban shirt gave him a laid-back vibe she wasn't used to him wearing. It gave him a rakish appeal she'd never noticed before. Her pulse quickened.

He gave her hand a squeeze. "Are you ready?"

She nodded, her heart pounding in earnest. Everything she'd anticipated for the last week was about to be revealed.

The building in front of them had the same old-world elegance that characterized so much of Havana. They walked through ornately carved wooden doors into a tiled lobby that stretched up into the second floor. Ahead, a wide marble staircase curved an invitation to ascend. A two-story message from Fidel Castro, titled "Patria o Muerte"—country or death—covered the wall.

Kate took every step carefully, grateful for Peter's arm once again around her waist. Inside the restaurant entrance, the hostess checked their reservation and beckoned them to follow her to the rooftop bar where they could wait until their table was ready. Kate scanned the restaurant as they walked through, looking for any sign of Emily or her party. None of the tables held more than one or two couples. But through the tall doors leading to the terrace she could see a long, empty table set for at least 20 people. That had to be for the BioCubaFarma party.

After they climbed another flight of spiraling stairs, they emerged on the roof. A warm sea breeze greeted them as they stepped onto the patio. Strings of lights threaded overhead cast a yellow glow over white furniture. The hostess led them to a tall table next to the concrete balustrade. From there they had a perfect view of the terrace below.

Kate looked at Peter in amazement. "Did you ask for this table?"

He shook his head. "I didn't, but it's perfect."

"Did you notice the empty table down there? That's got to be for them."

Peter nodded but didn't say anything as a waiter approached to take their drink orders. When they were alone again, he turned his attention back to the terrace. His eyes swept the space and lingered on the restaurant's wide windows.

"Hopefully they'll arrive before we get to our table," he said. "Otherwise, we'll have to be careful when they come in. Do you think she would recognize you?"

Kate's pulse quickened again. "I'm not sure. She obviously knew enough about me to send me those spreadsheets. But it's not like we've had a lot of personal interaction."

Peter nodded. "I doubt she's on the lookout. But you never know. If she spots us, we could be in trouble."

Kate swallowed, suddenly wishing she had her drink. "What do you think they'd do if she told them who we were?"

He pressed his lips together and shook his head. "I don't know. But I'd rather not find out."

The waiter interrupted her reply with their drinks. A Cuba Libre for Peter and a mojito for her. The first minty sweet sip helped to steady her nerves.

"This all feels so surreal," she said. "I never could have pictured us here a week ago."

He smiled, and his eyes held the hint of a teasing twinkle.

"It's been quite an adventure," he said. "I'm glad you let me tag along."

She held his gaze for a few seconds. "I can't imagine doing it without you."

He didn't reply, but his eyes searched her face. She saw her own questions mirrored in his gaze. Did he have any better answers than she did? Slowly, he reached his hand across the table and brushed the back of her fingers. The whoosh of blood pounding in her ears made her feel lightheaded. She watched her hand open, almost involuntarily. Like it had a mind of its own. Peter slipped his fingers into hers. They'd held hands all week, but this wasn't about maintaining a cover story.

"Kate," he murmured. "I never expected ... this. I mean, I don't want you to think I came her for any reason other than to help you find Emily Gibson."

She dropped her gaze, suddenly confused. Heat flushed her face. Was he looking for a reset because things between them had gotten out of hand?

"No, of course not," she blurted. "I didn't think that. I knew it was only about this case."

She tried to pull her hand back, but he held it fast.

"It wasn't only about the case," he said, slipping out of his chair and closing the distance between them. "That's not what I meant."

He looked down at her with so much intensity and longing that her breath caught in her throat. He reached out his hand and brushed her cheek. A whirlwind of conflict swirled in her heart. It tugged at the door she'd kept so carefully closed. She clung to the handle, desperate to keep it from swinging wide open. The last time an emotional hurricane swept over her life, it had taken her years to repair the damage. But maybe this kind of storm would be worth the fallout. Especially if she didn't have to tumble through it alone. She suddenly found herself wanting to let go.

Before she could reply, the sharp sound of laughter and excited chatter floated up from the patio. It sucked the power out of the vortex surrounding them, leaving Kate feeling suddenly bereft. Reluctantly, she broke Peter's gaze and looked down. A group of men and women had swarmed onto the patio.

And in the center, Kate spotted a flash of red. She sucked in a breath.

"That's her," she whispered.

When Peter didn't respond, she glanced at him. He was watching the group intently. Emily Gibson, unmistakable, stood next to an older man with wavy black hair, her arm threaded through his. The entire group stood talking for a moment, evidently admiring the view. Then the man with Emily said something that redirected their attention to the table and they took their seats. He guided Emily to one end and pulled out a chair.

"Looks like he's in charge," Kate said quietly, forcing herself to look away in case anyone was watching them.

Peter nodded. "It does. And she looks very comfortable in her new life."

"Definitely not dead." Kate said with a grin.

Peter chuckled and shook his head. "Definitely not. But I wonder if she has any idea what she's gotten herself into."

Kate took a sip of her drink. "Maybe if we're lucky, you can ask her."

Peter frowned. "Kate, listen—"

"I know it's a risk," she said, cutting him off. "But I have to try. The only thing we know right now is that she's not dead. That may be enough for the DA, but it doesn't tell us anything about why she ran, why she tried to frame Aaron Newhouse for her own murder. Or why she thought life in Cuba would be better than facing the consequences of lying about the vaccine trial at home."

Peter took a long sip of his drink and set it down with a sigh.

"I was afraid you would say that," he said. "So, what's your plan?"

Kate grinned with relief. She knew she was asking a lot, possibly everything. And he had nothing to gain from taking the risk.

"Eventually, she'll have to go to the bathroom, right?"

He raised an eyebrow. "I suppose."

"I'll follow her and see if I can get her to talk. Maybe, If I'm lucky, she'll agree to meet me tomorrow. I'll go alone in case she decides to turn me in. If I disappear, you go home and notify the State Department."

He rolled his eyes and shook his head. "Your mojito must have gone to your head. There's no way I'm letting you meet her alone."

"It doesn't do any good to get us both arrested," she whispered.

He squeezed her hand again, but this time it communicated nothing more than support.

"Maybe not. But you're not going alone."

The hostess's approach ended any debate. They followed her back down the winding staircase to the main floor, where the energetic strains of jazz played under the buzz of conversation. The hostess stopped at a corner table and gestured for them to take their seats. They couldn't see the patio, but they had a full view of the rest of the restaurant. It would be easy to spot anyone coming inside to use the bathroom.

They sat down and picked up their menus. Kate could barely focus on the options because she kept looking up to make sure she hadn't missed Emily Gibson walking by.

Peter chuckled. "Why don't we do this in shifts? I'll watch while you decide what you want. Then we'll switch."

Kate flashed him an appreciative smile and gave her full attention to the menu. Just the descriptions made her mouth water. She finally settled on chicken baked in a honey lemon sauce. Peter chose the fish of the day, which turned out to be sea bass.

"Do you want another drink? Some wine, maybe?" he asked, handing his menu to the waiter.

Kate suddenly thought of Brian and all their meals at Francisco's. She shook her head, and the waiter bowed and walked away.

"Something wrong?" Peter asked. "You made a funny face just now."

"Oh, no," she hedged. "It's just that I'm not used to eating at fancy restaurants. I never know what kind of wine I'm supposed to order."

He looked at her through narrowed eyes, like he was boring into her thoughts. She glanced down and fiddled with the napkin in her lap.

"Brian used to take you out all the time," he said.

She tried to suppress a blush, but it was useless. She cursed his perceptiveness. How could he so easily trace the train of her thoughts?

"True," she said lightly. "But I always let him order the wine."

Peter nodded thoughtfully but said nothing in response. She tried to read his face as easily as he'd read hers. No luck. She had no idea what he was thinking. It's not like Peter didn't know about Brian. But she hadn't expected her ex-boyfriend to intrude at such an inopportune time.

The electricity coursing between them earlier had completely dissipated. The sense of companionable friendship that had built over the week remained, but Kate felt like an opportunity had somehow slipped through her fingers.

While they waited for their food, Peter told her about some of the other parts of Cuba he'd seen on his last visit. His stories were entertaining, but they felt like little more than mindless chatter to keep them occupied while they watched the door to the patio. The waiter delivered their plates and their conversation lulled as they both savored their food.

"Is this what a stakeout is like?" Kate asked, cutting off another piece of chicken and putting it in her mouth.

"The company's not usually this good," he said with a sly smile.

Kate was about to ask him to tell her the story of his most entertaining stakeout when Emily Gibson stepped through the door to the patio. She looked momentarily lost until a waiter sidled up and pointed her toward the opposite wall. She smiled her thanks and walked across the room, never glancing around her.

She didn't appear to have any concern about her old life coming back to haunt her.

Kate glanced at Peter. He met her gaze with a worried frown. Her heart pounded so loud she was sure he could hear it.

"Now's my chance," she said, pushing back her chair.

He watched her every move, like he was afraid he would never see her again.

"Don't worry," she whispered, trying to sound more confident than she felt. "It'll be fine."

As casually and carefully as she could on her precarious shoes, Kate walked toward the bathroom. She was half afraid Emily would come back out before she made it across the room. But no one emerged by the time she got to the door and pulled it open.

The bathroom appeared empty at first, but as the door swung shut behind her, she heard a toilet flush. She stepped up to the sink and willed herself to take slow, deep breaths. She was drawing in her third when she heard the latch slide back and the stall door swung open.

Emily didn't see her at first. She was looking down at her clutch. When she finally looked up and realized she wasn't alone, she smiled vaguely and looked back down at her purse. Adrenaline shot through Kate, making her knees tremble. Emily hadn't recognized her. She fleetingly thought about turning around and walking back to Peter, leaving without putting either of them at risk. The impulse disappeared as quickly as it came. But before Kate could figure out what to say, Emily pulled a tube of lip gloss from her purse and turned to the mirror.

Kate followed her gaze, and their eyes met in the reflection. Emily's hand was halfway to her lips when recognition lit up her eyes.

"Kate Bennett," she breathed. It sounded almost like a sigh.

Kate nodded and gripped the edge of the counter as Emily turned to face her with a ferocious frown.

"What are you doing here?" she hissed. "How did you find me?"

"It's a long story," Kate said, suddenly getting an idea. "And probably not one we have time for tonight. Can we meet somewhere tomorrow for coffee? I'll tell you mine if you tell me yours."

Emily snorted. "That hardly seems like a fair trade."

Kate shrugged. "I do have a head start. But I'm willing to give a little more than I get."

"Please." Emily rolled her eyes. "Why should I tell you anything? Whatever I say is just going to end up on the front page of the newspaper. Probably every newspaper in America."

"You don't have to tell me anything for that to happen. As soon as I knew you were here, I sent a story in reporting that I'd found you." She kicked herself silently for not actually thinking to do that. If Emily had them arrested now, no one would ever know what happened.

Emily cursed under her breath. "That doesn't give me much incentive to talk then, does it?"

"It gives you a chance to tell your side of the story," Kate said quickly. "Otherwise, Aaron Newhouse will get the last word on why you fled the country and tried to set him up for your murder."

Emily sneered. "So the police actually bought that? That was just my backup plan to buy a little more time. Just to make sure I could actually get away. I figured they'd realize eventually that he didn't send those messages. But I hoped he'd have to put up with at least a little public humiliation until then."

"I can't really blame you for that," Kate said. When Emily didn't immediately respond, she scrambled for something that might convince her to talk. "I saw your mom before I left."

Emily's angry scowl softened, and she looked down at the counter.

"Did you tell her you thought you'd found me?"

Kate nodded. "She was beside herself at the thought you might still be alive. She told me to tell you she loved you."

Emily pressed her lips together tightly, and Kate wondered if she was trying to keep them from trembling.

"Look, you don't have to talk to me. But I've been searching for you for two weeks. I know Aaron Newhouse put you in a terrible position, and I do not want him to get away with what he did. If you keep quiet, he gets the last word."

Emily tilted her head to the side and looked at Kate through narrowed eyes.. They stood in silence for several moments before Emily finally sighed.

"I'm presenting my research to the team at BioCubaFarma tomorrow morning. But I can probably get away in the evening. There's a cafe near my apartment called Cafe Cortina. Meet me there at 7 p.m."

Kate nodded and tried to keep her expression neutral as she watched Emily swipe a fresh coat of gloss on her lips.

"I'll see you then," she said as Emily brushed past her and strode out the door.

Kate forced herself to count to ten before following. She half expected to see police officers waiting outside, but the buzz of conversation that filled the restaurant continued undisturbed. Nothing seemed out of place. But Peter looked like he was ready to spring out of his seat when he saw her. She smiled reassuringly and quickly took her place beside him. A slight sheen of perspiration covered his forehead.

"We have a date," she said, dropping her napkin in her lap to hide her churning excitement. "Tomorrow night. I convinced her to tell her side of the story."

Peter sat back and stared at her in amazement. "She didn't threaten to call the police?"

Kate shook her head. "It took some convincing to persuade her to talk. But she made no threats."

"It felt like you were in there forever. When you didn't come out right after her, I thought she'd done something to you."

"Were you going to come busting into the women's bathroom?" she teased. After the tension of the last few hours, bantering with him felt intoxicating.

He chuckled. "I would have."

Kate finished the last few bites of her meal and the waiter appeared as if he had been watching. After he carried off their plates, Peter leaned toward her.

"As much as I would love to stay for dessert, I think we should probably leave. I'd rather not be sitting here when their party gets up to go."

Kate nodded. When the waiter returned, Peter handed him a stack of bills and stood to pull back Kate's chair. She sensed his tension in the arm he draped around her waist as they walked toward the entrance. She glanced around but didn't notice anyone paying any attention to them. Peter barely slowed his stride as he swept them out of the entrance and down the staircase. He held her tightly to his side to keep her from stumbling over her heels.

When they emerged onto the street, he hurried them away from the building. The hair on the back of Kate's neck rose when she realized he was keeping as much as possible in the shadows. They walked two blocks in silence before Kate couldn't stand it any longer.

"What is it?" she whispered, fear squeezing her chest.

Peter slowed and loosened his grip. "Nothing," he said. "I just wanted to get out of there as quickly as possible and make sure no one was following us. I'm sorry. I didn't mean to scare you."

Kate took a deep breath and let it out slowly. A twinge of guilt twisted in her chest. He wouldn't be so worried if she hadn't insisted on talking to Emily. She looked up at him with gratitude.

"Thank you," she said simply.

"For what?" he asked, looking down at her with a questioning look she could just make out in the darkness.

"For taking a risk for me."

He threaded her arm through his and squeezed it to his side. "Always."

Warmth flooded through her. She knew he meant it. She just hoped he wouldn't come to regret it.

Chapter 25

After breakfast the next morning, Peter suggested they head out on foot and explore more of the Vedado neighborhood. The day held a sense of completion that felt almost anticlimactic. His fear over their imminent arrest had faded. If Emily had wanted to sound the alarm, she would have done it immediately. That didn't mean she wouldn't have police waiting on them tonight, but for now, they seemed safe enough.

"So, you've almost got everything you came for," he said to Kate as they meandered down a shade-dappled street. "What's the plan now?"

"You mean besides heading home and getting my job back?" Kate asked with a laugh. "That's the only thing I'm worried about now."

"Are you going to give Mattingly an opportunity to publish the story or are you going to call the Times?"

"Ha! As much as I would love to take this to the Times, I think I'd better give it to Mattingly. I want my job back, and this is my best chance for getting it."

"You think Mattingly might not take you back?"

Kate shrugged. "I guess it's a possibility. If he's still mad about me quitting. But I followed my instincts and got the story. He's got to know that was the right thing to do. He might not admit it, but giving me my job back would be the easiest way for him to say he was wrong without saying it."

"I don't know about that, but he'd be a fool not to take you back. I don't think you have anything to worry about. In fact, if I were him, I'd give you a raise. I'm sure you'll be getting job offers from all over the country after this."

She flashed him a grin that made him rejoice with her, even as it planted a seed of dread. How much longer would she stay in Galveston? Six months? A year? Last night had brought an epiphany. He wanted to know what it would be like to have her by his side every night, to hold her hand every day, not just as part of an elaborate cover story. The flashes of intimacy they'd shared over the past week had lit a fire he hadn't felt in years. He knew Kate had sensed the sparks, but he wasn't sure whether she wanted to fan them into a flame that would consume them both. That, he sensed, would take time, and an infinite dose of patience.

They spent the next few hours soaking up the sights and sounds of the neighborhood. They bought tostones from a street vendor and ate sitting on the seawall, their legs dangling over the edge. He talked her into getting another batido de mamey on the way home. Long, reflective silences punctuated Kate's enthusiastic commentary on the swirl of life flowing around them. He left her to her thoughts, although it took every ounce of restraint not to ask her what was going on behind her expressive grey eyes.

When they walked through the gate onto Elian and Carida's patio, Kate headed straight for her room.

"Last night, I told Emily I'd already written a story saying we'd found her," she said. "Seemed like a good insurance policy. Before we leave tonight, I'm going to do that, just in case. If anything happens, Elian can find a way to get it to Mattingly."

Peter nodded. It seemed like a good insurance policy. While Kate wrote her story, he jotted down his own brief account of what they'd found. Aaron Newhouse probably didn't deserve to get out of this scot free, but he didn't deserve to be tried for the murder of a woman who was very much alive, no matter what happened to them.

Marco picked them up several hours later. Anticipation filled her with a restless energy that made it hard to sit still in the Cadillac's wide back seat. Several times she pressed her hand into the top of her knee to still her frenetic foot tapping. She felt more nervous about tonight's interview than she had about the previous evening's stakeout. Confirming that Emily was alive was the easy part. Now she had to convince her to reveal things she'd probably thought no one would ever find out.

The cafe held down the corner of a block of austere apartment buildings. Despite its gloomy surroundings, the small building buzzed with bright chatter. Warm yellow light and seductive Cuban salsa music poured out the open doors and windows. They sat down at a table on the edge of the patio and ordered their drinks. Kate glanced at her watch almost compulsively. It was 7 p.m. on the dot. Emily was nowhere in sight. The waiter brought two steaming cups, and the minutes ticked by. Peter scanned the street and the cafe, looking for any sign they were being watched. His intense focus only fueled Kate's jitters.

She glanced at her watch again. 7:10 p.m.

"Maybe she changed her mind," she mumbled, kicking herself for not trying to get more details the night before.

"Or maybe she's just late," Peter soothed. "Don't give up yet. We don't how much freedom she has. Or whether anything might have held her up."

Another ten minutes dragged by. Kate thought the frustration and disappointment roiling in her heart might explode. She closed her eyes and took a deep breath, willing herself to relax.

"There." Peter's voice broke through her inner turmoil like a fire extinguisher snuffing out a flame.

She opened her eyes and immediately spotted Emily Gibson's bright red hair. She walked slowly, as though in no hurry, her lips set in a grim line.

"It looks like she's alone," Peter said as she got closer.

When she spotted them, her step faltered just slightly. A frown of confusion creased her forehead. But she kept moving, although she looked wary. Kate rose to greet her.

"I thought you might have changed your mind," she said, relief pushing the words out in a rush.

Emily shook her head, still frowning. She fixed her eyes on Peter. "I thought you would be alone."

"This is Peter Johnson. He's with the Galveston Police Department."

Emily recoiled as though he'd tried to grab her. He held his hands up in a gesture of reassurance.

"I'm here for Kate, not for you," he said. "All I needed to know I found out yesterday. You're alive. No one's been murdered. The rest of what happened is none of my business, officially speaking."

Emily glanced between them, calculating what he'd said. "You two came here together? Interesting."

Kate opened her mouth to say it wasn't what Emily thought, but the memory of what had passed between them the night before flashed across her mind. She glanced at Peter. His eyes held a question she knew she needed to answer. But she felt much more comfortable doing the asking.

"How did your presentation go?" she said, turning back to Emily with a redirect she hoped would get her talking freely.

"Good," Emily said, her wariness melting slightly as she pulled out a chair and sat down. "Really good. I explained how far we'd gotten and where I thought we went wrong. Their researchers have some ideas about what might have caused the problem. Hopefully, we'll figure it out quickly."

"Are you going to lead the team?"

"Well, not exactly," Emily shifted in her seat. "I'm just a member of the team, but obviously a key member."

The waiter interrupted their conversation to take Emily's order. Kate glanced at Peter, who was still scanning the nearby sidewalks. He nodded to her slightly, as if to say he'd spotted no threat. She eased back in her chair. Maybe this really was going to go as smoothly as she'd hoped it would. When the waiter walked away, she slipped a notebook and a pen out of her backpack.

"Do you mind?" she asked.

Emily sighed. "I guess not. If we're going to do this, I don't want you getting anything wrong."

Kate ignored the barb and flipped to a blank page.

"Why don't we start with the research? You're still trying to figure out what happened. But you think it's fixable?"

"Yes, of course. We're close. And we'll figure it out. We just need more time."

"That's what Newhouse said."

Emily snorted. "Too bad he didn't just admit that when we discovered the problem in the first place."

"Why didn't he?"

"Ego. He couldn't stand to take what he called a step backward, when he'd announced to the entire world that we'd succeeded. At first he believed we could figure it out in time, before we began the FDA trials. I knew it was risky, and I didn't like it. But I was willing to go along for a little while. I thought maybe we could make it work. But the closer we got to the big announcement, the more unlikely that seemed."

"So when did you decide you needed out?"

"When I realized he was completely blind to the reality of what was going to happen. There was no way we could keep it a secret forever. And once it came out, everyone would think we had intentionally lied. Which, in a way we had. It was going to be the end of both our careers. He was just too blinded by pride to see it."

"Why not just go to the FDA yourself?"

Emily shook her head and a hint of despair pulled at the corners of her eyes. "He told me if I did that, he'd blame the whole thing on me. He'd say I was the one who had failed and fabricated the results. He'd say he trusted me and I'd tricked him. It would have been his word against mine. He's one of the country's top virologists. Who would believe he had lied?"

"So you decided to run?"

"I decided to take what was mine and try to salvage my career as best I could," Emily said firmly, a determined edge sharpening her words. "I figured if I could go somewhere else and complete the research, it would prove I wasn't trying to trick anyone."

"Why Cuba?"

"They have a long history of medical humanitarianism. I knew that if they could be the first to develop a vaccine, it would go right to the people who need it most. Probably faster than if it came out of the U.S. And I figured if I could convince them that's all I wanted, too, they would take me in. Plus, I knew I would be safe here."

"Safe how?"

"From deportation. If the U.S. government pressed charges, Cuba would never give me up. Especially not if I became really useful to them."

"How did you even know who to contact?"

Emily waved her hand dismissively. "Medical research is a tight community. Geopolitics don't matter. I'd met someone at BioCubaFarma several years ago at a conference in South America. I reached out to him and explained what I had to offer."

"So, why not just fly here? Why all the intrigue?"

Emily smiled ruefully. "Aaron was becoming increasingly belligerent. Keeping a closer eye on me. Constantly threatening me to keep quiet. And I was worried that government officials might try to detain me if I tried to board a plane. It would have looked really suspicious."

"So you started going to the Broadside to make friends with the crew of a cargo ship?"

Emily flashed a grin. "I guess I wasn't as sneaky as I thought. That was actually my Cuban friend's idea. He said that would be the best way for me to escape."

"What happened after you met the crew?"

"I found out the captain's name and passed it along to my friend. He got in touch with the shipping company and told them to make sure the captain treated me well and kept me safe until I got here. An order like that in Cuba carries a lot of weight. After that, it was easy. One of the crew members met me the night I disappeared and took me to the ship. We sailed out of port the next day."

"What about your apartment?"

Emily grimaced. "I figured everyone would assume I drowned. But I needed a way to create suspicion. And I hoped it would eventually fall on Aaron. That's partly why I sent you the data, too."

"Partly?"

"I wanted people to suspect Aaron had done something to me, even if the police never charged him with anything. But I also wanted the world to know what he'd done." She paused and her gaze wandered over Kate's shoulder. Memories clouded her face, and for a moment she seemed to have forgotten their presence. Kate's grip on her pen tightened as the silence dragged on.

"I wanted to make him pay," Emily finally said. "He was methodically ruining my life. And I was determined he would not get away with it. How long did he stay in jail?"

"Probably not long enough," Kate mused. "Just a few days. But he's facing a murder charge. And since you're not actually dead, I think you probably got him back about as well as you possibly could have."

"And I have you two to thank for saving him from a trial."

Peter shook his head. "I don't think the DA would have taken it that far in the end. Without a body, the case was really circumstantial. And IT experts would eventually have figured out that you fabricated all those messages we found on your computer. Besides, I'm sure Newhouse would have eventually hired a private investigator to find you."

"He's the one who suggested you were still alive, you know," Kate said, watching Emily's reaction carefully. "I didn't believe him at first. It seemed so far-fetched. He claimed the vaccine trial failure made you doubt everything you'd been working toward."

Emily rolled her eyes, but the gesture lacked conviction. Kate searched her face as she flipped her hair over her shoulder, as though she was trying to figure out what to say.

"The only thing it made me doubt was him," she finally muttered.

Kate detected a kernel of truth, but she sensed that wasn't the whole story. She suddenly felt sorry for Emily. She might not want to continue her research, but it was the only card she had to play. That left just one question unanswered.

"What about your mom?" she asked softly.

Emily put her elbow on the table and rested her chin on her upturned palm. The defiance that had filled her eyes while she talked about Aaron Newhouse dissolved into regret.

"That was the only thing I couldn't figure out how to avoid," she murmured. "I knew if she had any inkling of the truth, the police would get it out of her. She could never lie convincingly."

"Seems like a high price for her to pay," Kate said, as the memory of Mrs. Gibson's tear-stained face floated through her mind.

Anger flashed in Emily's eyes, and she sat up straight. "I was going to figure out a way to tell her soon. It's not like I was leaving her forever. It was just temporary and vital for my future. I knew she would understand."

Maybe she would, Kate thought. But did that justify putting her through needless agony? Emily obviously thought it did. She believed her needs trumped everyone else's. She didn't seem to realize that was exactly the same perspective that drove Aaron Newhouse and put her in this position. Somehow, the collateral damage was always worse than the person inflicting it thought it would be.

Next to her, she sensed Peter tense. She looked up just in time to catch the look of disbelief on Emily's face as someone pulled out the chair between them and sat down.

David Knowles crossed his arms tightly over his chest and leaned back in his chair.

Kate felt like she'd grabbed an electric fence with both hands. She sucked in a breath. Stubble covered David's jawline. Dark smudges under his eyes suggested he hadn't slept much in the last few days. The last time she'd seen him, he'd teetered on the verge of a breakdown. The manic glint in his eyes suggested he'd finally fallen over the edge.

"David," Emily stammered. "What are you doing here?"

"Oh, you know, just looking for my dead girlfriend." His jaw muscles bulged as though he were grinding his teeth.

Emily had recovered her composure, and now a deep frown creased her forehead.

"How in the world did you find me?"

She sounded so annoyed Kate felt a twinge of sympathy for David. Emily clearly didn't feel the same regret over him as she did for her mother.

"Really?" David spat. "That's the first thing you're going to say to me? After everything you did?"

Kate sensed Peter shift in his chair. She glanced at him and saw that he'd angled his body toward David. A tingle of fear raised the hair on the back of her neck.

Emily huffed a sigh of exasperation. "Look, I'm sorry. Okay? I wasn't trying to hurt you. But everyone had to think I was dead or I never could have gotten away."

"Hurt? You have no idea what I went through. What your mom went through. Hurt doesn't even scratch the surface. You sacrificed both of us just so that you wouldn't have to face what you'd done."

Emily's mouth contorted into a snarl. "What I'd done? I didn't do anything! This is all Aaron Newhouse's fault."

"I'm surprised you could bear to leave him, based on the photos the police found on his computer," David sneered.

Emily's face turned crimson. She glanced at Peter and Kate. After everything she'd admitted to doing, this seemed to be the one thing she wasn't proud of.

"I didn't know he'd kept those," she mumbled.

"You lied to me all that time," David said, his voice rising with each word. "I knew there was something going on, but you denied it left and right. You even called me paranoid!"

Several people at neighboring tables glanced their way. Emily crossed her arms and scowled.

"Look, I was confused. I didn't mean for that to happen. And I didn't know what to do."

"So you just kept leading me on, pretending you loved me? I was getting ready to propose!"

He was almost shouting now, and most of the rest of the people on the patio gawked at them. Peter leaned forward urgently.

"David, we're attracting too much attention," he said. "Keep your voice down unless you want to answer questions from the local police."

"You stay out of this," David said. He was so angry he trembled as he turned his attention back to Emily. "I loved you with everything. I wanted to spend the rest of my life with you. I even brought the ring with me. I thought maybe you'd be sorry and we could start over."

Emily was shaking her head. "It would never have worked between us. I think I always knew that. Otherwise, I never would have felt drawn to Aaron. I am starting over. You should, too."

David was breathing hard, his nostrils flaring with each inhale. He leaned forward, hands on his knees. "I loved you. And you humiliated me!"

"Enough," Emily snapped. "This is pointless. I'm done here."

She pushed back her chair and stood up.

"Well, I'm not!" David lunged at her, and Kate caught the flash of something shiny in his hand.

Peter sprang out of his chair a second later, but not before Emily let out a strangled scream. David's hand flew back and forth twice before Peter crashed into him, sending all three tumbling to the pavement. As soon as they hit the ground, Peter and David rolled away in a churning pile of flying arms and fists.

Kate rushed to Emily's side. Blood already covered her shirt and her eyes were closed. Frantically, Kate put her hands over Emily's stomach. The sticky warmth made her gag.

"Help!" she cried, frantically looking around for anything she could use to stop the bleeding.

She was about to cry out again when two waiters dropped to their knees next to her. One pressed a towel to Emily's stomach while the other one put his fingers to her throat to check for a pulse. He yelled something in Spanish that Kate couldn't understand. But since others yelled back, and no one stopped trying to help, she took it as a good sign.

Kate barely had time to register the sound of heavy footfalls before someone grabbed her from behind and lifted her off her feet. She yelled in protest but caught sight of Peter about 20 feet away. He had David Knowles pinned to the ground, hands clasped behind him. The knife used to stab Emily lay on the ground, just out of reach.

Strong arms grasped Kate's wrists, and she felt the cool circle of handcuffs ratchet tight around them.

"Wait!" she yelled. "I didn't do anything. I was trying to help her."

As her unseen captor pulled her backward, two police officers pounced on Peter. He offered no resistance as they pulled his arms behind his back and handcuffed him. One yanked him to his feet while the other one put cuffs on David Knowles.

"Peter!" Kate gasped as she stumbled back, fighting against the arms that held her.

The police officers yelled to each other, and Kate heard the wail of a siren in the distance. She fervently hoped it was an ambulance and not more officers.

"Por favor, let me just talk to her." Peter pleaded as the officer holding him dragged him further away from her. His face looked calm, but his wild eyes told her he was more afraid than he wanted her to know. "Kate, don't struggle. It's okay. We'll get it sorted out. Everything's going to be okay. I promise. Kate!"

The officer restraining him paid no attention, dragging him toward a different car than the one Kate could now see in front of her.

She tried to squelch the sob that rose in her chest, but it was no use. It forced its way to the surface, ragged and full of fear. Tears streamed down her face and she cursed all the times she'd told herself she was better off on her own. At that moment, she would have given anything not to be alone.

Chapter 26

PETER PACED BACK AND forth in the small cell, trying to calm his rising frustration. He'd tried to explain, in broken Spanish, that he and Kate were innocent but no one paid any attention. He'd barraged the officers with questions about where they had taken her but they simply ignored him. Helplessness wrapped around him like a straightjacket, making it hard to breathe. The memory of Kate's twisted, tear-streaked face mocked him. He'd tried so hard to keep her safe. Now he had no idea where she was or whether he'd ever see her again.

Before they'd thrust him into the cell, the officers had emptied his pockets and taken his watch. He didn't know how long he'd been pacing back and forth. It felt like hours, but surely it hadn't been that long.

He replayed the whirl of events in his mind, from David's sudden appearance to his being forced into the back of the police car. How had he not heard David approach? He'd let his guard down just enough that he hadn't been listening for anyone to walk up behind them. When Emily appeared alone, he thought they were home free. She showed no sign of any hostility toward them. He assumed the danger was over.

He mentally kicked himself for the hundredth time. He should have known David was up to no good. He was angry from the moment he sat down. Peter just didn't realize how angry he really was. He'd stabbed Emily several times before Peter tackled him. If she lived, it would be a miracle. The fleeting glance he'd gotten as the police dragged him away told him she'd lost a lot of blood.

But by then the paramedics had arrived. Maybe they were in time to save her.

The sound of voices and footsteps in the hallway outside his cell made him stop pacing and run to the dented metal door. He pressed his face close to the small grated opening near the top and yelled.

"Hey! When am I going to get to talk to someone? I want to know what happened to my friend! What about the girl who got stabbed? Is she okay? Hey!"

The footsteps receded, and Peter slammed his open palm against the door in frustration. The sting of the blow radiated up his entire arm. He ground his teeth against the pain.

"Someone! Anyone!" His boiling frustration erupted in a primal yell.

Suddenly exhausted by the burst of emotion, he collapsed on the bench that lined one wall. He put his elbows on his knees and buried his face in his hands. He'd never felt so trapped and powerless. Even in his darkest moment, when he fled the only home he'd ever known under cover of darkness, to escape the rising tide of violence he'd helped unleash. He'd always had somewhere to run. Until now.

Heavy, gasping breaths filled his chest. His whole body trembled as the pressure of his own inadequacy pressed in on him. Overwhelmed by hopelessness, he slid to his knees and cried out to the only one who could save them now.

Kate sat as far away from the door to her cell as possible. She'd wedged her back into the corner and pulled her knees up to her chest. Wrapping her arms around her legs, she rested her forehead on her knees and closed her eyes. She had sobbed uncontrollably during the ride to the police station. When they'd brought her in and began searching her pockets, she'd begged them to tell her where they'd taken Peter. They acted like they hadn't even heard her. She'd forgotten all about her blood-covered hands until they uncuffed her and thrust her arms roughly under a spigot of cold water. A female officer had dropped a pat of soap into her hand and made scrubbing motions. She'd done the best she could, but traces of Emily's blood still lingered around her fingernails.

By the time they'd pushed her into her cell, her tears had stopped. A dull emptiness filled her now, oppressive and dark.

She had come completely to the end of herself and found nothing. No hope. No fire. No will to convince herself that Peter's parting words held even a sliver of truth. A twinge of sorrow seized her heart when she thought about his valiant attempt to convince her their world was not crumbling under their feet. If Emily survived, it would only be because Peter had stopped David from finishing his attack. He had risked his life to save her, and it might be the last sacrifice he ever got to make.

Icy fingers of despair folded around her. She knew so little about him. She desperately wanted to hear his story, to know what had driven him out of Africa. What Elian had urged him to forgive and forget. She'd probably never know now. And if she was about to spend the rest of her life rotting in a Cuban jail cell, maybe it didn't matter. But she sensed that Peter's story held the key to something she'd wrestled with since she was a frightened and heartbroken 12-year-old girl. How could someone live through something unforgivable and go on living? Really living, not just pretending to live. She believed Peter had stood before that very question and found an answer.

She had waited patiently for the opportunity to ask him. But now it was gone.

A ragged, shuddering sigh shook her body. She felt herself drifting into a hazy sleep. It gave her the sensation of sailing on her father's boat, rolling gently with the swells that buoyed it along. Scenes from their trip played through her mind. Sunlight illuminating the quiet sanctuary of San Cristobal. Heat radiating from brightly painted buildings. Peter's smile beaming down at her. She floated along after them, drawing in the ribbons of warmth to bind up her broken soul.

She woke disoriented, with a pounding headache. Her neck was so stiff it hurt to pick up her head from her knees. She willed herself to stand up slowly and walk around the tiny room.

The sharp sound of metal scraping on metal made her jump. The door swung open and an officer walked through the door carrying a tray. She set it down on the bench and backed out of the cell.

"Wait!" Kate cried. Her voice sounded too loud in the cramped space, amplifying the pounding in her head. She cringed but held her hand out in supplication. "Please. My friend? Where is he?"

But the officer swung the door shut behind her without saying a word. The bolt slid back home with a sickening finality.

Kate stood staring at it for a long while, willing the guard to come back. When she finally accepted that wouldn't happen, she turned toward the tray. It held a cup of water and a bowl of what looked like rice and black beans. She didn't feel hungry, but as she contemplated the bowl, her stomach made an involuntary lurch. She'd had nothing to eat since lunch the previous day. At least, she assumed it was Friday by now. Her cell seemed to be suspended in time.

She tried a bite of the beans, mostly just to appease her growling stomach. But before she realized it, her spoon was scraping the bottom of the bowl. She pushed the tray away and curled up in the corner again. This time, she rested her head against the smooth concrete wall. In moments, the darkness of sleep washed over her.

She awoke to voices outside the cell door. She focused all her attention on the sound but made no move to stand up. When the bolt scraped back and the door swung open, she expected to see the same female officer carrying another tray. Instead, a large man stepped inside the cell. He motioned for her to get up and turn around. In his hand, he held a pair of handcuffs.

Fear grabbed her by the neck and left her struggling to breathe. It took all her strength to swing her legs down from the bench and stand shakily to her feet. He could do anything he wanted to her and she would be powerless to stop him. Revulsion and fear made her stomach churn. But when she slowly turned around, he simply snapped the cuffs around her wrists. Wrapping his big hand around her forearm, he led her out of the cell and down the hallway. He wasn't gentle, but he wasn't rough either. Efficient, businesslike. He had the air of a man just doing his job.

They walked down one dark corridor and turned left, then walked down to the end of another long hallway and turned right. After passing a few doors, the officer stopped at one and knocked.

"Entrar," a deep voice responded from inside.

The guard swung open the door and firmly pushed Kate inside. Two men sat at a table. One wore a police uniform. The other, Kate recognized instantly as the man who had been with Emily at La Guarida. He watched her as the guard quickly removed her handcuffs. She was so focused on trying to read his face that she didn't even realize anyone else was in the room until she heard a sharp exhale and a fervently whispered, "Thank you, Jesus!"

At the sound of Peter's voice, Kate's heart leapt and every trace of fear vanished. She took three running steps and threw herself into his arms. He held her so tightly to his chest she could hear the thudding of his heart. Relief buckled her knees, but she had no fear of falling. After several long moments, he gently eased her back to her feet and loosened his grip. She didn't cling to him, but she wasn't ready to let go, either.

"Siéntate," the officer said. He sounded used to giving orders and getting immediate obedience. Peter guided her to a metal folding chair across from the two men and sat down next to her.

Worry quickly gnawed away her joy at being with him again. What if this was the last time they saw each other? It took all her strength to sit still and not blurt out everything she wanted to tell him. She willed herself to focus on the man from BioCubaFarma. He looked at her with interest, but she detected no hostility.

"Is Emily alive?" she asked quietly.

He nodded once, slowly. "She is. They operated on her as soon as she got to the hospital. As I'm sure you know, we have excellent doctors here in Cuba. They saved her life."

Kate took a deep breath and let it out slowly. "That's great news."

She glanced at Peter. He was nodding in agreement, but his face held a wariness. Emily's survival didn't necessarily solve their problem.

"I spoke with her briefly before I came here," the man continued. "She was still in much pain, but she wanted to know what had happened to the two of you."

He turned to Peter and regarded him thoughtfully.

"From what the police tell me, you saved her life," he said. "The man who attacked her has refused to speak. But she told me he was her former boyfriend. I gather he was not pleased about her decision to leave America."

Peter nodded but said nothing. The man turned to the officer next to him and the two spoke in Spanish for a few moments. The officer handed him a file folder. He flipped it open and reviewed the contents. He shook his head a few times and made disapproving clicking noises.

"So, you are a reporter," he said, looking up at Kate before fixing his probing brown eyes on Peter. "And you are a police detective! It seems you are in Cuba under false pretenses. Your visa cards say you are tourists."

"I'm not here in any official capacity," Peter said evenly. "Emily disappeared, and we thought she'd been murdered. In fact, we have charged someone with killing her. All I wanted to do was find out whether she was alive."

The man's face showed no emotion as he listened.

"And you?" he asked, turning to Kate. "What are you doing here?"

Her tongue felt like sandpaper as she tried to lick her lips. Her answer could be the key to winning their freedom, or sending her back to her cell alone.

"I wanted to know why she left," she said. Her voice sounded raspy and hesitant. She balled her hands into fists to beat back the fear. "Dr. Aaron Newhouse took advantage of her, for his own gain. He wanted to take her work and make millions from it. And he was willing to sacrifice Emily to do that. I wanted everyone to know what happened. I didn't want to let him get away with it. And the only way to do that was to hear Emily's side of the story. I came here to find her and hopefully to persuade her to talk to me."

"You did not tell this other man where she was?"

"No. But I did tell her mother I was coming here to find her. She must have told him. She believed he loved Emily. I know she never would have said something if she thought he would hurt her daughter. She was devastated when she thought Emily had been killed."

The man nodded and closed the folder. He sat back and eyed both of them carefully. Then he said something to the officer. Kate couldn't tell whether it was good or bad. Her heart started to pound. If he didn't believe them, they had no hope of leaving.

"You lied on your visa card," he finally said. "But, you haven't broken any other laws."

A trickle of hope began to drip into Kate's heart.

"Emily asked me to advocate on your behalf," he continued. "My friend here has agreed to let you go but suggests you leave the country as soon as possible."

"Our flight leaves tomorrow," Peter said.

"Yes, and until then, you will have officers assigned to watch you."

Peter nodded. "We don't want any more trouble."

"No, I should think not," the man said. "We have called your friend, the pastor, to come get you."

Kate tried not to let her surprise show. She thought they had been careful. But the Cuban officials knew who they were and where they were staying. Had their freedom been an illusion the whole time?

"Thank you," Peter said. His face showed no sign of surprise.

"Consider it an even exchange for saving Emily's life." He pushed his chair back and stood up.

"What will happen to David Knowles?" Kate asked.

The man frowned. "He will face trial for attempted murder. And I have no doubt he will be convicted."

With a nod to the officer, the man walked out of the room. Kate watched him go with amazement. It didn't seem possible that they were free to leave, just like that. But when the officer stood, he motioned for them to follow. Peter flashed her a tight but encouraging smile and held out his hand to pull her to her feet. The warmth of his touch filled her with strength.

They followed the officer down several hallways before emerging in a dingy reception area. Elian sat in a hard plastic chair, elbows on knees, head bowed. When he heard them come in, he started up. He leapt out of the chair with a cry of joy and embraced Peter in a tight hug. Kate made no attempt to resist when he turned and wrapped his arms around her next. It felt surprisingly good to know someone else shared the joy of their release.

The officer behind the desk motioned for them to come over. He set Peter's watch and wallet on the counter and then handed over Kate's backpack. She'd forgotten all about it, but the investigators must have picked it up from their table at the cafe after their arrest. Once they'd collected their things, Elian ushered them out the front door.

Kate blinked in the bright sunlight and shielded her eyes with her hand. It felt at first like the sun was right overhead, but once her eyes adjusted, she realized it was closer to late afternoon. They'd spent almost 24 hours at the police station.

None of them said a word as they climbed into Elian's Lada. Kate glanced out the back window as they pulled onto the street. Two officers in a police car pulled in close behind them, making no attempt to hide their presence.

"They weren't kidding about keeping an eye on us," Kate said, breaking the silence.

"No, they won't let you out of their sight until your plane takes off tomorrow," Elian said, his voice grim. "They made it very clear to me that they would watch all of us closely."

"I'm sorry we put you in this position," Peter said. "I never wanted to bring danger to your house."

Elian waved his hand. "God is watching over us," he said. "And you! We've been praying all last night and all day. The whole church. And God answered our prayers."

"He certainly did," Peter murmured.

Kate listened while Peter gave Elian a brief account of what had happened, from the time they arrived at the cafe the night before to their release that afternoon. She felt almost disconnected from the story, like it belonged to someone else.

"Emily Gibson is lucky you were there," Elian said. "If this David had found her at any other time, she would not have survived."

"No," Peter said. "I don't think she would have."

When they arrived at the house, the police car pulled in behind them. Elian ushered them toward the patio gate.

"Just pretend they're not here," he said. "They won't bother us."

Carida greeted them at the door.

"Peter, Kate!" she cried, hugging and kissing both of them. "Thank the Lord you are safe."

She led them inside, smiling widely as she nodded toward a dozen people crowded into the small living room. Kate suddenly felt like she'd crashed a family gathering.

"We have been praying," Carida said. "We gathered as many people here as we could. The rest are praying at home."

Peter smiled widely at them and brought a lightly clenched fist to his heart.

"Gracias, por sus oraciones," he said.

Kate offered her own faltering smile of thanks, even as heat flooded her cheeks. She couldn't believe all these people had been praying for them. They didn't even know her or Peter. But they'd dropped everything to beg their God to bring them home. Peter walked around the room, shaking hands and bending down to hug the matronly women. Kate stood there, feeling increasingly awkward, until Elian put his arm around her shoulders.

"This calls for a celebration!" he said, giving her a little squeeze. "Carida, call everyone. We will have dinner tonight at church and sing praise to the God who saves."

Kate cringed inwardly but managed to give their hosts a faint smile. Peter flashed her a grin.

"You don't think the police will mind if we leave?" she asked.

"No," Elian said, waving his hand again as he had outside. "In fact, I'll go tell them. And when we get to the church, we'll invite them in, so they can make sure you don't escape out the back."

He winked at her, and Kate laughed.

"Dinner at church it is," she said. "But first, I need a shower."

Chapter 27

About an hour later, Kate and Peter piled back into Elian's Lada. Everyone else had left while Kate was getting cleaned up. Elian waved cheerily to the police officers before sliding into the driver's seat.

"I promised to feed them well," Elian chuckled. "They are very loyal to their commanding officer. But they're not above enjoying an empanada with us."

"You're not afraid they might try to arrest us? Or anyone else?" Kate still worried they were running a big risk leaving the house.

"No. If they wanted you in jail, they wouldn't have let you go. They don't see you as a threat. But they want to keep an eye on you, just in case."

"What about you?"

He laughed. "They can arrest me any time. As long as I'm not demonstrating against the government or calling for democracy, they're not worried about what I'm doing."

"So you feel pretty free?"

Reflected in the rearview mirror, Elian's face grew serious. "We're not free. We still have to be careful. They watch the church, and sometimes they come and talk to me about what we're doing. They want to make sure we don't get cozy with any Americans. And that we are loyal to our Patria, our homeland. I have to be careful how often I leave the country. But other than that, they mostly leave us alone."

Kate stared out the window in silence as the crumbling and pocked housing blocks rushed past.

"You wouldn't last long here, though," Elian said after a few moments.

"Oh, why?" Kate asked in surprise.

Peter turned sideways in the front seat and smirked at her. "They don't like pesky journalists who are determined to report the truth no matter what," he said.

"That, my friend, is true," Elian said ruefully. "They definitely don't like reporters, unless they write for Granma. You are very lucky they let you go."

For a moment, Kate imagined herself back in that tiny cell and shuddered. She had always thought of freedom like a possession. And as a reporter, she'd put it to good use. Sometimes she waved it like a matador's red cloak in front of public officials. Other times, she wrapped it tightly around herself like body armor. She'd never thought about it as something she might lose. It just didn't seem possible. But now she realized how delicate and valuable it really was.

A few minutes later, Elian turned down a narrow road and stopped in front of a low cinderblock building with a gently sloping roof. It looked more like a warehouse than a church. They squeezed between cars packed tightly into the small parking lot and headed for the open front door. Kate glanced behind her and spotted the two policemen. They were climbing out of their car and making their way toward the building.

"Don't worry." Peter's low whisper next to hear ear stole into her spirit and calmed it like a snake charmer with a deadly python.

She glanced up at him and smiled. They hadn't had any chance to talk since they left the jail. She wondered if he'd been as scared as she was, alone in his cell. And was he as relieved to see her again as she was to see him? As if reading her mind, he put his arm around her shoulders. He said nothing, but his chest rose and fell with a sigh full of emotion.

A ripple of welcome greeted them when they walked through the door. Elian guided them through the crowd, shaking hands and sharing hugs. Peter spoke haltingly through a wide smile to everyone they passed. Kate watched with growing envy as he became more at ease with every conversation. After five or six, he looked completely at home, laughing and hugging as though he came here every week. Kate stood awkwardly at his side and tried not to think about how uncomfortable she must look. No one seemed to notice. The men nodded at her and smiled. Many of the older women patted her on the shoulder or squeezed her hand in theirs. Every face beamed an open and honest welcome.

When they reached the front of the room, Elian disappeared through a doorway to the right of the stage. The chatter of women bubbled out, along with the mouth-watering smell of simmering meat and warm bread. Kate's stomach growled.

Elian returned, leading Carida and half a dozen other women all wearing aprons. He raised his hands and his voice and said something in Spanish that Kate took to be an announcement about dinner. Elian motioned for them to join him and put one arm around each of them. Everyone around them bowed their heads.

Kate closed her eyes as Elian poured forth a prayer she couldn't understand. He started with jubilation but as he continued, his voice got thick and he paused several times to regain control. Tears welled in Kate's eyes. She couldn't understand his words, but she could understand his heart. When he finished, the room resounded with a hearty, "Amén!"

Elian wiped his eyes and wrapped his arms around Peter in another long hug. When he turned to Kate, he smiled and put his hand on her shoulder.

"God delivered you," he said. "Never forget that."

Before she could reply, he ushered them toward the back door. Carida and the other cooks had already bustled back through and stood behind big pans of steaming food laid out on a long plywood counter. Kate took one of the offered plates and shuffled down the line, gathering something new at each stop.

"Gracias. Muchas gracias!" Peter said to each woman as he followed close behind her. At the end of the line, someone pointed them through another door into a kind of courtyard surrounded by a low wall of cinderblocks. Big fans pushed the damp air softly across the open space. Naked lightbulbs dangled from open rafters under a metal roof.

From behind Peter, Elian ushered them to a long table at the far end of the courtyard. Kate dug into her dinner, for a moment oblivious to anything but her overwhelming hunger.

"I guess you enjoyed the jailhouse meals as much as I did," Peter said, smirking at her as he put a fork full of beans in his mouth.

Kate chuckled and put her fork down. "I didn't realize how hungry I was until we got close to the kitchen."

"Me neither. It's kind of hard to be hungry when you think you may spend the rest of your life in a 10 by 10 foot cell."

His voice was light, but the depth of the danger they'd escaped filled his eyes.

Kate looked at him for several moments as a swirl of thoughts and emotions vied for supremacy in her mind.

"I thought I would never see you again," she finally said, hoping that her gaze conveyed everything she felt but couldn't yet bring herself to say.

He reached over and put his hand on hers. His fingers closed gently around her palm and his thumb traced a slow path across her knuckles. Warmth crept up her back and neck and flushed her checks. An invisible cord filled the space between them. Every touch, every look drew it tighter, pulling her toward him with a sense of inevitability. It felt like floating in a dream, when somehow you knew you wouldn't hit the ground and could just revel in the sensation of weightlessness.

But the dream dissipated like a sea mist before the rising sun when Peter squeezed her hand and pulled away. Halfway across the room, she spotted Elian making his way toward them, a knowing and somewhat satisfied smile tugging at the corners of his mouth. Kate realized with a slight surprise that happy, chatting people had filled the other tables already. She hadn't noticed anyone else walk into the room.

Two other older couples trailed Elian and Carida, and they all squeezed around the table where Kate and Peter sat. Exuberant Spanish volleyed between them. Peter caught some of it, directed at him, and did his best to answer questions. Kate couldn't follow the conversation but gathered by the few words she could pick up that they were asking him about his parents and his life in America.

She marveled at the sense of community these people shared. Even Peter. It almost felt like a family reunion. She knew he'd been here before, and maybe he'd met some of these people then. But that had been well over a decade ago. How could they still care so deeply about him? It was like they considered him one of their own.

Peter never seemed ill at ease, unless he was the center of attention at a televised news conference. He wore a confidence that made him look comfortable in every situation she could recall seeing him in. But the way he sat and chatted now felt different. He looked like he was completely at home.

Kate had never known that kind of security. She felt safe in her own space, but this web of community she'd stumbled into shared a bond she'd never experienced. The hum of connection between the people vibrated around the room so tangibly she could almost hear it. And a longing to be a part of it echoed in her heart.

The next morning, Peter opened his eyes to find thin rays of sunlight shining through the shutters covering the window in his room. He lay there for a moment, relishing the soft pillow under his head and the freedom he had to stretch out his arms and take a deep breath. He rotated his shoulder gingerly. It had broken his fall when he'd crashed into David Knowles and sent them both tumbling to the ground.

He sat up, swung his feet over the edge of the bed and rubbed his hand over his head. So much had happened over the last 36 hours. And every part thrilled with hints of the miraculous. Emily's survival. His escape from David's slashing blade. Their release from jail. And Kate.

He closed his eyes and replayed the moment they'd shared during dinner. Her grey eyes always gave away more than he suspected she meant to reveal. But she had remained silent, beyond saying she thought she would never see him again. Sometimes he thought he had talked himself into believing she felt more than she really did. But last night, he sensed something shift. He now felt pretty sure of how she felt. The question was, how long would it take her to admit it to herself? And how long after that until she could admit it to him?

He stood up and stretched again. Patience did not come naturally. But this was worth waiting for. He vowed to tread lightly and pull gently. And pray for revelation.

He could hear Kate's voice in the living room, so he dressed quickly and threw the rest of his clothes into his bag. When he emerged from the room, he was ready to go.

Elian, Carida, and Kate sat around the table. They all turned to smile up at him as he approached.

"I managed to beat you up at least once this trip!" Kate said triumphantly.

He laughed as he pulled out his chair and sat down. "You're probably a lot more excited about going home than I am."

"You're not pumped about having to tell the DA he has no case?"

"Can't say that I am," he said. "But I am excited to see the look on your face when Mattingly gives you your job back."

"Ha! Well, we'll see about that," she said, dunking her bread in her coffee.

He took a sip of his own coffee and sighed appreciatively. Then he looked back and forth between his two friends.

"I can't tell you how grateful I am for your hospitality," he said. "Thank you for taking such good care of us. We couldn't have done any of this without you."

"Peter," Elian said, leaning forward. "You are like a son to us. You are always welcome. Just maybe come for vacation only next time, eh?"

They all laughed, and Carida dabbed at her eyes with a handkerchief. Kate kept her eyes fixed on her mug. He sensed saying goodbye would not be easy for her. Despite her fierce independence, she'd discovered something here she wanted. He could see it in the hungry way she watched their interactions.

Elian glanced at his watch. "We'd better go soon. I do not want you to be late. And neither do your guards."

Peter huffed and drained the last of his coffee. Across the table, Kate eased back her chair and stood. She turned to Carida first.

"Thank you," she said, her voice husky. Before she could say anything else, Carida enveloped her in a hug. Kate seemed to melt into her embrace, and the two women stood silently for much longer than Peter would have expected. How long had it been since Kate had allowed herself to surrender to genuine love and concern?

He turned to Elian and found him watching the two women. When he caught the older man's eye, Elian opened his arms and Peter stepped into the familiar bear hug.

"Let go of the past," Elian said quietly, so only Peter could hear. "Leave your mistakes with the one who always knew you would make them and provided a way out. Only he can make it right."

Tears filled Peter's eyes. He had run from the past, tried to forget it. But he'd never let it go. Maybe Elian was right.

As he pulled back, his friend held his gaze. "You have a future," he said firmly. "If you keep looking back, you will miss it."

Then Elian stepped around him and held out his arms to Kate, who gave him a hug while Peter turned to embrace Carida. A few minutes later, they were climbing into the Lada. She waved to them from the doorway as they pulled away.

Their police escort rode their bumper all the way to the airport. When they pulled up outside the terminal, the two officers got out and watched them tell Elian goodbye. Peter smiled to himself when they followed them into the building, about 20 paces behind.

Kate looked over her shoulder, a crease of worry crossing her forehead.

"Just ignore them," he said. "They're only here to make sure we get on the plane. And I have a feeling they'll watch from the terminal until it takes off."

She smiled up at him and nodded. They waited in line at the ticket counter to get their boarding pass and then walked straight to the security checkpoint. The two officers stood off to the side while their bags went through the scanner. When they picked them up on the other side, the officers continued their slow-speed surveillance.

"Do you want to get something to snack on?" he asked, looking at the shops lining the hallway leading to the gate. "Doesn't look like we have too many options."

Kate shook her head. "I'm not hungry. But I thought about taking home a bottle of rum."

He chuckled. "Why not? You'll need something special to celebrate your first day back at work."

She grimaced but veered toward a shop lined with rows and rows of bottles. He hung back to give her some space. It didn't take her long to select one and take it to the register. The officers following them had also stopped and eyed her carefully. Peter smiled at them, hoping to dispel any suspicion. When Kate emerged from the shop, they walked straight to their gate and sat down to wait.

Kate unzipped her bag and nestled the bottle of rum inside. Then she pulled a notebook and pen out of her backpack.

"If I'm going to have this story ready by the time we get back to Galveston, I'd better get to work," she said, glancing up at him.

"I won't interrupt," he said. "But I expect some credit when you give your Pulitzer acceptance speech."

Kate rolled her eyes, but a smile played on her lips. Without another word, she flipped open the notebook and bent over it. She must have already worked out the beginning in her mind because she wrote for several minutes before pausing to think. He slipped a book out of his backpack and pretended to read. But secretly he watched her work. When she stopped, he wondered about the words and phrases she was puzzling out. When her pen returned to fly across the page, he felt a little thrill. He couldn't wait to see the story in print. It would be Kate's moment of triumph. But sharing in the journey made it almost as sweet for him as he knew it would be for her.

She had persevered through doubt and opposition and risked her most valued treasure to find out the truth. Eventually, she would be ready to apply that same single-minded pursuit to the bigger questions of life. Until then, he would do everything he could to encourage her to keep digging.

Fifteen minutes later, Peter gave their police escort a jaunty salute as they walked down the gangway and onto the plane. As soon as they took their seats, Kate took up her writing again. She didn't say a word to him the entire flight. But as they prepared to land in Cancún, she finally sat back and rubbed her eyes. He raised an eyebrow in inquiry but waited for her to break the silence.

"Finished," she said. Satisfaction made her eyes sparkle.

He held out his curled knuckles for a fist bump and she laughed.

"So what's the plan?" he asked.

"As much as I'd love to spring this on Mattingley in person, I think I'd better try to call when we land," she said.

"Alrighty. I'll get us something to eat while you make the call."

"Thanks. For everything." She looked up at him with a hint of the intensity from the night before. Then it vanished behind an impish playfulness. "You know, you make a pretty good assistant."

He shook his head with a chuckle. "That's funny. I was about to tell you the exact same thing."

Kate took a deep breath as she watched Peter's retreating back. They'd found a table in the food court next to a planter that screened some of the surrounding noise. She looked down at the phone in her hand. Everything hung on this call. She opened her contact list, swiped down to Mattingly's number, and tapped the call button.

It rang three times before he picked up.

"Kate Bennett!" his voice exploded in her ear. "You have some nerve calling me on a Saturday. Where have you been? We've been trying to get in touch with you for the last week."

"I've been in Cuba."

"Cuba! I knew it. Didn't I tell you that was dangerous?"

"You did. And it was. But I've got the story. It's yours if you want it. If not, I'll take it to The Times."

"What? Now just hang on a minute. You still work for me."

"Do I? I thought I quit after you threatened to fire me."

"Well," he cleared his throat. "Why don't you tell me about this story?"

Kate smiled. She considered making him say out loud that she still had a job, or even pushing her luck and demanding a raise. But her triumph was sweet enough as it was. No need to rub it in. She started to give him the basics of what had happened, but he quickly interrupted.

"Wait. Who's we? Who went with you?"

Kate cringed. She knew he would not be happy about this. "Peter Johnson. Detective Johnson, I mean."

Mattingly swore.

"The chief sent him to find out whether Emily Gibson was still alive. That's kind of an important detail in a murder case."

Mattingly continued to grumble.

"Well, I could have just waited to get the story from him when he came back," she said. "Then we could have gotten it along with every other media outlet at the public news conference. Instead, I got you an exclusive with details no one else will have. And we'll have it at least a day before anyone else."

Mattingly sighed. "Next time, let's try not to get so cozy with the police, ok?"

Kate glanced up and spotted Peter threading his way through the crowd toward her. No promises, she thought.

"Do you want to hear the rest of the story or not?"

Missing researcher found alive

Emily Gibson says she fled Galveston to avoid taking the blame for the Ebola vaccine failure | By Kate Bennett

HAVANA, Cuba—Missing researcher Emily Gibson, feared dead after she disappeared three weeks ago, is alive. *The Gazette* found Gibson in Havana on Wednesday.

She appeared well and admitted she was working with researchers at the state-owned pharmaceutical company, BioCuba-Farma, to continue developing the Ebola vaccine. But on Thursday, Gibson got an unwelcome visit from her ex-boyfriend, fellow University of Texas Medical Branch student David Knowles.

Knowles had also tracked Gibson to Cuba, and in a fit of rage, attacked her with a knife while she was having coffee at a sidewalk cafe.

Gibson sustained several life-threatening stab wounds but survived. Paramedics rushed her to the hospital, where doctors performed surgery to repair the damage. They expect her to make a full recovery.

Police arrested Knowles, who faces a charge of attempted murder.

Shock and relief

UTMB administrators learned about Gibson's discovery when the *Gazette* contacted them late Saturday.

"Of course, we are relieved to know she's alive," UTMB spokeswoman Claire Dupont said. "And we are shocked both about her decision to go to Cuba and the apparent attempt on her life. We will work with the U.S. State Department to find out whether there's any way to contact her or find out more about her situation."

UTMB stands to lose millions with the vaccine trial's failure. But because of Cuba's strained diplomatic relationship with the United States, the school is unlikely to persuade officials there to send her home—or stop using proprietary information Gibson gained while working here.

Dupont declined to describe Gibson's actions as theft but said the school would consider all its options.

Newhouse vindicated

Galveston prosecutors charged Dr. Aaron Newhouse with Gibson's murder last week. District Attorney Nathan Mahoney is expected to drop those charges later today.

Speaking through his lawyer, Ben Castleman, Newhouse said he was not surprised to learn Gibson was alive.

"My client has always maintained his innocence," Castleman said. "Of course, he didn't know where Emily Gibson might have gone. But he long suspected she had run away on her own accord."

Castleman said Newhouse would prepare a more thorough response to Gibson's claims against him in the coming days. As for Gibson's plan to continue working on the vaccine, Castleman did not mince words.

"That is intellectual property theft," he said. "My client's position is that the proprietary information Ms. Gibson took to Cuba does not belong to her. She is working with stolen material, and the research community will judge her for that."

Mounting pressure

Gibson came to Galveston after graduating from the University of Texas three years ago to work with Newhouse on his Ebola vaccine project. She was the youngest person on his team. But Newhouse called her a vital part of his work and credited her with helping him achieve success. Given her lack of experience, media reports hailed her as a medical research phenom.

But the vaccine trial's success was short-lived. Gibson told the *Gazette* she was the first to discover that the immune response initially recorded in their animal trials did not last. By then, they'd already applied to start human trials under the Food and Drug Administration's supervision. Newhouse believed they could solve the problem and persuaded her not to say anything until they'd run more tests.

Gibson said she agreed, hoping he was right about a quick resolution. But when further tests revealed the same problem, Gibson said she started to get nervous.

That began weeks of heated debates between the researcher and her boss. She said she wanted to tell the FDA, and he did not.

Gibson told the *Gazette* Newhouse threatened to blame the problem on her and tell everyone she'd tricked him into thinking the vaccine worked. She feared everyone would believe him because of his status as a world-renowned virologist.

That's when she began making plans to disappear.

Escape plan

At first, Gibson said she only planned her own escape. But as Newhouse increased the pressure on her to stay quiet, she decided to make it look like he'd had a hand in her disappearance.

She planted fake messages on her computer that appeared to show Newhouse threatening to kill her.

Meanwhile, she contacted a fellow researcher in Cuba whom she'd met at an international conference. When she explained the situation, he said she—and her vaccine data—would be welcome at BioCubaFarma. Then she arranged to meet the crew of a cargo ship sailing between Galveston and Cuba and secured a passenger berth.

The night she disappeared, members of the crew picked her up near where she was staying with friends on the island's West End. They went straight to the ship and sailed out of port the next morning.

Before she left for her weekend at the beach, Gibson said she made it look like someone had ransacked her apartment, to raise suspicions about what had happened. And she mailed data showing the vaccine's failure to the *Gazette*.

'No words'

Pamela Gibson, Emily's mother, had no idea her daughter was alive. When prosecutors charged Newhouse with her murder, she believed her daughter was dead.

"I have no words right now," Pamela Gibson said when told her daughter was alive but had suffered a near fatal knife attack. "All I can think about is getting to Cuba to see my baby."

Gibson said she regretted keeping her plan from her mother but insisted she could not risk anyone knowing what had happened until she was safe in Cuba.

That included David Knowles, her boyfriend of more than a year. The investigation into Gibson's disappearance revealed she had an intimate relationship with Newhouse while dating Knowles. That news had devastated Knowles, who was planning to propose.

Gibson admitted becoming involved with Newhouse had been a mistake. She said she didn't realize he'd kept any of the photos she'd sent him during their relationship. Investigators discovered the images while looking for evidence on Newhouse's computer.

The discovery of Gibson's infidelity apparently sent Knowles over the edge. When he confronted her in Havana, he said she had humiliated him.

Still up for grabs

While Gibson plans to work with Cuban researchers to solve the vaccine puzzle, Castleman said his client also plans to continue his work.

"Aaron Newhouse has spent his life trying to find a cure for this terrible disease," Castleman said. "He plans to return to the lab now that his name is cleared. Emily Gibson may have a head start, but he fully intends to get to a working vaccine first."

But where that work might happen remains unclear. Although Newhouse has been cleared of murder, he still committed a serious breach of UTMB policy by engaging in an intimate relationship with someone who worked for him. He also exhibited a lack of ethical judgement in lying about problems with the trial.

Claire Dupont said UTMB's board would have to think long and hard about his future at the institution.

"While we recognize the importance of his work, we cannot ignore what appears to be grave flaws in his character," she said.

As she told her story in Havana, Gibson remained unrepentant—even defiant—about her decisions.

"I had no choice," she said simply. "Aaron Newhouse was trying to ruin my life. I could not let him do that."

Chapter 28

KATE PICKED HER WAY carefully down the steep concrete steps that led to the beach. The wind whipped her hair and fluttered the newspaper tucked under her arm. On the sand below her, a lone figure stood, hand raised to his eyes to block the sun's glare. From 50 yards away, two dogs slid to a stop and tussled over a bright green ball. The one that managed to grab it first pivoted on its hind legs and ran back toward the man, who clapped and called his encouragement.

When he turned to throw the ball again, he spotted her and waved.

The dogs returned more slowly this time, tongues lolling. Peter walked toward her, a contented smile lighting up his face.

"I see you picked up a copy of the paper," he said when he got close enough for her to hear him over the wind and waves. "You should check out the front-page story. It's a bombshell."

She grinned. "Oh, yeah?"

He motioned her over to where he'd dropped his backpack on the sand. He pulled out two collapsable bowls and filled them with water for the dogs, who lapped noisily and then threw themselves down, panting. Reaching into his bag again, he pulled out a blanket and spread it out on the sand. Kate sat down next to him, and they watched the waves in silence for a while.

"In case you haven't checked your email, the DA is holding a news conference this afternoon," Peter said.

Kate nodded. "Was he mad?"

"Not too bad. He wasn't happy that you broke the story, or that we went down there together. Neither was the chief. But I pointed out that you were the one who figured out the Cuba connection in the first place. I told them you'd earned the exclusive. There's not much he can do about it, anyway."

"Mattingly is trying his best to seem unfazed, but he's totally thrilled. He called me first thing this morning to tell me the publisher had called to congratulate us."

"Us, huh? I gather Mattingly didn't tell him you'd gone down there on your own dime, after quitting?"

"Well, he probably didn't make a big deal about it. But he won't try to hide it. He can't. The question is, will he let me expense my plane ticket and pay me for the time I was down there."

"He'd better. Or I'll make sure everyone knows the paper took advantage of you. He ought to be giving you a raise. Once the new job offers start pouring in, he'll wish he'd done more to keep you here."

A tremor of unease vibrated through her, an alarm from her emotional security system warning of danger ahead. She met his gaze and held it, ignoring the sirens blaring in her subconscious.

"I'm not interested in another job at the moment," she murmured.

"No?"

She shook her head and looked back at the waves. He leaned toward her until their shoulders touched.

"That's the best news I've heard all day."

Acknowledgments

Writing a book while working full time and having a full-time family is tough. I couldn't have done it without support from my husband, James, who held down the fort every Thursday for writing night. Keziah, thank you for understanding that writing is my ballet. Mimi, thanks for pinch hitting when daddy got stuck at school.

Rachel Le, Katie Gaultney, and Mandi Landry—thank you for your honest feedback and careful reading of the first draft!

Brad Gaultney, thanks for sharing your memories and pictures of Cuba.

To all the friends who encouraged me and asked about my progress, thanks for believing I could do it.

And finally, thanks be to the God and Father of our Lord Jesus Christ. He is *the* Author, and without Him, no story has a happy ending.

Want to read more?

Don't miss book one in the Galveston Crime Scene series!

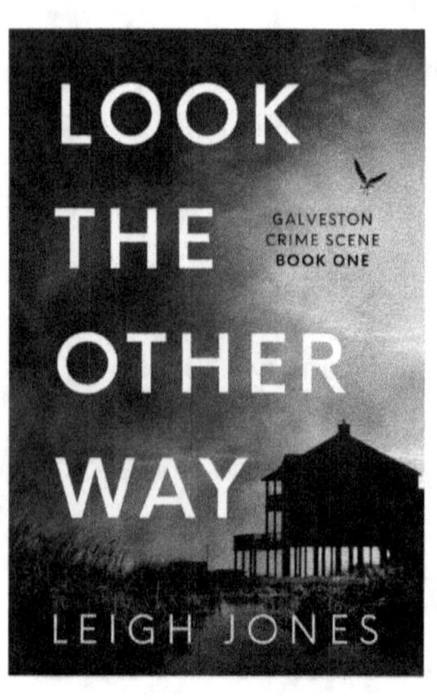

A young woman found bleeding to death on a stranger's front lawn uses her last breath to whisper two words: I'm sorry.

That's a first for reporter Kate Bennett. She's determined to find out why a murder victim felt compelled to apologize. And she can't wait to splash the news of an arrest in 48-point type across the front page of the *Galveston Gazette*.

Detective Peter Johnson has seen his share of human carnage. He knows from experience justice isn't always that swift or simple. When the case goes cold right from the start, he clings to faith that the killer will eventually face a reckoning.

But that's not good enough for Kate.

Vowing to find the answers he couldn't, she quickly discovers the truth costs more than some people are willing to pay. Can Johnson convince her that justice is still worth fighting for, even if she can't see it on this side of eternity?

Keep reading...

Can't get enough of Kate Bennett and Peter Johnson? Learn more about how they met and what drives them in two prequel short stories!

The Jumper tells the story of Kate's first day at the *Galveston Gazette*.

He Must Pay gives you a sneak peek into Johnson's past.

Read them both for free when you sign up for exclusive access to the Galveston Crime Scene!

Join now at GalvestonCrimeScene.com

About the Author

Gripping stories grounded in faith

Leigh Jones started her writing career in elementary school with a story about an enterprising hamster making a bid to take over the world. But after college, she set all dreams of fiction writing aside to chase the daily adrenaline rush of seeing her byline in print. She covered school board meetings, city council intrigue, and the occasional  heart-warming feature for several daily newspapers in Texas. She even covered a few murders and one very big hurricane.

She never considered returning to fiction until she became an editor and no longer got to see her byline on the front page. Facing serious adrenaline withdrawals, she began plotting her first novel. Eight years later, it finally hit the virtual store shelves as *Look The Other Way*, book one in the Galveston Crime Scene series.

When she's not writing fiction, Leigh works as the features editor at WORLD News Group, a national Christian media outlet that practices biblically objective journalism. There she shepherds long-form story projects for print and podcast.

She lives with her husband and daughter near Houston.

Learn more at GalvestonCrimeScene.com.

www.ingramcontent.com/pod-product-compliance
Lightning Source LLC
Chambersburg PA
CBHW072054190726
48294CB00005B/1509